Incarnadine hands stirring the great before,
the cinder of life a thousandth sown.
A vessel set forth betwixt here and yore,
I heave unto you all I have never known.

Supreme Weaver Kalthused
Excerpt from "Without Beginning"

Darrell Drake's
THE FLAMEFORGED SAGA

Book I
WITHIN RUIN

Book II
EVERAUTUMN

WITHIN RUIN
BY DARRELL DRAKE

PART ONE

CHAPTER ONE

The Caged Bird

The revered ruler watched, vigilant specter over an icy white operating table. Red, let by the morbid tangle of discord where weapons whirred and clanged, blushed the charnel below. Even the quiescent sea, frozen to stoicism, could not hide its embarrassment at the staunch hubris of mortals. A scowl of disapproval beheld the struggling forces, led by impetuousness to unforgiving disaster. Kalthused turned regretfully from the folly. When the scent of bloom returned and the great sea opened its maw in a swallowing yawn, they would have a proper burial.

She caught him, halted his retreat with an immovable hand placed knowingly on his chest—where it hurt most. "Kal," prodded the perplexed elf, the succor of her inquisitive pitch diving under her palm. He knew what excavating words would follow. "What are you doing?"

"Leaving."

Ankaa was his partner atop a fresh throne, and though their mottled marriage was the cause of conflict and ire, subjects knew she was of strong heart and able mind. She peered at her lover, auguring the tumult obscured by his hood without trouble. It was unlike him, abandoning loyal if slapdash soldiers to fate, a reliably pernicious beast. To his subjects, Kalthused was a father, savior—a saint, they sometimes called him. More radical accounts painted him as otherworldly, even before his ascension to shepherd of a youthful, flourishing nation.

The tenacious elf wouldn't allow him to crush noble ideals he'd resolutely followed for a decade. Not out of fear for her. With evident care, she raised gloved fingers to his cheek, festooned with a thick winter's growth. "You're going to regret this."

Kalthused sighed, blowing forth a hazy plume of wyrm's breath. "The regiment didn't follow orders. If I don't punish them, more will follow."

"Dear," reminded Ankaa, "they admire you because you care. Because you're the kind of person who would personally wade into that mess and extract every remaining Elusian. You can punish them later." Burrowing fingertips scratched teasingly at his beard. "And you aren't fooling me."

"Fooling you?"

"We've avoided battle, stuck to the northern hinterlands where only border guards patrol. And now you're turning your back on your virtues."

The aggrieved followed her appraisal, a trail of acoustic treats to frowning lips. He admired the windswept locks that writhed in delight about her angular features. The king knew where she was headed; that he could rely on her to temper and set right his wayward course.

"What does it tell our warriors? That you think so little of the end of my sabre. I will forgive a besmirched image if it eases your mind." The elf frowned, retracting her consoling touch and the fragile embers it wrought. "Howbeit, I cannot brook this. You will not shed ideals I've come to treasure for my safety."

Kalthused had sensed the tension when he turned north, the unspoken tingling that scratched at his nape when the avoidance of risk became a priority. He had relied on her tenacity many times before, yet part of him, all of him, wanted her to relent in this pursuit.

How many more skirmishes would it take to extinguish her flame? Before he found her standing at the tenebrous gate of no return? This was his utmost terror, the grinding, rotted brown grin that cursed his dreams above a vacant casket. There were no names, no insignias or engravings, but Kalthused knew who it was for. It wanted her. He sighed, for he knew he never had an option. The king couldn't submit to night terrors when the more pressing, tangible problem of his betrayed lover stood before him. Alienating her could end just as tragically.

Kalthused nodded, a signal of resignation. He would allow her this, but would not leave her side. "As you wish," he said in a relenting mutter, turning back toward the foray.

"Please do not be upset. I only—"

"I'm not," the king interjected. "Just promise you'll stay by my side."

"Always," agreed the elf.

"We've gone so far together, Ankaa."

Positioning herself by his arm, the queen looked up at her brooding companion. "You cannot let fantasies control you."

"I know, dear. I know." Kalthused offered Ankaa a grateful smile, pulling her close by the waist.

"What would you do without me to right your course?" the fur-padded girl grinned.

"I don't want to find out," replied the ruler, growing somber once more. "Let's see what we can do about suturing this grand disaster." Kalthused turned to his personal company, elite armsmen who watched from just down the cliff overlooking a sea hardened to placidity. He issued a signal, crossed arms that indicated a wedged assault from two sides. Archery was too dangerous with the ranks mixed as they were. The contingent reacted immediately, turning for the path to the beach.

Kalthused watched their departure with reticent uncertainty. A supportive squeeze from his queen reminded him that there were more pressing matters. The battle commanded a very tangible threat, one frequently given to snip the tender thread of mortality. A danger with greater proximity than troublesome dreams. He sighed. The din *called; a groaning war engine that, Kalthused knew, had to be quelled. For the good of his subjects.*

Descarta emerged from the vivid dream to find the oathkeeper across from her trying feebly to conceal his disappointment. As if that weren't enough, an unmoving shadow had fallen over her and she craned to see Virgil, her sovereign, frowning.

"I see you don't find 'Gods unto Gods' as captivating as the pious oathkeeper. Nor do I." Virgil placed his hand on her shoulder, from which she jerked away, eliciting another frown. "But you could be more discreet when napping while the good man helps you learn what you have forgotten."

As she grunted her discontent, he swiped the tome she had been reading. "What's this? *Kalthused?* Ah, the founder of our realm. I guess one cannot fault a queen for wanting to know of our kingdom."

The lass snatched her book back. "It's none of your business. I am your queen, not your child."

"As you wish. You should know history as written is never transparent. It always favors the victor."

"He was surely a better sovereign than you," retorted the girl.

Virgil expelled a defeated sigh. "Yes. He was." He waved a bejeweled hand in dismissal. "My inadequacy as your king aside, I must consult with you. Oathkeeper, I am grateful for your time. You may leave now."

The priest bowed once then briskly sought the exit, surely relieved to be leaving.

The king took the oathkeeper's seat across from his queen. She had begun reading "Kalthused" once more.

He admired the sparrow. She was truly an iridescent gem amid the turmoil of his besmirched realm. A cataract of winding hazelnut tresses framed mesmerizing amber orbs, a slightly upturned nose and rosy, dimpled cheeks then fell into a basin upon beseechingly downy shoulders. Her chassis was enveloped in jade chiffon which hung from her neck and tumbled down the petite physique of youth. This was all fortified by the radiance that dominated her person. Descarta was a foreign creature here, out of place among the morose sort who had seen better days.

In stark contrast, Virgil looked the head of a blighted nation. Though he was not unattractive. Before Descarta, many suitors found him quite the dashing sovereign. His mane was a raven mess of finger-length talons that clawed capriciously about his angular face. Sleep deprivation was manifest in the darkened candelabra set beneath dim cerulean eyes which resonated intellect. He carried himself with the assertive authority which was rightfully his as not only the king of Elusia but the supreme weaver—a sorcerer recognized as the most sagacious within the Triad of Sorcery. All of this was cast in a shroud of dolorous defeat.

"Des," he began, "I know you're aware of the disease that has crippled Elusia. I would like for you to be more involved in working toward a cure."

"How so?" she replied without looking from her tome.

"I plan to journey to Vanathiel to personally implore the minister apply their knowledge toward ridding Elusia of its plight. I would have you join me. The impact of both king and queen requesting assistance would be far greater. If you would agree, of course."

"Outside?!" she blurted with more enthusiasm than she would have liked. Then in a more sedate inflection, "Oh, I guess it couldn't hurt. Anything is better than this stench-ridden prison you've locked me in."

Virgil curled his lips slightly toward his cheeks. "Good. I look forward to it. We depart in a sennight." He left the comfort of the chair and halted at the egress to survey his queen. Once again, her gaze was planted directly on the recollection of Kalthused the Undaunted. "Enjoy your book, my blossom. Until tonight, then."

The royal maiden waited for the wooden portal to clap shut before she verily leaped from her seat, excitement coursing through her limbs. Finally, she would venture beyond the walls of the damned fortress city. Descarta could roam anywhere within the palatial ramparts encompassing the inner keep, a tiny realm with little to see. There was a courtyard, adorned with myriad flora, a bethel where the hymns of the Maiden reliably hummed every hour and the castle grounds, lusterless and boring. All else was contained in her tomes.

Descarta burst from her room and dashed through the castle causeways, dodging servants and visitors who either ducked away or shook their heads at the behavior of their queen.

Virgil's wards, Almi and Merill, were technically her wards, too. The twins were elves, and while far older than she, they hardly looked it—such was the way of their kin. So she treated them as friends, the only friends she knew in the oppressive environment. They were tricky, those two. Descarta was uncertain whether it was due to a characteristic of elves or a mere personality trait, but they were beyond mercurial. At times, they treated her as a chum, giggling and telling her of the happenings beyond her stone cage. She could feel companionship brewing during those moments. The following day they might approach her with such unchained hostility that she would be afraid for her life.

With little regard for their caprice, she rushed into the courtyard where they spent much of their day practicing swordsmanship and archery. "Merill! Almi! Where are you?!"

"Here," Almi called from amongst a patch of violet flowers, peering with intensity at a bobbing bumblebee.

Descarta had a mellifluous voice of the perfect pitch and weight. However, she always found herself envious of the twins. Their timbres exuded a soothing, innocent calm even when upset with her. They were nearly the same height, Descarta, Almi and Merill. Yet the sisters were willowy, supple in the right places. She was just short, skinny and modestly endowed.

"Why are you yelling?" questioned Merill, entering the courtyard behind Des.

Almi appeared in the same training gear as Merill: a skin-tight affair that matched her olive pigmentation and served to crush Descarta's confidence even further. She trotted over to her sister and wrapped an arm around her waist. Merill grinned widely at her sibling and they exchanged a curiously lengthy embrace for twins who rarely parted.

When they finished mollycoddling, the queen was bouncing on her heels in impatience.

"Well?" Almi slid her free arm around the beaming girl to tug her close as well. "Spry Des is spry. She always says this place is where queens are sent to rot, their fetid, maggot-infested corpses used first as toys then fertilizer for—"

"Okay, okay. I get it," whined Descarta in exasperation. "And I cannot believe you memorized that." The three shared a brief grin before she continued. "Virgil asked me to leave the ramparts with him. On a trip!"

Almi and Merill changed moods swiftly, and Almi's coiling limb dropped from around the queen's back. Their slim countenances transformed from affable to sinister, angled eyes narrowing in response. "Did our Virgil say that? We weren't invited."

Merill's words drove a lance into Descarta's chest and brought forth an overwhelming feeling of anxiety. They had such intractable control over her emotions. "M-Maybe he hasn't had a chance to tell you," she muttered, smiling meekly.

As abruptly as before, the twins were beaming. "That's it!" exclaimed Merill. "Our Virgil never interrupts us here. We will ask!"

The pair set off hand in hand with Almi tossing cooing thanks before they exited.

Descarta could feel her rigidness fall away as the two departed. They were never like that in front of the sovereign. To the Sundered with them. She wouldn't let it sour her mood. She was going to travel!

...

The sovereign of Elusia lounged in his throne whose high-back doubled as a support pillar which soared to the lofty ceiling above. All around the bronze chair were depictions of past kings and their contributions to the realm. When he departed, his legacy would be made manifest in bronze as well. His lids were shut in reverie, absorbing the silence of everything around him but the popping braziers lining his audience chamber. The high magus would arrive within the hour, and it was never quiet when all three of them were in the same room.

The weaver's precious quiescence shattered as the heavy wooden doors to his throne room thrust open and groaned on ancient hinges.

"Our Virgil," Almi and Merill moaned while stretching his name over the excessive amount of time it took them to approach the throne. Almi flung herself into a hop and landed draping lackadaisically over his lap. Merill took a seat on his armrest.

The sorcerer pinched the bridge of his nose and allowed himself a long, steadying breath before looking to Merill, then Almi. "Yes, my songbirds?"

"We want to come. Why hasn't our Virgil invited us?" Almi complained while she wielded her most enticing pout.

"Come? Where?" the king replied, averting his eyes to the dome above.

"Don't tease us!" Merill exclaimed. "We're not for teasing! Our Virgil can't leave without us! Not with her!"

"You'll be fine here. I won't be gone too long."

"Aha!" Almi wrapped her slender arms around Virgil's neck and dragged his gaze back down. "You must let us! We haven't been on a voyage with our Virgil for so long."

"During our last excursion, you complained incessantly about the weather," he retorted.

"Not this time. We promise," Almi pouted from below.

"We promise," Merill echoed. "Please don't leave us," she begged.

A baritone voice rang from the portal to the throne room. "They've arrived, sire," announced the castle's seneschal.

"Very well, Hazael. See them here." Giving the steward no further attention, Virgil found the twins staring at him impatiently, awaiting his decision. "You are a troublesome pair."

They nodded and beamed, accustomed to the particular inflection shift.

"So be it," he muttered. "Now off with you. I have three bickering rodents to attend to before we leave."

Almi and Merill each clung to his neck and kissed his cheek before hopping off the throne. "We're very grateful to our Virgil!" the wards recited in unison before bouncing off and between a group of niggling sorcerers. Virgil watched their departure with a satisfied smirk. He never planned on leaving them behind. Telling them as much would have deprived him of their dependably amusing banter.

The weavers entered, followed by the seneschal who secured the doors behind them and took his place vigilantly to the side.

These three magus were Virgil's subordinates in the Triad of Sorcery, a warren for those with magical aptitude. Its purpose was twofold: an omnivorous collection of knowledge concerning the three factions of weaving and to act as a control to keep the sovereign in check. Thus, his role as supreme weaver and ruler was unprecedented.

Dalstan, a twig of a man, was bristling. He headed the Aether faction, a sphere of weaving which granted the bearer control over nature.

In contention with the man stood Oagan, his polar opposite and head of the Terra faction, a sphere of weaving used for thaumaturgy ranging from divination to manifestation.

In the rear waited Violah, quiet and calculating. She represented the Fusion faction, a cohesion between Terra and Aether.

At present, Dalstan was twaddling on about the supremacy of his chosen weave of influence because it was natural and hence not a perversion of the world around it. He went as far as to posture that the creeping blight was due to Oagan's dimwitted apprentices.

"Magus, quiet," Virgil interrupted with no response. "Magus, quiet," once more, still without heed. The supreme weaver stood. With him the surrounding braziers bellowed a roaring flame. "I will not ask again," he added, maintaining a neutral volume.

Virgil locked a despotic glare at each of them in turn before continuing. "I have not invited you here to take part in needless debate over whose school of thaumaturgy is superior." He returned to his throne and waited without speaking.

Several onerous moments of awkwardness followed between the three high magus before Violah stepped forward. "Sire, may I ask a question?"

"Ah! Someone who understands etiquette! Yes, High Magus Violah. Pose your question."

"Sire, why have you brought us here?"

"A sensible, straightforward question, too! Well Violah, I plan to visit Vanathiel and behoove the minister to help us develop a remedy for this deleterious rot." He paused and nodded to the seneschal. "But first, I must uproot the rot among my subordinates."

Dalstan and Oagan exchanged brief glances before recognition twisted their features. They lifted their robed arms to pluck at the weave. A trivial and inconsequential effort. Their defensive bubbles shattered in a chromatic flurry of glass-like confetti with a casual wave of Virgil's hand. A flicker of movement followed and resulted in one spellcaster standing with the steward's blade protruding from his mouth like an iron tongue. The remaining quaked in the grasp of winding stone tentacles, his body contorting in ways it was never meant until it was reduced to gore and bone.

Violah stumbled backward, no longer so sure of herself. She struggled to conjure a riposte but the steward was somehow already behind her, blade to her spine. The iron-tongued cadaver to her side collapsed to the ground.

Virgil shook his head. "Do not be foolish, Violah."

"I have served you! Only you, sire! I have, I have—"

"Be quiet, woman. I'm not going to harm you. You will maintain your position, and I will install two new leaders of our deceased comrade's factions. Competent weavers who aren't so quarrelsome. While I am away, the three of you will govern by my will. If you refuse or betray me, you will be as Dalstan and Oagan. Understood?"

Violah's head bobbed obediently. "Of course, sire. I am loyal only to you."

"Now go," the sovereign ordered. "I will have Hazael inform you on the matter in more detail before I depart."

The remaining high magus bowed her obsequiousness three times then hastily let herself out.

"That went well," observed Virgil.

Hazael knelt to clean his blade on Oagan's robe. "Agreed."

CHAPTER TWO

The Caged Bird Freed

Reclined in an artfully embroidered chair, layered black robe strewn about him, Virgil whispered a near-perpetual string of archaic incantations. The jovial flicker that danced in a nearby lantern had long expired, giving way to the still blanket of twilight.

Beside him, Descarta stirred amid a mire of silk duvet. "I can't sleep with you doing that."

Virgil angled his head to the supine form on the bed beside him. "You've had no trouble in the two years since I began."

She rolled over to face him and further entangled herself in the duvet. "Yes. Two years of creepiness. Yet you still haven't restored my memory. So it has no purpose in keeping me awake."

"I am sorry, blossom, but memory restoration has never been attempted. Surely, you understand the complications of entering a new area of magic. There are no guides, no maps—it's uncharted."

"I remember nothing. Nothing. For all I know, you could be whispering gibberish to yourself every night," the girl huffed.

"It is for your good. And it is working, albeit gradually," Virgil assured his queen. "Is something else troubling you?"

"No." Descarta drew her cocoon tight and clenched her eyelids. At first, it was mortifying. A man she didn't know lurking beside her like a hauntling and chanting nightly in some menacing language. But that had long fell to routine. Now she was roiling with anxiousness for the arrival of morning: the day of departure. She envisioned the snow-capped crags of the Maiden's Peaks rising before her, vast prairies sweeping all around and no ramparts forcing her to stay put. A feathery itch on her nape truncated the fantasy. Irritated, the queen reached to scratch it, but the feeling exploded across her body, briskly forcing her to sleep.

Virgil retracted his touch from her delicate neck and resumed his ritual.

...

The following morning, the queen and sisters had gathered in the common room after preparing for the trip. Almi and Merill were strangely calm, settled like throw blankets over a violet upholstered couch with arms dangling from the side. From their vacant stares the diminutive queen gathered this was not their time of day. After some time dawdling, Descarta schemed an idea to shorten the delay. "Your Virgil is still asleep. I hope he didn't have second thoughts about the expedition," she lured, smiling wryly.

The sisters crooked to see her, glossy-eyed with lethargy. Languor gave way to recognition, and in a wild display of energy they dashed off to bother him.

She watched boastfully as they scampered off. They weren't the only ones capable of manipulation.

Descarta had shed her usual attire for trappings more suited to the road. A pastel viridian pinafore—she felt the color favored her eyes—loosely wrapped her chest, suspended from two buttoned shoulder straps. Its knee-length skirt flared into several layers at the hips, each lined with bunched obsidian lace. Under that were matching leggings and mid-height traveling boots. She had secured her copper hair with a length of black fabric which then rest over her right shoulder, reaching to just below the frock.

The queen strolled around the common room like she had since dawn, arms swinging energetically at her sides. Every other window hung a tapestry depicting a miraculous exhibition of magic, and Descarta had seen them all countless times. Yet she stopped to peer at each to pass the wait; her nerves allowed little more.

It wasn't until after she'd left the third such tapestry, a brilliant rendering of a spellweaver with hands to the sky and a phoenix of flame leaping from them, did Descarta realize she wasn't alone. Stationed by the adjacent wall, Hazael stood silently. Small sack in hand, he was evidently prepared to depart as well. The steward still wore his traditional charcoal trousers and vest, lavender side-button shirt and scabbard on his hip. The only exception was the scaled pattern of chain mail that created a ridged outline against his torso.

Hazael offered a courteous smile and bow. "Good morning, your majesty."

"Thank you. Good morning to you, too," Descarta said and curtsied. She had seen him often in the ramparts, and they never exchanged many words. When they did, he was always terse and cordial. "Is the king on his way?" she asked.

"Your sire will be here. Don't worry. We are early."

"He's just making me wait to torture me."

The seneschal didn't reply, only turned his head toward the nearest window.

...

The worn sovereign opened his lids to see Almi and Merill watching anxiously on their bellies to his sides, chin-length golden hair awash over their sprightly, angular faces. The two had donned knee-high boots and identical crimson tunics a shade deeper than their enchanting eyes. "Morning," Merill crowed. "You're awake."

"I've been awake," Virgil mouthed through a chasmal yawn and stretch. "Only resting."

"We waited for nothing," sulked Almi.

"No, you were patient. That is an improvement." The weaver emphasized the praise by patting her straw-colored crown.

Almi simpered and sniffed. "This bed doesn't smell like our Virgil anymore. Smells like berryflowers."

"That makes sense. I feel I shouldn't ask, but what do I smell like?"

"After the rain," replied Merill, rolling onto her back.

Virgil grimaced. "That . . . also makes sense. Though it's not quite flattering."

"We like rain," Merill explained. "It's wet."

"You are silly ones," Virgil mused. "Tell the others I am on my way."

...

Soon thereafter Virgil arrived in his supreme weaver's robe: a raven, many-layered affair with a dozen upturned stretches of claw-like fabric reaching out around the bottom. Down the front ran two rows of buttons to make removing the garb less encumbering. He had also shaved, an act which made his high cheekbones all the more vivid. "Let's be off then." he ordered.

Descarta was the first to cross under the rampart portcullis and into the city beyond. Below the hill to the keep ran two rivers. Between them lay the clamor and spectacle of the Elusian capitol, Saradin. She started to rush off, but Virgil took a firm hold on her arm. The diminutive girl tried to tug herself free. This time he did not relent. "No, Des. Not until we've left the city." To her dismay, he pulled her to his side and wrapped his arm around her, swallowing her in his robes.

"Virgil?! What are you doing?!" she screamed at her sovereign, fuming. "I did not permit you to hold me!" She struggled against his hidebound grasp. Images of being subjugated and dragged back into the cursed ramparts flooded her mind.

"You think you can just—" she began. The objection was curtailed when he willed the weave into the fingers encircling her upper arm. Tension sloughed off the girl and onto the cobblestone below. She angled her subdued eyes upward to the weaver, the beginning of tears accumulating. "That isn't fair. Not at all."

Virgil regretted meeting that awfully morose stare. "Please don't despair, blossom," he said as he loosened his grip. "I did not expect you to dash ahead of us like that. I understand you want to be unshackled. And I understand you dislike this proximity, but it really is necessary. As my queen, you are as much a target as I am. Much as I would like to say I can protect you from afar, it just isn't true. When we reach the prairie I promise I'll let go."

"Don't we get a parade of soldiers?" asked Descarta.

"Typically, yes," Virgil responded. "With the tension between Kaen Morr and a dwindling population, we cannot afford to remove them from our borders. The paltry military force stationed here would not even be worth the effort. Just stay with me. Please."

Descarta nodded her understanding and whimpered weakly within his voluminous robes. A lingering feeling of uneasiness still disagreed with being bound so closely.

"Thank you, Des." Virgil motioned to the seneschal and sisters who were suddenly very austere. "Proceed."

Hazael took the point, his palm resting alertly on the hilt of his sheathed sword. The twins formed the rear of the protective triangle. Almi nervously tapped the beastly, many-fanged mace which dangled about her hip while Merill held an arrow notched in her recurve bow. The royal escort began their descent toward the base of the bluff whereupon Saradin perched. There the gate waited.

This wound the cohorts through the din of its main avenue. Though it gave the envoy a wide breadth, ahead and behind them the street was a boisterous cornucopia of folk. Anyone within range of the escort groveled as they passed, only to return to their tasks immediately after. There were times when Descarta could see packs of women glaring derisively at her when they thought she wasn't looking, and sharing hushed remarks. At other times a caustic jeer would emerge from the noise. But no one was foolish enough to approach. Venomous glares and angry curses aside, the queen was thrilled. Everywhere around her an exotic import was on display or a street performer was vying for attention.

An abrupt turn left the boisterous throughway and started toward a belvedere-capped gate. The single shift dissolved traffic almost entirely.

Descarta thought her innards would heave from her throat. Then the induced comfort of Virgil's fingertips once again injected his commanding weave into her frame. This time she did not protest. They pressed onward slowly, giving the queen a chance to absorb the scope of her pestilence gripped domain. The cobblestone here was imbued with a sickly umber hue and lined with the lesion infested infirm who reached for the party with emaciated arms and called with ghastly, dry coughs. Soldiers dragged the dead to deep trenches for incineration, while weavers experimented with heretofore ineffective cures.

After what seemed weeks to the glum queen, they finally passed under the colossal portal and were beyond the outer wall of Saradin. The scourged, stacked a dozen high, lingered in her mind.

Virgil came to a halt beneath a statue of the Maiden. The sculpture portrayed an elven woman with a forgiving smile, hands clasped over her waist and a deluge of hair reaching just beyond her hips. "How can you allow that to happen to Elusians?" Descarta questioned under the scrutiny of the Maiden, their prevailing deity of empyrean love.

"I am attempting to cure it, Des. That is why we have embarked," said Virgil.

"Why haven't you let me try to heal them?"

"I assure you, we have many able healers at our disposal. They have failed, continue to fail."

"But I want to help them," insisted Descarta.

"Then pray."

"I don't know the Maiden, Virgil. I rarely visit the bethel," she answered.

"That is of no consequence, my queen. You are their shepherd. Do what you can." The weaver gestured toward the alabaster monument. "Place your hand on the Maiden and request her assistance."

Descarta nodded her assent and, for once, did as he suggested. Head bowed in reverence, she appealed to the Maiden to find it in her providential authority to purge the affliction from her subjects. To wash the tormented souls hale again. Initially, there was no reaction— exactly what one would expect from a celestial being. Then the supplicant queen felt a spark in her bosom as if the Maiden heard her plea. Descarta issued a smile to the statue then dolorously returned to her sovereign's side.

The cohorts set off once more, widening the gap between the group and the shrinking parapets of Saradin. As they did, Descarta recalled the destitute souls left behind. News always made it to the inner ramparts, but the plight was far more devastating than she imagined. She didn't have the strength or perspicacity to be their monarch yet. It had even taken a magical nudge from Virgil to prevent her from disrespectfully evacuating her morning meal. In hindsight, he had prevented displaying that inadequacy to those who depended on her leadership. "Thanks . . . for back there," she murmured from his side, soft enough that only he could hear.

Virgil nodded his acceptance and released the dainty girl from her shelter of enshrouding mantle. "It's safe now. Just stay near, blossom." The queen took a few quick strides forward, giving herself plenty of space and turned a full circle, skirt flaring around her. Her melancholy evaporated as she absorbed a chilled autumn zephyr and unobstructed sunlight. As far as she could see, fields of vegetation met the horizon. The only exceptions were the summits before her and Saradin behind.

"This is glorious!" she exclaimed to no one in particular. "The paintings do no justice to the countryside! Oh!" Descarta stooped to pick an orange flower with broad petals. "Dunkelhen! These only grow in our prairies! Nowhere else!" Descarta boiled excitement. She had dreamed of this for the past two years. The wide grin may as well have been gilded onto her rouge cheeks.

Spectating with more than a passing interest, Virgil was pleased with himself. The trek through the city lacerated the girl, he knew, but the resulting succor was worth it. He was well aware of her temperament, of how oppressed she felt within her palatial cell. Beyond her scornful words, there was genuine suffering. To have no memory, cohabitation with a king she didn't know, her universe restricted to what she could experience within a dour fortress—this was liberation well-earned.

In envy, the sisters had already occupied the spot Descarta evacuated. This forced the king to check over his shoulder periodically. The prairies were vast flatland, though, so anyone would be seen approaching from afar. "Why didn't our Virgil hold us? Like her. We were afraid," Almi probed in a wounded inflection, equipping doe eyes.

"You know why. You can defend yourself," Virgil explained. "She only possesses a modicum of restoration magic."

"You think she's better," Almi whined.

Virgil sighed. "You can all be quite bothersome at times."

Merill pressed her face into a layer of robe. "But you think she's the lovely bothersome," came her muffled reply.

"You are equally lovely."

"That's what you always say. Evasive. We don't like it," Almi protested.

"You said you wouldn't complain," the spellweaver reminded them in a severely censuring tone.

Whimpering, the elves retreated from his side and followed a few paces back, saturnine gazes transfixed on the earth below. The party continued like this for the day, with Descarta merrily loping about like a capering sylph while the others traveled without exchange.

...

The journey from Saradin to Galvant's Pass, the lone defile leading through the otherwise insuperable mountain range defending Elusia's eastern border, was two days travel. To ease the journey, a large inn had been established mid-way between the pass and city. The building, Spiced Cat, was a single floor structure far longer than wide. The walls were built of mammoth trunks harvested from the temperate forests southwest of Saradin. The interior was partitioned into four sections: an administrative office, social area, kitchen and sleeping arrangements—the largest by far with room for thirty tri-level bunk beds. It was here that the group stopped for the night.

The shimmering daysphere had just reached its nadir, casting a stream of carmine and violet hues across scattered clouds lazing amid the vesper above. A stoked hearth provided an aegis against the approaching chill of an autumn evening. Descarta, thoroughly drained from the day's exertion, had forgone the beds and verily collapsed onto a couch by the entrance where she snoozed peacefully. Merill lounged atop Almi, head on chest, over an area of floor which they claimed as far away from everyone as possible. The pair sprawled there, brooding. Merill busied herself with tracing ginger circles over Almi's flanks while they both did their best to avoid interaction.

In better times, soldiers would have been stationed here. Instead, there was a volunteer who ran the inn. She seemed a haggard old crone in a gown, but was dutifully cordial to her sovereign and his entourage. She also knew to obey when he asked that they be alone, so the weathered woman took refuge in her office. Virgil and Hazael sat across from each other at a dining table. Between them, steam ascended in errant wisps above two mugs of K'lazzen Tea, a mild elven brew. Virgil stooped over his, held between his hands to capture the radiating warmth. Hazael sat straight in his seat and paid little attention to the tea. He was more piqued by his lord.

"You hurt them," the seneschal stated.

Virgil contemplated the supine twins who jerked their watchful eyes away. "It will pass."

"Of course, but you've never spoken to them in that way," countered Hazael.

"It will pass," the king repeated.

"If you don't care about them, why don't you simply toss them aside?"

"They need me," the spellweaver glowered at his steward.

"Virgil. I've known you for how long? Someone needing you is negligible. You've done deeds that would make the Sundered blush."

"What's your point?" groaned the king before sipping his tea.

"That you need them as much as they do you," explained Hazael, still ignoring his tincture. "While that means little to me, your changing disposition does. To be forthright, I'm worried you cannot handle this journey."

"I'd advise you to be very cautious of the words you use."

The steward grimaced. "Look at you. How many anguish invoking trials in fetid piss holes have we endured together? Yet I have never seen you in such poor condition."

"I admit I have felt better," Virgil sighed.

"What of her? Is it worth it?" The seneschal motioned toward the dozing queen.

Virgil regarded his queen's dainty back, the alluring rise of her hips. He drew a half-smile at the way she curled in repose. "She is well for now. The nightly weaving is taxing, compounded by the weariness wrought of losing sleep. But it is not something I can just cease."

Hazael nodded his agreement. "Is she progressing?"

"She is. I have taught the girl to weave. Elementary weaving. I have explained the concept of the fabric, how it is the binding force of our universe. How we can manipulate it by using the ribbon that joins us to the fabric as a catalyst. She has an affinity for restoration, conceivably protection if trained." Virgil took a sip from his mug. The brew was bold with a sweet tincture of laurylroot. "It has fortified her ribbon, making the task less of a burden on mine."

"It's a shame I can't help," Hazael lamented.

"You could mollify my stress by not having these silly superfluous conversations. I am doing what I must, as I always have."

Hazael studied the sovereign, who now watched the downcast sisters. Everything that mattered to him was shouldered by the fatigued king. The reality of his helplessness was unsettling.

"Hazael," the sorcerer interrupted. "You are a good friend."

The steward grinned in reply. "I have no choice."

"Choice is an adolescent illusion anyway," Virgil retorted. He noticed the seneschal's untouched mug. "Laurylroot. You never had a taste for it. I'll give it to the sisters then."

The sovereign cautiously grasped the steaming, too-full tea and walked it over to the sulking pair. He knelt a robed knee beside them and placed the K'lazzen concoction on the stone floor. They didn't acknowledge him. "Is it really that bad?" he asked. Virgil blew an exasperated breath. He reached with his left hand to stroke Merill and ran a ridged course up and down her spine. The remaining hand administered like treatment to Almi, digging trenches into her sandy hair. It took a novice cantrip to infuse his fingertips with warmth, so he did them that favor, too.

The elves mewed, an unmistakable indication that they approved and their sour mood had been allayed. Merill curved toward the satisfying sensation, closing her eyes and emitting a prurient hum. Almi angled her neck to press greedily into the warm touch, likewise humming her pleasure.

Virgil pacified them a bit longer before returning to his feet. "There's tea for you. You'll like it."

"More!" the twins fervently, and huskily, begged.

"Des is sleeping. Not so loud." The spellweaver made to leave them to their drink but stopped short. They clawed at his mantle, writhing toward him. "I shouldn't have addressed you that way. Forgive me, dears."

"Our Virgil is so good to us," said Merill, now awkwardly positioned atop the struggling Almi who grunted in frustration underneath.

"I'm relieved. Now I must tend to your queen." Virgil paced to Descarta, who was still captured by dreamland. The wool blanket provided by the crone had slipped below her waist, so he pulled it up to her neck and watched her fidget. She was worth it, worth everything. He took a seat on the floor with his back to the couch and noted that its simple comfort was superior to even the lavish chairs of the palace. Or perhaps he was just that fatigued. Once again, the sovereign wove a string of verses with the disciplined artifice and fluency that illustrated him a master of his craft.

Having indulged in their tea, the twins slinked to the table where the seneschal kept watch. He winked at them and looked on in amusement as they finished Virgil's as well. Almi and Merill then hurried over to the couch and found a spot on either side of the murmuring weaver, using his thighs as pillows and stretching a limber leg over his.

Virgil felt the weight on his limbs although he could not see it. Around him stretched an endless realm of white and red. It was so simple and yet so mesmerizing. Most importantly, it was omnipresent. The sanguine curtain fell all around him, shivering an eternal vibration. The hollow areas weren't really white. The weaver knew they too were red. These empty stains just existed beyond his perception. There had been others who were better at visiting the fabric and auguring its features. Though the list of weavers who had ever entered this realm numbered only two dozen. Eight of them severed their own ribbon, leading to a brief encounter and an immediate death. He tugged at his consciousness, willing it gradually upward. After much effort, he reached the dim, faintly trembling ribbon that wound to Descarta. This is where he directed his weaving, mending her bond with the utmost care.

...

A rich, beckoning aroma emanated from the kitchen and burrowed into her nostrils, wrenching Descarta free from the mandibles of her dreams. She found herself wedged between two bodies. An arm lay across her face, which she tossed away, eliciting a drowsy grumble from the slumbering elf it belonged to. Descarta sat up and crawled over Merill and off the couch, steadying herself while the resulting vertigo retreated. "Bothersome elves," she mumbled. Merill mouthed something incomprehensible before emitting a shiver and squirming closer to Almi.

Descarta rubbed the irritating blur from her vision and shambled over to the hearth where Virgil reclined in a comfortable chair. "What's that smell? And why are they sleeping on me?"

There was no response from the weaver. He seemed bewitched by the low flame. She watched its flickering reflection in his eyes: forlorn windows that channeled a great inner turmoil. "Virgil?" she pressed. "I asked a question."

This drew those dejected windows directly to hers, and they bore into her, depositing the chill of despair. Then he blinked and it was purged, given to the cathartic deluge like her forgotten memories. "Morn, blossom. Why are you standing there?"

"You—" she bit her bottom lip, pensive. "No reason. The smell woke me, I guess." She gestured at the twins. "Though how I slept at all with them smothering me is questionable."

The sovereign shrugged. "The girls must have joined you during my watch. I left them on the floor."

"Well, tell them I dislike it," the queen complained. "I'm not a teddy bear."

"I'll do that," he managed, though it seemed his attention was partially ensnared elsewhere.

"Virgil!" she condemned, post-rest irritability breeding frustration. "Pay attention!"

"Excuse me, blossom," he replied. "I don't mean to be rude. I'm just very tired."

"You don't look well," she observed.

"I don't look well? It almost sounds as if you care. Has my lovely queen had a change of heart?" he mused.

Descarta blew out of her nose. "I'm just being circumspect. Almi and Merill would like to see me in a pond somewhere, or smothered against their bosoms. Hazael would probably watch in indifference as they bound boulders to my legs. It's only natural I worry about the person keeping me alive, even if it's only so to strive toward thieving my chastity. Survival."

"I cannot say I wouldn't mind thieving your chastity. You are a brilliantly sultry girl, you know. Those delightfully luscious thighs. I have needs that cannot be fulfilled by watching your enchanting bosom rise and fall at night," Virgil jested, smiling at the girl.

Her cheeks flushed crimson and she turned away, clenching fists at her sides. "Oh! I can't believe you! That's, that's, it's lecherous and—oh!"

Having just awoken as well, the seneschal chortled from behind at his queen's reaction to the teasing. "Don't be dismayed, my queen. I have seen him perform. And I must say, it is enough to make one aspire to be that moaning form beneath his ravenous husk," he quipped.

"What?! How do you know?! Why are you doing this?!" she yowled. "Let's eat. Let's eat and leave. Let's go. It's time to go." The queen paced a winding path around the room, shaking her hands as if to shed their taint.

...

Another day of travel deposited the envoy at Galvant's Bulwark, an antiquated spire which stood at the vanguard of the Elusian defense. Descarta gawked at the many-tiered keep. It seemed a gargantuan stone conifer with battlements expanding from branches in every direction and covered in enfilade slots. Hundreds of military camps dotted its radius, and nearly every tower looked occupied. Yet again, illustrations could not master the grand scale or looming authority of the fortress. She imagined arrows let loose from a thousand, thousand bows obliterating the ranks of an invading force as they tried in futility to exit the defile.

When the cohorts drew near, a horn sounded. The clarion boom echoed off the surrounding mountains. Virgil beckoned the queen to his side, and she obliged with only minimal hesitation. This time she had been warned and prepared herself for the uncomfortable closeness. Ahead, the colossal iron gates screeched and cogs wined as a portal big enough to fit all of the Saradin ramparts thrice over was set ajar. Seven figures emerged as insects from the swallowing chasm and shuffled briskly toward the cohorts.

"Who are they?" Almi asked.

"Our warm welcome," explained Virgil. "Josiah should be among them."

"Josiah!" Merill crowed. "We haven't seen him in years!"

"Twenty-three," the king specified.

Descarta thought to inquire exactly how old the twins were but chose to pursue that later as the group drew near.

"I'm glad you made it before sunset, sire!" greeted a lean, ebony man wrapped in the trappings of an Elusian scout: earth-colored long-sleeve jacket with hanging hood and pants of a similar hue. A matching girdle lined with pouches encircled his waist and a small harp hung over his back. He carried himself with an air of self-satisfaction and was fastidiously neat. The scout's head was bereft of hair save for a square patch of black beneath his bottom lip.

The seven knelt before the king as he addressed them. "Thank you for the greeting. You may rise." They did so. "However, as I instructed, I would rather not endure these toilsome formalities," Virgil projected as he scowled at the sorceress behind Josiah. While his scowl only met High Magus Violah, all seven fidgeted nervously. "It will be discussed later. We would like to rest."

"Understood," replied a stout, muscle-bound bear of a man wearing the uniform of a force commander. "My quarters are yours for the night and I will serve you personally. If you'll follow me, sire." The commander about-faced and started toward the spire's ingress.

The high magus and scout followed along with the royal escort, now augmented by four accompanying soldiers.

As they walked, Violah fiddled with the crochet cuff around her wrist. "My king, I only meant to—"

"We will discuss it later, Violah," the sovereign replied with a virulent hint.

"Y-Yes," said the high magus, taking care to keep her head lowered.

Descarta watched the woman from Virgil's embrace. She had seen the weaver around the ramparts often. Her third lesson in fundamental weaving was under Violah. The lady wasn't like the other weavers who often roamed the halls. She was capable and bore her pride well—just confident enough to fall below haughty. Now she looked shattered and afraid, as if every step was harrowing.

...

At the middle of the spire's interior stood a hollow cylinder that soared to the zenith of the Bulwark, a diplomatic gesture from Vanathiel. In it waited a capsule that, with the aid of weavers, could transport its contents to any level of the fortress. Before the apparatus was fitted, stairs were the only way of scaling the tower's many levels. The sovereign stopped to examine the five individuals standing in a pentagon around the device. "I am to entrust my queen's life to novices?" The mages present winced at his words.

"They can handle it," the commander replied in an attempt to assuage the king. "Apprentices are generally used. However, we pulled a fresh rotation of the garrison's best weavers for your transport."

"I am grateful for the consideration, Commander Byrnn, but that will not do. I will handle it myself." The commander parted his lips to object, but Virgil lifted a hand to silence the officer. "The lifting is achieved through weaving the water below into a geyser, correct?"

"You are correct, sire. The cavern below is flooded."

"Up, then. I would like to retire soon," Virgil insisted. The king, queen, seneschal, twins, scout, high magus and commander all packed into the transparent unit. Descarta crooked her neck to gape at the astonishing tunnel that rose higher and higher until converging into a point. She envisioned a Vanathiel metropolis with many similar foreign apparatus snaking every square. Clutching her tighter than before, Virgil sucked in a steadying breath and widened his stance. There was an incipient rumbling, the sound of churning liquid escaping from somewhere below.

Almi and Merill held one another tightly, braided together and eyes widened frightfully. "So spooky," whined Merill as she quivered in her sister's arms.

Then the water rose, foaming and bubbling around the perimeter of the container. At first, there was a crawling ascent. That swiftly became a perilous charge as they were propelled with speed enough to blur everything outside the chamber beyond recognition. Floors zoomed by until a fierce gust abruptly buffeted from above, negating the thrust the geyser granted. Descarta felt her weight escape momentarily and clenched her angry stomach while the sensation faded.

"I nearly forgot there was a roof!" Virgil chuckled heartily. "Off then so I can send this contraption back down." Hazael looked through narrowed lids at the weaver yet offered no comment.

With everyone in the officer's quarters, the sovereign lowered the capsule to its base. The task complete, Descarta felt a burdening portion of his weight perch upon her shoulders. She produced a quizzical look, straining under the pressure. Virgil tried to smile in return, but it was lost to a grimace. "Sorry, blossom. Just a minute longer," her sovereign whispered so that only she could hear. She watched and waited as the contortion dissipated to neutrality, the burden lifted from her frame. Weariness sheltered, the sovereign turned with his queen to face the waiting crowd. "That's taken care of. I hope you have more than rations to serve."

Byrnn nodded. "We sent for fine meals in expectation of your visit, sire."

"Fantastic. Have it prepared," the weary weaver ordered. "Violah, I'd like to consult with you in the commander's office."

The high magus trembled and followed the king in obsequious silence. Descarta watched the thick portal close and felt a cord of sympathy strike for the woman.

...

Virgil had succumbed to the relief of Byrnn's armchair, enjoying the cozy succor. Violah lingered by the door, taciturn and dolorous.

"Sit," Virgil instructed after a long wait.

The high magus obliged, high-necked dress frowning under her lowered chin.

"Explain yourself," came the next sibilant demand.

"I only wanted to show gratitude for my sire's benevolence," she murmured in response. "The horn was the commander's doing, I assure you!"

"The commander is your subordinate," reminded Virgil.

"I know. Sire, he wouldn't obey me."

"Now you know my quandary. What to do with those who refuse to follow orders."

Violah's gaze shot up, uncannily wide. "N-No, sire. I beg you. I'll d-do anything!" Tremor-wrought hands reached to her collar and fumbled with the binding, pulling it open as sensuously as a quaking woman could to just below her navel. Bare chest exposed, she blushed and averted her tormented eyes to the floor. "T-Treat me as v-vulgarly as you like. J-Just please spare me." To her credit, no tears came. Though the tremors did not cease.

Virgil, face in palm, simmered in reticence.

"Does this not p-please you?" The trembling woman stood and let the dress fall from her shoulders into a mound about her ankles. Slowly, she sunk to her knees, sliding her palms forward until her rear rose to a provocative summit. "I'll do a-anything, be anything you want."

"Violah," he breathed in exasperation, "I am your king. If I wanted you, I would ravish you. I would not require something so trivial as your consent." He worked the hand back from his tired face through a disheveled mane.

Violah audibly swallowed.

"Clothe yourself," Virgil sighed.

She did as ordered and finished with an arm held across her chest, timidly obscuring what was no longer bare.

The sovereign dragged his seat across the floor and sat it before the tormented sorceress. Again, he settled into the chair, this time leaning on his knees. "Look at me, Violah."

Her gaze fluttered madly between him and his robes. The scythe-like design reached out for her.

"Look at me!" he growled, squeezing her jaw in his hand and making her peer into his bloodshot orbs. Finally, she sobbed and the cataract of tears came forth. "What happened to you, Violah? I thought you strong."

She knew what he was doing when it began. And she was both supremely grateful and utterly ashamed. A pulsating wave permeated from his grasp, quelling her debilitating fright. A weaver could not slake their own emotions, and the proud woman was beyond conscripting the influence of another. Virgil did not ask for permission. "Thank you, my king." she muttered, confidence and vitality partially restored.

Virgil nodded and released her cheeks. "Maybe now I can speak without you rattling on like a gibbering urchin. If I may finish: 'Impaled by marksman' isn't the elegy I want emblazoned on the bronze throne of Saradin. Announcing my arrival to every spy or turncoat garrisoned at the Bulwark certainly gave them the opportunity to make it so. I could execute you for treason. But I am going to attribute the act to poor judgment." The king frowned. "I didn't think fear would enfeeble you so."

"I am able!" she countered. "I just . . . when you . . . what you did to Dalstan. I've never seen agony like that. The gore has never left my mind. When I think of failure, it paralyzes me."

"I like to think myself a connoisseur of agony," Virgil said in acceptance of the unintentional compliment. "Commitments made in fear are more likely kept out of fear. In your case, however, I can see mercy would be more suitable. So I have an offer."

The woman looked perplexed. "Mercy? An offer, your majesty?"

"Yes. That means you may decline. Though why you would defy mercy is beyond me. I would have you as an agent. You may still observe your power as high magus and maintain autonomy. When I need you, you will be there. You will always have my interests in mind. As recompense, I offer the title of supreme weaver within the year. And the assurance that my agents are treated with the respect they have earned."

"Sire, you are more deserving of the title. I have seen your prowess in weaving. And what of the doctrine? You are bound to the position until death."

Virgil scoffed, waving away the law as insignificant. "I am bound to nothing, Violah. Myself notwithstanding, you are leagues beyond any other weaver in Elusia, permitting you control this enervating fright. Yet you know how politics can elevate the impotent. So what is your answer?"

Violah wasted no time in replying. "A generous offer, my lord. I am most beholden to your kindness. Please," a flicker of her hidebound nature broke though, "make your enemies mine."

"Then it is done. You may go," Virgil gestured toward the door. "And Violah, do not let me witness that ever again."

"I will not," she agreed.

...

Meanwhile, the others had found places at the dining table. Descarta was watching the office door in trepidation. Josiah, sitting to her left, noticed. "Your majesty, is everything okay?"

She faced him. "That woman, Violah, she seemed mortified. And Virgil was incensed when we first arrived. Will she be hurt?"

The scout shrugged. "Perhaps. Perhaps not. Regardless, she knew the punishment for failure. It is beyond us, however, so there is no point in worrying."

Descarta sighed. "I don't have a choice then. I never do."

Josiah summoned a disarming smile. "Virgil would not be happy to see his queen so morose." He paused but began again. "Oh, my manners. I am Josiah, your king's scout for over two decades now."

"Nice to meet you, Josiah." She stumbled over the question before finally blurting it out. "Um . . . two decades? Virgil, Almi and Merill, they don't look very old. Why is that?"

"I can see how that would be flummoxing," Josiah replied. He scratched the side of his head. "Your liege, well, his intimacy with the fabric may curtail his aging. Could be why he looks just over thirty. That's only conjecture, mind. He's never told me outright. Almi and Merill, on the other hand." Josiah grinned at the twins who stuck their tongues out. "The reason these gorgeous little nymphs still look seventeen is because elves mature to that age and never look a day older, even after they expire."

"Oh, I suppose that would explain it. I haven't read many books on elves," Descarta said, wondering enviously how many years they'd seen. "And would you call me by name? I dislike formalities."

Josiah nodded and flashed his most charming smile at the elves across from him. "Almi, Merill. Not a moon passed without my thinking of the two enchanting maidens waiting anxiously for my return. This heart has never relented in its ardor for my kittenish truffles. Tell me: are you ready to be mine?"

"Never! Never! Stop harassing us! Now we remember why it was good our Virgil sent you away. We are his, his only," Almi hissed caustically.

"I see you haven't changed," Josiah smirked, his words lost on the aloof elves.

"Sent you away?" inquired Descarta.

"It wasn't banishment, I assure you. As much as I'd like, I've never done anything lecherous to those truffles. Our mutual agreement is that he pays for my travels; I'm a bard of sorts. In return, I search for artifacts, remnants of lost civilizations and send them back to him. Usually forsaken grimoires or arcane baubles—nasty, dangerous treasures."

"To voyage to uncharted lands and remote nations. It sounds delightful," the petite queen dreamed.

"That's what everyone thinks," Josiah replied. "I left when I was a hale, handsome lad roiling with ambition and wanderlust. Twenty-three years later and I'm only handsome. It's not all a glorious trek. It's fending for your life in snowstorms with frostbitten feet or escaping enraged natives. Waking to ants on your face or trying desperately to find food or water. Or all those things." He smiled then, running a hand over his bald head. "I can't say I wouldn't do it again. I have seen the magically illuminated streets of Tyr and subterranean ruins untouched since the Maiden walked among mortals. And don't get me roused over the salacious men and women. Multi-friggin'-farious."

"I, uh, won't. What do you mean you can't say you wouldn't do it again?" asked Descarta.

"This is my only remaining task. Escorting your group, I mean. When we're finished, I am no longer bound to Virgil. I plan on retiring here, where it all began," explained the bard.

"I like Elusia," the queen pondered, "but I'd like to see more of the world. All I know is within Saradin."

"I think you'll find yourself sufficiently riveted by a few stops on our way to Vanathiel," the rogue promised.

...

"Couldn't this have waited? Josiah was going to perform a ballad," Descarta complained while taking the narrow stairs behind her sovereign.

"His ballads alone justify leaving."

"Why? Didn't you hire him?"

"Yes, I did."

"Then why? Isn't he lauded?" snapped Descarta.

"He has a habit of performing the melodies that trouble me," replied Virgil.

"It's surprising anything troubles you. You only care about yourself. It's rude to pull me away just as he starts to sing. The tune was catchy, too," Descarta lamented, tracing her fingertips over the aged ashlar lining the stairs.

If Virgil had a response, it was never offered. Thus the remainder of the lengthy climb was spent without exchange. There were only the malicious shadows, cast by the saunter of restless torches. Time passed slowly for Descarta, who had little else to do but stare at the robed back ahead while wondering what draconian task he had authored for her.

"Virgil?"

"I think we're nearly there," he announced.

"You think? Do you even know where we're going?"

"Here," Virgil said as he halted and gripped the handle of an iron door. He unbolted the latch and pushed, the seldom used hinges emitting a high-pitched whine. The chamber before Descarta would have been unassailable darkness if not for the remnants of illumination from a torch just down the stairs. Still, its contents remained indiscernible.

"So you have brought me to a dungeon."

Again, Virgil offered no exchange.

"Why are you so quiet? Aren't you going to console your queen? Make her believe you care? Why are you bringing me all this way only to ignore me?" Descarta appealed, growing disturbed by his taciturn demeanor.

Virgil entered the veil and disappeared from her sight. She was alone now, and the cavorting shadows were suddenly unbearably sinister. "Don't leave me out here," she complained, and her voice cracked half-way through as she rushed in after the sovereign. Inside, there was a great still, like the chamber itself was numb. She reached out, searching for something to touch to gain a measure of bearing.

"Virgil, I'm afraid. Stop this." A tiny flame appeared farther away than she expected. He had maneuvered around quite well without seeing. The sovereign willed the ember forward and instantly the room was awash with light reflected off amplifying mirrors.

Descarta sucked in an astounded breath. She stood under a magnificent dome set with a consuming fresco. Countless images coalesced into a collective cycle, illustrating the same beautiful elven maiden throughout the seasons of many years. She would never have expected to find art so striking in an inviolable machine of war. But here it was. Beguiled, the queen paced, followed the depictions that stirred a maelstrom of feelings. Each act of the fresco, though a part of the whole, emanated its own will. And they all effloresced into a single moving entity. She looked to Virgil, who sat atop the marble floor with one leg out and his hands locked in his lap. He was watching her with intensity, back against an altar to the Maiden with an illuminating apparatus in its hands.

"This is magical, Virgil. What is it?" she inquired, unable to mask her emanating awe.

"Many things, blossom," the sovereign solemnly replied. "To most, it is where the sovereigns of Elusia recite their most intimate vows. Between the two of them, no one else."

"Does that mean we were here when I became your queen? Are you trying to renew our vows? Because I am not ready, Virgil. I don't know that I'll ever be. Or that I want to be with someone like you. Despicable." If she had thought nothing troubled him, the utterly shattered look her comment invoked proved her very wrong. She bit her lip, wishing she could rescind the baleful words. Descarta conceded even he did not deserve that.

"I know. I can never be like Kalthused, right?" he averted his eyes to the mural and pressed on, but the wound remained salient. "That's why I brought you here. I thought you would recognize her from the portraits in your books about the legend king. This is all Ankaa, his queen. He had this dome built for her. Kalthused commissioned it atop Galvant's Bulwark in this secret passage so that it was safe, hidden from anyone but the kings and queens whose devotion was consecrated here."

Descarta felt too foolish to reply. Instead, she lay and absorbed the story above her which depicted scenes from Ankaa's youth to her brutal demise. With unforgiving talons, it dragged Descarta to her amnesia—that she had no chronology of her own. "Will I ever have my life back?" she asked.

For a time, Virgil lingered in grim hush, long enough for the gloomy queen to expect no response. "When this journey is over, you will have a life," he finally assured the diminutive girl. "You should pray at the altar before we go. Don't forget what we left in Saradin." The remote, indifferent tone he answered in was unlike any way he'd taken her insults in the past.

...

That night, Descarta tossed sleeplessly. The biting unrest she felt since the chapel prevented weariness from taking her. In a huff of impatience she kicked her covers away, shivering from the chill. "Virgil," she called to the weaver who sat beside her, embroiled in trance.

There was a temporary still while he reeled his spirit back to its vessel. Virgil looked at her, distant and plaintive, as he had since her lacerating words. "Yes, blossom?"

"Are you unwell?" she asked.

"Not at all," he replied, his lips curling into a smile that didn't belong. "Do you need something?"

"No," she responded. "I just—" she started, wriggling back under her covers, suddenly feeling very exposed. "I just want to apologize.

Okay, Virgil? I'm sorry. What I said earlier, in the chapel, it was thoughtless."

"I am not a child, Des. There's nothing to be sorry for. Your feelings are yours to express."

She had already started shaking her head before he finished. "I just wanted to hurt you. To make you suffer. I don't understand how I feel." Virgil put forth no response, so she pressed on. "But I don't hate you. Even though being locked up like your property made me resent you. I don't hate you." Descarta wasn't sure why, but she felt like sobbing. Maybe it was her shame. That her resentment had transcended something she thought her sovereign had earned. Where she lost her memory, he lost a wife. At that moment, she felt worse than him, a vengeful witch that was naught but her lamentations.

"Then I am glad," Virgil said in the sincere, pacifying inflection he usually addressed her with, "that you do not hate me. Now rest, please. The morrow brings more walking."

...

The next morning found the cohorts once again heading east, with the spire at their rear and Josiah in tow. Flanking them throughout the defile were the Maiden's Peaks, precipitous crags that stood as sentinels against foreign enemies. Descarta marveled at the crooked, cloud-fishing mountaintops. "I'm sure Galvant is unhappy, wherever he rests," she postured.

"Why do you say that?" Josiah, who had just returned from his position as advance scout, asked.

"Look at what he uncovered. A view that makes the heart leap, a channel to a new world. If it weren't for him, Elusia would have never taken shape. Now the pass that holds his name is infamous only for countless deaths wrought of countless wars."

"An unfortunate outcome," agreed the bard, "but I don't think I would mind. It is worse to be forgotten."

"What do you think?" Descarta asked, turning to Virgil who followed a dozen paces behind her.

Virgil, scratching the renewed stubble on his cheek, pondered the question. "Whether my legacy is heralded as a boon or malady, I think I would rather be forgotten. Immortality, even as an idea, seems an onerous thing for those living in its shadow."

"A peculiarly murky answer, sire," Hazael commented from his side. "I think you are just lazy."

"People should be allowed to die," arrived Virgil's glum reply.

"We're going to live as long as our Virgil does. Who cares about the rest! Silly philosochatter!" Merill exclaimed from the rear of the party.

Virgil expelled a brief chuckle and Descarta smiled with apparent interest. She thought he exhibited more vigor today, if only slightly. For an unexplained reason, that was something she wanted. The diminutive girl recalled reading the account of an analogous dementia wherein the hostage took on a fondness for its captor. Was she exhibiting symptoms? Descarta deftly squashed that possibility. It was more likely she didn't want to become something she would regret. She wanted to control the one element she could: herself. To conquer eight-hundred days of resentment and emerge beyond its will. In her introspection, she didn't immediately realize Virgil studying her. When she did, Descarta briskly turned away and resumed her stroll, feigning indifference to the four behind her. It was true she couldn't despise him, but she wasn't going to befriend the sovereign either.

"What's funny?" asked Almi, wielding her brutal mace over her shoulder in a feigned attack.

"He's probably amused by your single-mindedness," replied Josiah, alert eyes wandering the crevasses and promontories around them.

"We're his loyal ones," Merill issued, tossing a pebble at the bard which landed in his hanging hood. "You bed any man, woman or feathered turnip lizard!"

Josiah fished the pebble out and snapped it back to bounce harmlessly off of Merill's tunic. "I do it well. I've never left a feathered turnip lizard unsatisfied."

"Our Virgil does it best," Almi mewed.

"So good," Merill concurred, letting out a deep, beguiled sigh.

"What?!" Descarta shouted, steaming at the twins. "What does that mean?!"

The twins giggled and intertwined their fingers, swinging their arms spiritedly. The queen then set her smoldering orbs on Virgil.

He avoided her spear-tipped gaze, pretending to be occupied with Hazael. "This conversation has really degenerated."

The steward nodded. "You're on your own."

"Don't get upset, blossom. They're just speaking in fantasies. Isn't that right, dears?" Virgil commanded more than asked, scowling over his shoulder at the vivacious grinning twins, who were evidently very happy with themselves.

"Right! Fantastic!" they echoed.

At the forefront of the group, Josiah erupted in a powerful guffaw, drawing Descarta's pestilent glare from her evasive king. Josiah tried to regain his composure, but his brow would not stay straight, dimples would not hide. Not so easily vanquished, his belly lurched and a whooping laugh spewed forth.

"Why is my king's infidelity so amusing?" Descarta simmered.

"B-Because," Josiah tried to explain. He was not faring well in his skirmish with the crippling wave of laughter.

"Because your face, my queen, has taken on the contorted shape of a banshee. For all of your cantankerousness toward his majesty, you care might a bit about him bedding his lascivious wards. Who are succeeding in their efforts to rouse you," Hazael explained.

Josiah bobbed his polished head and pointed a shaking finger to the seneschal, confirming the supposition.

Descarta could feel the warmth of blood swarm her cheeks which she promptly concealed with her palms. "You!" she growled at the twins, but she couldn't suppress the giggle that betrayed her elation. She felt she belonged here, on an eventful sojourn with companions who conveyed more than servile deference or fabricated hospitality: adventure. She was surrounded by odd individuals—some she didn't even trust—but it still stirred the conflagration of friendship deep within. The turbulent queen wanted to sunder the walls she'd erected in captivity and accept the consequences, however dire and unpredictable. But it was a risk she could not yet wrestle her frightful heart to endure. There were no certainties, no promises that betrayal wasn't a footstep away. And for the emotionally reclusive girl, that was unacceptable. Descarta had to be absolutely certain she was not being deceived, primed for another session of barred doors and unrelenting tears.

...

The tunnels they'd blundered into assaulted Descarta with impenetrable darkness. All she had to lead her was the vice grip Virgil secured on her wrist and the ephemeral firelight his explosions cast. The stench of charred flesh and sulfur filled her heaving chest with every painful breath. She was sure she sucked in more than air with all the silt her sovereign's fiery weaving set afloat. Descarta could feel the sweat on his palm, hear his labored breathing over the blazes ahead of her and clash of steel behind her. But he pulled her onward, stringing livid oaths at the assassins between every earth-shaking fireball.

"Virgil! There's a golem among them! It's downed Almi and Merill!" arrived Josiah's warning as he closed the gap in the group with impressive speed. "And it's here!" There was a grunt and nothing further from the bard. The pursuing construct grew near and the tunnel began to moan and quake under its thunderous strides. One such tremor left the queen prone and on her back, vision spinning from the fall. A blast from ahead threw light onto the metallic contours of the golem. All she could discern through her twisting perception was the towering creature's silhouette, iron limbs thicker than her torso and raised high. She was going to die. They all were going to die. And it was all her fault.

...

Guffawing finally subdued, Josiah advised the queen that she should be farther back. He should be at the front, scouting. Descarta shrugged off the warning, claiming a few steps were of no consequence. Then she heard it, a clicking beneath her boot. The next second she was tumbling down a pernicious slide of stones.

"Hazael! Ward us!" she heard Virgil cry as he dropped behind her. Obediently, the seneschal shouted a grating word. In response, boulders that should have crushed her raged a hair's breadth away, as if touching the girl was forbidden. Then she hit the bottom, tumbled into a roll and ended with a mouthful of dirt. Descarta slowly rose, shaking, to brace herself on scraped elbows, spitting and coughing.

"Des!" The call vaguely sparked in her mind, lost within the ringing and headache.

"Des!" came again the behest. That was her name, she realized. Someone was calling her.

"Here. I'm here!" she groaned. Footsteps echoed in the gorge. She couldn't tell whether they were growing nearer or farther away.

Something wrapped around her wrist painfully tight and she shrieked as it drew her to her feet. She began to fight it, but the chasm above was enough to brighten the countenance before her. Virgil was there, dragging her toward him, one eye closed under a stream of what could only be blood. He was looking past her to the point above, where they once stood. She hesitated, following his focus to a line of figures in attire resembling Josiah's.

"Assassins!" warned Virgil. "Almi, Merill, guard our rear. Hazael, do not let them die, damn you! Josiah, just be useful!" His commands stirred the death above, and they rappelled down the hole amid the recovering companions. She watched, entranced, as she stumbled to follow her sovereign whose insistent pull sought to dislodge her arm.

Merill's bow twanged thrice in rapid succession. Accordingly, arrows sprouted like delighted flowers from the chests of three dropping assailants. Almi engaged the first enemy within range before his boots hit the ground. She bellowed a high-pitched cry and hopped with feline grace. Coming around in a wild swing, her beastly mace tore its fangs through skull and was back in a flash, ready to devour anew. A rogue to the side went limp, something prodding its armor from within and trying to escape his belly. When he fell, Josiah stood behind him, bloodied dagger in hand. Hazael had his long sword aloft, but made no attempt to advance. She could hear him weaving, though, feel the weave answering his call, and knew that he was doing his part. Then she was tugged around a corner and the clamor was lost. A snarl from ahead brought her back to reality: that she was no spectator. "Run, girl! I cannot just drag you along! I need you to run!"

CHAPTER THREE

Artificial Hands

Descarta clenched her lids shut and pulled her bruised, scraped arms to her face in a feeble barrier, awaiting the crushing blow. She wondered if it would be agonizing, being splattered under the palm of animated iron. She prayed it would be swift and clenched her fists, but an end as mush and entrails strewn across dirt and stone never arrived.

In its place there was a booming flash, bright enough to blind her behind closed eyes. Biting heat crashed over her in a splash, drying her flesh and stealing her oxygen. The diminutive girl opened soot-sodden lids to see Virgil, shaking palm held toward the animation, spewing forth a whirling inferno. The blaze was focused on the construct, yet it seemed to have a will of its own, flaring hungrily in every direction as though the weaver's control was slipping. It coursed off the ceiling and took the shape of the tunnel: a spiraled vortex with golem, weaver and Descarta caught within. The queen, despite being aware of the danger, was frozen in fright. She could only watch the exchange.

An enraged arm descended toward Virgil, who side-stepped just out of the way, knees wavering beneath him aside the newly formed crater. The flaming geyser sputtered as the weaver tried unsuccessfully to renew its waning flow. The orange radiation emanating from the golem and the many small fires provided ample illumination. Descarta finally gathered the wherewithal to back away from the construct, and crawled to the sloping tunnel wall to whimper her discontent. Their assailant had lost an arm, half its head and a sizable chunk of its torso, yet it did not seem to slow. Conversely, Virgil looked beleaguered, robe sizzling under embers, a blistered, charred hand hanging to his side. He labored on one knee in front of his supine queen and drew great, onerous breaths.

Another mighty swing from the hidebound iron beast forced the weaver to lurch to the side. He evaded the blow, but his weight-bearing leg faltered and sent him floundering into the nearest wall. Undaunted, he pushed away, screaming a cord of pain and defiance, and unleashed a globe of conjured water which effectively quenched the roasted metal. A great cloud of steam resulted, obscuring everything just as well as the darkness did. When it dispersed, the construct stood a giant, inanimate statue rendered rigid by the spell combination. Descarta climbed to her feet and gasped for air, realizing she'd held her breath during the confrontation.

His foe vanquished, Virgil collapsed to his hands and knees, easing himself down to the tunnel floor. "Des," he called coarsely between drawing shallow breaths. "Des, are you alright?"

"I'm here, Virgil," she answered as she rushed to kneel beside him and patted down the embers burning about his robe. "I'm uninjured."

"Good. Good." He was calm for a short time, recovering from the skirmish. Then his face contorted in recognition of the bard's earlier words and he sat up. "Almi! Merill! Where are they?"

"They haven't come, Virgil. I don't know."

The sovereign struggled to his knees, but found himself too drained to go higher. "Could you help me, blossom?"

She agreed, pulling his robed arm over her dainty shoulder and assisting him to his feet. "We have to go back. They may be alive," Virgil said, peering behind the incapacitated golem.

"What of the assassins? What if they're after us?" Anxiety was vivid in her reply. Her king's enervation was lucid. She was burdened with practically carrying him.

"It doesn't matter. They're back there, Des. They need me."

"And what will you do for them, Virgil? Will you fight? You can't even stand without my support," argued the queen as she readjusted her grip on his raven mantle.

"Then you will support me."

"That's not the point! You can't—"

"I must!" the weaver contested. "Almi, Merill . . . they deserve better than to die my martyrs. They've lived bound to someone who denied them happiness. I must try."

Descarta opened her mouth to protest, but it was stymied by a loud grumbling from the charred roof above the frozen construct. The earth shook and ruptured, shedding boulders. Virgil willed himself forward, attempting to cross before an impasse materialized. Sensing the danger, his queen jerked him away from certain death, easily redirecting the weary sovereign. Balance forfeit, the weaver fell to his knees facing Descarta. A wave of dust and pebbles careened past as the tunnel caved in behind him.

Standing above her king, Descarta didn't need the extinguished flames to reveal the man before her as forlorn. She nibbled indecisively on her bottom lip, hesitant to reach for him, comfort him, though she believed she should.

Relieving her of the pressure, Virgil grabbed her arms and pulled himself up. She could feel the charred flesh of his hand slough onto her skin and it made her cringe. "We're leaving," he muttered in a tone that resonated misery.

...

Almi plucked a moist length of liver from her mace, tossing it aside and scrunching her oblique elven eyes in disgust. She hissed at the fading figure that lay below, a man who was patting his shredded side in a futile attempt to pull it back together.

"More?" Merill inquired from her perch on a tiny plane, arrow still cautiously nocked.

"I don't think so," Hazael sounded from under her, peering at the chasm above them. "Or they've all had second thoughts after watching your savage display."

The mace-wielding elf smiled and wiped a splash of blood from her cheek. "My weapon hasn't bitten in so long. Your compliment makes it happy!" Almi, center of melee for the duration of the foray, emerged with only a swollen eye, minor cuts and a limp courtesy of the stampeding golem.

Boot scuffing on rock caught the attention of all three. Merill raised her bow, prepared to intercept another assault.

"Don't kill me, please," Josiah groaned as he stepped from the tunnel and into the cave's dusty illumination. He was massaging a whelp on his now misshapen head. "That damned tin bastard kicked me."

"He kicked us, too. You aren't special," chided Almi.

"I didn't want to be kicked," Josiah sighed.

"Weren't you told to help Virgil?" the seneschal interjected, glaring at the bard.

Josiah returned the glare with like force. "I was asked. Not told. You aren't my superior." The rogue took a seat on the rubble-strewn floor and retrieved a jar of slimy green poultice from one of his many belt pouches. He dug two fingers in, scooped a dripping gob of the goo and began smearing it on his concussion. "I yelled to him, warned him, I think. Then the golem kicked me aside with one of its strides. One painful tumble later and I awoke to find the passage had suffered a cave in. I did see the construct among the debris, though. It was incapacitated as far as I could tell."

"Astounding," the steward replied as he snatched the poultice and tossed it to Almi. She sniffed it and recoiled, gagging on the putrid smell. "You aren't supposed to smell it, Almi. Just apply it to your wounds. Or get Merill to do it," said Hazael before turning back to the bard. "The creatures—well, devices—possess a nearly impregnable resiliency to weaving. It must have been the cave-in."

"You don't have to tell me. I discovered the damn things. Sundered curse them," replied the grumpy bard.

"We knew our Virgil was astounding all along," crooned Merill. She had come down from her perch to apply the jam-like muck which Almi refused to touch. The wounded elf pinched her nose shut while being doctored.

"Super astounding," Almi added nasally.

Hazael deliberated the darkened passage while stroking his clean-shaven chin. "Can we follow them?"

Josiah shook his head at the impossibility of the question. "Not happening. Massive boulders there. And even if we manage to move them, it'd take many hours and we'd risk another collapse."

"We can't just leave him! He's our Virgil!" Almi argued while Merill finished her nurturing with a gentle kiss. The elves hugged one another, foreheads touching. "All of this excitement," Almi whined in a carnal hum.

"Exciting," Merill agreed. The elves sighed in unison and frowned at Hazael. "We want our Virgil."

The steward deliberated, pacing the gorge. "We fell under Galvant's Pass near the desert. The tunnel looks to be artificially made—earthfolk, of course. That means it either leads to Stonenoggin or one of the many mines in the ridge. So the logical conclusion would be to set off for Stonenoggin and seek help. Your Virgil will push on whether we're with him or not. His next stop must be the earthfolk establishment."

"Makes sense," concurred the rogue, producing a length of rope and tiny grappling hook from yet another pouch. "It's fortunate I'm a resourceful bard. The spoony types are useless."

...

Virgil staggered forward, arm slung around the slumped back of his shambling queen. Hours had passed in this state, following a path whose exit was neither forthcoming nor promised. A meager flame floated above the sovereign's damaged hand, illuminating a sphere around the pair.

More than a couple times, Virgil cast a wistful glance to their rear. Descarta couldn't help but wonder what exactly the uncommon elves had meant to him. It seemed a complicated relationship. One he had forfeit for her, she accepted. He ordered the eccentric pair to stay behind while he dragged her onward into this tenebrous abyss. To send someone who worshiped her to their death. She could have never done that, the duty of a sovereign. "Virgil," Descarta started, still peering ahead. "Virgil, thank you. For saving me." He had rescued her, rescued her and left everyone else behind.

"Kalthused couldn't do that," he proudly and venomously replied.

"Not the response I was looking for."

"It's my first victory over the bastard," Virgil said as he took another weary step. "He could not protect his blossom. I could."

Descarta sighed and halted. "You win this one. Here, give me your hand." She grasped his forearm and pulled the injured appendage before her. The little fire bobbed gently to the side, a silent observer. "I told myself I'd never do this for you under any circumstances. Consider it payment for your deeds today."

Carefully wrapping her hands around his, Descarta hunched forward in concentration. Her calming breaths were like a morning breeze on his burned skin. Virgil watched, spellbound by the act, as ethereal wisps of pale blue emanated from her ginger application. The weaving capered across his flesh, mending all it graced until a healthy pink layer replaced burns and boils.

"You have been practicing." Virgil smiled at his dainty queen. His ember's paltry radiance played stark shadows on her blooming features. Soot-covered and glum, he still found her impossibly ravishing. "I will not forget the gesture, my blossom."

Descarta dropped his hand and helped him onward once more. "Don't get any ideas," she said. "You have two years to make up for."

...

The trek to Stonenoggin was an arduous one set across the Skrillsill Desert. Dormant dangers were abound: colossal ant lions, heat exhaustion, sandstorms and bandits, all ostensibly poised to strike from just beyond the nearest dune. Yet these were insignificant happenstances before the unremitting cavils of Almi and Merill. They whined, they complained, they carped and they cried.

"Virgil! Virgil!" the elves called fervently and erratically, hoping their dear king was within earshot. "Virgil! Come back to us!"

They pleaded at times, trying to coerce themselves back into what they perceived as lost favor. "Virgil, you're precious to us. We've always been yours. Always!"

Another vacillating mood was the time of tears, as Josiah had titled it in an attempt to placate himself. A period of mourning composed chiefly of inarticulate moans and wailed nonsense.

Their utmost endeavor, though, was a passionate display of pulchritude. The licentious elves equipped a sensual timbre and enumerated every dirty, taboo deed they would do for their master, to their master.

The bard knew madness then, he could sense it nipping at the peripheral of his sanity. A half-day of relentless grief was grinding against his skull, made worse by wearying travel and a sore lump aside his head.

"We're going too slow!" Almi crowed from behind.

"Stop! Just stop! You haven't ceased your childish carping since we left the gorge!" Josiah snapped. "Two decades! For two decades I have journeyed with half-wits and brigands, and not one was nearly as bothersome as the two of you!"

"But our Virgil! We must find him! He's too far away!" Merill screamed in response, her eyes tearing up for the fourth time that day, the time of tears reborn.

Almi hugged the morose elf and pouted too. "We cannot see him."

"Have you no sense at all?! What do you think we're doing?!" Josiah spat, incensed at the twins' compulsion.

Hazael pushed a flask of water at the bard. "Drink. You're growing dehydrated. Berating them isn't solving anything. They can't control it any more than thirst."

Josiah nodded and tilted the flask to his mouth, savoring the invigorating liquid. "Can't you do something about them?"

"Not with their lives intact."

The bard cast an inquisitive glance at the steward.

"No, Josiah."

"I won't tell if you don't. 'The sisters succumbed to sand worms. No bodies to be found, sire. We're terribly sorry,'" rattled the rogue.

"He would be using a bucket of your organs as courser feed."

"It'd be a content bucket," remarked Josiah, returning the water. "Do you think we'll reach Stonenoggin before sundown?"

"Plausible. We shouldn't be far now. And Josiah," Hazael peered back while treading through the sand, "You were banished those years past."

"We were friends. Virgil wouldn't be that severe," the bard said, dismissing the warning. "He gave me an opportunity to travel, give my ballads some substance. I accepted."

Hazael smirked. "Is that what he told you? You were either friends or useful, that much is true. Elsewise, he wouldn't have sent you far, far away. But I know what they were to him at the time, and you crossed a line."

"What are you trying to say?" asked Josiah.

"I've seen you leering. Maybe that's why their infatuation is troubling you. My advice is simple: let it go. There will be no second chance."

"Are you threatening me?"

"As his seneschal, I am warning you. Because in his absence it is my place to exact punishment." Hazael punctuated the point by tapping a thumb on his scabbard. "I would rather not."

...

For the fifth time, Virgil's chin slumped to his collar and curtains settled over his vision. Almi and Merill were there, painted beautifully across his lids. They flashed fairylike grins from the courtyard garden where they lounged on their bellies. The king had entered the fabric many times; the realm made traversing dreams simple. He was aware. Knew where this was, when it was, that it was merely a recurring memory. And he knew why. They were gone, and this is where he'd taken everything from them. Perhaps that's why they'd clung to the courtyard, why he avoided it. The weaver couldn't be what they yearned for. He no longer had the capacity. But the sovereign found himself challenging whether he'd put forth a genuine venture. Descarta, as understandably vindictive as she was, had revived rotted, antediluvian emotions. The devoted elves toiled for years and he sentenced them to die. Normally, that note would fall flat among the harsh chords of cynicism and forgotten ethics, but the echo of a wayward course rang sharp. An alternative passage where he had been what they craved, needed. Where he hadn't defied the twins' boundless love.

Frustration, stabbing and shrill in its relentlessness, surged forth, and he willed the dream to disperse. Mourning would not free him of this endless tunnel or restore his queen. He could feel Descarta's presence when he came to, standing above him tentatively. "My queen," the weaver said, more to himself than to the waiting girl. It was by his will that she was queen. The hidebound, adventurous young sprite had bewitched him, and he couldn't allow lamentation to jeopardize what little affection he had earned.

"What is it?" she asked. Likely for the third or fourth time, as her voice gained a slight edge.

"I have to rest, my queen." Virgil could sense her shift nervously before him.

"Of course you do. We aren't walking any further. I can't just carry you when you doze off, you know." Descarta shifted again, boot scuffing against the stone below. "I can't see when you're sleeping."

"Are you afraid?"

"No," she muttered, though her denial wasn't very convincing. "I just can't see."

"I'm sorry, dear. Come, sit near me." Virgil patted the uneven, pebble-strewn earth to his right as though it wasn't so unappealing. "I won't be sleeping, so you needn't worry. I have to administer your treatment."

"Not tonight, Virgil," she insisted. "Tomorrow, after you've had some rest."

"Every night, Des. I cannot break the ritual or we start over. From the beginning," warned the weaver in a solemn tone, making it clear he wouldn't discard two years of toiling for a slight reprieve.

The dainty queen hesitated, then sighed resignation. "Very well." She took a seat beside him, grunting as she searched for a suitable position. She swiftly discovered there wasn't one. Descarta reached across her chest and held her opposite arm, blinking against the darkness. Detestable sleeping arrangements aside, it wasn't much different than any other night, though she couldn't tell whether the moon was above them. Virgil was stationed at her side, murmuring, while she awaited reverie.

Only now her mind was awash with clamor. The twins were gone, and she hadn't decided what that meant to her. They were often rancorous, destructive brats who extracted delight from her misery. Yet just as frequently they were sweet, affectionate creatures who would stroke away her troubles. And could she truly fault them for their enmity? She was, albeit unwillingly, an obstacle to a relationship they had likely sought before she was given birth. She couldn't subscribe to their feelings. She knew dementia lingered there, but she also knew they loved him. If Virgil's disposition was ever nebulous, this day made it salient. He'd chosen her over them.

He did try to return, and the torrent of rock would have surely killed him. The time surrounding that event made it evident he had lost something he treasured.

It was possible the peculiar twins weren't the only losses. Hazael, the introverted steward who had cared enough to tease her. Josiah, the jovial bard who she'd only met yet who had treated her as a lifetime acquaintance. By her edict or not, their sacrifices were hers to remember.

CHAPTER FOUR

Miraculously Morr

Descarta sucked in a breath, stirring from her dreamless slumber and rubbing her eyes against the dim light. She stretched like a feline emerging from its nap and weaned out the ache worn into her bones by the rugged stone bed. Luminous golden eyes squinting in a yawn, she leaned to her left where Virgil had succumbed to weariness. Emitting a sleepy grunt, she brushed a messy tangle from her soiled cheek. The ribbon that had bound her hazelnut tresses was lost during their desperate escape. Now they fell in a dirty gossamer tumble around her fair countenance and shoulders.

"Liar," she mumbled. "You said you would be awake." It wasn't until then that an alarm was raised. So inured to waking to sunshine, she regarded the nearing torch as ordinary. "Virgil," she whispered to the dormant sorcerer. "Virgil, someone's approaching! Wake up!" Descarta spoke more fervently but his state remained unchanged.

One of the figures pointed at her, speaking to its partner in a voice like agitated gravel. "There!"

Descarta knew panic. She scrambled to put her boots beneath her, assuming a confident posture and doing her best to wrangle an authoritative pitch that wanted to break in fear. "Come no further! I'm a weaver, and I won't hesitate to use my power!" she growled, conjuring a harmless shroud of bluish energy around her raised palm.

The figures halted in trepidation at her command. It gave the queen a chance to examine them behind the glow of their torch. Closest stood an ogre of a man, presumably amused, as he wore a wide grin betwixt gray-bearded cheeks. His hulking mass was protected by a bronze half plate contrivance strapped over a navy arming doublet. A snarling demon crested his only spaulder, connected to a vestibule and hourglass gauntlet. Matching bronze sabatons and breastplate emblazoned with the earthfolk insignia, an erupting volcano, were the only additional plate attachments. Descarta imagined the goliath metal-forged mallet harnessed to his back demanded a wide berth.

Behind the man was an earthfolk wayfarer. Within the earthfolk den, wayfarers were often utilized as scouts, merchants or any vocation that didn't require great strength. They discarded the disproportionate upper body of their knuckle-walking brethren, titans, in exchange for a more humanoid form which delivered greater dexterity. Cracked, rocky masses like petrified bark sealed earthfolk, wayfarer and titan alike, as children of the mountain. Even the diminished anatomy of a wayfarer was imbued with more power than most any human or elf.

Still flashing a smile of white teeth, the human took a step forward. "Ah, the fair Maiden is my ally this day. I had a feelin' you would be in this abandoned causeway." He gestured toward the wayfarer, speaking in a resonating timbre. "Gurlax here said following my gut was asinine!"

"I said it wasn't empirical," replied the earthfolk. Descarta thought he was grumbling, but it could have merely been his coarse voice.

"You're thinkin' they're the same thing," laughed the man.

"Who in the Sundered's fetid pits are you, and why shouldn't I unleash a flurry of foul thaumaturgy at your foolish hides?" Descarta growled in agitation, trying to maintain her facade.

"What temper!" the human exclaimed before chuckling, hands on his hips.

"She is afraid, sir."

"I know, I know. She's fiery when afraid!" The human quelled his grin. "Forgive me. Kiern Hafstagg is my name. Call me Hafstagg. And please, dispel your petty pixie dust. It isn't suitin' you, and I won't be healed to death. We're here to rescue you, fair queen of Elusia."

The diminutive girl spouted an oath, releasing her hold on the weave. She still stood resolute above the unresponsive king. "Why should I believe you?"

"The thing does not wish to be saved," Gurlax observed in his perpetual grumble.

"You said she was frightened, brother. The lass fits the description, so we can't just be leavin' her here."

"All humans look the same to me."

"Bah!" snorted Hafstagg. "Beyond beautiful. Willowy chassis, modest thighs, tiny chest and fierce yellow orbs. A tiny sapling unfathomable in her capacity to enchant," he quoted. "Just as the king described two years ago. And the frock! You can't claim that, in these forsaken tunnels, someone who looks like the queen has mugged her and is now wearing her dress."

"A doppelganger?" suggested the wayfarer.

"Why are you twaddling on like I'm not here?!" yelled the queen, blushing at the odd but flattering description. Was that really how Virgil viewed her?

"Sorry, little one." Hafstagg lifted his hands, palm out, in a gesture of peace. "I've been told I take grim situations too lightly. Please don't think poorly of me." He took a tentative step toward Descarta. "We are not assassins. If I were willin' it, you would be like . . . like . . . Gurlax, your kind has a penchant for these analogies."

"Like a brittle winterflake before me," offered the earthfolk.

"That," said Hafstagg, edging closer. "We're one of many teams who set out last night to retrieve you and Virgil. At my command, of course. Debts to settle and all."

Logic affording no other option, Descarta nibbled on her bottom lip, a bastion of anxiety, and backed down from the imposing warrior. "He's not waking," she explained, absently stroking her forearm.

"Well, he's not dead," smiled the man. "His chest rises and falls. Happened once after the alliance thwarted another advance by Kaen Morr. Foolhardy bastards. We'll carry him to Stonenoggin." Hafstagg bent to heft the weaver, calloused fingers outstretched to scoop him up, hovering over a hole in his sleeve. When those thick phalanges contacted the sovereign they rendered the giant man paralyzed. Hafstagg mentally reeled as thousands of images poured over his mind, many blurred to meaninglessness while a fraction were as clarion as they day they'd been forged. As the film was delivered, a discordant note struck his core at regular intervals. The chord, a bittersweet plucking, called to his spirit with growing intensity at each resurgence. The warrior was afraid his spirit would be ripped from its vessel if pulled any harder. A heartbeat later—hours in his temporal distortion—and the engorged chord reached its final sforzando before dissolving into fading ache.

To the observing pair, it seemed like his posture and countenance transformed in an instant. He gathered a vast lungful of breath and held it, attempting to mend his shaken nerves.

Gurlax folded his stony arms, growing impatient. "Would you just pick him up?"

Descarta stepped toward the perturbed man, still stroking her arm in anxiety. "Um, sir. Is everything alright? I could—"

"No!" huffed Hafstagg. "No. Please don't burden yourself." He tentatively touched the same spot without reproducing the effect. It seemed safe, but he couldn't risk the queen seeing what he had. Hafstagg scooped Virgil with evident ease and forced a grin onto his face. "Ha! Weavers! They're like tiny flufftail rabbits! Was that a good one, Gurlax?"

"Mediocre."

"Bah!" snorted the warrior.

The trio set off for Stonenoggin with Descarta hurrying to the side of the hammer-wielding fellow. "What you said earlier," she murmured, "was it true?"

"Which part?" Hafstagg asked.

"About me."

"Yes, you're a brittle winterflake."

"No, not that." Descarta dropped her volume to an embarrassed mumble. "Virgil. Did he really say I was gorgeous, and the other things?"

"Of course!" bellowed Hafstagg, delighted at her timidity. "Though he's not for sayin' himself, I'm sure. Always had a chilly touch." He then lowered his tone as though it would prevent the figure in his arms from hearing. "Just don't tell him I told you."

The queen smiled, and a hint of rouge touched her cheeks.

...

"Ankaa!" bellowed Kalthused as he parried an incoming spear, beat it wide and shuffled in to disembowel its owner.

"Ankaa!" he called, brewing desperation clutching his pitch as he tried to shout over the din of battle. Aided by three royal guards, the spellblade trudged forward, fighting relentlessly for every bloody step.

"Ankaa!" The saturnine king had forgotten how many times he reached out for her. He could only measure the definitive misery creeping into his gut. It was rending, the culmination of every bloodthirsty legionnaire taking a stab at his heart. For she only had to respond—merely acknowledge his cries. Which she did not.

"Ankaa!" His commanding timbre was beginning to crumble under terror. Kalthused conjured a spray of water at the nearest raider. Chilled by the deep winter weather, the torrent washed over the man and left him a frozen cadaver.

"An, Ankaa," stammered the spellsword. Mirth was driven from his call, but he pressed on, weaving another crest of frosted

froth. He'd been fighting for so long, too long. Coupled with despair, exhaustion was beginning to leaden his limbs.

"An . . ." Finally, he and his guard broke the line. If it weren't for the haunting medley of labored breaths, or her scarlet-stained furs, Kalthused would have thought his queen ravishing. Sunflower strands spread in petals from her pained countenance. Ice shined iridescent around his supine goddess, slowly blemished by her fading vim. Wrapped as she was, Kalthused could have mistaken the dreadful scene for their diurnal, early morning greetings. When, comfortably swallowed by wolf pelts, she would issue her dazzling grin and bring about the dawn.

Ankaa. A thought unarticulated. He could no more call for her than she could come to him.

A mumble brought Descarta from her book. She laid *Kalthused* across the bunched lace of her frock and watched Virgil. He did not stir, only gave a slight tremble and returned to stillness. Kalthused could not prevent his queen's demise. Virgil had done precisely that, and at a harsh personal loss. The girl could not deny him that victory.

His caretaker was out, so she sat aside the biography and stood over the unresponsive sorcerer. Virgil was making it difficult to resent him. And Descarta needed the very resentment she found herself doubting. She reminded herself that this man had verily imprisoned her for the only years she'd known. Mere moons ago that would have been enough to extinguish her misgivings.

Now, hovering above her captor, she found certainty slipping.

...

Emptiness surrendered, retreating from its intoxicating throne where it served well as a numbing despot. The vacancy was claimed by a cavalcade of burdensome awareness: longing, regret and an acute headache. Virgil groaned and blinked at an umber sky. His body seemed heavier, as though sacks of grain were strapped to his chest.

Clarity returned gradually, revealing the sculpted ceiling of an artificial cave. The room wobbled and tilted in his vision like a deteriorating pendulum in its final throes. Virgil rolled his head to the left, control slowly seeking its way back into his body. The last flicker of sentience he remembered was being stuck in the fabric, too exhausted to will his spirit back to its vessel.

On a stool to his left sat a homely middle-aged woman in filthy dress and apron, bloodied cloth in her hand. "Oh, your majesty. Not even an hour's rest. You should sleep."

Virgil nearly succumbed to the order. Reverie was a rapturous idea. Perhaps he could find the quiet place again, the emptiness. Descarta, watching over the shoulder of his caretaker, reminded him that it was foolish, that he'd gone too far to give in now. Not yet.

"An hour? You forget he left me all alone in the tunnel so he could nap," corrected the diminutive girl from behind the nurse.

"Don't be hard on him, lass. He should be recovering," chided the woman.

The weaver felt his bubble of awareness expand further as more senses were restored. The grain-filled sacks stirred on his chest and watched him with expectant sanguine gazes. "Virgil," Merill whispered, the wake of a crying spell fresh on her voice, "Virgil, we're yours always."

"Always our Virgil's," Almi emphatically pouted.

"Don't leave us again, please. We were so afraid. We'll be good. We'll do anything," Merill begged, nuzzling his stubble.

"Anything," Almi again emphasized.

"Don't leave us," Merill repeated.

"Don't."

"We belong to our Virgil."

"Yours," petitioned Merill.

"Okay, you've made your plea, girls. Now let him rest," the orange-headed nurse sighed.

"Yours," whimpered Merill, sniffling.

"Forgive me, your greatness. We tried to get them to leave, or at least wait like normal folk. They wouldn't budge and put up quite the fight. We didn't want to hurt them, sire," explained the woman who still toyed with the stained rag. The king wondered how many more titles she'd prepared for him.

"I'm sorry," he whispered as the last remnants of cognizance returned. "I'm not going to leave you. You're special girls."

Watching, Descarta spotted the struggle in his distant gaze. She couldn't gather its origin, only that it was for them. His assurances were blatantly scripted responses, like he was concealing something just beneath the surface. Considering his demonstration in the tunnels, she thought he'd be ecstatic to find his clingy wards every bit the warrens of vivacity he left behind.

"Blossom," called Virgil, lancing her contemplation. "What time of day is it?"

"Late morning. We had to surface for a moment to switch tunnels."

"Good. We could be out of the Skrillsill by nightfall." Virgil sat up between Almi and Merill, muscles objecting ardently. The blanket he'd been covered with tumbled into a mess about his lower waist. "I've been undressed," he noted. "Why?"

Descarta inhaled audibly, and every inch of her exposed skin glowed a saturated red. Her sovereign was in impeccable condition, if a bit emaciated. Serpentine ligaments responded to the slightest movement, winding and bulging around a lean frame. The queen expected a lanky man and misshapen gut with all the time he spent in his study. She also spied a curious constellation of three circular scars on his back.

The elves were blushed for a different reason. They pressed their lithe bodies against him, issuing excited giggles. "Oh, it's been so long." Almi huskily breathed.

"Use us again," Merill pleaded, tracing her fingertips seductively over his deltoid. "Make us scream again."

"Hey!" Descarta objected. "Again?! Stop that! Stop now!"

The nurse, too flabbergasted by the sisters to reply, finally collected a response. "W-Well, you were unresponsive. I had to

examine you for injuries. It's procedure, your empyrean lordship sir."
She added another supplicating title to the growing list. "Your robe
isn't in good shape, but it's plenty intact. Hanging behind you, your
grace."

"We want to start," Merill pruriently breathed as she straddled
Virgil's lap.

"Stop!" shouted the flustered queen.

"Everyone out but Des," ordered Virgil.

"She didn't even ask!" cried Almi, wrapping her arms around
her sister's tummy and pouting over her shoulder.

"Go. Now," the weaver replied in calm, even inflection.

Depressed, the elves slinked off him and toward the egress,
movements provocative. They stopped there, Merill behind Almi,
chin hooked on her shoulder and slender digits exploring her sister's
torso. "What if we let Des join?"

The sovereign scowled his answer and the nymphean twins
fluttered plaintively through the door.

"Virgil," the petite queen started nervously, "don't make me . . .
I'm not ready for this." A barbed shiver rocked her frame.

"I just needed them out, blossom. Now turn around while I
dress," he explained, reaching for his threadbare mantle.

She did as he said, blushing further at the sound of his feet
hitting the floor. An intoxicating blaze called in her lower abdomen,
and Descarta wrapped willowy arms around her hearth.

"Honestly," the sovereign commented as he slipped into his
garb, "do you have such little faith in me?" Fastening the final button,
he approached the fretful girl. "You can face me now."

She turned around and he was right in front of her. Startled by
his proximity, she kept her sight on his chest.

"Des," he said. The sorcerer recounted the sojourn hitherto. He
surmised it wasn't what she had envisioned when they set out.

"Huh?" she answered, clenching her hands anxiously at her
sides.

"We won't draw attention in the market here. I think we can
manage a visit before we leave. And I'm certain we'll find something

exotic to eat." He paused, examining the ill at ease queen. "Would you mind joining me?"

Descarta nodded, turbulence lifting. "I'd like that."

...

Hafstagg contemplated his tankard, sloshing about the reliably inebriating Solstice Ale. The phantasmagoria he experienced was chiefly cryptic and above comprehension. Only shards of the display spoke with clarity, and what was clear troubled him profoundly. Virgil's memories added scope to a tale not unlike his own, one wrought of the same inescapable despair. Yet unlike the warrior, the weaver sought to transcend his burden. Even with such an unorthodox approach, Hafstagg knew he couldn't fault the king. The distraught warrior would surely follow a similar path if he had the capacity.

"Have you found what you're looking for?" inquired a baritone timbre.

The warrior looked up from the tincture to see Hazael seated beside him at the bar. "In here?" he swirled the ale around and offered a morose grin to the steward. "Not yet, but I figure I never will."

"Then why endure the torture of lamenting what you cannot change?"

Hafstagg shrugged. "It's my fault he's gone. I should suffer." He took a gulp of Solstice, reveling in the burning sensation that singed his throat and gave the brew its name. "The least I can do. All I can do."

The seneschal frowned while rotating his glass thoughtfully. "I know someone like that. The disposition atrophies your heart."

"Maybe," conceded the warrior, "but I'm thinkin' to forget would be an affront."

"Don't forget. Forgive."

Hafstagg nodded, not convinced. "So why are you here?"

"International diplomacy. I can't say much more."

"I forget I'm only rabble now," chuckled the beastly man. "No longer knight to the sovereign."

"That was your decision," reminded Hazael.

"One I regret today." Hafstagg sighed in a mighty, fermented breath. "I may fight for Ignus, but I'm only a mercenary." The warrior considered the revelation gifted by his sovereign's fragmented memories. "My hammer aches to smash heads in Virgil's name."

"You abandoned your service without his consent, and now you want to return?" The steward shook his head in disbelief. "No, I'll not risk making myself a target. Be grateful he didn't send someone to drag you back. His Majesty steamed for days."

"I nearly wet myself when I saw you and the girls, to be honest," admitted Hafstagg in a lighthearted tone. "Thought you were here to deliver a sentence."

"You did rescue his maiden. Speak with him; he may allow it," suggested Hazael as he rose from his stool. "Knowing him we'll be gone soon after he wakes."

...

He watched the freshly-washed auburn tapestry willingly conform to her movements and admired its luster. His spirited sparrow led him along a meandering path, head jerking to the nearest storefront as she searched for anything that would capture her attention. She halted at a booth with peculiar mammals hanging from their tails. Descarta gawked at the exotic creatures, tapestry giving way to a radiantly animated visage. The captivating siren produced a fascinated smile, angling her head to get a better look at the cute marsupials. The observer imagined the smile was for him, allowed himself to sink into the fabrication.

He reached a chimerical hand forward, losing his fingers in those lustrous curtains. The smooth flesh of her ear drew coils around his wrist and invited him further.

"Ah, she has a knack, sir!" The nasal voice of an elven merchant sliced the fantasy. "A knack for choosing the grandest of creatures.

These marsupials are sought after by elven nobility as bedside companions!"

He was lying. They were dirty swamp dwellers, and the only reason they weren't hostile was because they were given sedative. Virgil scowled at the vendor as his hatred for the race rose. Their barbaric superstitions were the reason Almi and Merill could never be normal. He wanted to garrote the unctuous bastard just for interrupting his dream. Instead, he swallowed the rising disdain. "She's only looking," arrived his terse reply. Then to Descarta, "Blossom, would you like some food?"

The girl pulled her attention from the furry creatures and stared up at him. "I've had nothing since the tower. Could we?"

Virgil appreciated the vigor of her gaze, the flame of a nearby lantern reflecting in a rapturous dance. He'd nearly lost that to a construct the night before. Yet here she was, wonderfully iridescent. And he still couldn't convey his roiling affection.

Descarta wasn't the only one being watched. She witnessed the tumultuous flow in his stare, trapping secrets manifold. He never told her anything. She was his oblivious queen, expected to follow him without pondering his decisions. She wanted to recall her past so badly. "Virgil, something's troubling you, isn't it?" she pressed. "Why don't you tell me anything?"

Virgil smiled at her and squashed the turbulence. She was a perceptive girl. "I was just thinking of a nice meal. You shouldn't worry yourself." He glanced beyond her to the plaza ahead. "Should we try there?"

She bristled and wondered if this was how she was treated before her amnesia. And if so, why she had ever found him a worthy companion. The queen didn't know why she tried to show compassion. "I'm not familiar with any of these cuisines anyway. Being barricaded in a palace can do that."

If her response bothered him, Virgil didn't show it. "You'd like what Kaen Morr has to offer. Despite our standing with the nation, I miss their culture." He started toward a venue entitled Miraculously

Morr. "A great variety of desserts there. You enjoy fruit-filled rolls, don't you? They have something similar."

Following closely, Descarta studied the massive stalactites crowning the cavernous caw. Marveling, she meditated whether the formations ever fell or if they spectated for millennia. The pair passed beneath a glowing lantern that obscured her view of the dome above. Lanterns were everywhere, illuminating what would have otherwise been a very dark, very large pit. When the flare was gone, they reached the portal to the restaurant.

Miraculously Morr was an astute name, as its dour interior reflected the state of affairs in the military dictatorship of Kaen Morr. Only one patron was present, so the pair seated themselves at a small table farthest removed. The owner soon approached and took their orders, with Virgil requesting a brioche dessert for the queen.

Descarta contemplated her layered skirt, fidgeting uneasily with the filigree. "This is the first time we've had a real meal together. In my limited memory, I mean."

"It is," the weaver acknowledged. "Does it inconvenience you?"

The girl shook her russet crown. "I'm just used to dining alone."

"Isn't that what you wanted?" he inquired, worried he'd mistreated her.

"It was lonely," Descarta admitted, thinking back to all the meals shared with a burning candle. "But I didn't want the alternative." She raised her spellbinding orbs to Virgil. "Were you lonely?"

"Not particularly."

"You didn't set a place for me in case I changed my mind?"

Virgil frowned. "You shouldn't spy."

"I didn't," she grinned. "It's just what I'd imagine a person doing when they wanted someone lost to return."

"Clever girl," he sighed. "Why are you prying?"

"Virgil, I don't understand. If you want me to trust you, why do you withhold everything from me?" Her smile vanished, lost to disappointment. "It has the opposite effect."

"What do you want then?"

"The truth. Not all at once, but show me you mean well."

Any reply Virgil meant to conjure was truncated by the arrival of their orders. They ate in reticence, Descarta picking at her grilled fish while her saturnine sovereign considered his options. He wanted dearly to please her, to tell her everything. Yet he had greater responsibilities which bound him to a distance. Even if he could somehow breach those rises, even if she accepted the truth, what good would he be to her? "Des," he called, deciding the least destructive response would be one that conveyed those thoughts.

She looked up from her meal, a cauldron of grief.

"Des," he repeated, using the name to galvanize his admission. "I'd like to be Kalthused. He could be the happiness you deserve." Virgil summoned a plaintive smile and diverted his attention to his stuffed brambleshrooms.

The queen was uncertain how to respond. She didn't expect him to entertain her. Descarta peered at the brooding man who leisurely consumed his lunch. Never before had he, even in such an indirect and wounding manner, willingly communicated his feelings for her. It occurred to Descarta that she'd never given him the chance to. Mayhap she hadn't been forthright either, rarely showing gratitude for his kindness because she considered her resentment warranted.

Hesitantly, she reached forward to place a quavering hand over his. The weaver was frosty under her fingertips. She issued a gentle squeeze to steady her trembling. Descarta realized she'd been unnecessarily antagonistic toward the man. He didn't seem to glean satisfaction from her imprisonment. When she noticed him hoarding his thoughts, it was always coupled with melancholy. And the chalice he finally put forward exposed both a desire to be her king and the resignation that he couldn't fill that role. She worried that meant Virgil had given up on her.

The sovereign gave the dainty hand his attention, offering it a perplexed grimace. Her contact was gossamer velvet, like it hovered there, brushing just over the skin. Virgil swallowed and locked his sight on the emanating warmth of Descarta's touch, too discordant to look at her.

Descarta identified the skirmish and prodded him. "Virgil," she said, leaning into his vision. "Hey, look at me."

After struggling with apprehension, he obliged. An array of conflicting emotions churned behind cerulean orbs.

"Forgive me," she started, tiny shoulders shivering in uncertainty. Descarta gave his fingers another brief squeeze, an act which calmed both of them. "I've shown enmity where I should have shown gratitude," the queen confessed, offering a dimple festooned smile. "You needn't be anyone but yourself, Virgil. Just don't shut me out anymore."

He struggled with an urge to unleash a cataract at the girl, to return her candor and affection. To venture withheld ardor for her magnificent shine, to confess his fondness of brushing the spine of her latest read, of scouring its tangy vanilla pages to explore her every world. How he longed to occupy those domains! To bring forth the thawing bloom her every delightfully buoyant laugh gave his heart when he watched his enchanting queen from afar. How he looked at her! She was a coming together of components so incredulous he oft thought her a fantastical figment fabricated to ease his abject spirit.

Howbeit, Virgil could no more liberate the words than visit her berryflower tresses. So he chose to tease her instead. "Should I call the chef? Did he lace your fish? I don't recall requesting an aphrodisiac."

"Virgil," she complained, "I'm being serious." Her smile remained bright, though.

"You're . . . well," he cast rapidly at her hand, still resting like a gossamer cloud over his, and back. "You're a lovely girl, Des. Beautiful throughout. I haven't overlooked that." He invoked a half-smile which ended as more of a smirk. "I'll try to be more open. For you."

The queen retracted her touch and shied timidly away from his stroking words.

During that moment of quiet abash, dessert arrived, the fortuitous silence killer. Descarta looked at it curiously. "What's this?"

"Brioche des Rois," Virgil explained. "Bread with chunks of fruit baked into it and topped with frosting. I thought you'd enjoy it since you find fruit rolls so appetizing."

"How do you know that?" she asked, slicing a piece away and warily tapping it to her tongue.

"You live in my keep. And you're my queen," the sovereign offered as if that were explanation enough.

"They're my treat to myself," she said before taking a bite. "Oh! This is—we must have this at the castle!" she beamed, mouth joyfully stuffed.

"I'm glad you enjoy it, blossom," Virgil said, preoccupied. He had tread a pernicious path this day. The king knew he'd choose her all along; she was a darling. He couldn't justify the relationship until today. Because before today there was no mutual relationship, he knew—only the marriage of misgivings. He wondered how Descarta would feel if she knew the consequences of her actions. So much more grand than simply stirring his heart! Virgil would tell her everything when she was ready, would usher her into his world and out of her tenebrous existence.

The weaver allowed a twisted smiled at his faulty self-assurances. How quickly he clung to the budding girl, so desperate was he to extirpate an uncertain future. Virgil was bewitched by her, the feeling manifested by a brief show of affection. So greased were his cogs of deception by her tender touch he'd nearly forgotten his dilemma.

Of one thing he was certain: time paid no heed to its creations, only shambled on virulent hands, poisoning everything it contacted. And time had injected its venom for so long that his spirit was a dilapidated shard of life. When Descarta saw him for who he was, what would she think? Would the judgmental creature accept him, or would she banefully reject him? He would exit the mire and be forced to truly decide soon enough. Until then, he accepted that it would be best to at least bestow a fraction of his feelings on the queen. Either it would be a sweet succor or it wouldn't matter at all.

"All finished," Descarta chimed. "Are we leaving soon?" She flashed her dimple-festooned smile.

The sovereign nodded and shut his lids, flushing the turmoil from his mind. He could only wait. Toiling over matters beyond his control just chipped pointlessly away at already waning energy. Virgil ran his fingers through the deep raven talons about his face, yawning at the thought.

"Hey," Descarta mouthed through her own yawn, "you're making me do it." She stared at him, realizing just how exhausted her sovereign was. If she wasn't so resentful, she would have thought Virgil handsome when she first saw him. Now the dark candelabras supported dimming candles betwixt obtrusive cheekbones. "Actually, you don't look healthy. You probably shouldn't even be walking this far after yesterday. Would it hurt to rest for a few days?"

Virgil sighed. "The thrill of adventure does tend to make one forget the goal. Remember our course is urgent."

Descarta looked to her lap, ashamed. She thought of the thousands suffering the blight's grip in Saradin. It'd almost entirely fled her mind when she was gifted the liberty to explore. "I'm sorry," she muttered wistfully.

The weaver frowned and stood from the table, ravaged robe jostling about his body. "Blossom, there's no reason to be sorry. I am tired, very tired. But monarchs are inherently weary. That's why they have queens to rest for them." He reached into a concealed pocket and withdrew a small leather pouch. "Come, we'll order more brioches for the trip."

...

"Brioches are breads, and breads are brioches, and breads and brioches are both types of breads!" the thrilled twins recited in unison as they cavorted around the king and shared the titular treat.

"Our Virgil bought us pastries because he loves us," Almi crooned before devouring half her share in one giant chomp.

"We love you, too," Merill beamed at the sorcerer as she tucked herself under his arm. She playfully kicked her next step high to illustrate her excitement.

"How do I always manage to forget the effect sugar has on you silly songbirds," Virgil sighed, giving the slender elf a squeeze. He hadn't forgotten. Their high-spirited display warmed a grove reserved for his wards, one he thought vacated by the trials of the day before.

Merill leaned into the sovereign's robe, happy to be reunited with the man. She hummed an impromptu string of notes that almost seemed pleasant under the sway of her tuned diapason.

The queen observed from behind Virgil, perplexed by their everlasting whimsy. From the sisters' own extravagant and detailed reenactment of yesterday's foray, Descarta wondered how they switched from bubbly to brutal so casually. Yet another enumeration to fortify her list of reasons to envy the succubi. For the sake of her ego, she chose to ignore that they protected Virgil while she cowered prone beneath a magically animated golem. Descarta confessed that the sisters exuded an air of cuteness when like this, though. Virgil paid them little heed, but that was his prevailing temperament. She pondered whether he found that trait endearing—being cute.

The observant queen wasn't alone in her scrutiny. Josiah looked on with interest born of jealousy and angry confusion. The ostensible truth Hazael revealed in the desert still vexed the bard. What if the last twenty-three years weren't a gesture of friendship but an imposed exile? When he was young, he had courted the girls. They were never responsive, always wearing a disgusted or disinterested glare as he recited his latest poem, written solely for the ravishing elves. Josiah knew they harbored no contempt; the elves were simply incapable of loving anyone but their king. While the thought was frustrating, what really incensed the rogue was that he might have been the victim of vengeance from a man he considered dear. Sure, his odyssey might have yielded ballads enough for the rest of his days, but he had acquired them in the name of his sovereign.

Josiah reminded himself that Hazael could be lying and using the bard as a marionette. Upheaval was common in broken nations, and it wasn't unheard of for a seneschal to forcefully capture the throne of a despot. He cast a surreptitious glance at the steward. Tacit, as usual. The bard wouldn't allow himself to succumb to distrust so smoothly. He would remain circumspect, and form his own conclusions.

The cohorts were approaching the tunnel which wound to the sun-scarred surface when Virgil halted, peering with menace into the portal. "What do you want?" he commanded more than requested.

"Never time for pleasantries, eh, my lord?" said Hafstagg, wearing his trademark grin as he stepped from the tunnel entrance. "I saved your life."

"And I have long allowed you to live. Your debt is canceled." Virgil waved the hand seated around Merill's waist. "Now go."

"I can't, Virgil. I have a duty to fulfill to my king."

"You forfeit that honor long ago." Virgil unwound himself from the elf and took a step forward. The air thickened around him, pliant and eager. "Grant us passage or I will unmake you."

The big man chuckled. "You see yourself as a god now, don't you? Given the circumstances I reckon you are, my lord." Hafstagg assumed a confident gait toward the weaver, sweat beading around his forehead. "I'm thinkin' even gods are fallible, and I know why you allowed me to live these years. Should I say it aloud, or would you spare a chat?"

Descarta sensed the tension, the atmosphere being drawn away from her. She took a tentative step back, seeking to remove herself from the conflict. The queen bit her lip as the giant man loomed well above Virgil. The tension pulsated and intensified, a tangible mass surrounding the pair. Hafstagg knelt before Virgil, head still reaching the sovereign's chest. Descarta detected a trace of a whisper emerge from between them, too fibrous to understand. It persisted for a brief half-minute then ceased. In response, a hush permeated the hanging tension and stripped it from the air as briskly as it appeared.

"Hafstagg will be joining us," Virgil said while the warrior stood and smiled at the sovereign.

"You won't regret it, my lord," Hafstagg replied through great white teeth. "I'll take the front then. Pulverize them assassins," he said as he took the lead.

Merill nibbled on her pastry and pressed her head under Virgil's arm until it slipped through. She glanced up at him with curious sanguine eyes. "Is it really okay? After what he said?"

Virgil nodded. "That's why it's okay, dear."

As if she had asked the question, Almi gave a fervent bob of her head without looking back.

"To Ignus then," the king proclaimed, breaking the egress.

Descarta and Josiah couldn't help but wonder what required clandestine discourse yet could also be disclosed to the sisters.

Hazael only frowned.

CHAPTER FIVE

Necessary Sacrifices

The dreadcleaver tightened the heavy woolen cloak about his emerald brigandine. The dark mantle was a poor aegis against the frosty gust breaking land on northern shores. Atop his crossed knees lay twin battleaxes fashioned with serrated blades. They were what afforded him and his ilk the meritorious title of dreadcleaver, adept and fear-inspiring. Dreadcleavers were known as battlefield charmers. When their axes whirred and spun a deleterious dirge, the ensuing massacre made it seem like foes split themselves on the notched blades.

Shivering before a feeble campfire, the man pulled his cloak tighter for the seventeenth time that evening.

"This is ridiculous," grunted the bundled form to his left. "We'll be icicles before dawn. We should be swinging axes, not trembling like kittens around a dying fire."

A third figure nodded its concurrence across from the other two. "If I don't wake up tomorrow, I'll be a very persistent ghost. Piss ectoplasm into your tea."

Lastan sighed a cloudy puff of chilled breath. "I, too, would rather be a messenger of vengeance than sit idly under the spire of Galvant's Bulwark," he confessed. "Look around. Thousands of campsites. How many sit and wait like us?" He gave the comrade to his side a pat. "It's only the first night. Just follow your orders and revenge will be yours."

"Oh, I'll have it," grumbled the hunched warrior.

"Just remember to share," smiled Lastan, retracting his hand and performing the habitual tightening once again. He could be inside the tower where the winds weren't so biting, napping cozily beside a warm hearth. Lastan, ever the responsible leader, had chosen to endure the nasty weather among his subordinates. They were a raucous group, disciplined in warfare but with a penchant for skullduggery without. He knew his presence was enough to augment their patience. The dreadcleavers would complain until he censured or consoled them, but they knew to obey his orders, complaints or not. Warnings were hardly forthcoming from the stern captain.

The mounting bloodlust was palpable. All around him, calloused phalanges were occupied with stroking engraved axe handles, pacifying the fury within. Lastan counted himself among the tumultuous spirits. He, like the rest of his crew, was ready to rupture the oppressive nation and put a stop to its barbaric policies. His countryside was a warren of vitality once, impregnated with the prosperity of a hundred hamlets. They were all despoiled now, reduced to seedy, predator-friendly circles amid a man-made swamp. Many of his men were from those boroughs, had returned from their tour to find all they fought for strewn across a flooded, putrid sepulcher. Corpses were abandoned to be bloated, decomposed or eaten by critters. The few survivors had no chance to care for the dead; they were busy running.

Hardly an exception, Lastan was there during the catastrophic march. He was impotent then, a hardly trained militiaman forced to watch as his wife and daughter were ravaged and gutted alive. The captain would never forget the shrill cries, the way they eventually submitted to the soldiers like bereft dolls and the hollow stares of lifelessness where vivacity once pooled. He would have stayed there with them, weeping until the deluge took him too, if he weren't dragged out by the soldiers. Again, he was the powerless spectator, leashed with a dozen other of his kind atop a rise that afforded a safe view of his hamlet. They punctured the dam and the fury behind it was unleashed. An insuperable flood lurched forth, reclaimed the valley and everything that once mattered to the desolated man.

Ever since his escape, clarity defined the long course before him. Like the restless souls he sought to temper, his utmost endeavor was the downfall of that baleful nation.

For Lastan would not forget.

...

All around, rugged terrain studded with the bluffs of insurmountable plateaus defined the fertile land of Ignus. Under the earthfolk, fertility was a horizon of cracked stone and arid barrens. The gravel-voiced race thrived in these conditions, surrounded by a mammoth incubating womb of mineral deposits and boulders.

For a troupe of five humans and two elves, these were not optimal conditions. The septet erected camp at the base of a plateau, utilizing the wall as a bulwark. If assassins persisted, one point of entry was rendered null, barring an attack from on high. After scouting for an hour, the bard assured them no one with mortal dexterity could ascend any side of the formation.

Descarta slumbered peacefully on her cushioned bed roll, and a thread of drool grew from the bottom corner of her lips. Willowy arms wrapped her head, embracing it like a stuffed toy. A dozing elf draped a slender leg over the queen's chest. Another ornamental girl lay crosswise Descarta's lissome thighs, head buried within the layered skirt. Her tunic-wrapped frame and unprotected limbs spread beyond the roll and over rock-strewn ground, travel-worn feet resting in Virgil's lap.

"How can they sleep like that?" Josiah whispered, wrinkling his brow at the contorted bodies.

"They're resilient," answered Virgil, the only other party member awake. The king's lethargic stare angled at the creamy splendor of the moon while he absently stroked the silky calf of Merill's interposed leg.

"You should be sleeping, you know. The next watch is yours," said Josiah. His gaze was fixed on the sovereign's petting touch.

"And leave my queen to your lecherous hands?" Virgil turned a slight smile to the bard. "I'd rather not."

"I wouldn't want another twenty years of punishment." Josiah inwardly flinched, regretting his choice of words as much as he'd intended on using them. He should have exhibited more subtlety, strummed a less stringent tune.

The caustic meaning was not lost on Virgil. He exhaled a breath of exasperation, returning his gaze to the sky.

"So that's how you reward friendship. If they displease you, they're handled with the utmost severity."

"Friends don't do what you did. I would have killed you."

"Oh, so I should be grateful that, instead of death, I was gifted a lifetime of exile by a friend? Forgive me if I don't grovel, my lord." Josiah leaned his bald head in worn palms. "I was young, and I loved Almi. I only kissed her. I didn't fondle or invade her."

"No, you forced yourself onto the girl. You stirred memories better left dormant." The weaver gently patted the curled elf's side, stimulating a tiny murmur. "And she was my queen once. Both were."

"What? I never heard that."

"It was very brief. Wonderful girls. Abysmal queens," lamented Virgil.

"You punished me out of jealousy then?"

"I just explained. You were reprimanded for forcing yourself onto Almi. If only a kiss, it fractured walls she'd erected against her childhood. You revived agony long buried." The king allowed a self-deprecating smile to curl his lips. "I would have welcomed someone who could take care of them. Someone who could give them the affection they desired. Affection I was incapable of. But the cursed masochism binding them to me doesn't allow it."

Josiah frowned. "I wanted to get through to her, to excite a response to my love. Hurting the girl wasn't what I intended. How was I to know?"

"The harm was done. It took years to reverse." Virgil concentrated on the rhythmic rise and fall of the napping elf's berry-dyed tunic. "How wretched a malady. She ached for contact, would hover about me, begging with those tormented carmine eyes. Yet even a brush of skin would set her affright, shuddering and sobbing." He looked at the sulking rogue. "You did that to her. She may have forgotten out of necessity. I don't have the luxury."

"I had no idea I hurt her so," the scout said in an austere inflection. A fraction of the burden of blame shifted from the king to himself. "Why not heal them? You command the might of a kingdom. Surely someone—"

"Do you not think I have tried?"

"Send them away. You only torture them here with Descarta around. They'll have to—"

"I have," Virgil groaned. The salvo of complaints was growing cumbersome. "A grave mistake. Not a week later they were returned for execution. Mutilated one another, murdered their foster family." The sovereign closed his lids, seeking to purge the gruesome image. "I pardoned them, of course. Had their wounds mended. Reattached . . ." He clamped his lips shut, truncating the thought. He did not want to relive the memory, but it was not his subject, would not relent to his command. The weaver's phalanges trembled on Almi's side as he was transported to an operating table. He instinctively turned away; the scene was familiar, mortifying. Heedless to his objections, it pressed on. The weaver endured as he always did, in recognition that it was a self-imposed affliction. Virgil knew he brought more ruin to the sisters than Josiah could in the transient years of his life.

"Reattached?" came the call of reality. The bard squinted at him, obtrusively perplexed by the word.

"That's enough, Josiah. I can't change our past. Deal with it like we all do."

"By hoarding it in a vault and pretending it never happened?" the bard smirked.

"Precisely," Virgil replied.

"Maybe that would be best, if unhealthy." Josiah nodded as he peered at the contorted tangle of bodies beside the despot. Virgil was right, he knew. It was childish enmity, caught in an exile which may have been warranted. He tightened his focus on the jade pinafore amid the cluster of appendages. "Does it not trouble your dainty queen that they're always near? The twins are still as sultry of figure as the day I left, and they're so very clingy. What's the secret to preventing her from gnawing your throat while you sleep?"

Virgil allowed his gaze to concur with the rogue's, observing the girl in her reverie. "There's no secret. Mayhap she trusts me. Though my prevailing supposition would be that a large, vehement part of her despises me too mightily to care."

"Ah, so you too brook the forced distance," Josiah grinned at his friend, allowing camaraderie to illuminate his grim mood. "I don't feel so down knowing I'm not alone in my longing."

The weaver drew an affected smile across his countenance. "No, you aren't." Virgil lay back, and a wistful suspiration crawled as hissing spiders from his throat. "Wake me when it's my watch."

...

Descarta parted sand-hemmed lids to a red tunic and olive arms cradling her head. She started to protest, but hushed discourse halted the outburst.

"No, you forced yourself onto the girl. You awoke memories in her that were better left dormant."

She knew the calm, somber voice belonged to Virgil. Descarta watched as his fingers gingerly stroked the elf's side directly in front of her.

"And she was my queen once. Both were."

A flock of agitated butterflies flitted about her belly. She had no idea the twins were once more than wards to him.

"What? I never heard that."

And the response could be none other than Josiah. Even when troubled, there was a gentle melodic ring to his speech. Descarta listened to the exchange and gained purchase on the history of two girls who had bewildered her endlessly. The elucidation wasn't what she hoped. The queen let her disdain slip a notch, then another, then another, culminating in pity and guilt. She contemplated the elves about her, sisters who agonized for an unobtainable goal, and questioned how deeply their loneliness pervaded.

Albeit here they were, entangled affectionately with her, an enormous impasse to their ultimate goal. Perhaps it was simplicity that allowed them to forgive an ongoing enemy. Whatever the cause, they were better than she was. The revelation of their disinherited status and everything that title meant shook her. The twins were once his queens. He'd likely slept with them, loved them. One resounding uncertainty would not relent: what did the sisters mean to him now?

"Though my prevailing supposition would be that a large, vehement part of her despises me too mightily to care."

The admission wounded Descarta, surmounted only by the dripping despair it was shrouded in. Hadn't she been uncharacteristically kind to him earlier? She'd conveyed compassion of her own desire, put forth genuine effort to be a sympathetic queen. Inadequacy worked its way into her thoughts, leading Descarta to a similarly dour mood. She shut her eyes and begged repose to take her from the whirlwind of dismay.

...

Tentative footing on a precipitous promontory wasn't exactly the sense of adventure she sought. Her boots often found shifting rubble on stairs which should have been, at such perilous heights, adamantine. Descarta was told this speciously ordinary plateau was home to the Underrise, epicenter of the earthfolk nation. She found the claim absurd.

"Why are these crumbling?" Descarta asked as she took another shaky step. She thought a race with propensity for crafting stone would yield better results. "Not at all impressive for a capital." Descarta's next step encountered little resistance, and her foot plunged through the brittle stone toward a pernicious fall. She gasped, reaching her arms out in panic for anything that would prevent the bone-shattering impact.

An arm encircled her waist, pulling the mortified girl briskly away from the breach. She trembled and peered at the detritus along its lengthy descent until the rocky rain bounced where her corpse would have been. Descarta pressed closer to the strong smell of ozone, not caring that it was Virgil. She clenched her lids and shivered, anxiety manifesting in deep swallows of air. She wanted him to magically sedate her like before, but no such treatment was forthcoming.

Virgil gently stroked her side, giving the shaken girl a reassuring squeeze. He wanted to console her; however, the sovereign knew the encounter would make her more alert. "Careful, blossom." Hand steadying Descarta, he nudged her upward. "Step as I said, please. Keep your weight on your rear foot until you know the next is safe. We've almost reached the top."

The queen followed his words to the apex of their climb where Almi and Merill waited impatiently with disapproving stares. They'd bound with the feathery, sure-footed grace of lithe sprites to the entrance as if it was a trivial task. "Come on!" Merill yelled, hopping next to Almi.

"Patience, little ones," Virgil called back. "Or I'll toss you off."

"Ohhh!" Almi harrumphed. "Let her fall next time! She's so slow! We're better!"

As riposte, Descarta hugged herself close to Virgil, sticking an antagonizing tongue out at the twins and throwing a generously devious middle finger to the pair.

The twins exchanged astonished glances, mouths agape.

"V-Virgil!" Merill exclaimed. "Did you see?!"

"See what?" the sovereign grinned.

"Don't tease us! Are you on her side now?!" Merill objected, hands on hips.

"B-Barren whore! Pestilent—ohhh!" the mace-wielding sister fumed, tossing snowy hair about in a frustrated shake of her head.

From behind the royal pair, Hafstagg released a hearty chuckle. "Glad I chose to follow you, your majesty. Entertainment in all forms."

Merill pouted and cuddled her saturnine twin, scratching ferociously at the back of her tunic.

In return, Almi expelled her exasperation by rubbing an angry face fervently in the crook of her sister's neck. Each muttered mostly inscrutable curses about having lost everything to Descarta, who was vividly portrayed in the elven language as an ugly slut-potato.

"Oh, calm down, you two. We're only jesting." Virgil turned his attention to the girl beside him, whispering now. "Please be gentle, dear. They are fragile." He grinned at the image of her noxious retort. "That was not in character."

Descarta offered a grin of her own, sinister yet containing all the sparkling shimmer of a star. "I need to let the three of you know *I'm the queen.*"

The weaver was caught off guard by the choice inflection, which he did well to conceal. "I cannot contest your point. Tonight would be as propitious as any to begin the consummation, then." He suggested in a libidinous tone—no longer whispering, while gliding his fingertips sensually over the side of her slender thigh.

"Ahh!" Descarta yelped. She hastily fled from his side, blanched, up the remaining steps. "Don't, you're, I—" she pulled her palms to her face.

"Look at her! Lass is rouge-fleshed head to toe!" the warrior chortled.

Hazael and Josiah each added a supplemental chuckle to the embarrassment.

"Aw . . ." Almi cooed as the sisters pulled the queen into their cuddle, entwining themselves with her. "Teasing you, too."

"They're mean." Merill lovingly scratched the slightly shorter girl's scalp, a mysteriously soothing sensation.

Descarta peered through narrowed slits at the king, who responded with an apologetic half-grin. She bet he thought he was clever, weaving the three of them together like one of his arcane passes. The queen groaned and hid her face in Merill, vexed by the lingering spark his caress ignited.

The elf slid her velvety hands down Descarta's spine, running a circuit over her waist. From behind, Almi wrapped an olive-skinned leg around the queen and nibbled on her ear.

Merill breathed huskily, settling her forehead on Descarta's. The seductive twin pulled curve-hugging digits up the contours of the viridian frock, ending their course cupping the girl's disconcerted face.

"What are you doing?" Descarta mumbled through half-covered lips.

"We'll be your friends," the rear sister mouthed into her ear, an act invoking a prickly response over the affected area.

Merill nodded with fierce sanguine orbs. "Friends."

"Huh?" The queen furrowed her brow.

"Share," Almi instructed in sultry susurration.

"What do you—"

"Share," Merill whispered emphatically, drawing parted lips near to a kiss.

The encircled girl tried to pull away, but she was ensnared by the twins' trap.

"We'll show you everything he likes. Teach you. It'll make you feel good. We promise," the elf continued. "In return, be fair."

"Share," Almi pleaded from behind.

"Deranged creatures!" The queen wriggled between the pair. "Let me free!"

Virgil, having just reached the platform, cast a censuring glare at the twins who promptly removed themselves from Descarta. "Enough, you two."

"She's damaged," Almi complained. "Damaged."

"Broken," agreed Merill. "We tried to help."

Having escaped the elven mire, the queen rushed back to Virgil. The absurdity of running back to the king wasn't lost to her, and she expressed an inward sigh at the predicament. How little she had when her comfort was the one who'd imprisoned her. She stuck beside him as he led the companions into the tunnel. "Why do they hate me so?" she asked where only he could hear.

"Hate you?" Virgil sighed. "Blossom, they must adore you. I've never known them to take on another pillow."

"I don't like that," she noted.

"They find you cozy."

"I still don't like it. They're too intimate with me."

"I can't honestly say I fully understand them. It's their way of showing they accept you. The only person they've ever been that way with is me." Virgil nodded in affirmation of his supposition. "Otherwise, I believe they would have attacked you by now."

"Should that make me feel better?" Descarta cringed and imagined Almi wearing a visceral, sharp-toothed simper while bludgeoning her with the fang-enhanced mace. "Can't you do something?"

"I'm afraid not."

Descarta huffed, exasperated by his indifference. "Because you don't care to. Because you love them, your perfect little queens." She tightened her fists, recalling the way he'd spoke of them when he thought she wasn't listening, how he'd nearly braved a cave-in for the damned elves. "Because I'm not them. Because—"

"Please," Virgil sighed. "Not now. You don't . . . later, dear. Later, I promise." He outpaced the queen by a few steps, and she fell behind, morose at being shrugged off.

Descarta dropped a roiling amber stare to the ground. He didn't even care enough to tell her it wasn't true. He hadn't changed at all, so distant and aloof.

"You must think our king a fiend," came a baritone voice from her side.

Descarta dragged her glum cauldrons to see the steward, wise silver eyes peering down a crooked nose. He was smiling, but she could tell it was affectation. "Often," she replied.

"Cruelty isn't a garment you wear well."

"He just walked away; he didn't deny it! He's the one being cruel!" she countered, incensed by his accusation.

"Look at him, girl," Hazael cast his gaze at the lone figure ahead. "Destitute. I have seen him endure unspeakable torture; yet he never lost his vigor."

"I doubt he ever had it. He's thoughtless and likely growing senile."

"No, he's drained. Drained from this journey, from expending his energy fighting—for your life I might add. Has it not occurred to you he has foregone nearly all sleep for you? Intelligence would dictate he console you; it would be evident to him if he were hale."

"What are you saying?"

"I'm saying that was not a good sign, my queen. Virgil would not abandon you to your misgivings. You are . . ." Hazael cast askance, searching for a diplomatic term. "You are precious."

The brooding queen inspected the shambling figure before her, shoulders hunched under the heavy robe. "What should I do then? Just accept his treatment?"

"Practice understanding. To him your words have form, wicked as daggers or soothing as zephyrs." Hazael gave her a plaintive stare. "Be wary which you choose."

"You're very familiar with him for a steward," observed Descarta.

"I've shared a weird friendship with the man for many years. We are kindred spirits, I would say." Hazael frowned. "I'll talk to him for you. He's been avoiding me since the incident with the construct, though."

"Why?"

"It bothers him when I'm right."

"Halt!" a deep, gravelly voice shouted from ahead. "This is not an entry. Fleshlings must use the—"

"Oh, be quiet. I'll have none of your backwards, haughty condescension. Be a good pebble and inform Bromyr that he has visitors," Virgil calmly disputed.

"Disrespectful rodent! You'll address the Impervious properly or I'll—"

"You'll do as I say. Now tell him Virgil, King of Elusia has arrived and seeks a meeting."

Descarta and Hazael caught up in time to see a brutish earthfolk titan stomping away in rage.

"Not in the mood for discretion, I see," commented Hazael.

"Not in the mood for derision either," Virgil muttered in rejoinder.

"Very well. It seems nothing I excel in is acceptable," joked the steward, spreading his arms to the side in defeat.

Virgil spun on him, ablaze with anger. Slinking tributaries of fire spread in veins across his hands. "Your irreverence is neither entertaining nor acceptable. It ends here."

The seneschal didn't flinch, only discreetly moved his palm to the hilt of his sword. He answered the blazing snarl with a composed scowl.

The weaver lifted twitching, ember-touched fingers toward Hazael.

"What's going on?" Hafstagg asked as he and the others approached the leading group.

Descarta took an alarmed step back, fright telling her to avoid harm. She pictured the twisting inferno he wove versus the construct. Hazael's advice was fresh, though. She commanded an influence over her king. The girl didn't want to see her companions hurt. She imagined the five as scorched cadavers much like the assassins they'd encountered in the tunnels. Descarta was terrified, but she had to slake his anger. She finally had an existence, knew the feeling of friendship. He couldn't take that from her. She would not permit it. The queen took an agonizing step forward, warily placing one boot before the other.

"Don't," Hazael hissed through clenched teeth as he grabbed the girl by her wrist.

"He won't hurt me." Descarta projected the response to the incensed king. "Right, Virgil?" She wrenched from the steward's grip and moved forward, shaking. She stood in front of the weaver, who gave her no heed.

"Hey," she called from beneath his upraised hand. "You're tired, Virgil. I'm right, aren't I?" She reached up and grabbed his robed arm, tugging it down. The embers snaked to her, crawling over the girl. Descarta gasped, but the dancing cloak of cinders was merely a warm sedative.

The sovereign dropped his baleful stare to the beseeching girl.

"Hi," she smiled, patting his sleeve. "Calm down, alright? He didn't mean any harm. This is silly and pointless."

Virgil growled a discordant rumble. "Remove yourself."

"No." The dainty girl moved closer, clutching his arm against her chest. "You don't want to hurt me, do you?"

"Oh, but I do. Ungrateful, spoiled, hateful little witch." Virgil spat, gaze flaring with his venomous curses.

She flinched despite herself. "Do it then," she lured. Descarta lifted his claw to her chin, pulling trembling fingers about her jaw. "Burn me." She imparted a steadfast stare, struggling to keep her knees from shaking.

The conflagration writhed about her in an agitated swarm. The weaver tightened his fingers about her jaw, compressing delicate cheeks between them. A dense still persisted, Virgil drawing concentration. He exhaled slowly and quenched the weave until the fire was fully extinguished then retracted his grip. "I'm sorry, blossom," the weaver whispered, casting downward in guilt.

"Your Majesty," a wayfarer produced with as pleasing a tone as one could expect from earthfolk.

Giving the diminutive maiden no further notice, Virgil turned toward the voice. "Yes?"

"Greetings. I am steward to the venerable Impervious." The creature bowed its boulder-like head deferentially. "He is presently indisposed, but invites you to stay in the royal suite."

"For how long?"

"Not very, I assure you."

"That will do then," Virgil replied.

"If you'll follow me, sir," the wayfarer instructed as he about-faced to lead the troupe.

...

Josiah strummed an acoustically evocative tune on his harp. The melody was imbued with enough magic that one would think he had plucked the fabric, weaving it with the aptitude of a talented thaumaturgist. He crooned a solemn ballad which rose and fell along the harmonious contours of the tune.

Unconditionally bound, phoenix and raven,
To the same damning thread, to catch craven.
Tethered as they were, two could not fashion,
A course to forbidden passion.
Thence they wrought forevermore,
Fervor bidden to never soar.

Descarta hummed the wistful melody to herself, elbows resting on the edge of an elaborate balustrade. The sight below was mesmerizing, an inspiring feat of architecture and dedication. The cylindrical chasm could fit all of the bulwark capital of Elusia and plummeted as far as the tallest spire into a radiating pool of magma. Hundreds of slate bridges formed a cross-hatch of causeways so that only brilliant beads of the sloshing molten rock below shone as fiery pearls to an observer at her elevation.

The diminutive queen set free a melancholy huff, wallowing in disappointment. This should be a moment of elation, looking down from royal chambers at the limestone web of the Underrise. Yet she found her thoughts drifting to the sealed portal where Virgil sought refuge. Descarta conceded that she was depressed because of him—denial was impossible at this point. Being threatened was painful, but the insults stabbed a glacial lance into her bosom. Did he truly think so lowly of her? He didn't even put forth a genuine apology, only an apathetic sorry.

Hafstagg appeared beside her, unnoticed in her introspection. "Feelin' down, my queen?" He presented a toothy grin and leaned beside her, which brought the monolith to his knees.

She politely returned the smile and returned to the criss-crossed bridges below.

"Music can't be helping." Hafstagg turned and waved to the bard. "Pluck something lighter, would you?"

"Oh, sorry," Josiah nodded. "Thought she'd like to hear something about Kalthused. Well, I thieved this piece from a pair of delightful fairies." He plucked a higher melody, notes bouncing and bobbing in a flitting bumblebee's gait.

Brioches are breads,
and breads are brioches,
and breads and brioches
are both types of breads!

The twins clapped excitedly and giggled in fascination at the stolen lyrics.

"We'll be famous!" Almi bounced in approval.

"What've I done?" Hafstagg voiced regretfully as his scrutiny returned to the forlorn queen. "Don't be so depressed, tiny one. Surrounded by comrades who care, yet you toil alone."

"They only feign empathy because I'm their queen," Descarta sulked. "Besides, I don't need anyone to coddle me."

"Hah! Virgil has rubbed off on you!"

"I'm nothing like him," she sneered.

"Sure, lass." The warrior's sarcasm made it clear he wasn't convinced.

"I'm not."

"He's locked himself away from everyone but a persistent steward. You're avoiding the group as best as you can. And neither of you want to talk, or think you should." Hafstagg grunted and produced a self-deprecating grin. "Yet your subjects just pass the time in anxiety, too insignificant to be let in on your troubles."

"I don't see you as insignificant," Descarta replied. "I'm just not comfortable discussing it."

"I can't let that pass. Couldn't sleep tonight knowing I didn't cheer you up," said Hafstagg.

"Why do you care? You've only just met me."

"Let's just say you remind me of a charming young lad I used to know," answered the warrior, recalling blurred, frayed memories.

Descarta furrowed her brow. "That doesn't make any sense. Who is the charming young lad?"

"So now you want me to share while you hoard your misery like a mighty dragon." Hafstagg shook his bearded chin. "Thick-headed, yes. But I'm not that thick, lass."

...

Meanwhile, Virgil reclined in tranquil meditation on an armless divan imported from the northern reaches. Over the intervening hour, he'd subjugated the mental clamor down to an eldritch shimmer, a faint scratching that moaned for attention.

"How long are you going to ignore me?" Hazael carped from across the room. The steward had chosen to sit atop an empty stone desk, a sign that no incumbent ambassador was present.

"As long as I am able," answered the sovereign.

"Ignoring the problem isn't going to fix it."

"It cannot be fixed," replied Virgil, "and discussion isn't going to change that."

"This isn't some negligible peccadillo. You nearly attacked us," the seneschal said, disbelief manifest in his tone. "How can you act as though everything is fine?"

"She calmed me."

"And next time? Or the time after that? How long until—"

"I know!" Virgil screamed, wisps of magically disturbed embers upsetting his raven hair. The distressed weaver took heavy, steadying breaths against the onset of vertigo. A salvo of shrill, unchained emotions wormed around his consciousness, seeking a way in, leaking their noxious fluid through the cracks. "I know," he repeated, softer, as he labored to enslave the force.

"I've never known you to be so temperamental. What's going on, Virgil?" Hazael said as he approached the supine man. "Let me examine you."

"No," the weaver insisted. "Apart from fatigue, I'm fine."

"I think we've passed the point of fatigue."

Virgil took another deep breath, utilizing the exercise to calm the gibbering, upset spirits. "The pressure on my ribbon is growing unbearable. Their emotions are bleeding into me, becoming my own. Vicious, violent and powerful emotions."

Worry painted the steward's visage, marionette lines growing dark. "Do you plan to gather tonight?"

"I must. You know that."

"We could try again later when—" the steward shook his head. "No, that's impossible." Hazael peered reluctantly at the king. "What of the girl? Will she last?"

The sovereign pictured her petite form as she coddled him, eased him back to sanity and away from a colossal mishap. The visceral terror whirling in her eyes as she pulled his hand around her jaw sickened him. So steeped was he in enhanced rage at the time that he still couldn't gather whether the urge to kill her was genuine. "She will," he nodded. "She must. Just as I must persist for her."

"Virgil," the seneschal began in a grave tone, palms on his knees. "You've strayed, haven't you?"

"Don't be foolish," replied the sovereign. "She is a tool, an apparatus. Am I that good of an actor?"

Hazael chuckled, a gesture dripping with uneasy doubt. "Quite. You know what this means to me, friend. To reclaim what is mine." He envisioned the toppled braziers, burning tapestries and ear-lancing shrieks. They'd stolen everything from him, executed his mother—the rightful queen, a just queen—all to accomplish a forsaken coup. And for what? The authority to levy taxes on merchant guilds. He'd never forget the dolorous stare she'd given him as the axe descended to sever her vertebrae. He would have been next.

"You aren't the only one seeking to supplant the past, Hazael. Don't forget that," Virgil muttered from his repose.

"Right," Hazael agreed. "I shouldn't doubt your dedication. It was thoughtless."

"It's not important," Virgil said. "We'll both have our prize. I assure you, I've explored every contingency."

"And I will be your sword and shield until we're rewarded for our diligence," Hazael added. "Get some rest."

"I've been trying to," groaned Virgil. "And send the queen."

The steward didn't respond, only smirked. Kindred spirits set upon a noble path. There were times when, faced with the king's grim reticence, Hazael forgot they were comrades.

Hazael had other thoughts, too. Deeper, the rustic mechanisms of creaking doubt lashed together memories, ending in potent redirection. The smiles, the simple gestures—acts seemingly remote and disconnected—were strung together into a lucid framework. What if the ruse wasn't designed for Descarta, but for him? Would the king betray Hazael? Would the king betray his own aspirations?

The steward shook his head as he closed the portal, returning to the common room. He paused, staring in silent deliberation at the stone door. Virgil wouldn't fail him.

...

Descarta welled in turbulence by the door, seething with questions she wanted to wield as refined blades against the prone king. Approaching, she imagined plunging the vorpal uncertainty into his gut and showing the lofty sorcerer the hurt his spiteful insults initiated. But fear overcame the girl, commanded her paralyzed. It was a nebulous sensation, roots spreading in all directions so that she knew not the cause. The fear of fingertips set about her cheeks, vengeful digits whose touch delivered death, the fear of answers, impartial truths which could scarcely be rescinded. Or the fear of change, the loss being cast aside would bring about—a paradigm she didn't want to entertain.

"Blossom," Virgil began, startling the queen from her musings, "what are you doing?" He sat up, hanging his legs from the divan. "That's creepy. Now I know how you feel when I watch you sleep."

Descarta clenched her fists, brooding over the light greeting. He acted as though nothing happened, as though the way he treated her was of no consequence. Releasing an angry, frustration-fueled groan, she riposted with a bitter slap to the weaver's cheek. Harrumphing, the queen showed Virgil her back.

Thousands of pinpricks protested across his cheek, but the king didn't mind. The sharp ache in his chest was what tore at his spirit. He set his sight on her lower back, the twinge of resignation setting in. He conceded this would be best, that the less attached she was, the less hurt she would be. He imagined her gossamer cheek resting against his palm once more. Virgil knew that wouldn't be, not after the truth was thrust upon her.

"Aren't you going to say something?" she muttered in a breaking voice after her calm returned.

"What is there to say?" he responded, maintaining a neutral inflection.

Descarta spun on him, sorrowful dew accumulating at her ducts. "That you didn't mean it! How could you? How you could do that?!" Unable to suppress the deluge of fear, the dew gave way to a torrent of tears. "How could you call me those things?! I've tried to change!"

The sovereign studied the girl in apparent distaste. "You are what you are, blossom. Ungrateful, spoiled, hateful." He winced at the frosty rejoinder, fought off the urge to embrace her, to assure her she was wonderful in every way that mattered to him.

Descarta froze, shocked. She peered through a blurry lens at the sitting figure and waited for him to laugh or simply tell her he didn't mean it. "Why, Virgil? Why did you change so quickly? What did I do?" she mumbled, covering her face in embarrassment at crying while he watched in disapproval.

"Come," the weaver ordered as he stood. "We're visiting the Maiden."

"I don't care anymore. Let them die."

"We're going," insisted Virgil, grabbing her wrist and injecting a gratuitous amount of sedating weave into the girl.

She opened her mouth to protest, but all that emerged was a weakened mewl. The weaver wore a dejected grin where she couldn't see, pleased that the girl gave him an excuse to numb the agony he'd wrought.

...

Virgil toiled behind his diminutive love as she idled without passion before the Maiden's statue. There were no other terms for her now, no farces or fabrications he could employ as devices of deception. The sovereign was prepared to forfeit everything he'd designed in exchange for the girl and accept the absent life that followed. Perhaps he would be content with the erratic elves as companions. They would never leave him. He sighed at the idea; it was a chimerical notion. A reactionary vindication against unfair terms. The weaver missed the days when he wasn't so self-aware, when he'd wrap himself in the solace of misdirection. He wished he could revert to the simple comfort of ignorance.

"Go on," he pressed. "Pray. Don't lose sight of what's important."

"Why?" she asked through the consuming numbness. "Why should I care what happens to them?" The queen stepped toward the empyrean beacon. "She will not heal them, anyway. The Maiden is either oblivious or doesn't care, else there would be no scourge." Regardless, she obediently touched the statue, which conjured the same warm spark deep within that each prior engagement with the ivory representation of the ambivalent goddess had.

Behind the girl, Virgil's mind reeled. Descarta galvanized the temple into releasing its quarry, and he was tasked with serving as a vessel. The multitude soaked him in an unabated flood of raw, coarse antipathy. The weaver hissed, hatred invading his mind in ivy, finding the tiniest of fractures in his mental barrier and snaking in, prying them apart. His vision spun. A phantasmagoria of the stark white and reds of the fabric, multifarious memories shook from thousands upon thousands of rage-bearing limbs.

"What's going on?" Descarta inquired, still saturated with the imparted feeling of wellness. She knew something wasn't as it should be when the yarn of crimson fluid unfurled from his lips. Yet Descarta just spectated, too seeped in the weaver's manipulating spell to do more.

"Des," choked the sovereign, a name he invoked as a defensive rite and final lamentation. Virgil's crumbling shield found stability in the utterance, though, a single word of power which gave him the second of strength he needed to skirt the assault. With no intention of squandering the opportunity, Virgil cast an ethereal web about his assailants and began the arduous weaving that sealed them within his carapace.

An hour later, and a fiendish harvest behind him, the resurgence of physical wherewithal brought with it a hammering ache in his core.

Shuddering, he waved for Descarta to follow. "I assume you're done, staring at me like that." He swallowed, the metallic taste an obtrusive reminder of beckoning mortality. How Virgil yearned to answer the chime of its call. "Back to the quarters then. Visitors likely await our return."

The enthralled girl gave a servile nod and took her place behind the departing man. A recovering shard of consciousness wanted to say something, to initiate discourse. It was quickly squashed by the soothing vibration coddling her mind.

...

"King Virgil!" greeted a pebble-grinding shriek as the king and queen entered the reserved quarters. An earthfolk sprang in front of him, eyes of amethyst alight with the enthusiasm of youth. The creature's frame was humanoid, indicative of a wayfarer, and the bioluminescent crystal growing in patches on its head designated its gender as female. "King Virgil! Look!" chattered the rock-hewn girl. The obsidian earthfolk cupped talon-like phalanges before her torso. At her behest, miniature ashen snowflakes spawned above her palms, undulating down in elation into an ivory mound.

"Impressive," admitted Virgil while admiring the capering emberflakes. "The first of your kind to manipulate the weave." He paused, reaching forward to gauge the temperature of her palms. Still like iced stone. "I wouldn't let your father find out, princess."

"It's a decade too late for that, weaver," grumbled a voice forged in the maw of mountains. "You've already poisoned my little orediggger," said the titan as it stepped behind the princess, fully double her height with oversized obsidian limbs as large around as Hafstagg's barrel chest. "Mundin has been captured by the vile magic since you left."

"I poison everything I touch, great Bromyr," Virgil replied. "The folly lies in introducing her to me."

The Impervious' protruding lower jaw lanced the seriousness of his voice with a crooked leer. "Caverns embrace you, Virgil."

"Caverns embrace you, Bromyr," the king repeated, an earthfolk greeting of good will.

"I'm proud of her, to be honest," said Bromyr as he patted the crystal-laden crown of his daughter. "We must progress as a race. Though our myopic nature too often prevents it." The hulking mass of stone leaned forward, peering beyond Virgil. "And who is this?"

"My queen," answered the weaver. "Descarta."

"Ah, your elves were telling me of her." Bromyr bowed, a motion that cried like scraping stone. "Caverns embrace you, Descarta."

The girl stared blankly back at him.

"Does the queen talk?" grumbled Bromyr.

Virgil looked behind him to Descarta. Perhaps he'd been too liberal with the analgesic application. Or she was exhibiting signs of another probable outcome: depression. "Des is not feeling well," he explained, bringing his attention back to the curious titan. "She'll be better soon."

"Apologies, little one," the goliath offered. "I thought you were being rude."

"She wasn't," insisted Virgil. "Could we enter?"

The obstructive earthfolk stepped out of the way in complaisance, granting the king and queen ingress.

"Where are the others?" asked the king after entering.

Almi and Merill, lying belly to belly on the polished limestone floor, grinned in impudence from their respite. "Said farewell. Supplies, I think," Almi muttered in disinterest. "We wanted to wait for our Virgil."

"Loyal elves love you," Merill mewed. Lounging atop her counterpart, she seemed especially pleased with herself. "The rock king told us! Told us about you!"

The weaver scowled at the hazy, potentially dangerous comment. "Did he?"

Bridging her back, Almi peered so that her eyes were mostly white, struggling to look at the upside-down entrants. "You fought beside him against Kaen Morr! With fists gauntleted in granite!"

"With valiance!" quoted Merill in fey approval. "The tale was grand!" The willowy elf lengthened the last word as she zestfully spread her arms.

"I see," muttered the king, glaring at the stony giant.

"Oh, don't get fussy," said Bromyr as he settled into an oversized chair fashioned out of the cavern wall. "I did no harm by telling them. Besides, they should know you have a side worth honoring."

"The skirmish wasn't one of honor," sighed the weaver as he, Descarta and Mundin sat across from the Impervious.

"Boulderdash!" exclaimed Bromyr. "It was glorious!"

"You think all battle is given to glory," countered the sovereign, leaning back in exhaustion. "Heedless of the outcome."

"Hmph," grunted Bromyr in disagreement. "Never were one to value other cultures."

Mundin pored cross the sovereign at Descarta. "Hello, miss."

Descarta was jostled from languor by the polite voice of tumbling coal. Drawn to the greeting which shattered her shell, the queen blinked in confusion when she saw the princess. "H-Hi," she stammered. Lashes broken, the events during her analgesic state were suddenly transmitted as though liberated from a queue.

"You have a lovely dress, miss. Father doesn't allow me to wear such beautiful garb." The Ignusian girl gestured in disdain at her armor-infused leather skirt. "Virgil must love you," she babbled, squeezing her skirt and slanting toward Descarta. "One day, I'll have someone like that. They'll send me all sorts of frocks with frills and lace and bows. It'll be wonderful."

"Yeah," mumbled Descarta, directing a saturnine frown to her boots. "He must."

"We only have tunics," inserted Almi from just beyond Descarta's feet. The prone elf reached up to toy with the black lace lining the queen's many-layered skirt.

"Only tunics that match," lamented Merill, tugging at her sister's sleeve for emphasis.

Descarta furrowed her brow at the pair. They were notorious for thoughts vacillating between base and byzantine. Disposition gloomy, she slapped irritably at the kneading fingers. The girl just wanted to be given time alone. Even having been discarded, she was still denied that.

Bromyr exhaled a breath of disapproval at his daughter's aspirations. "Again with the ceaseless urge to betray our customs."

"Rooted by me, I'm sure," commented the weaver.

"It's only entertaining if I say it," grumbled Bromyr. "Now," began the titan, shifting to fold golden-veined limbs over a menacing chest. "Nine years and you haven't visited. Yet you appear this day without warning." The leader paused, extracting further words with care. "You are always welcome here, Virgil. Still, I know you care not for my realm. What, then, do you want of me?"

"I'm seeking a cure for the malady of—"

"You know that is beyond us," rumbled Bromyr.

Virgil glared at the domed ceiling, allowing deep breaths to dissipate the unrest born of interruption. He despised meeting the oaf, so embroiled in the warlike tendencies of the folk that direct conversation was troublesome at best. Fortunately, the burden of discourse wasn't so glaring when their goals were less disparate. "And in doing that," he pressed on, "I have inadvertently invited Kaen Morr to my realm. They will attempt to seize the nation within days. If you can hold them off while I obtain the cure, we could unite our forces upon my return."

The shale leader released a sigh of flowing sand. "Fighting aside you again would be magmaficent. Tossing meaty humans, punting frail elves." Bromyr shook his giant head. "Great satisfaction to be had. Not an expedition Ignus would support, at any rate. Even my will cannot move earthfolk to champion a weak nation."

"Elusia pried your crumbling country from devastation," reminded Virgil.

"Many still view it as a shameful decision of a crumbling leader. I'm sorry, sorcerer; it can't be. You understand the burden of rule, don't you?"

Following an exasperated outbreath, Virgil directed an inquisitive gaze at Almi. She grinned and nodded her head vigorously.

"Yes, Virgil! For you!" He knew she'd agree. He would have known even if she wasn't briefed the day before. Not that he required her compliance. Moreover, the sovereign saw no harm in making them feel autonomous, appreciated. He returned the cheerful smile with one of his own forlorn brand. The weaver did not miss the sullen misery set about his queen's strained features when he smiled at Almi. A resurgence of guilt tore at the king, an accosting torment he knew he deserved.

"Very well," muttered Virgil in noxious rejoinder to the immovable titan. "As a member of the earthfolk, I challenge you to Oghlatkun."

"What?!" spat Bromyr, golden veins pulsing in concord with outrage. "What audacity?! To think you would even—"

"I have the right," pressed the weaver. "Every member of this nation does. Or would you forfeit?"

"You have no kin to fight in your name," contested the Impervious, fuming.

Virgil waved the titan's attention to Almi and Merill. "The sisters are my wards. Not family by blood, but they are still family. Almi will be my gladiator."

"Don't do this," threatened Bromyr.

"Please?" plead the princess from the weaver's side. "I don't want to fight."

"Your hypocritical, thankless subjects and their ever-noble Impervious have forced my hand." Virgil glowered. He had hoped there would be no need to submit Almi to the potentially fatal rite. Multifarious capacities were spurred by the decision—none were pleasant. "You understand the burden of rule, don't you?" the sovereign quoted virulently.

Incensed, Bromyr closed his gigantic fists, resembling the iconic Ignusian volcano before its cataclysmic eruption. "In my own stronghold! You would challenge me?!"

"Not you," reminded Virgil. "Your offspring. I have not been cantankerous. I request support that I earned through, as you put it, valiance. You deny me."

Bromyr simmered, enraged but unable to combat the weaver's halcyon justification. "I am bound to accept," he eventually replied, evacuating his seat. "Tomorrow." The titan snatched Mundin like a bag of feathers and stomped out of the quarters, ground trembling in his wake.

"How troublesome," groaned Virgil.

"Troublesome," the twins agreed.

Concern drawing crevasses on his brow, Virgil left his seat in favor of the reflective stone next to Almi and Merill. For some time, he deliberated in quiescence about the challenge. Unable to convince himself he was satisfied with the choice, Virgil planted a hand by Almi's head for support. Leaning so that the content was deflected by his torso, the weaver murmured to the pair. "Girls, are you certain? I can stop him."

The elves peered up at him, clad in caramel smiles.

"What?" asked the king.

"Nothing," giggled Merill from atop Almi's chest.

Virgil blew a breath of frustration and shifted to rise, but the twins coiled tentacle-like appendages around his arm.

"Wait," protested Almi. "We want it." Her timbre hadn't been so serious for years. Since the weaver erected an emotional barrier between himself and his wards. She released her hold and enclosed Merill in an embrace that represented her resolution. "We want to show you."

Merill constricted her fist around Virgil's wrist. Fervent carmine orbs set on his own, unblinking. "Show you we can be worthy."

The sovereign grimaced. The eccentric elves were worthy; they commanded admirable dedication. Dedication that was not lost to the troubled weaver. Nevertheless, he needed them as they were: in a state of pliable desperation. The knowledge, unremitting in its strident, festering guilt, pained him. Through countless tools and ruses, they persisted, provided companionship in a landscape dominated by icy white desert.

"We will," insisted Merill, and the intensity of her stare flared aside her assurance. "We'll do anything for our Virgil."

"Even if it's for someone else," added Almi. "Even then."

Virgil nodded, patting Merill's back. "Good."

No longer capable of listening silently to intentionally obtuse dialogue, Descarta cleared her throat. The grunt ensnared the attention of the slate-bound trio. "Would you tell your forsaken queen what is going on?"

Cosseting fingertips brushed up and down the side of Almi's cottony neck, infused with the warmth of pulsing lifeblood. Virgil observed the ensorcelled elf, admiring the way her lips twitched ever-so-slightly in response to his petting. "Almi has agreed to participate in an earthfolk ritual," the sovereign explained. "A duel with the peculiar princess you just met."

An acute amber gaze followed the pendulum-like stroking. Its aggrieved owner wanted to snatch the hand away. Descarta wondered when exactly she'd fallen to the sinister onset of jealousy. Further, at what point had resentment evolved into an underpinning supportive of jealousy. Disgruntled and perplexed, Descarta settled her chin twixt the smooth palms of royalty. "Why?"

"The ritual requires our progeny represent us."

"No," the queen shook her head, "why must she fight?"

Virgil frowned, still attending the elf's contentment. "Securing Ignus as an ally is imperative. Because of Elusia's current frailty, the earthfolk will only support us if we prove our merit."

"I see," muttered Descarta. She wanted to scorn the dapper elves for settling so comfortably under Virgil's cosset. Yet the diminutive girl couldn't deny them their reward. They served Elusia better than she.

...

Having returned from gathering supplies, Hafstagg, Hazael and Josiah joined Virgil in the communal bath. Earthfolk engineers, ever enterprising to harness the gift of stone, crafted channels of magma-generated heat to warm the open bath. The sovereign, submerged to his neck, tried to enjoy the respite. Beset by discontent, he missed the evenings when he could languish, comfortably numb and aloof to everything but one goal.

"So," Hafstagg began from the side, "are you certain about this?"

Pretending to be lost in thought, Virgil withheld his reply.

"Virgil," Josiah called with concern. "This isn't fair to them. Only one contender can leave that arena. What if it isn't Almi?"

The weaver exhaled frustration, steam dispersing from his breath.

"You can't just treat them with disregard," argued Josiah. "How can you be so cold after all they've given you?"

"The king is doing what must be done," spoke the steward from opposite Virgil. "He has greater duties to his nation."

"At what cost?" retorted Josiah, a dangerous edge to his tone. "Who is he to decide who lives and dies?"

Hazael shifted, a casual movement that brought a scar-covered arm within reach of his blade—just in case. "Virgil is our king. Do not forget that."

"Enough," Virgil groaned. What he would have given for tranquility. A place of cessation, where niggling and quibbling were forbidden entry. "Almi and Merill chose to participate of their own accord."

The bard scoffed, reply envenomed and condemning. "You knew they wouldn't deny you, and you took advantage of that. How can you be so callous?"

Spirits crowed anxiously. They pawed at Virgil's mind with hungry, malformed hands of malice and misery. "I said enough," he muttered, inflection wavering under the growing pressure. "I . . ." The weaver faltered in his rejoinder. Josiah plucked a dreadfully accurate reproach. As paramount as his mission was, Virgil confessed he couldn't imagine a day without either of the clingy twins. "I'm going to bed," he decided, lean physique emerging from the cloak of disrupted water. The king snatched a towel and swiftly left the dour atmosphere behind.

"What do you gain from that?" asked Hafstagg in a censuring pitch.

"You think it right? Sacrificing Almi because she wouldn't dare disobey him?" defended the rogue. He was astounded they all found it acceptable. That she was an adventitious pawn, destroyed when the stratagem fit.

The bearded warrior frowned his disappointment. "I'm thinking you're too self-absorbed to see above your own affection for the lass."

"The Virgil I know would have killed you for your disrespect," offered the seneschal. "How you can be so thick as to not see his turmoil is beyond me."

Hafstagg nodded in concordance with Hazael's admonishment. "I'd wager he wants to muck up the battle more than you. What separates him from you is his ability to prioritize."

Josiah grunted his surrender. "She'll win, anyway."

CHAPTER SIX

Regret

Descarta peered from the obscuring tent of her blanket at the chanting king. His actions carried her to a world of befuddled wandering. She couldn't comprehend his demeanor, contrary even now. So swiftly he had changed from passive adoration to outward aggression. And there he sat, still weaving with the purpose of restoring her past.

His divan was shared by two entwined elves whose contented purrs rumbled in their throats while they nuzzled his chest. Before tonight, he'd shown his queen enough respect to prohibit the twins from sleeping with him. Another rending change brought forth by some unspoken slight. It wasn't until being tossed aside that Descarta understood she wanted to be where the sisters were. He treated her well, fought for her, endured these diurnal sessions and never asked for anything. But Almi and Merill were always there, giving their utmost for a king whose mind was elsewhere. The sodden queen contemplated the trail. Was it due to her trenchant distrust expressed in the tunnels before his outbreak? Or mayhap she didn't fawn over him like the ever venereal elves?

As if in clairvoyance, Merill's sanguine gaze appeared, and she presented a fairylike smile to the morose queen. It could have been a normal smile, bereft of clandestine purpose or malediction, but to Descarta there was no denying the victorious gloating the elf emanated.

Sensing the sleepless girl's malcontent, Merill crawled over her sister who grunted and slapped at the air. She slinked onto the bed and joined Descarta under the covers.

"What do you want?" the queen sneered, turning away from the elf and shut her eyes.

Merill inched closer, pressing against the delicate girl's back and wrapping her with an arm. "You're sad," she said, squeezing tight. "Virgil says sad elves are bad elves, so sad Des must be bad Des, too."

"We want you to be happy," whispered Almi, suddenly in front of Descarta. The elves enclosed her in a protective cocoon and gingerly stroked her hair. "Be happy, okay?"

"Oh, pretend you care now that you have him," snapped the queen, jerking her head away. "How sweet of you."

Almi cringed, hiding her face from the insult. It wasn't the reaction Descarta expected.

"Have him?" lamented Merill in her ear. "Our Virgil . . . hasn't loved us for so long. So long we've been waiting."

"So long," whimpered Almi in a wistful inflection that clawed at Descarta's heartstrings. The dolorous elf dug her cheek into the queen's silky hair.

The awareness in two girls who seemed little more than symbiotic creatures shattered Descarta's image of the twins. She was awestruck by the revelation, one which painted them as steadfast remora with resolve worthy of extol. "Then why fawn and dote over him relentlessly?"

Almi retracted her visage from the berryflower scent. Her expression was one of bewilderment, the inquiry an affront. "He is our Virgil," she offered, as if it explained everything. For the impassioned sisters, he was a catholicon.

A velvet-clad arm weaseled under the queen's warm neck, another around her chest to engage her in a generous hug. Following a slight sniffle, Merill soared away to her refuge, years long dilapidated by the bite of sorrow. "Our king loved us once. He will again."

"He must," came the soothing elven tune of concurrence, spiced with heartbroken bitterness. Almi partook in the return to ruined times, sharing the temporal journey with her sister. "It's so nice when he pets us," she sighed. "Like laying in sunshine."

Descarta frowned in self-flagellation. The chronically bound girls appeared much smaller to her now, much less intimidating than when they first set out. In ignorance, she had viewed them as simpletons, unable to perceive anything beyond Virgil. Sure, Almi and Merill were still joined to him as truly as if they were sewn together. Yet they were bound while brooking the pain of unending rejection.

The queen raised delightfully gossamer fingers to stroke Almi's hair, rousing a murmur of approval. "Remember the tunnels when we were split?"

Almi nodded, pressing into the girl's touch.

"Virgil tried to go back for you. He would have dived under the collapsing roof if I didn't stop him." She grinned at the captivated carmine stare that seemed to undulate in the orange glow emanating from magma far below. "If he wasn't so weak at the time, he would have thrown himself under the torrent of boulders for you. He said you deserved better than him."

The elves were withdrawn for some time, communicating on a frequency reserved for the two of them. Apparently reaching a conclusion, Merill clung tighter to the diminutive queen to press a moist cheek against her upper back. "Thanks," the elf managed before an eruptive sob shook her frame. "Could you . . . share?"

Sniveling, Almi snatched the queen's arm and attached herself to it. "Please," she begged, "don't make us wait until you die."

With a deep, disgruntled sigh, Descarta clutched the covers about her chin. They held a penchant for morbid and upsetting ways of requesting her aid. The queen imagined they would wait, calculating the brevity of her human lifespan as just another bothersome rise to climb. "Don't wait," she mumbled. "It's already your turn. I'm just . . ." The dolorous girl paused, auguring the term for her discarded state. "I'm nothing."

Almi shook her head, snowy bangs flashing like pell-mell flitterbugs across Descarta's nose. "That's silly. Des is everything . . . it's why we must wait."

"So please," Merill whimpered from behind, "share."

Exhaustion forbade the queen from contesting their assertion. "Fine, fine," she said to entertain them, "I'll give it some thought."

"Elves are good friends," assured Merill and Almi in unison, cozily fitting themselves around the glooming queen.

...

The high mage fidgeted, habitually toying with the lacy cuff encircling her hands. Violah was fond of the mannerism. The simple gesture was a charming trait, yet also a complex misdirection device. Deception was like weaving an elaborate spell, many tangles, loops and passes that when combined yielded trenchant results. The habit often made her seem uncertain, could lend to timidity or augment her aura as a desirable mate. When needed, it could do all three.

Now, with the grim figure before her, she only needed its most fundamental of conveyances: nervousness. "Your concern is appreciated, Captain." She sighed, drawing her lips into a troubled grimace. "However, when the dreadcleavers were commissioned, orders were clearly given. They will brook their restlessness."

Lastan pulled a plaintive canvas over his travel-worn face. Something was bothering the weaver—he didn't need thaumaturgy to divine her mood when she tinkered restlessly at her sleeve. Yet it wasn't him, he was certain. She was an accomplished sorceress, and he would likely be ash, mutton or both before he could set his ferocious axes spinning. The dreadcleaver had been delivered a missive from an anonymous origin promising swift and cataclysmic justice. Swift was a relative term, though, and he couldn't mollify his band perpetually. Lastan knew clandestine machinations took time, and he was equipped with steadfast patience. "Our orders aren't clear, ma'am. The trouble lies there," the warrior spread his hands, "and all around us."

"I am aware," conceded Violah, "that your men are driven by bloodlust. And that they are like leashed hounds, idling at the foot of the Bulwark as they are." She leaned forward, striking gaze seizing Lastan with its vigor. "But they will remain so until the order to attack is given. Understood?"

Lastan tilted his head in deference. "I do." He had his misgivings concerning how long his subordinates would remain pliable, but the dreadcleaver thought it circumspect to refrain from challenging the high mage.

"Your underlings will be unchained within the sennight," Violah offered in comprehension that his difficulty wasn't a result of incompetence. A hound will only obey its master for so long when a meaty treat dangles just before its nose. "Keep them tame for a slight longer."

"As you command, sorceress," replied Lastan. "May I take my leave?"

"You may," she answered, already surveying a scroll amidst the heap of documents strewn about her desk.

With no further words, Lastan exited, grateful to not have incurred her wrath. Tension was poignant among his troops, but he would rather confront them than the weaver. For all her worry, she was adroit in the arcane arts. He could sense some candor there, though. And it made him want to explore her personality to greater effect, beyond the manipulative parlaying and authority. Perhaps when this contract was terminated, he would pursue a more intimate arrangement.

For the time being, keeping the dreadcleavers sedate was work enough.

...

Almi stood on her toes with fingers entwined behind her king's neck. Her many-fanged mace dangled hungrily in the leather wrapping securing it to her hip. Merill hovered behind her, nervous digits fidgeting with her sister's tunic. Their companions spectated from farther away, shrouded in awkward silence, with Descarta having inched forward to catch the exchange.

The elf craned her neck to peer at Virgil. "Watch me," whispered Almi. "Watch me, okay? Out there. I'll be out there for our Virgil."

Virgil nodded.

"Merill and I, we'll always be yours."

Virgil nodded.

"We'd do anything for you to look at us like before," sniffed Almi. She pushed her face into his chest and used the thick robe as a refuge for tear-glazed cheeks. "We love—"

"I know," interrupted the weaver. "I've never forgotten." He frowned, misgivings tearing at his resolve. Virgil had always persevered, clung immovable and aloof to lofty aspirations. Yet, on the dangerous precipice of success, he shook. The weaver recalled the tunnel encounter, his initial disregard for their lives and what it could have cost him. Was he really willing to risk them again? Even if Merill remained—and he had his doubts considering their connection— Virgil knew she would not be the same.

"We'll be yours always," Almi muttered, emerging from her robed refuge. The girl smiled, a solemn, enchanting thing, and rose to her toes. She paused there, lingering in tantalizing proximity, enlarged scarlet orbs prospecting his own for deposits of affection. "We love you," the elf whispered. Almi angled her head to brush tender lips across his, catalyzing poignant memories. "Always," she repeated emphatically.

Virgil sighed, an act he seemed to take part in more and more frequently. He patted her sides and pushed her to arms' length, searching for an appropriate response. "I'll be watching," was all the sovereign could manage.

The mace-wielding girl bobbed her head before pivoting and throwing herself around Merill. No words were exchanged; yet Virgil was sure they communicated well enough without. Parting, Almi skipped off into the hexagonal arena where preparations were nearing an end.

He wanted to call her back, to subjugate the regret that churned in his craw. To at least give her proper thanks. The weaver rarely did what he truly wanted. Instead, he froze, a useless sentinel enervated by malaise.

Merill tugged on his sleeve. "Virgil, you must watch." She tugged again, turning him by his arm. He followed her lead, but his mind was elsewhere. Virgil counted every selfish step that widened the distance between him and Almi.

Descarta watched him depart, troubled by the intimate half-secrets shared and the evidently miserable atmosphere. She pivoted to the trio behind her. "Why are they so grim? Almi isn't leaving."

The bard rubbed his bald head, naturally first to reply against the decision. "Figures, the illusive bastard didn't care to tell you."

"Tell me?" asked Descarta.

Intending to lessen the blow, Hafstagg stepped forward, cutting off Josiah's forthcoming response. "Little one, Almi is competing for a grand purpose. If she lives, we'll have secured Ignus as an ally."

"Lives?" questioned the queen. "Lives?!" she spat, recognition contorting her features. "How can you be so wretched?! She's a person! A wonderful person! Not some diplomatic commodity!"

"Be calm," advised Hazael.

"No! You cannot tell me this is acceptable!" she shouted. Descarta dashed toward the sloping ramp taken by Virgil and Merill.

...

"Our Virgil saved us, pulled us from the darkness." Merill delayed, allowing the seconds where her sister would have offered a supportive phrase pass. "Gave us everything. And we tried to be good. We tried so hard." Another uncanny pause for Almi followed. "Our Virgil has always been there. Always made us safe and fed. Even when we were failures. This time we won't fail you, our Virgil." She nodded in affirmation and gave the weaver's wrist a squeeze.

The sovereign halted, pulling his anchored ward to a stop in turn. Almi and Merill were ever enigmas. He never truly understood their hidebound attachment. Probably because he was too preoccupied or too afraid to ask. During sleepless nights in the study or through countless attempts by masked enemies at unseating him, they were always present. They provided company, dawdling the hours away while he sought to refine rituals. The frolicsome sisters were an intractable aegis against assassins and loneliness. Yet they thought they were maladroit, undeserving. Virgil knew why. He had forsaken them by ignoring their affection. He was no better than the elven bastards who ruptured their persona as children.

Yes, Almi and Merill never failed him. They were the one constant, the adamant sprites he could rely upon in any situation. He was the failure, the unabated menace. So accustomed to stepping on others, he'd mistakenly placed them underfoot.

"Virgil!" demanded Descarta, shattering his introspection as she appeared behind him. "By the Sundered, what is wrong with you? Are you really this cruel behind that mask of kindness? I may deserve your malice, but these two—" The queen suspended her tirade to place herself between Virgil and Merill. "These two worship you! You should praise them! Not use them as political fodder!"

The king sighed. Apparently, he had a penchant for making those he cared for feel inadequate. These byzantine quandaries were never given form when he simply did not care. "And who are you to question me?"

"Your queen!" harrumphed Des.

"Only in title," retorted Virgil, the words corrosive as they slinked over his tongue. He reminded himself that, as much as he abhorred the treatment, it was for her. Hitherto, he'd been selfish. But he would make certain she didn't suffer a relationship with a vile and undeserving king.

Descarta flinched as the biting malediction took purchase on her spirit. His responses were always so coddling, so complaisant, and she'd grown used to being treated gently. Descarta wanted desperately to go back, to rescind the venomous responses and lack of gratitude. She'd warmed to him too late, her opportunity to blossom long withered.

"We want this," said Merill in confidence as she moved around Descarta, lithe frame set against the king's raven mantle. "We decided. Not our Virgil."

The diminutive queen blanched. She contemplated the response and how influenced it was by Virgil. Her vigor was drained, her reply meek and without charge. "You want what he tells you."

Merill nodded her accord. "We are his. This time, we chose. We want to be special."

"There are other ways of doing that," muttered Descarta.

"For you," whispered the elf, looking to her boots.

Virgil frowned at the portrait of ruin. It was all his pursuits ever yielded. "Are we going?"

The elf grabbed his wrist. "Yes, Virgil." She shot him a glimmering smile and started again up the ramp toward their elevated booth. Descarta followed closely behind, disturbed by the twins' slapdash decision to throw Almi into danger. All for someone who would toss them aside. He exhibited such polarity in his actions. And yet she still felt a compulsion to find his favor, just as Almi and Merill did. Mayhap the three had more in common than she thought.

...

Almi's wicked backhand sent her skull-shattering mace just above the ducking princess' head. The earthfolk intended to riposte, but Almi harnessed the momentum by deftly throwing her leg into a right rear round kick.

Mundin retreated into a backward roll, rising with a defensive upward swing of her heavy bronze staff. The maneuver was set to connect with the advancing ward, who had been intent on controlling a proximity where the staff was crippled. Almi was an elf, though, gifted with refined dexterity. She cartwheeled to toss her lissome body over the technique. Spinning with the weight of her weapon, Mundin thrust the staff behind her. Realizing the incipient swing was a feint, Almi tried to shift direction. But the vicious jab squarely struck her abdomen and sent the girl into a tumble.

At first, adrenaline mollified the injury. As the elf attempted to rise, however, she emitted a pain-startled cry and whimpered under the pressure of a demolished rib. Agony spread arresting ungulae out in crippling waves from the impact. In her malaise, she searched the cheering crowd for Virgil and spotted him sitting in tense turbulence, trained upon his ward. Almi found vim there, in knowing he was watching. She could not let him down.

The injured elf regained her wherewithal just in time to roll away from a ground-shattering thrust. She sprung to her feet, sustained fracture little more than a nuisance before her determination to gain Virgil's favor.

Mundin stalked forward, ensorcelled by a mineral earthfolk warriors ingested to incite battle-rage. Charmed or not, Almi would have shown no mercy to the princess. She was an adversary who must be defeated regardless the cost. Anything for an untarnished smile from her king. Not the sorrow-soaked, feigned countenances he'd long given them. Her purpose was to free him from discord. While this savage display was but a tiny offering, she firmly believed the granular victories would one day amount to something. She had to believe; else her sole dream was forfeit.

Almi dashed forward, ignoring the blaze in her side, voracious mace poised for a crushing overhead blow. She roared a banshee's shriek to accompany her charge. The obvious feint didn't ensnare Mundin. Instead of dodging or parrying, she stepped forward with a powerful thrust of her polearm. Almi followed the feint with another, spinning a pirouette around the incoming staff that spun her many-fanged mace toward the princess' right arm. The obsidian girl hopped backward, finally entangled in the intricately woven design of the clever elf. Almi ceased her half-hearted swing and executed a teep kick to her retreating foe's chest which knocked the girl off balance and onto her rear.

The bronze stave clambered to the stone and rolled away. Mundin tried to escape, but the razor-toothed mace bludgeoned her shoulder and excited an explosion of black dust as it ripped into her stony hide and threw her onto her back. The princess howled a shrill cry of dragging chalk. Almi stood above the shaking creature, readying her truncheon to end the competition. Around her, an austere aura washed over the crowd. Earthfolk glared and sneered in both disbelief and rage that one of the lesser races bested their prized princess.

Almi flashed a triumphant grin. Virgil would be pleased.

She brought her mace down for the killing blow, a strike which would easily blast the girl's head to dust.

The victory was halted by a resonating voice wrought of earth. "Cease this!" echoed throughout the arena in the commanding timbre of the Impervious. The titan approached the gladiators, Almi frozen with her wicked mace held aloft, Mundin quavering below. "That's enough. You have won," he bellowed. "Don't kill her, please," Bromyr followed in a less harsh tone. The crowd burst into clamor. Jeers and praise for his unwillingness to submit to century old laws converged in a wild din.

Uncertain, Almi looked to her king, awaiting his edict.

The sovereign scowled, vexed by the outcome. He doubted the Impervious would have interfered if the tables were turned. Worse, he felt diminished by the knowledge that he might not have done the same for Almi. He would have liked to have the elf kill the princess out of spite. Sighing, he gave her a nod and beckoned for the elf to return.

...

"Virgil, Virgil!" called Almi as she trotted toward the sovereign, animated with delight. "Virgil, I did it!" As she reached him, the elf lifted her arms for a hug. No longer affected by adrenaline, the action bore thorny burrows of agony into her side. Almi's features twisted under its sway, and doubling over, the elf barreled into Virgil.

The king groaned. The back of his head throbbed from its contact with the floor. Almi whimpered atop him and quivered from the fire in her ribs. She struggled against the jagged shards of broken bone, straightening to look up at Virgil with a watery iridescent stare. "Did I do well? Did I?" she pleaded more than asked. The shaking girl sunk her fingers into the sorcerer's robe, kneading and tugging vehemently on the fabric. "Is our only one pleased?"

Virgil swallowed as the suffering maiden sailed him to black seas. A worry prodded him—one that he'd managed to avoid for decades. That one day soon he might go too far and forfeit the lovely creature's life. The concern arrested him not due to its likelihood, but merely because he cared. Seeped in years of fermenting apathy, he had suddenly become so irresolute. Perhaps this was the result of shutting yourself in dusty, candle-lit rooms for a lifetime. "You performed wonderfully," he said, gingerly stroking her swollen side with magically imbued fingers. The king's command over restorative weave was no better than a novice's, yet it did well to diminish the pain. "You always have."

The lithe elf swooned, emitted a satisfied mew and nudged her cheek against his stomach.

Descarta entered the staging area to see Almi, one leg hooked around Virgil, exposing a sultry olive thigh connected to a voluptuous rear only just hidden by her raised tunic. She started at the incriminating image, and the pestilent acid of fear welled in her bosom. "W-Whats going on?" she stuttered, emotion manifest in her inquiry.

"Almi fell," explained Virgil. "She's hurt." He patted the elf's sunny crown, lightly combing the strands.

The queen approached and appraised the pair. She found herself confounded by the rare compassion expressed as he petted the resting twin. Virgil wore a countenance of uninhibited concern, unusual for someone who, she had begun to discover, lived a constant masquerade. Sometimes she forgot he was human, that he could ever hold such raw feelings for another person. Such love, she thought, as she pinpointed the catalyst with palpable envy. It made her wonder why he'd even allowed the ritual to take place. She could scarcely untangle the king's contradicting actions.

Led by the pattering of her boots, Merill burst into the room, sliding to a stop beside her sister and flopping haphazardly on the girl she so dearly missed.

Almi expelled an enfeebled cry, and squirmed to remove the agonizing weight.

Merill yelped and withdrew from the elf akin to traversing broken glass. "What did he say?" asked the girl, bending to brush her nose sympathetically over Almi's upper arm.

The radiance of the wounded elf's grin would have been enough to transmit the news. "Oh, Merill!" she exclaimed in a mellifluous timbre unmarred by pain. "Our Virgil gave us praise."

"Gave it?!" gasped Merill, edging closer to touch heads with her sister. "Really?"

Almi bobbed affirmatively. "That we're wonderful always."

"Always?" gasped Merill again, emitting a pleased mew. "Our Virgil is so generous," she crooned, contorting her neck to beam at the king.

"As cozy as you are, darlings," said the sovereign, "the champion needs adequate healing. Merill, fetch me Hazael quickly." This time the pattering faded as the elf, brimming with energy, bolted off to obey the command.

"Virgil," started the queen, watching the shallow rise and fall of Almi's back, "why do you do this? Why allow this torment?"

With a burdened sigh, the king brushed dandelion curtains behind Almi's smooth ear. "Because the alternative is inconceivable," he finally answered.

"Inconceivable? What could possibly be more important than your wards?" she demanded, genuinely confounded by his incongruous behavior. When he didn't respond, she sought his image.

Immediately, the king turned his sight back to Almi, assuming a veil of neutrality. But not before she caught his glowing blue cauldrons, kindled with the despair of terrible longing. "Must I entertain your invasive questions?" he growled.

"No," Descarta murmured as she turned to leave. "I'll look for Hazael, too." She shambled away, brooding. She couldn't talk to him anymore. A great ache pressed on her chest, threatening to consume the terrified throbbing beneath.

Almi tensed when the queen's footsteps disappeared. "Is our Virgil mad?" she questioned in trepidation.

"Of course not. Don't worry yourself."

She did, though. For a moment, the man beneath her was foreign. "You do not like her?"

"I do."

"Why talk like that then?" poked Almi.

"Well," replied the dolorous sovereign. "It's complicated."

A moment of taciturn followed before Almi spoke again. "Our Virgil does not speak to us like that."

Virgil injected another wave of healing through her side, dimming the returning ache. "No, I don't."

"So . . . so we are not liked?" whimpered Almi.

"That's not what I said."

"Treat us the same. Like us, too?" pleaded the elf from her respite. "We like when our Virgil says we're wonderful. It makes us warm inside. But that means we're not liked."

Virgil sighed at the confused girl's broken logic. "That isn't how it works."

"But—"

"Just rest, dear. I like you plenty."

Almi nodded her acquiescence.

...

Hopping about merrily, the twins gaped at the churning pit of magma below. "Look at it! So bright! So orange!" chirped Merill, an arm slung around her sister's waist.

Almi leaned over the railing running one of the capitol city's hatch of bridges. "It's like jam!" She kicked her feet behind her. "I bet it tastes fruity."

"Spread it on brioches!" suggested Merill.

Hafstagg chuckled at the vigor-given pair. "Lively today, aren't you?"

Merill bounced her reply. "Our Virgil likes us!"

"Beat that rock lady," added her sister while spinning a pirouette and swinging her arms.

The bard rapped a simple tune on his harp. "You're quite the fighter, Almi. Earthfolk are known for their tenacity. You're fortunate you didn't die."

"I didn't," agreed the girl, not catching onto the gravity of his statement.

Behind them followed king, queen and steward. "I'm indebted to your healing artifice, Hazael," commented the king. "She was in such pain."

The seneschal shook his head. "We all have a place here. I simply served mine."

Virgil watched the girls cavort as if they hadn't suffered at all. To them, the day before was a boon, a victory with loot reaching beyond diplomacy. "It was folly to allow her to enter. Her life could have been squashed," he contemplated. "I'm a detestable king."

"No," countered Hazael. "It is precisely that which makes you a worthy king. To do what must be done without forgetting they are more than pawns to you."

"Could you be more unctuous?" groaned Virgil.

Hazael scoffed. "When have you known me to take your favor seriously?"

The sovereign decided to shift the conversation. Descarta had already been subjected to enough for now. He had no desire to torture the poor girl with his affection for the elves. "Well, we accomplished what we came for."

"What did the Impervious say?" asked Hazael.

"He was understandably terse." Virgil recalled the titan boiling atop his throne. The earthfolk patron expressed that he knew Virgil did what had to be done. Words, the weaver knew, spoken with little real meaning. Bromyr likely wanted to leap forth and smash him. "Ignus will march the day after tomorrow."

"And Bromyr?"

"His rage will pass once he's fighting."

Descarta took in the surrounding structures. Everywhere, crevasses were filled with residences or shops adorned with ornate designs. Forges lined each level of the spiraling pit, drawing forth magma to be worked into instruments of varying purposes. Earthfolk roamed about, most paying the group little heed. A few gawked at Almi, recognizing her from the arena, but the rest simply went about their mundane affairs. The establishment was a giant hive primed for war. Nevertheless, she found respect for the beauty of their diligence. They never stopped adding to the shaft by pulling from their treasured stone.

"Descarta," came Hazael's voice.

She broke her attention from the city and looked to him. "Yes?"

"Would you like to have a look around before we leave?" offered the steward.

Descarta thought it odd Hazael asked instead of Virgil. He was ahead of them now, the twins humming and hanging from his arms. She would have liked to explore at his side. "No, Hazael. I'm fine, thanks." Sightseeing no longer seemed enticing.

"As you wish," said the steward before withdrawing to catch up with the king. "She declined."

"I see," sighed Virgil. "We'll be heading out, then."

The elves groaned from their perches. "But we just arrived!"

"This isn't a trip of leisure, songbirds," reminded the king, drawing another complaint from his sides.

"Virgil," started the seneschal in a furtive volume. "Why did you have me offer at all?"

"Isn't that why she's here? To see foreign lands?"

Hazael frowned at the response. "I know you're being clever. What worries me is my uncertainty concerning the goal of that cleverness."

"You worry too much," said Virgil. "Everything is proceeding as I designed."

Hazael grunted in distaste. "Sometimes I forget that you have an empyrean design, dear lord. One too lofty for us mortals."

"Be quiet," replied the king, looking askance at the diminutive girl behind him. "I'm doing what is best, anyway."

The nebulous response stoked his anxiety. Hazael liked to designate himself as one who could read the weaver. Recently, his confidence had faded. The murky answers were enough to unsettle the steward. They could have been harmlessly woven or lashed together to please him and make no admissions.

Hazael shook his head. He should trust Virgil; the man had never failed him. With so much at stake, however, he couldn't quell his paranoia.

The cohorts exited the heart of the Underrise via a tunnel with the words "NE Passage" chiseled in rigid script. In the place of torches, slits and angled mirrors of polished steel gave the magma yet another purpose: natural lighting.

"Where are we going now?" inquired Descarta who had taken to the front of the group alongside Hafstagg. She was a tiny thing juxtaposed against his hulking physique.

"Vanathiel," answered the towering man. "Our final destination. Is that right, my lord?" he called over his shoulder, grinning at some unknown joke.

"Yes," Virgil tersely replied.

"Another long walk," grumbled Josiah. "My life has been one never-ending walk."

"There will be more elven women than your eager loins can handle," guffawed Hafstagg. "You should be excited!"

The bard deliberated Almi. The cursed girl had soured the race for him. He would never have her, he knew. "I think I'm finished with elves for some time."

"Finished?" gasped the hammer-wielding warrior. "You cannot tell me you will pass through the city of elves without swaying."

"I will," sighed Josiah.

Hafstagg expelled his heavy chortle in response. "I do not believe it."

It didn't take long to pass between the core and bulwark of the Underrise. Descarta and Hafstagg exited first, and were blasted with the brilliant midday sunlight. The queen winced, lifting a hand to shelter against blindness. A sudden movement to her right followed by the ring of clashing metal startled the sightless girl. Hafstagg yelled for her to stay near. More voices were added to the tumult as Almi and Merill shouted gleeful cries. Having adjusted to the unfiltered light, Descarta turned a full circle, sucking an anxiety-ridden breath at the chaos around her. Assassins—dressed in the same black jerkin as before—had already fallen around her feet. A horde still remained, surging from above in a deadly buffet. Descarta's chest heaved in horror as she screamed and begged for someone to pluck her free of the madness.

A stern-faced assassin lunged from the tumult at the frozen queen. Daylight glinted off his wicked blade, serrated edge lined to puncture her throat. Transfixed by terror, she watched as a gargoyle would, spectator to her own approaching demise. Seconds of grief passed, yet the shimmering blade held its menacing posture. Suddenly, as if ripped of his soul, the assassin collapsed into an unmoving husk. Raven tendrils retreated from the withered form, running an obedient course to their origin. Descarta followed their sanguinolent path between shuffling feet and draining corpses to Virgil's outstretched fingertips.

The weaver traversed the distance with purpose. Beside him, Almi worked her mace furiously to disrupt the onslaught of sellswords. Virgil paid no heed to the advancing death, entrusting his life to Almi and Merill, whose bow twanged in accord with a bloody melody of startled gargles. The sorcerer was focused on a more precious flame, that of his paralyzed blossom—the assassins' secondary objective. He flung the blighted thread from his hand as an arcane whip, dismantling the spirit of any who neared the girl.

"Des, stay near," ordered the king when he reached her. He spoke with magically-augmented clarity above the cacophony. Behind him, those equipped for melee had aligned in a semicircle. Merill stood with her back to his, shaft notched, ready to plug any gaps in the defense. "Wake up!" yelled Virgil in desperation. "Now is not the time!"

"We could use some help," cried Josiah. "Sling a spell or two, Virgil!" The bard wailed a discordant note that set his nearest foe off-guard and ran the stunned woman through with a swift lunge.

Growling, the sorcerer pivoted and lashed out with his ethereal whip, rendering another assailant empty. "Descarta is our priority here," boomed his frustrated reply. Virgil considered the promontory they'd been cleverly herded onto. A devastating spell could jeopardize its integrity. "I can't—"

...

The fragrance of berryflowers assaulted her with a pact of peaceful security. She curled her lips into a contented smile, cooing at the compassionate digits stroking her scalp. Descarta blinked, waking to a world of crimson velvet and stark white.

"Poor girl," lamented a euphonic voice of heavenly resonance.

Descarta hadn't registered that the calming touch must have belonged to someone, that the supple lap she rest in was not her own. Fright did not claim her, though, for it was beyond this place. She rolled onto her back, toward the ministrations, and looked up to the woman grinning plaintively back down.

"We finally meet," greeted the elf.

"Nice to meet you," said Descarta, admiring the visage that, even when set with sorrow, beamed with beauty. With her angular elven features, radiant golden hair and crimson eyes, the queen thought she resembled Almi and Merill. Just softer, gentler and shroud in grace. "Who are you?" she asked in a calm tone.

"Someone who cares," answered the sweet vibrations and further stroking.

Descarta nodded, peering at the youth-given canvas above her. "Is this the fabric? Virgil said it would be like this. Why am I here?"

"Inquisitive creature." The woman ceased her stroking, instead running fingers like lily petals over Descarta's rosy cheeks. "Yes, and you are here because you willed it."

The queen caught the faint clinking of metal in time with the elf's caress. Upon further inspection, she realized the woman was bound by neck and wrists to obsidian chains. "Why are you restrained so?"

While her smile did not fade, the prisoner's shimmering orbs conveyed great turmoil. "Because I am—was precious."

Descarta wanted to comfort her, sensed a welling of wrongness that the descended angel would scar herself with such sadness. How easily she had become attached to the serenity exuded before her probing question.

"Do you love him?" inquired the celestial elf, still petting the prone queen.

"Love him? Who?"

"Your king, blossom. Virgil."

"How do I know?"

The woman frowned, pressing a feathery palm to Descarta's bosom. "Does it ache here when he denies you his affection? When you think of him discarding you?"

Descarta swallowed, grimacing at the thought. At the lacerating words her king adopted. She nodded her answer.

A troubled breath escaped the elf's lips. "That one is beyond me. Of all people, he should know you are a brittle creature."

"You know him?"

"I did once," replied the prisoner, and the vibrant smile returned to her fair features. "He will need you soon."

Pressure accumulated under the bound elf's palm as she spoke, gleaning energy from the eldritch realm. "I have waited alone for so long. As gratitude for your visit, I will gift the means to show him your feelings. If you so choose."

"I don't under—" Descarta howled in agony, writhing against the immovable force lancing her chest.

"I am sorry, hollow one. This is the only way," the woman explained as she gingerly wiped the beading sweat from Descarta's forehead with her free hand. She sunk gradually, penetrating the wailing queen's spirit until her arm was buried to the shoulder. Until she reached the faint flicker within. "Go forth," she whispered. "Love."

...

Descarta drew in a breath to scream once more, but the tearing at her soul had evaporated and left only the evocative scent of berryflowers. Still saturated with a feeling of well-being, she admired the exhibition. Virgil had an arm suspended before her, a subconscious gesture that illustrated his protectiveness. The other wove a complex pattern of frothing, putrid blackness. The growing substance churned behind each pass, seeking to return to its source as he spread it wider and wider. One final gesture left a disk of purest black. To Descarta, it seemed a portal to another place, one dominated by a starless night. He thrust an open palm into the conjuration. The dark pit responded with a jettison of tendrils similar to what the weaver summoned before, only by the dozens. Each sought an assassin and attached as leeches to their targets. A winding helix of flame manifested in his outstretched hand. The mighty heat exuded by the trifling candlefire was enough to instantly dry out the queen's eyes. He then lifted the dense mass with great difficulty and shoved the burden into his oily disk.

Impossibly bright light exploded into life, eclipsing the foray in an impregnable glow. The subsequent vacuum brought clarity and replaced berryflowers with sulfuric stink. Droves of sellswords exploded into clouds of snowy ash and charred equipment. Merill released a delighted chuckle, spinning amid the charnel blizzard. Virgil nodded, satisfied with the result, while the others worked against the remaining foes, still a sizeable force.

The smug complacency was punished by a twang, the dirge of a nearby bow. Desperation fueling him, the sovereign leaped at Descarta and bowled her over. The baneful arrows missed their mark, knowledge which relieved Virgil.

But the thrice dealt stabbing in his back was excruciating. More than that, it was stunning.

A coat of poison, he realized.

Then he was falling. Plummeting with his petite sparrow tucked between his flightless wings. Caught by the noxious nectar, he couldn't prevent inertia from taking him over the cliff. Momentarily, he accepted the fate and the liberation it would bring.

"Virgil!" shrieked a mortified Descarta. The promontory's farewell was a fuddling swirl of stone and sky. Vermillion leaked into blue, blue into vermillion, until her surroundings were but streaks of the colors.

The spinning nauseated her. The weightlessness nauseated her. The swiftly approaching end to her kaleidoscope descent nauseated her. "Virgil!" Her voice reached, saturated with fright, for him to somehow extract them from danger. She did not know why or what she yearned to persist for. Still, Descarta was certain she did not want to become a tetherless puppet upon the unmoving Ignusian earth.

The last despairing call gripped him. His precious blossom needed him, called for him. As it had always been, he could not ignore her. Could not reject the endearing girl her right to flourish. So he pooled his desire, worked against the onerous poison seeking to dilute his resolution.

"Virgil," begged Descarta, arms locked securely around his back. "Please do something." She clenched her lids tight, shoving the disorienting blur of stone away.

Leisurely zephyrs converged under Virgil's will, forming swift gusts which were woven into an enthralled tempest of powerful winds. The forces roared a high-pitched complaint. Wind's mercurial nature made it the most arduous element to manipulate. Virgil faltered, nearly allowing the hodgepodge of recruited gale to escape his control. Punctured organs, upset spirits and his own subconscious condemnation were all against him.

He pressed through the muddiness of thought, clenched his jaw and commanded subservience. The tempest howled contrarily but did not disband. Obeying, it cushioned them, negating their velocity bit by bit until they struck the rock-strewn ground in a bruising tumble.

Descarta coughed, orange-brown dust scattering under her lips. "Ugh," she groaned while rising to a sore hip. "Ouch, ouch, ouch." The queen shifted her weight to her rear, submitting to the objections of her thigh. She didn't sense any serious injuries; she was intact. The weight of that revelation was made lucid when she gazed at the promontory they'd said farewell to. No one could have survived an impact from that height. A moist wheeze to her rear notified the girl of her king's location.

He'd tumbled farther than her, ending the roll on his side.

She hobbled over to him, kneeling before the recumbent king whose turmoil-shroud stare followed her movements. "Are you injured?" she asked.

The sovereign opened his mouth, producing a mirthless gurgle and an escaping sanguine stream.

"V-Virgil?" stammered Descarta before releasing a distressed gasp at his crimson reply. She leaned closer to examine him. "What's wrong? Virgil, please." It was then that she discovered the broken shafts protruding victoriously from his robe. Dread rose in her throat, a bile she couldn't evacuate.

"What do I do? Virgil? What do I do?"

A grunt from below caught her attention. Virgil struggled to bring a trembling hand to her cheek. He smiled, thinking it a preferable demise: to finally revel in the feather-inspired endowment of her skin. The slight blanket of her parted hazelnut curtains along his knuckles was heavenly.

Descarta did not pull away from the chilly digits whose touch deposited scarlet streaks across her face and hair. She lowered her eyes, perplexed and embarrassed by the forlorn farewell. Why he tread such a circuitous path around the contours of her heart was beyond her.

Virgil cast out another mouthful of decay. He knew he was fading, venom rendering his functions inoperable one by one. He always thought hatred would define his final thoughts. Hatred of a world that stripped him of every morsel of happiness he happened upon. With the end finally arrived, he knew only deep-seated regret. The sorcerer failed in everything. And that meant Descarta would not last one moon without his extra-dimensional weaving. While she assumed his dedication was to restoring lost memories, it was in actuality a life-extending technique. A day without would be her last.

Now that she had no future to bring to ruin, he wanted her to know. To reveal what he kept discreetly packaged behind his back for so long. Sometimes he would flash the ribbon-wound parcel, praise one of her many engrossing traits or do something unnecessary but indicative of his captivation. Never had he went as far as presenting the bundle.

Rouge-coated lips parted to form his waterlogged confession. "How I've failed you, my blossom." Virgil lifted the petite queen's downcast chin and forced her to meet his eyes. He wanted her to see the honest fervor he beheld her with. "Though my regrets are many," he rasped. "Utmost is withholding my love for you."

If she responded, if she accepted or rejected his terse confession, he wasn't aware. He was being escorted away, pinpricks of sunlight withering to impenetrable darkness.

CHAPTER SEVEN

Brought to Light

The great whirling hammer indiscriminately battered a half-dozen sellswords into a perilous spiral. A nimble assassin bobbed beneath the span of bronze only to have her fair complexion ruined by a giant gauntleted fist. Hafstagg bellowed triumphantly. "'Tis a good day for smashing!"

Something clattered against his back, deflected by the bronze plate. He turned swiftly, hefting the massive bludgeon for another punishing blow. Fully intending to introduce another meddlesome rogue to oblivion, the bulky warrior nearly clambered off-balance when no one was behind him to receive the blow.

He chuckled at the discarded bow, evidently used as a projectile at the hands of a frustrated young elf. Merill stood, hands on hips, scowling at the man. An unshackled wind escaped gleefully over the cliff, flapping the tunic in its wake around her lithe olive thighs. "Kill stealer!" she complained, stomping toward him to retrieve her weapon. "I had her marked!"

"A shame I was quicker," Hafstagg grinned. "You should practice more, little one."

"Oh!" The girl huffed and scuttled off to assist her sister.

Tunic sodden with gore, Almi was utilizing the hilt of her mace to punch holes in the skull of an already dispatched assailant. The corpse shook and rattled under her strikes, a festive postmortem dance that led Merill to believe the man was still alive. She skipped over and used her heel to assist in the superfluous pummeling, jabbing repeatedly at the torso. Almi, who had straddled the man's bloodied chest, ceased her barrage and leaned back, hanging her head to look at an upside-down image of her sister. "What're you doing?"

"Helping," grunted Merill as she stomped the body.

"Oh," smiled Almi, chin-length hair swaying under her head. "We finished?"

Merill stood on the bruised abdomen, surveying the death-strewn outcropping.

Nearby, Josiah was cleaning his dagger on a fallen sellsword, fiddling with pockets and relieving satchels of their contents in search of loot and information.

Hazael cut down the final enemy with a horizontal slash which cleanly split his throat. The assassin scratched at the wound in disbelief while wheezing misdirected gasps of oxygen. The seneschal left the floundering creature, content in the finality of the show. While the remaining sellsword gurgled incoherent curses and pleas, lowering a curtain on the pernicious performance, Hazael examined the heaps of second-rate killers. He did not spot the talons of Virgil's robe or lace of Descarta's pinafore. "Where are Virgil and Descarta?" prompted the steward.

The squatting elf leaped from her prize, trotting around and calling out the name of her king at regular intervals. A few calls later and Merill imitated the girl, lifting bodies in her search.

"He fell, along with the girl," came a belated response from Josiah. He was reading a roll of parchment he'd procured from its hidden pocket.

Hafstagg stalked over to the bard, brow furrowed in distaste. "When were you going to tell us this?"

"He was hit three times by arrows," said Josiah. "Then he took Des off the cliff with him. What use is there in telling you he's dead?"

"Dead?!" shrieked Merill, shaking her head vigorously. "Virgil doesn't die! Tell them, big man!"

Almi nodded. "Tell them, big man! Our Virgil can't die!" Together, the twins shuffled along the promontory, peering at the debris below.

"Folly! Hubris!" whined the bow-carrying girl. "That they think our Virgil so little!" She spoke the words merrily; yet her eyes were already leaking.

Her twin pointed, gasping. "Our Virgil!" Almi pulled Merill down with her, lying so their chins peeked over the deleterious drop. They waved their arms frantically and echoed calls that couldn't reach the figures far below.

Hazael stood beside them, noting the movement displayed by his queen. "I would like to investigate more," he began, "but I see someone. And I don't recall any assassins in green frock."

"I found a missive," offered the bard. "Encoded. It's nothing I can't decrypt given time."

Hafstagg hefted his colossal hammer and started toward the winding descent. "Let's be off then. No time for dawdling."

...

Wearing a cloak of silent melancholy, Descarta sat hovering by the departed sovereign. She watched his deep blue eyes, vacant and devoid of the dreary sagacity she once squandered. The frowning girl tried to convince herself it was for the best. He always seemed so dissatisfied, always a servant of sorrow.

Descarta wanted to believe he'd escaped unending torment. Dearly, she sought that conclusion. The ardor that teemed behind cerulean portals when he held her gaze would not permit it. When he uttered his regret, Descarta knew it was without solace. Thus he had forbid her the same.

She contemplated his tragically late parting message. The sovereign—her sovereign—was no august leader, defined as he was by apathy. Nevertheless, he was attentive, considerate to her needs. As often as she tried to push him away, he was always there.

The girl reached out apprehensively, thinking of how vigilantly he watched over her. How he willfully sacrificed himself for her. There had to have been some benign purpose behind the cutting way he'd addressed her over the last day. With certainty, Descarta would miss him. Her heart ached as she daintily touched his face and pressed her head against it. "I'm so sorry," she whimpered, sobbing into his dark mane.

Suddenly and alarmingly, a blizzard raged before her, vision awash with the energetic fluff of winter. Layers of fur provided ample insulation against the frigid storm.

"Kalthused?" called a sonorous voice from her side. She turned her head and admired the vixen. Even wrapped in pelts and leather, the woman was a bastion of beauty. "You seem unwell."

Descarta met recognition then. Somehow, she'd been thrust into another place, perhaps even time. She was a ghastly prisoner trapped in a foreign body. It felt heavy, powerful but mostly confining. As much as she struggled, she couldn't influence her vessel or escape the phantasmagoria.

"I'm fine, my blossom," responded her husk, pulling the elven queen close. "I just have a bad feeling about this." The founder of Elusia gently kissed his queen's crown. "Is this right, Ankaa?"

The elegant lass grinned at him, snowflakes nesting in her hair. "Oh, my paramour. If only all rulers had your noble spirit, these wars wouldn't be necessary."

Descarta sensed a wave of worry wash over her, channeled from the body she inhabited. "They just need a flower worth fighting for."

A flash of blinding despair transitioned to another location, another time.

"A-Ankaa," whispered her perspective. No reply came from the blood tarnished woman below. "Ankaa," he repeated, furiously shaking the unresponsive damsel.

Descarta's consciousness recoiled, drowned in a flume of commanding hopelessness.

Kalthused cradled his dirtied, limp lover, her head lolling unnaturally over his elbow. The scene grew muddy, glazed with the moist film of loss. The king sucked in a labored breath. Shivering, he brushed his lips over hers. They were cold and cracked, dead bark dragging along his skin.

Again, the queen found herself assaulted by anguish, a keen locomotion that deposited her elsewhere, elsewhen.

Decay dominated the thick ruins, untouched for ages. Vines wound over depictions of sorcerers, having long reclaimed the lost polis. Ahead, an elderly man whooped, his robe jumping with the motion. The avatar approached and peered down a steep ravine into a field of spires, each taller than Galvant's Bulwark.

"We've done it!" exclaimed the old erudite, barking at the overgrown valley. "The Sundered's Citadels! Kalthused! Do you know what this means?!"

Descarta was amazed by the panorama. It was truly a feat that so many towers could have been erected.

"Yes," responded her carrier in a timbre worn by years. The sovereign reached out and gave his companion a pat on the back before shoving him over the side and into the promise of death. Kalthused followed the tumbling man, watching as appendages were mangled and organs ruptured, until he was content there would be no surviving.

"Ankaa," he whispered. "I'm coming, blossom."

Loneliness. Vast, impregnable loneliness stretched over an enormous emptiness.

"Virgil," mewed a tiny foundling from below.

"Virgil," followed an accompanying snatch for attention.

A groan escaped Descarta's new carapace. "I'm trying to sleep, dears. What do you need?"

"Her picture," complained Merill, shifting uncomfortably under the blanket.

"It watches us," added Almi.

The king sat up, easing the two elves from their nest.

Descarta thought they seemed younger, smaller, more jubilant—if that were possible.

Almi and Merill peered up at their mate, youthful crimson spheres afire with affection. "We love our Virgil so," cooed Merill, crawling to Virgil's side to cuddle against him.

"Does our Virgil love her more?" whined Almi, pouting and squirming into his lap.

Virgil thoughtfully stroked her waist-length hair, drawing an appreciative hum. Descarta thought the longer style suited them, made the girls seem more like enchanting dryads.

Merill wriggled in her semi-translucent, lilac nightgown. "Does our Virgil?"

Descarta sensed something surge through her, a distraught tow of ill.

"No, dears. You needn't worry. I loved her once," the sovereign paused, reaching to apply the same pacifying touch to Merill who happily accepted. "Then there was the memory of that love. Then the memory of a memory. Now there is nothing."

There was another tow, this time of guilt, as Virgil cast gloomily at the rendition of his deceased queen. The source of that guilt was indiscernible to the helpless visitor—whether it was for Ankaa or the sisters. The fastidiously preserved painting conveyed more than just a gorgeous elf unblemished by the passage of time, though. Descarta surmised that Ankaa was the girl she'd visited before their perilous fall, the chained prisoner.

"So . . ." murmured Almi.

"If you wish it, I will," agreed Virgil. "Now, please. Let us rest."

Merill purred into the king's ear as he reclined. "Our Virgil is so good to us." She extended a succulent thigh over his abdomen, hiking her gown provocatively.

"So good," concurred Almi as she rose like a predator from his lap. "We want to thank our Virgil." She straddled him, inclining so that her cheek pressed against her sister's tantalizing thigh.

Beseeching, eyes imbrued with cinder stared expectation as she swayed her raised rear, an oscillating heart-shaped metronome.

Descarta tried again to retreat from her role, frantically reaching out with mentally conjured claws for an exit.

"My queens are such temptresses," smiled Virgil. "Tomorrow, though. I've been up for two days."

The girls nodded obediently, wiggling again into their duvet atop him. "We love our Virgil," Almi mumbled through a yawn.

"Truly, we do," said Merill.

"I know, dears," the king responded.

Bewilderment followed, the aftermath of disparate feelings coming to conflict.

The next leap left Descarta staring at herself, a strange sensation. She remembered the day. It was her first venture outside since losing her memory. The bronze sunshine was so invigorating, splashing its soothing warmth across her face.

"Is our Virgil preferring her?" inquired a familiar tone. "A new favorite?" whimpered Merill from his side. "We were here first. We love our Virgil."

"Doesn't our Virgil remember?" pleaded Almi as she pressed against the weaver.

Virgil offered no response. He couldn't hide his emotions from his passenger, however. The overflowing cauldron of uncertainty, of pain. Most of all, of ambivalence.

He did love them. Intensely. But they reminded him of Ankaa. The sovereign did not know what that meant. Were they merely replacements, or was he truly enamored by the twins?

"We've sacrificed much for her. Tens of thousands. We'll sacrifice much more before we're through. How do you feel about that?" asked Virgil.

Almi and Merill shrugged, earnestly embracing their beloved. "Who cares," muttered Almi. "Our Virgil knows best."

The sovereign sighed.

Another jump. This one was turbulent, as if the force binding her was losing its purchase.

Again, she watched herself. Her chest rose and fell slowly in the comfortable bliss of respite. The wards wound lasciviously about her body, but Virgil's attention was fixed on his queen. Descarta recognized the setting. It was only yesterday she slumbered there, entwined with Almi and Merill in the halls of the Underrise.

The spectator welled with unspoken longing as he frowned at the reverie-taken girl. Longing that bridged into his passenger, murmuring his desire in sullen tones. Often he peered at her so, yearning to dismantle his own barrier and be a true king to her.

As selfish as he could be, the sovereign cared too immensely to confess. If she ever accepted him—and he knew the odds were nigh impossible—she would eventually discover his dark secrets and turn away, disgusted. More importantly, she was the perfect girl, and she deserved better. She deserved a fair opportunity at a future without taint and ignoble principles.

A future beyond his scattered, wrecked spirit.

Virgil sighed, rubbing weary eyes. Two years had passed since he had a full night's rest. The weaver imagined lazing about for days with his diminutive sparrow, a messy heap of blankets as their ultimate refuge.

He growled at the fanciful procrastination, turning away from the bed and the alluring sight. The ritual required concentration, something he wouldn't exhibit while indulging silly fantasies.

Descarta blinked. The temporal journey came to a halt and returned her to the present. Frightened, she clambered away from the dead weaver, feeling violated. The metaphysical journey began to coalesce, less befuddling when she wasn't strung along through rifts in time. The tragic irony was not lost on her. That Kalthused, the legend she always raised above her king was, in fact and by some eldritch magic, before her the entire time.

The blur of tears could protect her from the image of his cold corpse. Yet they were nothing before her thoughts.

His loss.

His solitude.

His suffering.

His love.

She wanted to know more, to fill in the chasms. To ask him to express what he hid from her, for her. She wanted to be the girl he'd longed for.

Descarta had tried to run, tried deception, tried fervent resentment. Now, she was forced to discard the lies, a girl enamored. Excuses, misdirections, all tossed to the nether, she could no longer paint him her eternal villain.

She swam in freshly invoked questions given by the obtuse visions. Mundane worries before her discovery. A discovery she couldn't disregard or lock away. Sniffling, the queen crawled a shivering path toward Virgil. Descarta collapsed onto the lifeless figure, wrapping her arms around his frigid body.

"Virgil," she sobbed, shaking her head against his shoulder. "Virgil, I'll be yours. Okay? So come back. Return to me."

Stirred by the command, something divine yawned within her dainty frame. Descarta shook furiously, seized by power. Roused from its slumber, it filled her, threatened to rip her apart with its overwhelming presence. Yet it was bound to her will. And her will was for Virgil to return.

Coursing over her tongue, the celestial weave pooled in her throat, forming a hardly contained bead of restorative weave. Descarta hovered before his parted lips, coated in a maroon film of dried blood. Shuddering, she expelled a gossamer wisp of pure weave that snaked to the king's lips and slipped inside until it no longer occupied her.

During the following still, Descarta began to wonder whether she failed. Maybe she was too weak, too inexperienced to use such mighty thaumaturgy.

Then Virgil inhaled a great, lung-filling gasp and allayed her fear. The sorcerer continued to draw heavy breaths, vitality punching at his spirit. "Des?" he asked in astonishment as the throes settled to a simmer. She looked drained, tired. Despite her wear, she smiled at him. He was relieved to be given another chance to appreciate her dimple-hugged shine.

The proximity of their lips hit her, and the shaky queen retreated to her knees, soiled viridian pinafore bunched around her like a blooming chrysanthemum. "Yes, Virgil? How do you feel?" She looked down, blushing.

"I feel . . . hale. What were you doing?" he asked, blinking at the curious absence of feathered shafts in his back.

"I, um. A prisoner. Ankaa. I met her. She talked to me, told me you'd need me. She touched my ribbon. Then we fell and—" the queen rambled, rapidly divulging her jumbled thoughts.

"Enough, blossom. That's too fast." The sovereign groaned, cautiously sitting up. He ached horrendously.

"Blossom. Your name for her," muttered the diminutive queen. "W-When," she faltered a moment, mustering her courage. "When you were Kalthused." Descarta couldn't manage to look at him. She was afraid of what she would see there. So she kept her head lowered, trained on the black lace between her nervous fingers.

"What?" he asked with unintentional venom. "When I was who?" His restored health was baffling enough. Now he was angry at what she may know if she'd discovered his true identity. Did she witness the same diorama as Hafstagg?

"K-Kalthused. I touched," she halted again, growing red, "o-only touched your face. It t-transported me places. Within your memories. Such ruin." She clutched her dress; the malice in his voice cut at her nerve. "I'm s-so s-sorry," the quavering queen stuttered between sobs. "I d-didn't mean to invade your p-past." Her mind was a whirlpool of feelings, all battling for supremacy. The wild din frightened her.

"Blossom," he sighed as he eased his throbbing torso toward her, penciling terracotta blemishes over his robe. "The past," he hesitated, apprehension tempering his movements. "The past doesn't change that you're my blossom now." Virgil eased one arm tentatively around her dainty shoulders. He wanted to smother her heartbreak away. Another sleeve enveloped her, and when she offered no resistance, he guided her toward his chest where he shrouded her in a rueful embrace. "I'm sorry, Des. I'm not angry with you. Just that you know."

She nodded, the gesture rubbing her face against his robe. Weeping, she exhaled a long, emotionally charged breath against his chest. "Why'd you want to keep it hidden?"

"I care for you. That's reason enough to hoard myriad secrets. An unwanted past is a terrible, inescapable beast," replied Virgil, setting his chin atop her head. The sweet aroma of berryflowers always followed her.

"Why—"

"You must have many questions, dear. I promise to answer them all," he gave her petite back a pat. "For now, you should rest. The spell you wove is limited to the mighty elven ancients. You haven't the stamina they do."

The queen, no longer wrought with weeping, nodded again in compliance.

"And Des," added the sorcerer. "Thank you." He didn't know how she managed to drag him back to the realm of the living, only that the girl did it because she wanted him there.

She gave a slight third nod, weariness taking her to slumber.

...

The musty odor of antiquated tomes and untended furnishings flooded Descarta's nostrils as she reclaimed consciousness. There was a feeling of weightlessness, a skyborne chariot whose locomotion was reliably bobbing. Around her, wrongness permeated the stale air, the trappings of a defiled building. The girl shivered involuntarily. Arms—her lofty cradle, she realized—offered an assuring squeeze. Her eyelids flickered open and quickly adjusted to the dim illumination of a far off light source.

Cast with harsh ridges of concern, Virgil looked ahead, lost in thought. She perused his features, something she'd rarely done before. Descarta could see beyond the stern, broken grimace now; she knew a smile rest there for her. A dormant creature whose visits to the surface were irregular and infrequent. But it was for her. A moment passed and her scrutiny was noticed.

Virgil brought a relieved gaze to his parcel, drawing the side of his mouth in an awkward grin under her stare.

She tore her eyes away, hiding rosy cheeks in his ozone-scented robe. The bobbing ceased, and she was lowered until her bare feet came to rest on dusty, chilled marble, a sturdy arm supporting her shoulders.

"How do you feel?" asked her revitalized king.

Descarta left her hideaway to meet cerulean orbs wrought with disclosed worry. This time she hovered there instead of retreating. For a reason unknown to her, she felt she should not disregard the uncommon display. Like it would belittle the affection.

"Des, are you infirm?" reiterated Virgil, tightening the support around her upper back. He reached up as if to touch her face, but halted half-way, curling his fingers and easing the hand back.

"I'm fine," said the queen. She tried to rise, but dizziness struck her. Agony flared in her forehead, throwing blinking spots before her eyes.

"We're in a hurry," imposed an agitated reminder from somewhere outside Descarta's pounding bubble.

"She's awake," snarled Virgil in a violent tone, heated emotions writhing just beneath the surface. "Blossom," he began in a milder octave. "Blossom, don't burden yourself." He lifted her again, delicately cradling his bundle.

Virgil took a step and paused, closing his eyes and drawing an unsteady breath. He reminded himself that it was nearly over, that he would soon expel his burden. The clattering of snapping maws would rescind their incessant cursing and no longer grab with greedy, fetid rakes in desire to devour his control.

"I'm sorry for holding you, Des. You've been unconscious for several days."

The girl nodded from her perch, watching the passage of web covered statues and decayed paintings. "Where are we?" she asked.

"An old palatial retreat of mine," explained the courier. "Rest," he advised his load. "What you did . . ." his words trailed off as he pulled together strips of a response. "Was dangerous and reckless. You could have never awoken."

"Virgil wouldn't put you down!" Almi complained from beside the pair. "He paid us no attention!"

"Three days!" issued a similar voice. "Only you for three days!"

The sovereign sighed, pointedly avoiding the diminutive girl in his arms. "Quiet," he ordered.

Almi and Merill groaned their discontent, but reluctantly obeyed his will.

"How can you be Kalthused?" questioned Descarta, returning to the temporal journey which, to her, had only just passed.

"I am not," replied the king. "Kalthused ceased to be the day his queen perished."

"Yet you're here," persisted the girl. "And you're him."

Virgil shook his head, taking on a pained visage. "You were correct when you said he was the better sovereign. We are not the same person. Not anymore."

...

"She cannot manage as far as Vanathiel," Virgil solemnly surmised. "You must activate the final beacon without us."

Hazael watched as the sorcerer scrambled through an examination. He would press or knead her with the utmost care, often assuming the vacant stare that signified a metaphysical trip into the fabric. The unusual delicacy with which he addressed the scrawny figure spoke for her pricelessness. "Do you plan to keep her?" asked the steward. "Des."

"Why do you care?" Virgil retorted while prodding at the unconscious girl's stomach.

The seneschal grimaced, rubbing weariness out of his lids. "Why wouldn't I?"

"Have you suddenly grown meddlesome? Grappling with newfound curiosity? Tell me, Hazael," the weaver's barking grew more venomous after a short visit to the fabric. "Is there some reasonable motive for your question, or do you simply aim to burden my clearly occupied mind?"

The onslaught of stress and imprisoned spirits was taking its toll, the steward reminded himself. He found no solace in the knowledge, though, for his fondness of the king still led him to worry. "Am I not your friend, Virgil? We've been at this for nearly two centuries. Friends inquire."

"No!" shouted the sorcerer, sweat giving his rage a glistening sheen. "You have been at this for two centuries! I have toiled for nearly five! Friends, as you call yourself, disappear, turn or die! Now do your part!" he commanded. "Do your damned part and claim your damned reward!"

This was familiar. It shouldn't have been, because the sovereign had nearly always practiced clemency. Not only was it against his personality, but the weaver was rarely pressed to raise his volume. Virgil's subjects respected him, and understood his gentle fury was to be feared. Virgil was breaking, and Hazael couldn't bear to see his chum lowered so. "This will be the largest harvest," warned Hazael while pulling his lavender vest taught. "Do you think it wise? You can hardly contain them as it is."

The king tilted his head, peering in disbelief through narrowed lids. "H-Have y-you," flabbergasted and incensed, Virgil could scarcely summon the words. He threw a sweaty hand in the direction of the supine queen. "Does she look like she can wait?!" he exploded. "She's swiftly fading! I will not be surprised if I cannot manage to sustain her until you reach Vanathiel! Which, behold, is going to take longer since you persist in lingering uselessly! Take Josiah and go!" Drained, Virgil finished his tirade by turning his back to Hazael. Frail arms supported his fatigued frame as he sought relief by leaning against the slab where Descarta lay. Occupied with her waning health and his passengers, he couldn't force the steward to obey. Virgil couldn't afford to expend energy unnecessarily when his queen approached ruin.

"Very well," said Hazael. "We'll make haste."

"Good," said Virgil.

He monitored the unconscious girl for the next day, pouring energy into her whenever he could spare it. His trips to the fabric grew further apart as he scraped at his arcane reserves. Descarta's unwinding twine was down to a tiny thread, its severed joints hanging in frayed strands. The knowledge that his efforts were nigh insignificant aggrieved Virgil. Yet he refused to cease the administrations. If all he could do was increase her chances by a minute percentage, then that would be his role.

...

Instantly, she was aware, as if yanked without warning from a state of obliviousness. Descarta could detect the ceiling above her, a stone canopy that lay somewhere beyond the impenetrable shadows which clung to its belly. The girl tried to move, to ascertain the nature of this foreign place, but she couldn't. The chill of metal was flush with her skin in intervals, rendering her immobile. Bound as she was, Descarta could only move her eyes. They darted around, searching for an explanation. All she discerned was an emerald glow from beyond her miniscule realm.

She whimpered softly, struggling against the intractable clamps. Her mind raced. "W-What's going on?" stammered the shaken girl. "Hello?"

There was silence, then a shuffle to her side. Descarta tensed and shivered in dread. She wasn't alone; some cruel creature was watching her. Footsteps echoed throughout what must have been a gigantic chamber.

They were drawing nearer, she realized. Closer and closer they teased her, haunted her. Chills skittered up her spine. Something was on its way, and she could do naught but await its sharp-toothed judgment. The arbiter approached, and its shadow touched her first. Gasping, she clenched shut her lids. Descarta didn't have to see it happen. The beast hovered over her, its heavy breaths penetrating her chassis.

"Des?" it asked. "Des, are you awake?"

The pitch was familiar, worried. It belonged to Virgil. Which didn't change that she was made helpless before him. He released a frustrated susurration and turned away. His footsteps began to take him in the other direction.

She didn't want to be alone.

Slowly, tentatively, Descarta opened her eyes. "Wait. Wait, Virgil," she called. "Don't leave me." Abiding, the king returned to her. He stood over her, sweat matting a mess of raven claws over his grim countenance.

It wasn't until he watched her that the willowy girl realized she could feel the bitter cold against every tender inch of her body. "What's going on?!" She flooded crimson, trying futilely to turn away. "What have you done to me?!"

"Nothing," Virgil quietly assured her. "Nothing, my love. I promise."

"Then why am I bare?" she begged, desperately searching for sense amid her panic. "Why can't I move?"

"I'm sorry," muttered Virgil, taking a seat beside her and brushing placating weave into her upper arm. "I'm sorry. I haven't been very good to you, have I?"

"I'm naked, Virgil. Naked and I cannot move. No, you haven't."

Virgil nodded and looked away from her.

"Please stop this. Whatever it is, please just stop," she urged.

"I . . . cannot," he replied. "This is the only way for you to live."

"To live?" asked Descarta. "You're speaking nonsense."

A pause broke the exchange as Virgil struggled with his reply. "To live," he repeated. "The nightly rituals weren't meant to restore your memory, but to extend your life." The sovereign swallowed. "The spell you used to revive me placed too large a burden on your tether."

"I don't understand. This doesn't make sense at all." The girl fought the iron clasps once more. "I'm only tired. Unshackle me."

Virgil shook his head. "I've been trying to repair you, dear. But you're deteriorating faster than I can manage."

"Deteriorating?" questioned the girl. She heard the despair in his voice, recognized the grave pitch. He was as helpless as her.

The sovereign was still, combating uncertainty. He dreaded what his queen would say when he clarified. She would likely think him a demon, curse him and never wish to see him again. He was nothing more, he admitted. A fiend. Yet he was without a choice. The rite he was preparing to perform would bring them both to death temporarily. Who knew what memories she would encounter this time? Which of his vile, detestable secrets would be laid bare before her? No, he would tell Descarta himself. If she were to ever accept him, it would be by his word, not as a bystander to his horrors.

"Yes, deteriorating," Virgil somberly said. "You have been since . . ." The king's resolve crumbled. She deserved better. She shouldn't even exist. This isn't what he planned at all.

"Since?" pressed Descarta. "Why won't you take these off? They're chilly, Virgil."

He cast a melancholy glance at her, opening his mouth to voice words that clung with desperation to his vocal chords. "Forgive me," he began. "I'm the cause of your suffering. Every wretched spur. You've been fading since I created you three years ago."

"Created me? That's impossible," argued the girl. It was impossible. Why was he toying with her? "Stop this at once. I just want to be freed." The tears arrived, distress fueling their flow. "Please . . . just let me go."

"I cannot," Virgil uttered. There was a clinking under Descarta's head and the metallic brace surrounding it fell open with a clang.

Relieved, Descarta rolled her head to look at him.

"Thank y—" she managed before drawing in a horrified breath. Rows and rows of glass cylinders were set behind him, emanating a bright green hue. Each held a lifeless, malformed body, or partially formed portions. He wasn't stringing her along. All this time, he wasn't trying to restore her memory. She never had any. "I . . . I'm not . . . real?"

Virgil reached forward, this time not relenting. Gingerly, lovingly, he stroked her head. "You are real, my blossom. Very much so. In all the ways that matter."

The girl reeled, eyes darting from tank to tank. She did not know what she was searching for, until she found it. Until its emptiness tore at her. The lone tank had no glow, no concoction; it was vacant. Somehow she knew it was the womb that birthed her. "You made me here?" she asked without stealing her gaze from the tank.

"Yes." Virgil was still mired in reluctance, afraid of making the slightest mistake in a conversation of utmost import.

"Why?"

There it was: the harbinger of bleak, blackened skies. Virgil closed his eyes and recounted the centuries of labor he would discard for her.

Would it really be discarded? Was she not a product of those endless nights, of ignoring an aching soul and fading morals? She might have been a mistake, progeny of happenstance. Still, her precious life would not have been stumbled upon if it weren't for those arduous years. No, she required no sacrifice.

That left the excruciating inquiry, dangling its bared heart for him to mar with his stinging touch. He retracted his hand, taking a seat on the iron tablet where Descarta lie, his back facing the troubled girl. "The moment I met you is still as vivid today as it was then. I happened to look up from the pile of scrolls that once covered this slate. You were staring at me from your container with those brilliant amber stars, brimming with life." The sovereign smiled, a sad thing only he could see. "Life that wasn't supposed to be there. You, like the thousand that came before, were to be a homunculus, a shell to hold Ankaa's drifting soul."

"So I'm only a tool, then?" replied the wistful queen. She'd dragged her attention from her birthplace to the sorcerer's slumped back. He'd lowered his elbows to his knees, burying fingers in his sweaty raven hair.

"You were," emphasized Virgil. "Until I discovered you were somehow given a spirit of your own. Your vigor, innocence, innate grace of being . . . they captured me. I . . ."

Descarta frowned at the hunched figure. "You abandoned her. You locked her up for me."

"I did."

The girl didn't know how to feel about that. It represented the sincerity of his love for her. Yet knowing he'd cast off Ankaa after centuries was no consolation. "Why?"

Virgil chuckled, a sound devoid of the heartiness it should have carried. "You spare me nothing, blossom."

"I'm here against my will and you won't tell me why. I may as well trouble you."

The morose sovereign nodded and turned to his queen. "Our time runs short. I'd like to tell you everything now. If you'll listen."

"I don't have any choice," Descarta pointed out. "But I would anyway."

Virgil crossed his legs beside her "You won't like it. I promise."

"I'll listen," she repeated. Descarta doubted it could be any more harmful than the life-shattering revelation he'd just given her.

"I don't think I'll be able to concentrate with such a ravishing lady laid bare before me," Virgil teased, trying to disperse the thick tension.

Descarta turned red, but maintained her composition. "I knew it. You're just a pervert. You better not have touched me."

Virgil only smiled. "Elusia thought I drew my final breath with Ankaa in my arms, already departed. That's what I wrote, a dreadful but romantic ending. As I've told you, history as written is never transparent. In fact, she died a battlefield away. My regiment won, but at the greatest loss I have ever known. I found her, impaled through the stomach by a spear, lovely face tarnished by agony and frozen in death. She died because I wasn't there. Ankaa died because I wasn't protective enough." Virgil looked to his queen. "For that reason, I couldn't let you leave the ramparts."

Descarta nodded, shying away from his stare and the conviction he asserted in defending her. As much as she cursed and resented him for it, he persisted. She didn't think it was the correct approach. It was thoughtful, nonetheless.

"I wandered for years without purpose. I irresponsibly abandoned my kingdom. Until I stumbled upon—or fell into, rather—a tomb of the weaver you call the Sundered. Multiple seals once barred entry, but the millennia must have taken them. Contained within were ancient tomes detailing the taboo spells that had him sentenced to death. They were never meant to be seen again. Scrolls holding secrets behind the creation of artificial life, age-defying magic and many unbelievably powerful concepts were all stored there, awaiting someone reckless and hopeless enough to use them."

"You," reasoned Descarta.

"Yes," said Virgil. "I needed to make everything right again. Is that wrong? To try and right a mighty blunder no matter the consequences?" He seized his queen's gaze, desperately wanting her to agree with him, to understand.

"I-I don't know," was all she could say before averting her eyes uncomfortably.

He should have known that would come. Nervousness lowering his volume and confidence, Virgil continued. "Unfortunately, he'd never actually succeeded in creating a homunculus. So I was working with notes on failures. The years became decades, the decades, centuries. I employed the Sundered's anti-aging spells. They did nothing for the mental stress. Somewhere along the damned journey I lost my love for her. It escaped me, and I could never find it again. There was only unrelenting infatuation." He stopped, examining the uncharacteristically reticent girl. The fear of his ugly deeds stood before him in a wall of briars.

She watched him intently. "Go on, Virgil. I want to know."

"I don't want you to," he replied, puffing anxiety. "It seems I have little choice, however." The spellweaver sat without speaking, fighting the formidable resistance within. He tried to further recount the past, but he was stricken speechless.

"What?" she inquired, divining his inner turmoil.

Virgil took a deep, steadying breath. He could feel it imbue his core with life just as his blossom's was fading. He had to tell her. "This trip wasn't meant to cure the blight on our kingdom."

"What?" she reiterated in dismay. "What else could it be?"

"We set on this dangerous trek to complete you, Des—to suture your tenuous existence permanently. This ritual requires . . . components in order to be performed, though; the same as transplanting Ankaa from the fabric and into you."

"Components?" asked the queen, unsettled by his difficulty with the word.

The sovereign produced a slight nod, an affirmation of the grotesque word. "Hazael and I engineered the Bethel, the myth about the Maiden and the Sundered. A ploy to plant statues of the Maiden's countenance across nearby nations. They would act as conduits. Think of it as casting a net to catch fish, only with departed spirits seeking the fabric. Yet the yield was not enough. We ignited antipathy, incited wars. I created the blight on Elusia. Anything to generate a larger harvest. That's all it was to us, Des, a harvest. We were gathering components, and we needed copious amounts for what I was attempting. What I'm attempting this day."

The sting of bile crawled up her throat. The sickened girl tightened her esophagus to prevent its rise. He'd warned her, and she knew something was amiss when Virgil, usually so confident in his intelligence, was shaken. Still, there was no way for her to expect something so thoughtlessly evil.

Virgil knew what her reaction meant. Yet he persisted. "It's for you, Des. To heal you once and for all. If I don't, you'll cease to be. And I cannot accept that."

"Don't I have a choice?" she asked. "You aren't the only one who has to bear this sin."

"No," he muttered. "You must endure this, my blossom."

"Then don't call me that anymore," replied the queen.

"What do you mean?" Virgil asked.

She didn't reply, offering only a disappointed glower.

Something cracked then, a penetrating fracture that spanned his spirit. It could have been his heart, but Virgil knew the souls had broken his barrier. They writhed and gnawed within him, chewing at his tether to the fabric. Time was running short.

Turning his attention back to the exposed girl before him, he wore a defeated grimace. "As you wish. I will return shortly and this will all be over." Virgil retreated from his seat atop the slate and reactivated the brace for Descarta's head. She had closed her eyes: the only way to effectively avoid him in her position. The dejected king hovered briefly, fighting his growing ache for something to change her mind. In the end, he left without saying a word.

When she was sure he'd taken egress, Descarta opened her lids. The shadows were there again, still hanging like bats on the dome above. They seemed deeper now, rendered tangible by the tenebrous exchange. His impositions were unjust, and he wouldn't acknowledge that. Virgil might have had his ethics eroded by time, but he couldn't expect the same from her. The queen's thoughts shifted to his reaction, like something within had collapsed when she rejected him. She didn't want that, regardless of what he was doing.

He was right. It didn't matter that she'd been created. She was sentient. She could feel just like anyone else. Descarta grimaced at the truth of it. She could feel love, and it was agonizing. Why did he insist on dragging her through these trials?

CHAPTER EIGHT

The Best Intentions

Virgil sunk into a lavish recliner set in the room adjacent to the alchemical workshop holding Descarta. He was exhausted in every way. The chewing, pestilent souls inside didn't bother him. Loss, tossed as a barbed javelin, pierced his chest. He should have known she wouldn't forgive his corruption. She was too pure, too caring.

Almi and Merill, who were sharing a brioche, tossed the pastry aside and scrambled over to their king. "Oh, oh," cried Almi, "you look unwell!"

"Not well," agreed Merill. The girls hovered beside him, flinching and jostling each other, unsure what to do.

"Come," said Virgil, closing his eyes. "You can sit."

The sisters didn't need to be ordered. Eagerly, they settled beside him and beamed at each other from their nests.

Virgil wrapped a robed arm around each, pulling them close. It occurred to him that this could be the last time he saw the frolicsome twins. The sovereign regarded each in turn, glossy scarlet stares meeting his own. He wasn't sure what to say—what could be appropriate for them? Eventually, he decided it didn't matter. They would treasure any words spoken solely for their benefit. "Dears," he began.

"Yes, our Virgil?" they answered, cozying up to him, trained on his face.

He smiled and stroked them both, cossetting their sides. "I've treated you poorly. Neglected you both, reproached your attachment when I should have given you praise and affection. If only I'd learned earlier just how deserving you are instead of looking elsewhere, I could have tried to be someone you could depend on." He sighed, clenching them in his arms. "I suppose I just want to apologize. If it were in my power, I would relieve you of your terrible burden."

The elves locked stares for a half-second—long enough to concur—before Almi climbed into his lap, legs set aside his. She reached up and cupped his face with both hands, focusing his quizzical stare on her own.

"What are you doing?" he mouthed. Her hands were beseechingly delicate. Despite her training, no calluses were set within the gentle touch.

"Being angry," she frowned. The girl didn't evade his stare. Instead, she kept her palms locked on his cheeks. "Remember when we were found?"

Virgil gave a slight tilt of his head.

"Sometimes we do. It hurts everywhere. Our Virgil made us a better place. With food and no hitting hands or fiddling fingers. And him. So kind is our Virgil. When he loves us it's like rolling in pillows."

Virgil couldn't levy the flow. Her confession struck him with such severity, such strident meaning that he wet her hands. It was rare they were so coherent, and never about this. "I'm sorry, I couldn't, I wasn't," he fumbled.

Almi shook her head. "Broken girls couldn't fix a broken Virgil. Only she could." The elf leaned forward to rest in his neck, with Merill climbing closer. "Seventy-six years, three months and two days with our Virgil. We'll stay always."

"She'll die," added Merill. "We'll still be yours."

The sovereign accepted their embrace. "You two truly are sordid."

...

The uppermost reaches of Galvant's Bulwark trembled and discharged a pearlescent stream which leapt toward the eastern crags. To Lastan, captain dreadcleaver and widowed father, it was glorious, a sign to feed. The glowing beacon signaled the time for insurrection. All around, his ravenous hounds were unleashed.

Lastan, too, would drink. For him, like his brethren, inebriation only came with the spilling of Elusian blood. And no ale was as filling as vengeance.

The dreadcleaver equipped his double axes and joined the revelry, sending the nearest slumbering knight to oblivion. An alarm sounded, but it was too late. For every dreadcleaver, five soldiers had fallen. And they continued their murderous course even as the troops roused and took arms.

Lastan set his notched axes into their whirring spin, lopping a defender's arm at the elbow and sinking into his sternum with a crack. He withdrew the axe from its cleft of bone and meat and grinned. "For the fallen!" he bellowed before discarding his cloak and displaying the proud emerald tabard of his kinsmen. Throughout the foray, similar shouts erupted and spread like wildfire.

With every gut-splitting, limb-severing swing of his ferocious blades, the panging for his stolen family throbbed. Elusians had marched on his land, poisoned it underfoot and taken everything from him. Kaen Morr was hardly magnanimous, but this vile nation was the greater evil. These soldiers had once stomped innocent lives with as much regard as crushing dandelions.

And so his nearest foe fell, brow split with disregard.

...

Violah watched from the security of her chambers, highest such room in the spire. Even if the dreadcleavers were to penetrate the walls, they would never reach her. The magus commanded weavers in a tower made to channel their magic. No, she only needed to await the coming earthfolk. The dreadcleavers were outnumbered, but their ferocity was unmatched by the ambushed knights. Even so, the fierce surge had been reduced to a gradual advance once the garrison regrouped.

The battle progressed just as Hazael instructed, with the greatest toll possible. When Ignusian reinforcements arrived, the mercenary axemen would be squashed completely. Then she would be supreme weaver and Hazael her sovereign. Violah enjoyed the prospect, though she would have taken many men over their present despot.

It might have been premature, but she'd already slipped into the talon-ringed robe of supreme weaver. The title would be hers within days, so she thought she may as well adjust to the heavy mantle.

Violah narrowed her lips in a pensive frown. She wondered how the earthfolk would respond to a salvo of arrows, siege weapons and magical conjurations. Soon enough, she would know.

"Surely, your revered Impervious," the weaver spoke in an unctuous tone. "We could not discern friend from foe in the tumult below."

On cue, a clarion horn rang from the jagged peaks beyond the Bulwark. The din of stampeding earthfolk rose above the battle below as they poured from underground passages and onto the flatlands surrounding the clashing troops.

Violah stood and took one final look in her mirror to ensure she looked the role of superlative sorceress.

"This will do," she said, grinning approval. "A woman as supreme weaver. Oh, they will surely enjoy this."

She exited her quarters, drawing dumbfounded stares from her subordinates. The weaver wore a scowl and stood tall, awaiting any who would challenge her garb. As expected, all were silent. "Onward then," she ordered. "Surely, we can move earth with greater accord than those brutish earthfolk."

Some displayed uncertainty, others disdain, others indifference, but they all respectfully accompanied her to the buttresses above the field of contest.

...

Virgil woke to searing streaks torn across his skull. He bellowed a raw, throat-cutting scream and jolted upright, throwing elves to the side. Shaking knees buckled under him as his entire body quaked uncontrollably.

The twins panicked, helping the dizzy king steady himself. "What's wrong?! What's wrong?!" begged Almi.

Hazael must have activated the final conduit and drawn the net in. The load was unbearable. Virgil was certain his skull would burst under the immense pressure. Had they really contained such a vast amount of souls? Saliva ran down his chin, preparation for an abruptly emptied stomach. "Fetch Hafstagg!" he growled between convulsing rasps for air.

The sisters bobbed obediently, rushing off to retrieve the warrior. Seconds that seemed to Virgil like decades later, the man arrived, kneeling beside the king. "Tell me what to do, Virgil."

"Bring," Virgil managed before a contracting diaphragm interrupted him. "Bring me!" He growled, again blustered by convulsions. "To her!"

Hafstagg immediately swept up the sorcerer with no effort, proceeding to rush him into the tank-studded room.

"Who's there?" echoed Descarta's worried pitch.

The warrior covered the distance to her operating table with great strides.

"Beside," Virgil spat, irritated by his debilitating tremors. "Beside her," he blurted.

Hafstagg did as he said and took a step back, worry apparent on his features. Almi and Merill twitched nervously, shrinking into one another.

"W-What's going on?" stammered Descarta, unable to make out the scene.

"He's beginnin' the ritual," explained Hafstagg from beyond her vision.

With quaking arms, Virgil did his best to steady himself beside Descarta. "This will p—" the king shook violently and clenched his jaw through a swell of inbound spirits. "Probably hurt." There was no time to explain further. The weaver laid a sweat-soaked palm on her exposed abdomen.

"Wait!" she panicked. "Please don't do this! V—" Her appeal was shattered by an ear-piercing screech as he breached the juddering queen's physical form and forcefully bore her into the fabric.

Unsettled by the grisly display, Hafstagg turned from the wide-eyed queen, ochre fluids frothing on her lips. She still shook behind him, remnants of the impossibly penetrant trauma.

"We're afraid," whimpered Almi, creeping closer. "What now?"

"Nothing," reminded Hafstagg. "Just as we were instructed."

"But our Virgil," Merill contested, following her sister.

"No!" censured the giant, snatching them both by the tunic. "These are Virgil's orders. Do you want to risk harmin' them even further by interfering?"

Almi and Merill shook their heads simultaneously, huffing and slouching over. They peered somberly at the motionless bodies. Virgil's head had fallen to rest unceremoniously against the iron cage around Descarta's stomach, while she stared with absent spheres frozen in horror.

...

Descarta feared she would be ripped in half. It was as though her spirit was being stretched across a mountaintop to the point just before the jagged peak ruptured her belly. There was no sense of orientation, no fingers or toes to curl, only her consciousness, pervaded by mind-numbing torment.

Then, it ceased, dispersed by a gust of transportation.

She was whole again, though hardly more than discarnate. Around her, the crimson and starch fabric stretched, surreal reflections of a realm just a snip away.

Ahead, a twisting storm of snarling spirits circled a familiar figure. He was cast in the shadow of the otherworldly tornado, but Descarta knew Virgil waited at its center. His enthralling whisper pulled her with the same clarity as though he hovered at her ear. The calling penetrated her, permeated her spirit and edged it closer and closer to the whirlwind. The diminutive queen was awash with their disgusting, visceral screeching, projected in cadaverous reek from the storm. One of the serpentine souls snapped at her and just missed her nose. Something warm brushed against her wrist and yanked her deftly to safety.

The homunculus sucked in a breath, caught with fright at the sudden touch. A distant part of her mind thought it was odd the twister of snapping souls wasn't unsettling yet her rescuer was. Mortified, she craned her head to the calming image of Ankaa. The queen—a true queen of Elusia, Descarta thought—was even more magnificent than their first meeting. The elf's sure grip secured Descarta like an errant balloon hovering before its desperate rise.

"Hello again, empty one." Ankaa furrowed her brow and tightened her lips in deliberation. "No, that's not you. No longer." The elf tapped her foot for a moment before grinning up at the perplexed girl. "Pretty one will do."

"Hi," responded Descarta, entranced by the undulations of her savior's sanguine dress. Ankaa was possessed of a gorgeous tranquility that soothed her spirit. "Your shackles are gone," noticed Descarta.

"And your clothes," chuckled Ankaa. "Pretty indeed to captivate him so."

"I-I'm sorry," stuttered Descarta, turning flushed cheeks away.

"That's not hiding the rest of your body, pretty one." Ankaa was amused at the display, and it rang with clarity in her dulcet chuckle. "Tell me, though, why are you apologizing?"

"I didn't want to take him," explained Descarta. "I'm no thief! He's yours. I don't want him. Do you know what he's done? It's unspeakable!" Descarta trained a begging gaze on her predecessor. "Make him stop. Please."

Ankaa frowned. "That I cannot do."

"Why?" pleaded Descarta. "Why must I endure this?"

"Because he loves you, it seems. And I would not stop him if I could. That man is no longer my dear Kalthused." The elf tilted her head to peer beyond the anchored girl before her. "He is Virgil, a persona developed within regret and ruin."

"I don't want that person either," mumbled Descarta.

Ankaa shrugged as if it was of no consequence, and the cloudy dress hopped with her shoulders. "You felt differently when we last met. Admirable qualities of a queen are compassion and clemency, I have been told. But it is not my place to lecture you. I merely thought to use my brief moment of freedom to thank you."

"Thank me?" She wanted to be frustrated. The woman before her was better than her in every way, and now she was toying with Descarta. Something emanating from the deceased queen prohibited that antipathy from gaining purchase. Instead, she held only curiosity. "Why would you thank me? It's because of me you won't be brought back. Virgil abandoned you after you waited for centuries."

Ankaa exhaled in exasperation. "Oh, pretty one. I do not know this Virgil you speak of." She shook her head to punctuate the point. "I know of him. I know of his sins. I know he planned to revive me. I know he'll now use me to ignite your wonderful spirit once and for all. But I do not know Virgil. I only know Kalthused." She shook her head again, golden locks swaying elegantly with the motion. "Time is waning. He calls."

Descarta heard it, the commanding susurration gaining volume within her, tugging earnestly. Having realized Ankaa purposefully did not answer her question, Descarta wondered whether she really was being toyed with. "Answer me," she demanded.

"Oh, you needn't get hostile. After all, I'm going to be with you from now on." She smiled, and Descarta averted her eyes, ashamed. She knew what Ankaa meant by Virgil using her now. She was a sacrifice.

"Do not worry, pretty one," consoled the elf. As if struck from behind, she suddenly stumbled forward a few steps. "He's grown strong," she gasped. The once queen cast an austere frown at Descarta. "Occupying you has made the hundreds of years worthwhile. Thank you for being such a sweet, lively vessel. More importantly," she began, "thank you for giving him what I no longer can."

Then, it was as if the resistance Ankaa applied shattered, and Descarta found herself swept into a maelstrom of loathing. Tossed about violently in the carousel of ghosts, she caught one last glimpse of the ravishing queen being devoured by thousands of greedy ghouls.

A mortifying shriek broke through the crowd of restless souls, thickening the atmosphere so that moving through air was like wading through tar. It wasn't until then, with the tumult brought to a near-halt, that Descarta discovered the term ground was relative in this place. Taking a tentative step forward, the nothing below her was just as reliable a platform as any. Her sudden relief at being in control masked the approaching sorcerer, who snatched her by the ankle and flung her to the crimson slate below. It didn't hurt when she landed. In fact, she hardly felt the impact at all. What hurt was how he'd treated her so roughly. It was a passing pain, however, when she noticed the talon-like jaws clamped shut on empty space—space she'd occupied just seconds before.

Virgil descended toward the girl as though unhampered by the thick air. He landed on a knee beside her, which hardly disturbed his robe at all. Parts of his spectral flesh were missing, replaced with savage wounds. His umbilical, the thread that bound him to existence, was reduced to a frayed filament.

Frozen in place, Descarta offered a helpless whimper and shook her head, a final appeal to be left alone. If the entreaty had any effect, it was inconsequential. Virgil wasn't even paying attention to the prone homunculus. Instead, his focus was set just above his love, following the swaying passes of her ribbon. It was frail, streaked with faded patches of pink and white, wholly unhealthy hues.

The sovereign did acknowledge her then, with a visage that begged for forgiveness. He would not allow her to fade, even if it meant forsaking her wishes and violating the poor girl. Even if it meant forcing a life wrought of innocent deaths upon her. Even if it meant her hatred was eternally his. She was his queen, and he would rather have her abhor him than nothing at all. It was selfish. He knew it was selfish. He no longer cared. Morals are what cost Ankaa her life. And what did she get in return? She was the liberator of a nation which had forgotten her within a generation. Virgil would not allow Descarta that lofty, naïve virtue.

His decision was made. The sorcerer swallowed, a purely superficial action that did nothing to diminish the lump in his throat. He reached above the paralyzed girl and tugged on the blemished ribbon. There was a plucking sensation as if removing a hair and Descarta became an empty shell. He held the cord in trembling hands, and studied the lifeless girl at his knees. She was gorgeous, imparted with an artificial splendor he could not resist. Virgil did not care that she was unnatural; some would call her an abomination, an affront to the order of the world. Her origin was of no consequence to the spellweaver. That steadfast affection wasn't due to being her creator, not out of obligation but circumstance. Virgil did not plan for the vessel to adopt a personality, an unforgettable union of lively intelligence and sweet compassion. Even suspended at arms' length during their tenure at the Saradin ramparts, he was certain she was special.

Spoiled as it was, this would be his final gift. Virgil set his jaw and reached behind his head, still carefully holding her ribbon in one hand. He fished around, finally catching a nearby spirit and began the arduously sensitive task of sewing her finespun thread to his.

...

Lastan slogged through the fallen, warriors plucked from each of the three factions. His infamous brigandine swung by one canvas strap, and its plate lining had been damaged beyond effectiveness. The dreadcleaver growled through a limp, favoring his left leg. He unclasped the crippled armor and let it slough away, as much a symbol of his fallen legion as the massacre all around.

Redemption would not come. He should have figured it odd, that Elusians would entrust a coup to mercenaries hailing from their most despoiled adversary. Upheaval was unpredictable in that way—deception greased its mechanisms. Lastan knew as much, but he and his crew were too blinded by revenge. They were pawns, purposefully thrown into the machine to upset some unseen balance. To him, it was simply chaos.

Ultimately, his band achieved nothing. What good was murderous revenge when you had no home to return to? It wasn't until the sodden moment, saturated with defeat, that he comprehended the futility with which he fought. Justice would never come; he could no more usurp an empire than revive his wife and daughter. He and his had achieved notoriousness through the gathering of small deeds.

They were still human, weak to treachery. And Elusia counted treachery high among its enduring evils. His notched axes moved of their own fading accord, batting aside the buckler of a belligerent knight and freeing his steamy entrails. Lastan watched the adversary twitch and moan, disgusted by his own brutality. They would both fall in service to devils that cared little for fodder.

When the earthfolk approached, Lastan knew something was amiss. The stampede was deafening. And the stone-gilded combatants could take on three dreadcleavers without chalking.

The mercenaries could have overtaken the knights. Their ambush was thorough, incisive, and enough to destroy the regiment had reinforcements not arrived. Then the Impervious belched his mighty roar and suppressed everything. The earthfolk wrought a flattening charge indeed.

But a single deception would not suffice for the meddling kingdom tinkerers. The lofty sorceress and her subordinates joined a volley of indiscriminate fletching with arcane might. Elusian soldiers, dreadcleavers and earthfolk all fell to their blighted betrayal.

Now, only thinned patches of contention remained. The area surrounding Galvant's Bulwark was littered with corpses. Lastan stumbled through the cadavers, kicking away the occasional, half-charred, half-impaled grabber. He followed a meandering course toward the haughty sorceress, vowing to at least fell the witch who had ushered his demise. His family was gone, and no amount of retribution would change that. Still, he could take the damned woman with him.

Lastan halted before the imposing tower, craning to see the magus looming high above. He clapped his axes together. "Come down, wench! Face me!" The dreadcleaver clapped his weapons again. "Face me, Elusian scum!"

He had her attention. She was staring at him, and Lastan grinned when she disappeared behind the buttresses. He would make her swallow his blades.

The following bolts of lightning should have been expected. Why would Violah risk confrontation when her weavers could dispose of him? Lastan cursed himself as he fell into the seizing throes of electrification. Teeth clattered and his fists opened and closed of their own volition. The dreadcleaver captain's last sensation was the smell of roasted flesh and the taste of liberation. They were waiting for him on the other side.

...

Descarta yawned, curving her back and reaching above her head to bump her knuckles on a wall of sculpted stone. The scent of decaying leather wasn't so strong here, diluted by the smell of herbs and incense. She sat up and pulled the thick quilt smug around her chest. The queen fluttered tired lids at her surroundings. It was a quaint accommodation, dusty and cobwebbed, whose furnishings were covered with tarp. The bronze cosset of sunlight illuminated the room and whispered to her bare arms, but its source was somewhere beyond the false window from which it emanated. Descarta expelled a contented coo. Her flesh exclaimed its joy at the quilt's embrace. Her lungs inhaled stale air with an appreciation reserved for a blissful spring breeze.

"What is this?" Descarta prodded at the feeling, trying to extract the proper description. "Wholeness?" The realization was a trigger, stripping away the cloudiness of her mind and bringing back the mortifying ritual she'd endured. Descarta instinctively reached for her ribbon, grabbing without success above her russet mess. Of course she wouldn't be able to feel whether it was there or not anyway. The rite could have been a nightmare, she considered, prayed, as she peered about her quarters. It was unknown to her, another foreign place among foreign places. Eventually, inquisitive eyes found the stand to her right. A cup of water awaited her parched throat, condensation forming a shimmering halo around its base. Descarta reached for the glass, but stopped when she noticed a letter labeled "Des" partly concealed behind its distorting refractions. Throwing modesty out of the window—she was alone after all—the petite girl let the quilt drop and grabbed both the water and stationery. She fumbled with the violet wax seal while swallowing the refreshing liquid in large gulps. She was beyond parched, and the water was delightfully chilled. Finally having broken the seal, the letter unfolded before her, revealing elegant script.

> *Descarta,*
>
> *There's every indication the weaving was successful. Your ribbon's complete reversal in health is remarkable. As of this day, it has been over four months since the rite was performed. For a time, I feared you would never leave your moratorium. In the last few weeks, you have shown signs of return, and I suspect one day soon you will.*

The realization, miraculous as it is, left me with a troubling dilemma. What do I do when you finally return? Eventually, I came to the conclusion that I could not see you. I would bind you here, unable to part with someone so immeasurably precious. So the decision is entirely in your hands. No longer am I going to bind you to my will, to lock you away because of the mistakes of my past.

I'll know when you've awakened, and Hafstagg will be waiting outside of your room. He will escort you anywhere for as long as you like, though you are by no means obligated to take him. But you must stay away from Elusia; you would be killed there without doubt. I hope you find something worthwhile in the life you've been given. Search for that, and if you find it hiding amidst despair and pain, do not let it go, my blossom. It's a priceless jewel.

If you so choose, you may also stay with me. I have treated you terribly, kept you isolated and submitted you to detestable practices. I've tucked you under a poisoned wing and wrongfully expected you to regard me with anything but venom. Misdirected it might have been, but it all came to be because I treasure you. The moment you regarded me with those brilliant orbs I knew you were special, and the past three years have only fortified that knowledge. I would very much like for you to stay here and give me the opportunity to right what I have done.

We both started anew when you were issued the spark of life. Let us continue our score of memories. Please. Hafstagg awaits. He's a brute, but he's loyal and forthright.

Affectionately yours,
Virgil

Oh, Almi and Merill insist on adding something to each of these letters. My apologies, dear. They're persistent creatures.

Descarta squinted to read the nearly unintelligible scribbles at the bottom of the page.

That dress isn't made for travel. Have this tunic. We're still rivals.

Descarta sighed, read the letter again then sat it gently on her lap. So it wasn't a nightmare. Thousands died so that she could live. She closed her eyes and images of the dead bodies, stricken with boils and discolored flesh, littering the streets of Saradin bombarded her. The plague, and who knows how many other travesties, now lay on her dirtied hands. So much death for one life wasn't right. She pushed the images away. They were dreadful, and she couldn't force herself to look at them any longer.

Until the ritual, she would have forgiven Virgil his peccadillos. He was a vile, cruel king, but she found something there to cherish. She had, and then he defiled her so thoroughly even as she begged him to stop. She couldn't blame him for holding on so dearly given his past. That didn't mean forgiveness was possible either. Her choice was clear then. As much as it hurt—and it was scathing—staying was no option. Perhaps the world outside would have something to offer her. Though if the journey thus far was any indication, she doubted it would.

For hours she sat in quiet apprehension. She had made the choice, but going through with it was not so simple. There awaited a finality which she wanted to avoid.

Trembling legs struggled to support her as she stood, atrophied during her lengthy repose. To pass the time and settle her simmering mind, she rummaged through the pack that had been thoroughly prepared for travel. Within, she found a viridian tunic of the same design as the sisters'. Slipping it on, and adding black tights for modesty, she pulled her hair into the low ponytail she left Saradin with.

"You can't just sit here forever," she told herself as she grabbed the bag by a strap and hefted it over her shoulder.

Hafstagg met her outside the door, sitting patiently on a dusty old couch within a hallway adorned with paintings of elves. He stood, rising like a tower, and produced a grin which quickly disappeared when he saw the sack slung over her shoulder. "Have you made your decision then?"

The homunculus nodded. "I have."

Hafstagg stood there, awaiting further explanation. When none came he grunted, shifting his weight uncomfortably. "Well? Are you needin' more time?"

"No," she muttered before her confidence could drain. "I—we are leaving."

The warrior grimaced and opened his mouth to reply. Nothing came out, though, before he turned and started down the hall. "As you wish. The exit is this way."

As she followed, condemning elven portraits sneered at Descarta at regular intervals, shunning the girl for her decision. She drew her arms around her chest in a shield against the jeers.

Hafstagg halted before an oaken portal braced with iron. Exquisite patterns were etched into the wood in a system of winding vines. "Before we leave, I'm to confirm this is what you want. You aren't required to interact with anyone here, but you are not rushed in your decision." The warrior recited the memorized phrase.

His timbre was grim, one which didn't fit him, thought Descarta. She wanted to wait, to be certain she made the right decision. But Virgil was here. The queen clenched her hands above her chest. It was lacerating to think of what he did to her. "Let's go," she muttered. "I want to leave this vile place."

Without responding, Hafstagg pulled on the heavy door.

...

The pitter-patter of bare feet on marble intruded on the cradle of stillness Virgil had allowed to take his mind. He suspected the clapping belonged to his resident troublemakers, recently his personal worrywarts. They could have belonged to ogres and the lackadaisical sorcerer wouldn't have cared. A disposition he scolded himself for; his life was no longer his to squander. The twin sets of footsteps skidded to a tumble beside him and ended in a tangle before his feet. Grunting and shoving, they barked complaints at each other before noticing his scrutiny. Four caring orbs shot to him, set within worried expressions. "Our Virgil is doing it again," Merill whimpered.

"We give our Virgil time, but he does this," Almi whined.

The king sighed, moving a heavy gaze to the empty bottle in his hand. "I'm being censured by a pair of barren elves who cannot operate by themselves. Oh, such a grand sovereign I have become." He bristled at the wine bottle. Three centuries of fermentation and it was still no more than liquid fertilizer. An angry toss shattered it among a pile of its deceased peers. How many more would he go through before his chasm was sewn? Virgil knew it was pointless. He'd tried the same method of grieving when Ankaa left with ill effect.

A wounded sniffle from below captured his attention. The girls shivered, shrinking away from the inebriated sorcerer. Virgil swallowed, regretting the insensitive remark—they could no more help their state than he could have swayed Descarta. He reached for them and they jerked away, emitting a frightened squeak. The king subjugated the urge to throw something again. He'd never know anything more than destruction, destruction and unending frustration. Almi and Merill did not deserve to be involved. They were only trying to be attentive, to be what they thought he needed. "Dears," he declared, and the girls quaked at being addressed. "Dears, I didn't mean it. You're my sweet songbirds, and I wouldn't have you any other way." He reached for them again, but was still met with trembling. "Please," he muttered. "Forgive me. I'm not upset at either of you. I should not have fouled you."

The pair examined his hand like cats appraising someone foreign. "Why does our Virgil do this?" Almi asked.

"Never talked stabbing before," worried Merill.

"Our Virgil is dependable and he cares. We know it," said Almi, hesitantly pressing her diamond studded face against his palm. "But why?" she whimpered.

Virgil carefully stroked her cheek, trying to remind the pair they needn't fear him. The past few weeks had taken their toll. Descarta was gone, perhaps forever, which left him free to wallow in the dark clouds of forlorn thoughts.

"We want our Virgil back," muttered Merill from behind her sister. "Our Virgil ignored us, but he never hurt us."

The sovereign nodded and drew himself from the chair, settling with his back to its base. "It takes exceptional girls to love a villain like you do. Perverse, but exceptional."

Almi hesitantly crept forward, confidence growing as she pressed her chest against the weaver's. A deep breath filled her with his scent, and she shivered under the sway of ozone and alcohol. She worked her face into his neck, pressing her lips to the warm flesh insulating his aorta.

"We want to make our Virgil happy," emerged Merill's soothing voice as she hung her chin on her sister's shoulder. Her deft hands, rigorously trained by notching arrows, had slid around Almi's sides and under the anxious rise and fall of her chest to unbutton Virgil's robe.

The sorcerer planted his hands on the sides of the nearest elf, meaning to lift her from his lap and remove the seductive sprite. Somewhere amid the hot breathing against his neck, Almi's gyrations and fuzzy thoughts, the voice that uttered reason was naught to be found. His hands instead searched beyond Almi, sliding down her sister's slender back to grasp her succulent rear.

Merill mewed in response, eagerly pressing her hips forward. "Use us. Please, use us again."

Snapping his fist up and fishing a handful of golden hair, Virgil abided by prying her head back. The girl squealed in exultation. All that remained was a desire to indulge, lust that squashed reason. With a yank on Merill's hair he rose and toppled them over, climbing atop Almi. Her sister, caught beneath, did her part by riding Almi's tunic to her waist. The impassioned king snapped an iron grip around the elf's throat, clamping her esophagus while they engaged in a furious kiss. Muffled whimpers escaped the asphyxiated girl's lips, soon fading along with her fervent grinding. Crimson eyes wandered about in a daze while Merill, grinning merrily, explored the choking elf's heaving chest.

Then Virgil pulled back, removing his hand. A strand of saliva still connected his lips with his ward's. Almi inhaled frantically, filling burning lungs and issuing a delighted gasp-moan. "More!" she rasped between breaths, wrapping olive thighs in behest around Virgil's waist.

It was all the invitation he needed.

...

Descarta took a tentative look at the man across the campfire. He was staring at the blaze in the same brooding way he had for the last week. She released a melancholy sigh, picking at the charred fish he'd prepared for dinner. The catfish was delicious; yet she didn't have the stomach for eating. "Why won't you talk to me?" she eventually asked. "Are you going to be silent as long as you're here?"

"Yes, I am," he replied.

"Why?"

"Because I was ordered," said Hafstagg. "And because I'm not thinkin' I want to talk."

The homunculus toyed with her tunic, scrunching the wool between her fingertips. "Am I really so loathsome?" she asked while suffocating in anxiety.

Hafstagg shook his head. "No." He angled his sight across the fire and found shame in his callousness. "No, not at all. I'm just a senile old man without the virtues you're havin'."

Descarta focused on her nervous fumbling, closing her eyes and allowing the warmth of the fire to play on her face. "You aren't mad at me for leaving? Was I wrong, Hafstagg?"

Hunched over his meal, the warrior produced a mirthlessly self-deprecating chuckle. "Only you know your heart, little one. As for me, well. I was never allowed the decision."

"What does that mean?" inquired the girl, throwing a glance at the warrior. "Never allowed the decision?"

"Eh, I won't bore you with my stories," grumbled Hafstagg. "It's getting late, anyhow. Perhaps—"

"Please," interrupted Descarta. She caught him with her lonely gaze, preventing his escape. "We've just been waiting, and I've had no one to speak to at all. Let me hear the story?"

"I promised Virgil I—"

"He isn't here. What harm will it do?"

Hafstagg sighed in resignation. "Fine, fine. But it isn't a tale worth recountin' to be honest." The warrior lost himself in the crackling campfire, returning to years lost. "Once, I was the captain of Virgil's personal guard. We followed him everywhere, a shield against the countless attempts at his life. Our ranks were constantly changin' during the conflict with Kaen Morr." The warrior shifted on the log that served as his seat, clearing his throat. "Met a castle chef around that time. Handsome lad and I was thinkin' he'd be nice to settle down with. We had somethin' special, but the keep wasn't a place to start a life together. He was thinkin' we should move somewhere quieter, safer. I asked to be relieved of my duties. Virgil denied me that." Hafstagg sunk lower, glaring at the circle of sand spread around the flame. "He denied me everything. Not a month later my chef was struck down by a fleein' assassin. I left that day and had only seen Virgil once before stumblin' upon the two of you in the tunnels."

Descarta frowned, not eager to look at the warrior. "Then why did you help us?"

Another dry chuckle escaped the silvery beard. "When I was sent to search, I was not pleased. Why should I be rescuin' someone who had given me nothing but torment? When I saw you there, I was excited. I was thinkin' it'd be easy to hammer the both of you and let the assassins take the credit." Hafstagg gave her a toothy grin. "You'll learn. Life takes you to dark places, and after bein' there so long, you know only the shadows." He tightened the straps around his arming doublet, occupying his hands in the same way Descarta did with her tunic. "Then I touched him. I saw what he'd been served. The Sundered, my loss seemed slop aside his. Thinkin' again, that isn't true. Our losses were each regrettable. Helped me to see Virgil had a responsibility of his own. Anyhow, your king forced me to stay because he was working toward a larger goal. And after seein' what he planned with you, I couldn't strike him down. Heck, I had to help him. For my own sake, too. Thought I could settle this spirit by helpin'."

"You knew about it, and you didn't think to stop him?" asked Descarta.

"I knew," admitted Hafstagg. "I was never thinkin' of stopping Virgil. The realms aren't all black and white like you're seein', especially not to fellas like us. What he did wasn't admirable, and it won't get him a fancy statue overlookin' Saradin. It surely soiled his reputation as a king. What he did was necessary because he loved you. Somethin' I should have done myself. Virgil gained my respect through his dedication, foolhardy as it was." Hafstagg caught the girl, now sailing an introversive sea, with his gaze. "Your decision is yours to make, and I was told to let it be. But girl, he was hale when I left. Didn't seem a day over thirty. The guard scarcely defended him so much as we cleaned up his mess. Yet here you are and he's lookin' a starved, sleep-deprived ghoul. I'm not telling you to return or lose your value for human life—hold onto those virtues, girl. I'm just sayin' a sacrifice is a sacrifice. You could have thanked him."

Descarta winced, drawing closer to the mesmerizing fire. "I guess I could have . . ."

"Oh, don't be worryin' yourself!" bellowed the man, sabatons clinking as he stood. "I'm sure he's grateful enough you decided not to stay in that coma forever! Tomorrow the zeppelin arrives, so get some sleep. That's when you decide where we head. A vast world before you." Hafstagg disappeared into his tent then, leaving Descarta to contemplate his words.

Tomorrow. She didn't know what a zeppelin was; just that she couldn't turn back after boarding. Wrought with anxiety, Descarta would not sleep that night.

Digging through her sack, she retrieved the one book she brought on the trip, *Kalthused*. The homunculus smirked, recalling her naivety. Virgil had warned her history was often written to favor the victor. He knew all too well. He'd offered that often when he discovered her reading his biography, she realized. Slumping her shoulders under the weight of invoked memories, the queen flipped to her bookmark, tucked right before the final chapter. She continued where she left off, the clash where Kalthused lost Ankaa forever then disappeared. An uneasy sorrow welled in her belly, thinking of her brief meetings with the deceased queen and the despicable way she suffered.

The biography's especially garrulous account of Ankaa's final words gave her pause. Verily so that she read them five times. "Implore not my name again. The brok'n heart will surely wane. For o'er its wake she is made. This iv'ry maid, so divine, embrac'd despite your darken'd mind. And should she learn your secr'ts vile, this blooming flow'r will only smile," Descarta repeated the section out loud. She thought it a strange farewell. Huffing, she closed the tome, not intent on reading the conspiracies surrounding Kalthused's missing corpse. She went to store the book, but the authored name lured her back. "Foehr D. Eskarduh" ran along the spine. "Foehr D. Eskarduh," she read aloud. "Foer Dee Escarduh. For Descarta."

...

An exasperated breath permeated the stillness dominating the abandoned summer palace. Descarta wasn't supposed to leave. He had expected it, but his heart was hardly primed. She was to forgive him, to care enough to forgive his many blemishes.

Virgil had done it again; treated them as they wanted. He despised what their early childhood left behind: sexual arousal through being beaten and abused. Yet, in his insufferable weakness, the weaver nourished that urge. He despised himself for it, no matter how utterly blissful it was to use them. The most wounding reality was that they needed it, needed him. The king couldn't deny the satisfaction they gave him, but he always ended these carnal skirmishes with great regret. It was enough to make him shed them as queens, after all. He looked to the snoozing elves at his side, fur-lined cloak pulled tight around their shoulders. Twenty-one years had passed since he last touched them in such a way. Sloshed or not, it was something a part of him still yearned for. With Descarta gone, he couldn't tell himself he wasn't trying to dilute her loss. Perhaps her passing presence made him capable of treating his elven wards as more than exotic pets. He remembered the day he lowered them to that level, when their dementia and resemblance to his departed queen forced him to. Virgil wouldn't forget how keenly he'd scarred them.

Ankaa wasn't there any longer. She hadn't been for years. Now, he only saw Almi and Merill as the sugary-spirited songbirds they were. Virgil closed his eyes and reclined, gingerly stroking Merill's shoulder.

PART TWO

CHAPTER NINE

A Grim Reunion

A pitch black ingress opened like a monster's maw before the girl. Somewhere within the cave was an entrance to the summer palace which likely still housed Virgil. Nervously, she ran a thumb over the hilt of her deadly sabre. So many uncertainties plagued the homunculus, and her fingers shivered ever-so-slightly under the mounting pressure. She was stronger now, strong enough to forgive and to understand. Still, this encounter was different than chasing game or sparring. There was no target for her sabre to strike down, no manifestation to burn with her inherited affinity for weaving. "Do you think he'll still love me?" she asked. "It's been five years after all. Is this a good idea?"

Allowing the girl a generous breadth, Hafstagg groaned his irritation from beyond her personal circle. "How many times are you going to ask that, little one?"

"I'm no longer little," she complained, looking with doubt to the concealed tunnel.

"You haven't grown at all, and look at you shivering like a flufftail." The warrior stared at the green tunic, hazelnut hair trimmed to match the day she left precisely. The girl had gone to great lengths to show Virgil she was still the person he loved. Hafstagg knew it

wasn't a façade; the way she gripped the tome, *Kalthused*, every
night—her comfort in a world so far removed from her norm—made it
clear. Yet she had changed, matured into an individual with the
determination to come this far, to come to terms with the fact that
reality wasn't perfect and neither was Virgil. "He would not forsake
you," Hafstagg eventually promised, as he had countless times over
recent weeks.

Descarta had grown accustomed to the brute's jests during
their travels, so they bounced harmlessly off her tunic. She knew he
was right, regardless. She was beyond aging, and her belly felt as if it
would burst in a flurry of flutterflies. Mortified, she spun on her
guardian. "I abandoned him! I wouldn't be here if it wasn't for him,
and I abandoned him! How do I apologize for something so
wretched?! How could he ever see me as anything but a heartless
failure?!" The girl shook, her tiny chassis unable to contain the
tempest within.

Hafstagg just stared at her. This was another situation he
encountered with greater frequency. Any reply would only fan the
self-flagellation. So many vesper conversations involved the girl
begging for another story about the king. It made Hafstagg wonder if
her infatuation clouded reason, if there was reason at all to be found
in a trial such as hers.

A dull thump to the side sent them both into a defensive
posture, Hafstagg taking a protective step toward Descarta.

Two elves stood over a downed buck that they must have been
dragging by the antlers. Hafstagg figured it was the source of the
thump, since the pair stared at Descarta with flabbergasted
expressions, hands and mouths agape.

The homunculus nearly did not recognize Almi and Merill,
lustrous blonde tapestries grown to their waists and bejeweled with
leaves. Smiling, she waved, approaching the twins. "You look so
different! If it wasn't for the tunics, I would have thought you wild
beasts." Reaching wide, she hugged them both, paying no heed to the
blood that spread to her tunic. "Are you well?" She squinted at Almi,

then Merill. Their necks were nearly fully bruised, a discolored mesh of purple, green and yellow. "What happened to you?" she gasped.

The sisters were still gaping at Descarta, crimson hands hung flaccidly at their sides. Almi's eye began to twitch, then Merill's followed suit. Slowly, the former eased her hand toward the savage mace dangling from her hip.

Hafstagg, no stranger to the motion, yelled for the queen. "Get back!"

Half-heartedly taking heed, the girl stepped back, just avoiding a wild swing by the enraged elf. The keen tip still bit, though, tearing two gashes across the bottom of her tunic.

"You don't belong here," growled Merill, notching her composite bow.

"We can't let you live," snarled Almi, hopping forward and dragging the many-fanged mace into a rising blow. Sandy hair flared behind her in a nymph's cloak as she dashed forward.

Descarta shuffled back, hand clenching the hilt at her hip defensively. "Wait!" she reasoned. "It's me! Descarta! Don't you remember?!"

She stepped behind another brutal swing. This one was a feint though—one she would have seen through were it not for her confusion. The girl was no expert at real combat, not experienced enough to retain her bearings when emotions pulsed through her veins. The intended attack struck her sternum with agonizing force, a charging shoulder which lifted her feet from the grass and crashed her upper back against the unmoving earth. She whimpered from her cumbersome position, chin tucked against her chest, surroundings assuming a nausea-inducing blur.

"Die!" Almi cried from above Descarta, and the homunculus figured she would have no choice but to oblige. She tried to conjure a defense, weave the elf into submission. Yet she found it impossible to concentrate. The point of sentience that strummed at the fabric had been rendered inaccessible.

"Enough," Hafstagg commanded. Having closed the gap to the downed girl, he disarmed Almi and whacked her unconscious in one dexterous movement. An arrow clanked against the menacing demon watching from his bronze spaulder. The hulking man turned toward its owner and narrowed his eyes at the remaining elf. He knew she would have split his skull if her entire body wasn't quaking.

"Leave!" she bellowed, her harsh tone nearly losing its mellifluous pitch. "He's ours! Ours! You just die!" She stammered the threats while notching another arrow, trembling elbows making the task impossible. Tossing the weapon aside, Merill instead rushed forward, steel-tipped arrow gripped in her palm. Hafstagg planted his feet apart, intending to intercept her. But the elf nimbly vaulted onto his spaulder and over, arrowhead raised high to run the downed homunculus through.

Descarta was ready this time. She unleashed a stunning wave of wind that disrupted Merill's descent, causing the elf to land unceremoniously on her stomach. Still wielding the makeshift skewer, Merill started to rise, but Hafstagg pressed a knee into her back, wrenching the dangerous arm behind her.

Sobbing, Merill flopped about, oblivious to the cracking objections of her immobilized shoulder. "Let me kill her," she pleaded, reduced to a sobbing whine. A torrent of tears spotted the dirt below her angular scowl. "Don't take him from us. He's ours. Our Virgil. Please, Des. Please die." The desperate elf lay motionless briefly, then renewed her resistance. Her shoulder issued a loud pop, signaling its dislocation and giving Merill the freedom she needed to pull her knees to her chest and execute an explosive flip, kicking her boots into Hafstagg's face. The blow was devastating; yet he retained the wherewithal to secure her ankles, which only led to more kicking. Descarta, recovered from her disorientation, rushed over and summoned vines to bind the girl to the underbrush. The sister spat, cursed and shook her head, but the coiling vines prevented her from damaging herself. "Die! Slut Potato! Nngloth'noxth!"

Hafstagg moaned, gingerly tapping what he knew to be a broken nose. He was fortunate, though. Her frenzied kicks could have driven the bone into his brain.

Merill had quieted, reduced to a repeating string of "Our Virgil" between bawling sobs. Hafstagg rose, a scarlet stream wetting his chin, and approached Almi. She was unharmed; albeit she would surely meet a headache when she awoke.

"This is not what I was expecting," muttered Descarta, standing reluctantly over Merill. "What does this mean?"

Hafstagg shook his head. "Never could understand these two."

"Des," whimpered Merill from below. "Des." She gazed up at the queen with pleading scarlet orbs, light playing on the tears welling there. "Des. Des."

The homunculus squinted at the girl. "What, Merill? Why are you acting this way?"

"Des," begged the elf. She looked at Hafstagg and shuddered, then back to Descarta. "He can't hear."

Descarta looked back to Hafstagg who shook his head again. "Just don't listen to her," he warned.

The girl dropped to a knee anyway, kneeling beside Merill. "I'm sorry. Your shoulder must hurt terribly. Just tell me what's wrong, okay?"

"Des," she whispered, eyes darting apprehensively to the warrior who watched her intensely.

The queen inched closer, ensnared by the elf's weakness. She wanted to know what changed so dramatically over the last five years. Why did they detest her with such ferocity? Why were their necks so bruised? Questions which would not be answered, she realized, when spit splashed against her cheek.

"Leave! Never return! We don't want you!" cursed Merill, spitting again on the emerald tunic. She slammed the rear of her skull against the earth. "Leave!" she ordered in time with the banging. "Leave! Leave! Leave! Leave!" Until a vine secured her head to the ground and wound around her mouth.

"Please don't despise me," sighed Descarta, lightly stroking the supine twin's wounded shoulder. "I'll mend this for you." The neophyte weaver could see the rage in Merill's glare, and it struck her deeply. Even so, she brought forth a pulsating azure light that righted the shoulder and healed the self-inflicted split atop the elf's skull. "See?"

"Go on," said Hafstagg. "I'll watch over these two. I'm thinkin' it wouldn't be a good idea to go in with them." Descarta nodded her reply, rising and starting toward the imposing cave. "Be wary," added the warrior.

Descarta only nodded, sucking in a breath and stepping into the tenebrous tunnel. She found the door soon after, its hinges groaning their defiance as she shoved the weighty portal inward. The torches burned dimmer than she remembered, darker than the detestable day when she made the mistake of abandoning him. Descarta crept forward. The sisters' reaction left her jittery and unsettled. It weighed on her heavily that their greeting was wrought with such enmity. The girl peered around and reminded herself she was not safe yet. Anything could be lurking these halls, a crypt to unspeakable sins. She stopped at the only door she remembered, the one blank slate leading to the room where she threw so much away. Descarta could not forget the bitter scowl the painting across the hall threw at her egress. Cautiously, she drew the door open. "Virgil?" she asked the space within. There was no reply. Only a scorched room greeted her, a bed's skeletal frame contorted amid a mess of ash and debris. The diminutive girl swallowed and shut the door. She did not think blaze-bitten quarters were a propitious portent.

Something beyond caught her attention. Fragmented dialogue floated on haunting wings down the abandoned hallway from somewhere ahead. She pursued its source, careful to tread furtively, and as she drew near it became lucid Virgil was the speaker. Anxious, she broke into a brisk jog, throwing the security of a clandestine approach aside. She couldn't hold herself back any longer. A sharp turn sent her into a massive cavern, stalagmites and stalactites meeting around her like the jaws of an ancient beast.

"Girls," Virgil slurred from further in. "Not now. I've . . ." The sorcerer paused, apparently seeking the proper greeting. "To the Sundered with it," he muttered. "This will not work. Those curves were not there . . . or were they?" There was splashing, a dissatisfied sigh and more splashing. "Almi, Merill. I cannot remember, dears. Were there freckles here?" More splashing came, followed by the clamor of liquid dripping on stone. "Almi? Merill? No games now, my dears." Descarta could hear his deep breathing pervade the cavern, but the sorcerer remained quiet for several unnerving moments. The girl wanted to call out to him, but she couldn't find the resolve to do so.

"Who's there?" he asked in a scathing tone. "I'll unmake you. I'll roast your innards through your mouth!" He let out an enraged roar, illuminating the room with a violent wave of flame which instantly dried Descarta's eyes out. He stood in the middle of the chamber, the workings of an ice sculpture set within a meager underground spring. The frozen statue depicted his homunculus as he'd last seen her: leaving with a sack slung over her shoulder. The back of the figure was meticulously carved, but the front was without the slightest detail. The image was exactly how he'd remember someone who left him, she deliberated.

"Oh, it's just you," the weaver groaned, taking a generous swallow out of his gem-studded chalice. "What will it be today?"

Descarta peered at him, taking in the radically transformed figure before her. The darkened candelabras had been lifted from his eye sockets and replaced with the hale hue of youth. The raven robe that once signified his position as supreme weaver hung in tatters from his waist by knotted sleeves. Beginning just below his right ear, a scar blighted his flesh in a scorched field, covering the upper half of his torso and the entirety of his right arm.

"Well, out with it," he ordered, stalking toward the girl. "Make my insufferable peccability known. I honestly cannot think of anything else you can rend me with. You've covered every last lamentation, you damned sprite—from my glorious failure at loving you to the exquisite ravaging of those sweet elves. What will it be today, then?"

Descarta sunk away as he neared her, fright sinking its crippling phalanges into her stomach. "V-Virgil," she managed. "It's me. I've come back for you."

The weaver stopped his advance at the diminutive girl's proclamation, tilting his head in confusion. "Oh, you! I am a clever one, aren't I? This is a new approach, my little illusory blo—blo—blo—floweret. I cannot wait for this lesson's torment! Is this a treat of what I could have had, then?" Virgil raised a charred hand to the girl's cheek, touching the tender flesh with reverence. "And to finally gift me this delightfully angelic visage. I remember now. Enchanting beyond reason. Come, you can string me along your condemning spinning wheel." He snatched Descarta by the wrist and pulled her to the sculpture, depositing her across from him. "Stay still and I won't ignore you." The broken sorcerer caressed the ice with the touch of an artisan, and it flowed willingly beneath his palm.

Taken by the eccentric sorcerer, Descarta observed for a long time without speaking. She admired and pitied the intensity of his stare, how deftly his hands moved to capture a passion lost. He didn't even have the good fortune to grasp that she stood before him. She wanted dearly for him to be the person he was when she left. She wished she'd possessed the courage and compassion to have never boarded that zeppelin at all. "Virgil," she said.

"What?" he answered, paying the girl little heed as he manipulated the frozen mask.

"Do you still love me?"

He looked at her then, forehead burrowed into deep defiles.

"I've never stopped loving you," she offered, taking a step forward. Her hopeful timbre was saturated with the affection secured deep within. "I just needed to learn to appreciate what you did for me. Will you forgive me, too?"

"I guess I still have a few tricks up my sleeve," he sighed. "I must discard modesty. I've impressed myself today. Now," Virgil declared, splashing toward the homunculus. "I will play along with your nonsensical jaunt. You deserve a reward for your ingenuity. There's no harm in rewarding oneself," he mused. Virgil grabbed the girl, fingertips digging into the tunic around her arms. The once sovereign captured her gaze and produced a smile so burdened with sorrow she bit back tears. "You can never forget her. Fade as you will, as you are, you must never find yourself without the load that is your love for that inspiring, precious blo—blo—blo—"

"Blossom," aided Descarta.

"Don't mock yourself, you half-wit," groaned Virgil.

She didn't know how it started, but she was moving, urging her chin forward. Desperation anchored its tethers to her joints and led the marionette into her king. Exhausted arms encircled the sinewy muscles of his side and back, inviting the weaver close enough to urge craving rouge lips against his own. She embraced him rigorously, sending her hands on an exploratory course through tangled hair. The passion-filled joining drowned her palate in the taste of century-old wine and the bitter twang of grief. Her amateur tongue hungrily followed his lead, plunging the homunculus into the blazing rapture of her first kiss. Descarta had awaited this encounter for years, imagined it on sleepless nights fraught with loneliness and diamond-studded cheeks. So it was with great trouble that she pried herself from him, releasing an unsteady breath just as a skittering spark ran down her spine. Parted lips glistening in the aftermath, she cast blazing orbs toward the weaver. "Virgil, give me a second chance. I'll never let you down again. Just let me return, will you?"

Virgil visibly softened, and his mirth sloughed off in a dreary susurration. "That was . . . your grandest performance yet," he murmured, untangling himself from Descarta's clinging arms. "I concede. You are the victor," the spellcaster responded in a defeated timbre. "That will be enough. Please, spoil my soul another day, rotten hallucination." He started away, dragging his saturnine carapace back to the sculpture when interrupted by high-pitched shrieking.

"Virgil! Virgil! Virgil! Virgil! Virgil!" echoed through the halls and into the cavern. "Virgil! Virgil! Virgil! Virgil!" the frantic call neared until Merill burst into the room. "Virgil!" she exclaimed in horror. "Virgil! Don't choose her!" the elf shouted. "We have dinner for our Virgil! We didn't leave our Virgil! We didn't hurt our Virgil! We love our Virgil! We were here! We were! Not her!"

"Calm down," sighed the sorcerer, rubbing his face irritably. "She's, she's . . . curiously inventive, but she's only an illusion. That's all, my songbird. How many times must we address this?"

"Virgil!" screamed Merill, huffing and scratching at her soiled locks of honey. "We're yours! Not her!" she hissed, pointing a crooked finger at the downtrodden homunculus.

The weaver followed his ward's bloodied finger until his eyes fell upon Descarta, whose amber plea pulled forcefully at his heart. Then it dawned on him: Merill was pointing right at Descarta. His grip slackened, silver chalice clattering to the unworked granite with a splash of burgundy spirits. The sudden change made sense now. "Des?" he asked with a shaking voice dripping with disbelief. "Des, is it you?"

"Yes," she affirmed, nodding her head. "I'm sorry. I tried to tell you." The diminutive girl closed on him. "I've learned the true meaning of the prose you wrote for me. I want to be your queen, Virgil. I want to right the mistake of ever wronging you. To be yours no matter your past."

Merill stalked forward, wedging herself between the two, possessively pulling the sorcerer's scarred arm across her chest. "We're his, not you," she announced, raising her chin to defiantly show the chromatic band of ownership wrapping her neck. "His."

Virgil didn't speak or acknowledge the hostile elf, so bewitched by Descarta's confession he was rendered dumbfounded.

"There you are!" raged Hafstagg, colossal hammer held aloft. "You're payin' for that, damn elf," he cursed. An arrow protruded from his thigh, broken off halfway up the shaft. "Virgil!" he bellowed. "They tried to kill her!" When Virgil exhibited no signs of replying, the warrior stomped over. Merill shrunk under the weaver's arm and hid against his back, peeking hatefully around his elbow. The ogre-like man switched his hammer to one hand, using the other to shove the despondent spellweaver out of the way and pluck Merill from her feet, dangling the kicking girl by the front of her tunic as if she were weightless. "I serve loyally and this is my payment upon return?!" scoffed the warrior. "If he won't be punishin' you, I will."

"You will do nothing," threatened Virgil with a virulent pitch that, partnered with the cracking stone at his bare feet, made his anger deadly clear. "You will put her down with the utmost care. You will never, never touch either of my wards again. Or, as my personal fucking chandelier, I will show you centuries of unspeakable agony. And I can be . . . quite inventive."

"Do as he says," counseled Descarta. "Further harm is pointless, isn't it?"

Hafstagg softened, realizing just how ridiculous he was acting. Gently, he lowered the elf, who took off toward Virgil the moment her boots touched the cavern floor. "See," she sobbed, pulling her arms in and pressing against his chest. The elf prodded the sorcerer with aggravated bumps of her forehead. "They want to hurt us."

Setting the bronze hammer to its rack across his back, Hafstagg turned to Virgil. "We were just arrivin' and those devils went insane on us. Weren't even—"

"Where is Almi?" the weaver interrupted. Virgil scanned the room, searching the shadows earnestly. "Where is she?!"

"Virgil, she's outside. She's unconscious, but she was trying to murder Des."

"She's here to take our Virgil!" protested Merill.

"Unconscious?!" Virgil boiled. He wrapped a steadying arm around Merill's shoulder, visibly quaking. The cavern roared his discontent, its many teeth rumbling in rage. The weaver palmed his face, grabbing at his temples.

"She's fine!" pleaded Descarta. "Almi hasn't been hurt! She had to be contained!"

Hafstagg set his jaw, eyes darting nervously to the many stalactites that threatened to crush them all. It felt as though runaway energy was spreading through the room, soaring to a deleterious peak without a limiter to regulate its rise.

Merill had begun to hum an inharmonious tune that eased the shaking, staring daggers at Descarta while she stroked Virgil's sides. "Calm, calm. Calm for us. You'll lose more if you do this again. Remember? Be calm, our Virgil. Calm for songbirds." She continued to hum, fervently rubbing her cheek against his scarred flesh and maintaining her piercing glare.

Gradually, the shaking diminished to an almost inaudible simmer. Still hidden behind his hand, the exhausted sorcerer addressed the group of ex-cohorts. "Merill, go to Almi and ensure she's unharmed." The girl nodded, grinning at the weaver. "Something amuses you?" he asked.

"Our Virgil didn't break!" exclaimed the girl.

"No," he agreed. "But a little elf will soon break if she doesn't leave now. Because with her standing here, I'm having great, great trouble overlooking her attempt on Descarta's life."

Merill's grin faded as she dissected the response. "I—we—y-yes, our Virgil!" she stammered as she ran off, tripping over herself twice before dashing out.

"Des," murmured Virgil from beneath his mask. "I'm sorry you had to endure my . . . all of this. I'm certain it's not the greeting you were hoping for."

"No," responded the homunculus, "you've nothing to apologize for."

Virgil stood wordlessly for a moment, searching his muddled morass of thoughts. Coming to the conclusion that he was in no state to deal with something insurmountably important, he turned to leave. "Forgive me, blo—blo—blo—" he emitted an exasperated grunt, tossing the attempt aside. "Forgive me. I want nothing more than to speak to you, to hear of your journey and to . . . affirm the outcome. Albeit, I fear I play the role of the rude host; I cannot talk in this condition. The elves will not harm you now that I know. Almi best be hale, Hafstagg." Without another word, he staggered out of the cavern.

"I am truly sorry," offered Hafstagg. "This is not what you deserved to return to. What happened?"

"I'm not disappointed," replied Descarta. She knew she wasn't lying to herself. He may have suffered mental trauma, but he still loved her. The genuine ardor conveyed by his confession would have been enough. If anything, his malady served to augment the touching declaration—for he thought he was talking to himself, entirely unshielded. She closed her eyes and imagined him before her, clutching her arms, telling himself to never forget his love for her. "No, he is just unwell. I know without the slightest misgiving he shares my affection."

The hammer-wielding guardian dropped to his rear, taking the pressure off of his wounded thigh. "He was showin' signs of mental stress after the ritual. I figured it was just over you. Judging by that forsaken elf's response, they've had trouble with him in the past. You felt it, didn't you?"

Descarta tilted her head. "I did. It was an avalanche with no resistance, growing and growing."

"He may still love you, girl, but don't be discardin' caution." With a slam of his fist and an agonizing roar Hafstagg pushed the arrowhead through the rear of his leg, tugging out the shaft. "Now that we're done with that, could you heal this?" he panted. "Then we'll see what we can be doin' about your infatuation with deranged spellcasters."

...

Descarta followed the eldritch hymn down foreign corridors. The tune carried an absurdly tuneless pitch, but the elven lyrics were entwined with a mysterious capacity to incite a state of drowsy sedation. More importantly, they belonged to the quarrelsome pair she sought. Twinkling pinpricks had taken over the dome above, sending their smoldering cousin to its diurnal reprieve. In turn, the passageways had assumed a state of near-darkness without the supplementary light of day. Descarta didn't need much illumination to navigate; yet the fey hymn coupled with empty passages did nothing to settle her.

The lullaby eventually placed her before two narrow-eyed elves, regarding her with open disdain from their belly-to-belly respite. Almi and Merill had ceased their hymn when they noticed her approach, never lowering their judging gaze. "What do you want?" asked Almi from beneath her twin.

Descarta shifted her attention to the phoenix emblazoned door beside their heads. "This is Virgil's room, isn't it?"

The elves ground their foreheads together in agitation.

"Could you let me in?" asked Descarta as sweetly as she could manage.

"Our Virgil told us to leave you alone," said Merill.

Almi rolled over, showing Descarta her back. "He didn't tell us to be nice. Thieving harlot-shallots don't deserve it."

Frowning, the homunculus lowered to the dusty floor. "You were nice to me before. I thought we were friends."

"No, not friends," said Merill.

Almi shook her head in agreement. "We took care of our Virgil. Not you. You broke him. He's ours now."

"You can't take him back."

Descarta's frown deepened. She concurred with the elves. They were here to protect him while she abandoned him. Prevailing fairness was uncommon, though, and she had been dealt enough unfair situations herself. Foremost, being thrust into a life-altering ritual and, utterly unprepared for real choices, made to make one that would drastically change the following five years. Descarta often wondered if it would have been better for Virgil to force her to stay. "I'm sorry," she stated, extracting a pair of brioches from a sack at her side and offering them to the elves. "I brought these from Vanathiel for you."

Doing a poor job of masking their excitement, Almi and Merill each snatched a pastry and ravenously bit into the treats. Thinking herself safe with the girls occupied, Descarta stood and started for the ingress marked with a reborn bird. Intransigent claws snatched her ankle, pulling her attention back to the elves. "We'll know if he tastes different," warned Merill, peering up through solemn scarlet orbs.

Descarta jerked her ankle away, huffing. She did not want to know what they meant by that. Hesitantly, she knocked thrice on the portal, so thick it was like knocking on a wall. She doubted the sound penetrated at all. "Virgil," she called. "May I come in?" There was no response, so she called again.

"See, he wants you to leave," snapped Almi.

"Shhh. Remember what our Virgil said," Merill gasped, covering Almi's mouth with both hands. "He'll be angry." Almi bobbed her head in understanding.

Growing tired of the berating, Descarta nudged the portal open, timidly calling out. "Virgil, I'm coming in." She slid through the entrance and it slammed shut, sending the girl into a jolted hop of surprise. Regaining her composure, she surveyed the room. Alembics, crucibles, retorts and a slew of unidentifiable alchemical tools and cultures lined smoke-stained walls. The noise hadn't stirred Virgil, who rest atop the one facet of the room befitting a king who transcended generations: an extravagant canopy bed as high as her chest with wispy lavender curtains. She approached the reclined sorcerer, who commanded certain caution even in sleep. The homunculus recounted her time with the man and noted she'd rarely seen him resting. He was always beside her, ignoring his sunken eyes and diminishing health to preserve her own.

Carefully, she raised herself onto the bed while trying to refrain from disrupting his sleep. A task of great difficulty, Descarta discovered as she wormed her way onto the mountain of a bed and through the swampy, ill-supported mass of sheets and blankets. The girl unstrapped her boots and tossed them off the side, flinching as they thudded on the floor. Sitting up on crossed legs, Descarta spotted a tome amid the stormy ocean of sheets. Curious, she leaned closer to discern the title, *Resurgere Ex Cineribus*. Throwing a furtive glance at Virgil, she plucked the book from its place among the waves. Descarta flipped to the beginning, where the tome's title was written in something she prayed wasn't blood. Pages of arcane diagrams and equations whose sight invoked queasiness were skipped until she reached a new section entitled "Homunculus Index". She flipped through nearly one-thousand detailed analyses until the last entry, the only one without an infuriated "FAILURE" scribbled over the notes.

> *Title: Descarta*
> *Iteration Number: 984*
> *Pod Catalog: 102y, 20x*
> *Date of Creation: 2868 M.E.*
> *Eyes: Amber*
> *Hair: Brown*
> *Height: Short*
> *Body Type: Thin*
> *Overall Condition: Unstable*
> *Fabric Affinity: Further observation required; results too high.*
> *Comments: Vital organs intact; physically without flaw. Improvement over past vessels by injecting imprisoned queen is manifest. Body will likely fail within hours. Will attempt to extract more data during autopsy.*
>
> *21 Evenglow: During fabric observation, a ribbon was discovered. It's the first with such a connection. Ribbon is damaged, likely an effect of synthesis. Will attempt to mend and follow up accordingly.*
>
> *24 Evenglow: Three days and it yet lives. Nightly mending results in longer lifespan. Will continue with temporary solution and further observation.*

24 Evenglow: Without stimulus it awoke. It's aware, as its eyes follow me relentlessly. Will proceed with removal from incubation pod.

25 Evenglow: It's sentient and possesses higher than basic functional knowledge and sense. Perhaps as a result of Ankaa's injection. The thing is curious, though, so I've had to lock it up. Still requires nightly surgery.

27 Evenglow: It seems to have a spirit independent of Ankaa's. The Sundered's notes mention nothing of this anomaly.

03 Ashentide: I have begun to teach the creature. Hazael thinks it a foolish endeavor, but tests have proven knowledge augments one's ribbon.

19 Crescens: She's taken to her lessons with exceptional aptitude. The girl is a genius; yet she remains frail. Suturing her tether nightly is laborious; need to find an alternative.

29 Crescens: Attempted to teach weaving to the girl. She plucks with remarkable ease—cantrips, of course, but spells that would have taken any other decades to cast.

11 Bloomsfell: She smiled today, the first exhibition of emotion. She doesn't talk much; her vocal chords are still healing, most likely. What's more curious is her innate understanding of language.

24 Bloomsfell: Laughter, delighted laughter. Descarta continues to impress.

Conclusion: Success. After a year of observation I have decided she cannot be sacrificed. She is my creation, yes, but she is real. I cannot find it in myself to extinguish such a brilliant flame. I believe I can permanently mend her ribbon by sewing it to my own with the spirits we've gathered. I will have to erase her memories prior to tomorrow, however. It would be better if she didn't know her origin.

Virgil had already revealed the truth to Descarta, but it wasn't until reading about herself treated as an object, another test result, that it truly weighed on her. She had always dealt with her amnesia by believing one day her memories would return. For her, there were no memories, no sunny days in vast meadows, cavorting around her parents' legs to remember. She had no past to lose. Looking to Virgil, she questioned which the larger torment was: a past stained by despair or no past at all? Descarta had since been given a past, though. And she decided with certainty that lacerating memories were far more penetrant than emptiness. The girl nibbled her lip in consternation, proceeding to the next page.

This journal has had no function for two years. I have found love again, wherever she is. The experiment yielded results I could have never imagined, and now my animated little blossom has departed. She's out there somewhere, living a life I cursed her with. To think I believed she would tolerate me if given the option. What a foolish man I have become.

Regardless, this log must serve a new purpose: an archive for a past I fear may slip away. Leading up to the ritual to inject Descarta with life, the spirits grew to an unbearable din. They raked at my mind from the fabric endlessly, with resultant instability. At times, weaving works as it would any other day. Then there are the instances when I find my purchase slipping, when the membrane that shapes the fabric to my will simply cracks. With it, my memories of that precious creature escape me.

I cannot remember her face. I have Almi and Merill describe it to me for hours, but what I know to be of undisputable beauty is only a milky blur to me. I will not lose my blossom. I must not forget. Thus, these pages will serve as the slate of time.

The log went on to describe random events with Descarta: the many times she would bark curses at him, the uncommon way she held eating utensils, her ravishing physique, the awe and excitement with which she regarded new ideas or places and hundreds of similarly scribbled memories. Then the writing took a sudden change, sharper and less legible.

Illusions, I'm faced with illusions. As if I don't know my faults! My failures! I am reproachable! She visits regularly, recounting all I have not done for her. I've tried everything, even attacking her. The act was moronic; for as I went beyond my means, the flames ever grew. And there's the senselessness in trying to destroy an illusion. I survived thanks to Almi and Merill, as I have for these two years since Descarta left. I have lost again. The term may be useless now, given I've been forbidden to say it to a girl whose wondrous portrait I'll never again visit.

With a despondent sigh, Descarta thumbed until she found another drastic shift. It seemed to have regained some lost legibility.

She returned today. I can see her face again. An enchanting manifestation of every last shard of my utmost desires. I'm afraid I cannot approach her. Even

*if I weren't inebriated and my skull didn't scream, I
would have no worth to offer. What do I say? That I,
your malefactor, your tormentor, your vile beast am
even less worthy this day than the cursed morn you
left? She says she's returned for me, and I admit finally
gracing my withered lips with the splendor of her rouge
counterparts was invigorating beyond explanation.
Still, I don't even have the capacity to call her my blo—*

The last three letters were scratched out, followed by pages of
"Blo". Attempts at writing what he was no longer permitted to
express.

The eerie elven lullaby had returned, carrying its frictional
caterwauling through the heavy portal with clarity and rousing Virgil
in the process. When Descarta finally withdrew her attention from
the troubling illuminations, she found him staring up at her. Startled,
she yelped and the tome fell open in her lap. "What are you doing?!
How long have you been watching?!"

Virgil sat up, supporting himself on his arms. "Not very," said
the sorcerer. "And I think I should be asking what you're doing,
sneaking into my room and invading my privacy."

"I-I didn't mean to," stuttered the girl, fumbling to shut the
book and shoving it out with both hands toward the drowsy weaver.

He sighed, accepting the tome and turning away from the girl,
hanging his legs off the bed. "Why are you here?"

Descarta peered at his back, gaze hovering on the constellation
of poorly healed injuries and the cinder-sown scar reaching around
his right side. "I wasn't sure how long to wait, and I couldn't sleep,"
she explained.

"No, Des. Why have you returned?" Virgil had begun scribbling
in the tome, the scratching of quill on paper adding cadence to his
intonations. "You are without equal—beauty, genius, compassion,
character—you embody the superlative form of a woman. And you
have the coffers of a queen. You would have trouble not finding a

courter in any land. I am, have always been, below you. Is that not why you left?"

Descarta blinked at the fallen king. He spoke as though her presence displeased him. Yet his flattering words took trenchant purchase. "There were suitors, Virgil, but none enchanted me as you have. Not one. I ventured for so long, crossing vast oceans and visiting nations aplenty. My boundaries were limited only by how far the zeppelin could fly. It was an ever-changing existence. Still, one constant persisted. That after training with Hafstagg, after rigorous studying, after exploring vast cities, after hearty greetings at quaint boroughs, after everything, the nights were for one person. For you, Virgil."

She edged toward the spellcaster, occupying the space at his side and dangling her feet by his. She stared at her lap and recalled the late evenings of yearning. "Initially, it was baffling. How could I miss someone who had subjected me to such horrors? Time passed and confusion faded as I was given ample opportunity to consider your actions." Descarta chanced a cast at Virgil. He would not look at her, so she pressed on. "In your own way, you've shown me boundless affection. As often as I tried to push you away, you were always there. Your sacrifices were unknown to me. I thought your affection an act of obligation."

Shyly, she tilted her head until it rest against his arm. "Above all you've done, your final act was the most difficult to overcome. I felt betrayed, forced into a role I did not ask for. Until I saw through my naivety. It was your grandest gift. And while ethically appalling, the ritual represented clarity of purpose. Once healed, you didn't force me to stay. You only wished me hale enough to exist without you, to be happy on my own."

"I don't think—" Virgil began to protest.

"No," the homunculus objected, shaking her head. She'd been awaiting this moment for too long. "To persist without you is to be unhappy. My inability to see that cost us both dearly. I've found

forgiveness. Could you do that for me, as well? I'm still the girl you
loved. I promise you."

"You would not willingly touch me before," the sorcerer
pointed out, "and you surely would not kiss me."

Descarta's ivory cheeks flushed a vibrant sanguine. "You're
wise enough to spot desperation when you see it, Virgil. Why do you
tease me so?"

"Because I am afraid of hurting you," the weaver lamented,
dragging a plaintive gaze to the homunculus. "Have I treated you so
poorly you value pain?"

The homunculus shook her head, mounting frustration
manifesting in streams of tears. "Why won't you accept my love?" The
sobbing girl clenched his forearm in her hands, trying unsuccessfully
to prevent the streams from growing. "I don't care what you've done.
I'll be yours, Virgil. I'll be yours." She looked up at him, and if he
thought to doubt her desperation, the boring ache of her stare painted
it vividly. "I haven't changed! I let no one touch me! I did my utmost
for you, Virgil! I'll do my utmost for you! What changed that you
dislike? Tell me and I'll right it!" she maundered. Then it crept into
her, a probing thread she hadn't felt in a very long time. The girl could
have rejected it; she had the capacity now. Instead, she embraced the
magic that willed her to sedation—she would not deny his affection.

"You are tired, Des. It must have been a difficult journey.
Anticipating the moment you would land, the stress of approaching
my cave and finding a tarnished king where you expected to return to
much more." Hesitantly he reached up to her cheek, stopping just
before his charred invitation touched the skin.

"Please," she smiled, enchanting orbs glistening with
anticipation.

Incumbent upon her desire, he tenderly laid his palm atop her
misery-moistened cheek, carefully dispersing the film with his
thumb. "I would never turn you down, my dear. If this destitute soul
will satisfy your ardor, it belongs to you."

Her amber stare beamed at him, instantly brightened. Sniffling, she wrapped her arms around him. "I was worried you'd forget me."

"Never," assured Virgil. "Now, you should rest. You look exhausted."

"I was too nervous to sleep these last few days," explained the homunculus. "How can you at all with their wailing?"

Virgil cast wistfully over her shoulder. "You . . ." The sorcerer took a deep breath and expelled his stress. "You learn to appreciate it. Now rest, please."

The girl gasped when warm tendrils spread from his fingertips as rays of gossamer sunlight, penetrating her spirit and settling her into the tranquil respite of windswept meadows.

Gently, Virgil deposited the sleeping girl among the maelstrom of duvet. The sorcerer lingered at her side for a time, beholding the hidebound flower. Her serene image strummed a calming harmony on his core. A melody in contention with the lullaby pervading his quarters. Regretfully, he looked to the phoenix-emblazoned doors. Unforgiving, this wretched fate that leaves no victors, only mauled survivors.

How could he ever choose between the two?

The weaver wished to be exultant. He'd dreamed of Descarta's return, of her confession and their subsequent voyage together. Yet it was always regarded as fantasy, a chimerical gumdrop set to dangle tantalizingly before the man while he catered to other obligations. Virgil left the lavender canopy and headed toward the exit. They weren't obligations, he reminded himself. Almi and Merill were commitments.

Virgil slowly shut the dense portal behind him and turned to the sisters who were impatiently bouncing on their heels, hands clutched behind their waists. The movement sent waves through their hair, jostling the leaves and twigs within. Big, bright stares of loving scarlet regarded him. "Good evening to our Virgil," greeted Merill. "We waited for you."

"And made dinner," boasted Almi, adding an especially exuberant bounce for effect. "Can we do anything for our Virgil?"

"We would do anything," they proclaimed in unison.

Virgil offered a half-hearted smile, plucking a dried leaf from Almi's honey tapestry. "I'm fine, my sweet songbirds. Why do you wear the mess of hunting? You should have at least cleaned the blood from your hands."

"Oh," the elves replied, each holding slender palms before their faces, examining the caked blood.

"We're sorry," Merill pouted. "We were coming back and that's when—" the girl paused gloomily, having recalled the error. "Then!" she said, glowing again. "Then, we had to sing for our Virgil because we love him!"

The sorcerer couldn't help but curl his lips at her display. The declaration wasn't news. The three had occupied those grounds half a century ago, and re-entered recently. This was an untraveled channel. He could cherish the two; see beyond their dementia to girls long nested. A loving, resolute pair who would give—had given—everything for him. "Your song was lovely. Very much so. Now, go clean yourselves and I'll see what you've managed to cook up." Apparently satisfied, the two nodded their understanding and turned to leave, but Virgil caught them with an arm around their heads and drew the sisters close. "You've been far too good to me," he said, kissing their sunny scalps in turn. "And you'll remain my special songbirds."

"Special," mouthed Merill as though she were a sommelier tasting the ripeness of the word, finally quaffing it in approval. "Special," repeated the lithe elf, rising to her toes to peck his cheek. "Like our Virgil."

Almi shared the same reaction before Virgil pushed them off and they capered merrily down the dim corridor.

The sorcerer faced his quarters, trailing dusty fingertips over the fire-born engraving. He offered himself to the flames of rebirth, leaning forward and placing his forehead on the door.

CHAPTER TEN

A Long-Awaited Invitation

Brilliant light stirred the slumbering maiden. Borrowed from the world above, its alien touch in the starless mansion suggested she rest just a slight longer. Squinting under the intense illumination, Descarta searched the atelier, finding that an alembic was throwing the harsh refraction. Tilting her head away from the blinding apparatus, she spotted Virgil perched atop a cluttered desk. He'd pulled his clawed robe to its intended wear, but all that remained was a tattered sleeve and some of the torso, following a singed line around the scar dominating his opposite side. Functionality utterly ruined by its encounter with fire, Descarta wondered why he didn't just find something new. He sat precariously amongst overflowing cylinders and cracked flasks as though he had little respect for what she assumed were potent substances. "Why are you sitting there?" she drowsily prodded.

Virgil regarded her as though she'd asked him an incredulous question. "I'm reading."

"I know," she replied, deliberating the grimoire spread across his lap. "Isn't that a dangerous place to sit?"

The sorcerer cast in an arc, surveying the mixtures. "Potentially, yes."

"You aren't as wise as I thought." Descarta grinned and shifted to her side. "You can sit here, Virgil. It's comfortable and less prone to hazard."

Again, the weaver offered a perplexed riposte.

Descarta groaned. "I'm not so spiteful."

His countenance remained hesitant as he hopped down and took a seat on the edge of the bed. "Are you certain it doesn't trouble you?" Virgil recalled how frightful she was during his nights as her silent sentinel. Closeness was harrowing for her in those times, and he learned better than to chance lying next to her.

"Relax," she urged. "I won't hit you this time, I promise."

"As you wish," the weaver responded, throwing her one more glance before leaning against the pillows. "Did you sleep well?" he asked, returning to the pages.

"Brilliantly," she cooed, revisiting the moment when his fire-touched fingertips wove her delicately, compassionately to reverie. She looked up at the sorcerer. The decimated robe wound alluringly around his torso, accentuating the serpentine sinews that formed ridges under his burned flesh. "Virgil," she breathed unsteadily. "Did you enjoy our kiss?"

The spellcrafter raised the ancient tome high enough to peer under its tattered edges. "Of course. You're euphoric, dear."

Descarta inched forward seductively, resting her chin on his chest and admiring how handsome he'd become when sleep deprivation didn't mar his face with deepened candelabras. Her petite bosom pulled in heavy, sultry breaths which captured his scent, entombing her deeper in the heat conquering her diminutive frame. The smoldering craving gathered in her abdomen, a kiln where her lustful longing grew into an overbearing flame. "Then touch me," she slurred in a licentious timbre. The request was supplemented by her slender thigh, creeping up the sorcerer's legs to wrap around them enticingly.

Virgil slowly closed his reading material, making great effort to control his desire. A familiar sensation sought his core, seating itself with a tantalizing pull. He ached to master her mesmerizing body.

The way her tunic bunched around her provocatively arched waist, clinging to the girl's bottom and revealing its luscious contour drove him mad. "Des," he began, matching her electric stare with his own scarcely contained spark. "Are you feeling unwell?"

"No," she purred while ascending his frame. Her roused breaths blew goosebumps onto his skin as she climbed the wiry rise. "How I've yearned for you to take me. So many lonely nights, Virgil. I want to be your queen." Without warning, she feverishly attacked his mouth, gyrations matching her tempo. She had to have him, needed him to unshackle the roiling inferno between her willowy thighs. Descarta didn't wait for his lead this time. Instead, fervor drove her tongue to coil around his as they engaged in a moist dance of passion. "Use me," she begged as she parted to suck air into delightfully burning lungs. "Make me yours in every way."

The weaver admired his diminutive queen, whose grinding rear persisted in its role of both illustrating and authoring her eagerness. Screaming to be freed of its confinement, her chest heaved above him in pressed objection against the viridian wool of her tunic. Passion-enthralled orbs sought him from behind alluringly shivering russet curtains, inviting Virgil into a corporeal feast. The weaver slid his hands gradually up her legs, taking care to brush along her inner thigh, to map her lean physique before disappearing under her tunic. Powerful fingertips sunk like talons into her supple bottom, sending a tremor through her body.

The homunculus trembled, head awash with desire as she ran her hands over his torso. "Please," she managed through shaking, wet lips.

Virgil could not deny her.

...

Descarta reached, her daze only permitting she fish to grasp something. She didn't care what; she needed something to squeeze. Finally, seeking nails clamped around a feather packed pillow, crushing it in ecstasy. "V-V—" she groaned. The remainder of his name eluded her tongue, replaced by a bewildered string of guttural grunts and unintelligible whimpers. She rasped an unsteady breath. An onerous task with her face half-buried in the pliable mattress, one lithe arm pinned awkwardly beneath her sweat-coated chest and a mess of damp hair clinging in an obstructive web. He was driving her to madness, but she couldn't articulate the words to implore him to stop, partly because her enraptured side dominated her will. It melted under his libidinous touch. The way his magically heated digits sought purchase on her raised hips, digging with zeal into her porcelain backside while he relentlessly drilled the tiny girl from behind—it was unspeakably consuming.

The sorcerer was empowered by her delirious moans and unfinished pleas. Virgil could not have stopped if he wanted to, and any part of him that might have was squashed by the heart-shaped invitation offered by an acutely arched back below. The way she peered at nothing in particular with glazed eyes, her husky, irregular breathing and the tender rear beneath his fingertips: it all captured him without protest.

An especially vehement thrust sent a skittering band of shivers up her back, which buckled under the sensation, shooting into a bridge while she shivered and emitted a string of meaningless sounds with no more purpose than to convey marvelously blissful surprise. Her unrestrained arm hit the bed repeatedly, a release for the shocking marriage of pain and pleasure which his last thrust ripped through her abdomen. "V-V—" she attempted again, coherent thought lost amid the tempest of ravenous love.

Sensing her exhaustion, Virgil guided the muttering nymph to her side and wasted no time stretching her moist insides once more. The latest in an array of invasive positions settled her betwixt defined arms which suspended him over the moaning homunculus. Sweat beaded on the ends of his sodden raven tangles, and the weaver had no intention of stopping. She was a source of pure intoxication. Descarta had pulled her arms against her meager yet invigorating breasts, hiding her face in absurd embarrassment while producing maddened moans and seeking his pounding eagerly with welcoming hips.

The dainty girl tried to focus on the arm in front of her, concentrating on the merciless kneading between her legs. A white blur had taken her periphery vision which augmented the feeling that she had been whisked away to another place, a world of divine pleasure domineering. Descarta wrapped weakened fingers around her king's forearm, setting biting nails into his skin to brace against the rocking beating she endured. Something warm and damp latched onto her ear. A part of her careening mind recognized it was Virgil as he took to heightening the roaring blaze in her gut by nibbling and licking her.

She was his now, and he was her cartographer. Virgil would know all of her.

...

"I was not the initiator!" blurted the irritated weaver as he peered inside the evacuated incubation cylinder. "And another thing," he started, spinning to further contest the accusation. Blinking, he bit his tongue, surprised to find Hafstagg standing before him. "When did you arrive?" Virgil grumbled, patting dusty hands on his dilapidated robe and scowling at the obstinate illusion with whom he was arguing.

"Only just now," responded Hafstagg, strolling next to the fallen king to examine the cylinder. "What're you lookin' at?"

Virgil turned to regard the vacant womb. "It's—" grimacing, he cast at his personal specter. "It's where I met Descarta."

The ogre of a man followed Virgil's gaze to see only unoccupied air. His mammoth chest produced a deep sigh. "Des is deservin' better," he muttered solemnly.

Bristling, Virgil spun on the man. He didn't shout though; he merely nodded. "She is," he agreed, trailing wistful fingers over the dimly lit glass. "This isn't what I sought for her. But I hear that plenty. I don't need you to remind me."

"From your apparition?"

"So you were listening," scowled Virgil.

Hafstagg sunk his shoulders in exasperation. Virgil had grown so defensive. It was giving the warrior second thoughts about his reason for approaching the sorcerer. "No, Des told me. That's not why I'm here, anyhow." He scratched his silvery beard nervously. "It's about Almi and Merill."

"They wouldn't risk assaulting her now that I know," shrugged Virgil. "And you'd best never touch them again."

"That's the thing," began Hafstagg, "I'm thinkin' your hands are the ones to be worryin' about. The twins don't boast over their bruises because you beat them."

Virgil shot a virulent glare at Hafstagg.

The warrior could see unrest stewing within Virgil. While he wasn't afraid of the man, he knew a fight would benefit no one. "Virgil," he gently explained, "I have ventured far with Des, and that has afforded me an appreciation for the lass. I'm not for recoutin' the details, but she ached for you tirelessly. I heard and witnessed enough of it to know. I don't want to see her hurt."

"The point is not coming quickly enough," pressed Virgil.

Hafstagg equipped his most austere tone. "You're goin' to injure her if you continue with the elves. Somethin' you may be unable to reverse."

"I am . . . aware," the weaver lamented, pressing his back to the container. "I—quiet yourself!" Virgil shouted at the empty space before him. "You be quiet!" He took several steadying breaths before speaking again. "What would you have me do?"

Due to the outburst, it took Hafstagg a moment to gather he was being addressed. "Have you do? Isn't it obvious?"

"Obvious?" Virgil retorted with a dry, self-deprecating chuckle. "Obvious? You'd have me discard those wonderful elves? You care not for their untrammeled embrace. You cannot credit the years they've looked after you, the numberless evenings whose closing capacity was their dependably discordant song. What of their immovable dedication—even when faced with death? No," Virgil spat, "you do not care to acknowledge any of that, because you, like everyone else they've known, only view them as creatures to be pitied, hated, used but never cared for." The dreary patriarch looked to Hafstagg, conquered by a solemn shroud despite his raving rejoinder. "I once thought of them with the same distant capacity. I have since learned my folly."

Hafstagg frowned. Virgil was right, and part of the hammer-wielding man thought him a better person for it. Yet the situation remained unchanged. "And what of Descarta?"

"Thus my predicament," answered Virgil. "Unearthing an appreciation for the sisters' . . . character has not diminished my adoration of Descarta. Hence this, this," he waved in disgust, "this hauntling that troubles me tirelessly." Virgil's fingers sought the obsidian mess atop his head, writhing there in discontent. "These incarnadine hands could never be free of their stains, and yet that girl has returned. How could someone brimming with such purity remain unblemished by my touch? Oh, I can still recall the noons when she capered about these halls, causing trouble for no reason other than to satisfy her boundless curiosity. Even when she learned resentment, when she tried to hide that bubbling enthusiasm from her sordid captor, it still lingered luminous as ever. Descarta is above anything a real human could be. She is the manifestation of my dreams, Hafstagg." Virgil shuttered his vision and summoned the image of her porcelain body slumbering in his arms. "That girl is magnificent."

Hafstagg wasn't sure how to galvanize a decision in Virgil, or whether it was possible in his wayward state. The man had regained his vigor. Yet he lost the luster and carriage of a sovereign. Staring daggers at unseen foes, Virgil seemed more human than he ever had as a king. Though he still possessed the haughty attitude, and he'd developed a swift temper since shedding the throne. Hafstagg produced his signature guffaw, clutching his paunch accordingly.

"I fail to see the hilarity here," the weaver muttered, not amused in the least. "Please, educate me."

Hafstagg contained his chuckle enough to place a gauntlet on the sorcerer's shoulder. "You've changed. I'm not for knowin' whether it's for the best, but you've changed. I can't respect what you're doin'. I can respect why." With those words Hafstagg departed, sabatons clanging against the floor.

"All three must remain unharmed," Virgil declared to the warrior's armored back.

"If you're thinkin' it possible," Hafstagg responded before taking the portal and bumping into Descarta.

"Oh. Hafstagg. Pardon me," she apologized, curtsying and slightly raising the calf-length skirt of the exquisite jasmine frock that loosely grasped her shoulders.

He gave her a sodden smile and continued by. Hafstagg didn't miss how shaken she looked. Descarta was scrambling when he rounded the corner. He wondered how long she'd been listening.

The girl sheepishly approached Virgil. She had planned on swooping in and impressing him with the dress, but the exchange she'd overheard dampened her mood. "Good evening," she called, raising her voice to a jovial pitch. Virgil frowned when he spotted the girl, looking her up and down. It wasn't the response she thought the garb would elicit.

"Where did you find that?" he asked.

"A chest stowed beneath your bed," she explained, feeling ashamed of searching his belongings. "I'm sorry. My tunic was dirty from, um, you know, and . . ."

Sloughing the frown, the sorcerer ordered her worry away with a wave of his hand. "You needn't apologize, blo—you look positively ravishing, dear. Truly, the gown makes you glow."

Descarta flared crimson, a slight grin curling her dimples. Virgil's praise brushed over her skin, silky words mollifying the turbulence within. The sorcerer no longer needed to weave her into submission; he needed only soft taps of the palate to manipulate her mood. "You're too flattering. It's just a silly dress," she responded.

Though blushed cheeks and drawn lips betrayed her. Descarta peered about, casting at the macabre exhibit of tanks occupied by undeveloped bodies, surgical instruments, alchemical apparatus and a lonely slab set with restraints. This was the ritual chamber, she surmised. She approached the slate, eyeing the broken shackles and blood-blemished table.

Virgil shifted uncomfortably behind her. "Des, perhaps we should go. Almi and Merill will have venison prepared."

"It's fine, Virgil," the homunculus assured, running slender fingers over the defiled slate. Descarta knew he was trying to protect her, but she had already accepted this fate. It was grim. It was reality. "What happened here?" she asked, tinkering with the cracked shackles.

"It is not a clean process," explained the sorcerer as he drew near to Descarta.

She followed the crimson-brown stain's sanguinolent descent into a dried puddle that could have swallowed Hafstagg thrice over. "There is much blood," Descarta observed.

Virgil inclined his head toward the gruesome mark. "Less than I recall," mouthed the weaver. "The intervening months were spent repairing you."

"Repairing me?" asked Descarta.

Virgil nodded. "Yes." He decided to leave it at that.

Descarta knew she was stalling, avoiding the possibility of being hurt, of confrontation. She decided she'd try to ease her way into the conversation she sought. "I read you were with me for a year before you took my memory," she prodded. Immediately, she regretted the accusatory diction.

"It was nearly a year," he agreed. "When I decided against your sacrifice, I also came to the conclusion that you should never know of your origin." Virgil appreciated the homunculus. The dress complimented her vigor, even if it was noticeably large. The pale jasmine set a soothing support to the hearth of hazelnut and amber that fueled a heart-warming visage. Indeed, the flowing sundress fashioned Descarta a normal girl. One who didn't know the despicable truths she did. He preferred her this way.

"Why?"

"You knew what you were, what your purpose was and you loathed me for it. Stolen memories couldn't rid you of that loathing." Virgil frowned, reaching to stroke the golden-brown cataract pooling around her bare shoulders. "Perhaps that's really why I reset your mind."

Descarta drew a breath at his coddling. It was still foreign, even if he had just ravaged her. Nevertheless, she enjoyed his touch, and the girl did her best to fight the tension it created. "What of Almi and Merill? Were you . . . with them then?" she questioned.

"Then?" The weaver coiled his finger in a lock of hair. "No. Occasionally in the decades prior, but not since your arrival."

"And now?" she pressed, mumbling her apprehension. When it was clear no response was forthcoming, Descarta turned to face him. Her closeness required she crane a sharp angle to meet his solemn stare. "Virgil?"

"You were listening," he stated.

"I didn't intend to, but as I approached . . ." Her voice faded and she diverted her troubled gaze. "I shouldn't have."

"No, the fault is mine. I should have never allowed myself to embrace them," Virgil lamented.

Descarta shook her head. "What you said was true. They're more deserving than I am." The dismal girl laid her forehead against his chest. "Are you going to reject me? I'm different now, aren't I? I'm broken," she pouted.

"Des," sighed the sorcerer, enveloping her shoulders and squeezing her against him, "I would never. And it's not at all true. Did you ignore what I told him about you?"

The girl tossed her head back and forth, hair flailing accordingly. She heard it all, but the seed of doubt had already taken root when his tribute arrived. "Did I not please you, Virgil? You can choke me, too. Do you like that?" She detached from him, snatching his hand and pulling it to her throat. "C-Choke me," she stuttered, saliently horrified by the idea. Fright did not stop her from closing her eyes and lifting her chin in offering. "I'm not as experienced as the elves, but they can teach me, can't they? I won't ask you to part with them. Just don't discard me." Descarta was ashamed at how ridiculous she must have appeared. She was terrified of parting again, though, so circumstances led her to greater worry. What if giving herself to him wasn't enough? "There must be some way I can be of use that they cannot." The despairing girl could feel the confidence she'd fortified over the past half-decade begin to crumble, its integrity ruined by uncertainty. Descarta imagined herself being cast off, watching as the cave taunted her with its shadowy maw.

"Des," Virgil murmured, followed by a distraught susurration. Worn digits clamped around her throat, causing the prostrating girl to empty her lungs in relief. The sorcerer then loosened his grip, giving her nape slight strokes. "Look at me, Des."

Obediently, she blinked her lids open, met by a countenance of profound sadness.

"What have I done to you?" demanded the incensed weaver. He gave his hands a disgusted grimace before releasing her. "You aren't Descarta. You're another hallucination. A poor illusion at that. None of this is her." Growling, he stalked off toward the homunculus farm. Cylinders shattered and dispersed their grotesque contents as crags bit from below, reaching under his will.

Descarta nearly succumbed to helplessness, watching as he destroyed yet another facet of his past. "That's exactly what you're doing," she murmured. The homunculus saw it in his inability to call her blossom, to remember her face, in the scorched room and now her birthplace. Slowly, he was erecting a palisade against what he thought he'd lost. The insight bolstered her resolve, reminded her that she didn't return to fail or fall to her own obsessiveness. Her affection had become an unnatural yearning, but she was still his blossom, whether he could tell her or not. Charging herself with his state, she paced to the raging weaver and snagged his sleeve, briskly turning him to face her.

"What?!" he snarled, incubation tanks popping behind him like sap-producing trees in winter frost.

"Forgive me, Virgil. You aren't the only one who has changed." She produced a shattered grin to punctuate her admission. "I've tried to grow strong for you, to overcome the immaturity holding me back before. Perhaps I have changed too much." The girl searched his cerulean gaze for understanding. "You weren't the only one affected by the ritual and the distance that followed. I accept you as you are: changed, perhaps irreparably. Can you not accept me? Someone who, under your counsel, learned disdain could become furtive affection, furtive affection could become fascination?"

Virgil simmered, chagrinned by the girl's forthright account. "That is more like you," he responded, smirking.

"I'm not certain how. Still, I am afflicted. Hafstagg told me I was being irrational, dangerously obsessive. I never believed him until now." She squeezed his arm, dropping her gaze. "I remain your blossom, Virgil. Just . . . blemished by imperfections."

"Well, if these imperfections allow me to explore you as thoroughly and vigorously as this morning, I've no choice but to embrace them," replied Virgil as the fetal fluids crept around his bare feet.

"Virgil!" she complained, the cinders flaring once more in her abdomen as she pivoted to conceal flushed cheeks. "You're so obscene and filthy and sordid and, and, and . . ."

"And what, dear?" exhaled the mage, bracing for another verbal assault.

She occupied shy fingers with knitting an invisible scarf. "And I find it strangely charming," she confessed in a nearly inaudible murmur.

Virgil allowed himself a sincere smile. More romantic words could not have rapt his spirit. For his utmost doubt was that she would ever accept his temperament, mangled as it had been by centuries of misfortune. His reach met downy shoulders and skimmed just above the jasmine sundress, setting about a plumed journey to wrap the girl, bewitching in her hidebound devotion, within his mantle. Virgil pressed his face into her golden-brown canopy, cherishing the berryflower aroma that had taken sweet residence there.

The homunculus reached up to grasp his arms. She felt content there, secured against him—safe and warm. "It doesn't please me, but I will not ask you to decide so quickly. I wouldn't want you to make the same mistake I did when I left." She knew she would never ask him to choose between her and the twins. The risk was far too great.

"Worry not, love. I would forfeit my life before letting you go again," he mouthed against her scalp, comfortably adrift amid the silky vines.

...

"We'll continue later," Josiah sighed, shooing the peasant girl from her duty between his thighs. He watched her departure lustfully, taking pleasure in the slight sway of her hips. "This had better be important," he groaned, foregoing the courtesy of strapping his pants.

Violah wore a grimace, but did not otherwise complain. "You have been shadowing me," she said.

"Don't flatter yourself, woman. Did you see her? Brilliant, and every bit the butter throat." The seneschal shook his head. "I've no need for a lady past her prime."

A flicker of malice caught the supreme weaver. Still, she remained calm. He was a lecherous rat whose loins were more rancid than the swamps of Wilheim. "Do not be coy with me, rogue. Your goons have all the subtlety of a mammophant."

Josiah scowled, but put forth no objection.

"Let me be frank, then. Your presence is grating, disgusting and I'm sure your butter-throated harlot awaits." The weaveress strode forward, her talon adorned mantle reaching malignantly, and seated herself on his desk's edge. "You've somehow discovered my connection to the assassins that visited our past king. I could end you. Here. Now. With trivial effort," she mused, rapping fingertips on rosewood. "Or—and I believe you would prefer this outcome—you join me."

"Join you? I find your arrogant stench no less revolting. And regicide is no petty crime."

"He's no longer king," countered Violah. "Merely a man whose existence threatens our present lord."

"Merely a man whose power I would not cross, whose ire supplants any torture you would enact," replied Josiah. They may have had their disputes, but the bard harbored no murderous desire toward the man.

"Let me handle him. Powerful weaver or not, he is mortal. And I've unearthed some of his rituals." She planted palms before the rogue, staring daggers at him. "Find the wretched crook and in return, you may have his wards."

Josiah suddenly found himself absorbed by her proclamation.

CHAPTER ELEVEN

Nothing Lasts

The artist had depicted her with a favorable glow, taking care to render the fallen queen with the vim she displayed in her abbreviated throes of life. Virgil couldn't recall the commission, the artist or the queen. He only recognized, by an innate synapse, that she was Ankaa, and he once belonged to her. The sorcerer wondered what she thought of him, of how he'd perverted her beloved and authored a rancorous beast. The noble elf must have watched in dismay as Kalthused sloughed values she treasured one by one, becoming the fiend with each broken tenet. Until the day when she scarcely knew him as much as he remembered her.

With a great sigh and a plume of dust, he pulled a tarp over the dilapidated painting. Virgil couldn't change what he'd done, and given the opportunity, he still would not. He may be a cracked, weathered and altogether detestable reflection of his past self, but it was this dereliction which allowed him to achieve great things. No mortal could have accomplished feats normally reserved for gods as he had. One had to transcend pitiful infatuations with good and evil if they sought immortality. When he considered Almi, Merill and Descarta and the fulfillment they'd given him, the sorcerer had no misgivings over the worth of his insidiously trodden path.

A year of tranquility had allowed him to nurture a faltering mind and quiet his burdensome passenger. Now, when Descarta caught his breath with her delightfully ebullient splendor, he needn't worry she was a phantom. Virgil owed this comfort—every comfort—to his trio of flowering dandelions whose dust was his nourishment.

Virgil regarded his reconstructed robe with appreciation. The repair was a poor attempt, a mottled claim to weaver's wear. Much as they had patched the charred mantle, his nectar-sweet seamstresses had stitched his soul anew.

As though summoned by his thoughts, Almi and Merill burst into the cluttered storage room, nearly toppling over the spellcrafter in their haste. Reclaiming his almost forfeit footing, Virgil then claimed their waists with an adoring squeeze. The elves giggled energetically in his grasp, hopping anxiously on their toes and darting widened carmine gazes between their sire and the entryway. "What has you buzzing, my songbirds?" The sorcerer released the wards, freeing his hands to explore their sap-colored curtains which had been shortened to just beyond angular chins. Almi and Merill issued charmed mews at the cosseting, jittery frames simmering to still placation under his attention. Virgil recalled Descarta mentioning taking the matter of their hair into her hands. It had grown unmanageable over the year since she returned, perpetually tangled and mired by leaves, branches and various assimilated oddities during their daily escapades.

"She sheared it," purred Almi from her meditative state.

"I see."

"Are we still pretty to our Virgil?"

Giving the sandy tops an assuring scratch, Virgil nodded. "Undeniably so, my scrumptious lovelings. Should I need food, you would surely fetch a month's worth, maybe two."

"Don't bake us!" protested Almi as she shook her head. "We're not for forking!"

"Don't spoon us!" added Merill, twisting away but taking care to remain under his touch.

Virgil let his amusement stir a grin. "Oh, but you're so tasty." Teasing them was leagues more satisfying than explaining the glaring issues with their response.

"Almi! Merill!" echoed an angry boom throughout the myriad of palatial causeways. Stomping sodden feet plodded just beyond the bellowing, drawing nearer with each watery slap.

"Dears?" posed Virgil.

The twins sniggered, sinking into his patchwork mantle until they peered from within a canopy of obsidian. "Shhh," sounded Almi from her nook.

Descarta stepped into the entrance, waterlogged sundress sticking to her melancholy frame. Tangled medusa curls writhed as irritable vipers about rosy cheeks and shadowy eyes. Sheaves of severed elven hair clung to the girl, saturated with enough umber muck to fashion the lass a swamp naiad. The girl looked from the peeking elves to Virgil. Drenched and dour, her dress ruined, she wanted to release the tears of frustration tugging at her ducts. Descarta had to be strong in front of the elves, though. She wouldn't give them the satisfaction of knowing they'd hurt her.

"Are you injured?" inquired Virgil with enough concern to assuage a portion of her anxiety. As she shook her head, he left the twins and strode up to her. A hint of hesitation snagged at his shoulders before she nodded, inviting the radiating warmth of his ache-consuming chest. His compassion favored her heart so that it jolted whenever he hugged her. For he was ever mindful of her jitters, the tightness that sometimes caught in her throat when he thought to touch the girl. Her skittishness born of self-loathing had been tempered, lessened by a year of careful caresses and wanton sheet thrashing. Through it all, Virgil had displayed vigilance in handling her illogical and unpredictable aversion to physical contact. There were times when he would pet her with reverence befitting a goddess, but any further and he always had the wherewithal to consult her permission. Yes, her raven had worked hard to thwart her uneasiness, efforts made lucid in the way his encompassing wreath infused her sopping frame with wellbeing. Still, Descarta valued his apprehensive embrace and the core-seated concern that fueled it. The gesture made her feel wanted. Stalky arms squeezed back and expressed her gratitude to the weaver. "They wound me in their hair and pushed me into the creek," she mumbled, holding a steady timbre before the twins.

With a sigh, Virgil gave her back a pat. "Forgive me," he whispered as he guided her from the room.

Brow wrinkled, Descarta submitted to his lead, scrutinizing the weaver. "Where are we going?"

"Where are you going?" echoed the sisters, peeking from the doorway.

"Away."

"We'll join you!" chirped Almi, springing from the dusty room and giving chase alongside her sister.

"No, you won't," hissed Virgil without stopping or turning to regard the pair. "You'll stay put until I decide what to do with you."

Tempo and luster stolen, Almi and Merill slowed to a halt, collapsing onto one another. "But . . . our Virgil," the mace-swinging elf whined from her sister's belly. The wounded moan was lancing, a lure which hooked onto the sorcerer's weakness for his tragically attached twins. He persisted, contending with the cloying urge to avoid souring their fragile smiles.

...

Fleeing streams splashed an inharmonious rhapsody as they leapt from auburn tethers. The escaping water ruined her reflection, but it mattered not to the girl. She was searching beyond the surface, piercing the crystalline spring for answers less transparent. Descarta cast a glance at the man who insisted on escorting her to the thicket. He sat reticent, hunched back respectfully facing the bathing homunculus. She understood him well enough to augur the source of his turmoil. Almi and Merill had gradually readjusted to her presence. Yet resentment still lingered there. This often left Virgil wedged between dissident parties, both cherished with fervor uncharacteristic of the foul king. If she had the strength when he needed her, the weaver would never have fallen. Descarta could have been his companionship. She could have been his poultice during troubled times. Instead, the golden-haired imps occupied the role of loving support. She did not deserve to be touched by one she'd abandoned. Descarta felt unworthy of the ember-granting joy his contact promised. "You shouldn't have left them like that," counseled the diminutive girl. "Please don't do things you'll regret for my sake."

"My accursed wards must learn somehow, blo—blo—blo—" expelling a groan, he shifted his seat. "This is your home, my sparrow. You should feel safe here. Safe and without worry."

Frowning at his response, the dainty girl rubbed a red-brown stain from her forearm. Its hue spread briefly through the water and was eventually quenched by the pool's clearness. "I do, my Virgil. I belong here thanks to you. So you needn't ask for my forgiveness. Almi and Merill will be as they are, and their faults are not your responsibility."

"Aren't they?" retorted the fallen king. "It is by my will they have a home here."

Descarta nodded to herself. If the elves lost his favor, they would surely be put out. Nevertheless, the sorcerer's unwillingness to abandon them wasn't a source of despair. She secretly hoped he'd never lose the sliver of humanity binding them there. Troublesome as Almi and Merill inarguably were, they were capricious sprites who could be just as saccharine. More importantly, they were just as much his foundation as she was. "I cannot say I have no desire to make this affair just the two of us," admitted Descarta, errant fingers inciting ripples around her waist. "Yet asking that of you would be an error. I can accept you for what you are, but knowing you have the slightest obligation to your feelings—to Almi, Merill or me—lends me great comfort. It is because of them I feel safe and without worry."

"You're a strange one," muttered Virgil.

"No stranger than a king who's seen centuries pass living alone with three pretty girls," responded Descarta as she emerged from her bath, wrenching her russet waterfall and slipping into her lace festooned pinafore.

"You paint me the lecherous old pervert," grumbled the weaver from his spot in the surrounding copse.

"Then I've used all the proper colors," she replied, taking to her knees behind him and prodding at his back. Descarta envisioned him above her, dominating her as he did on the twilight trysts when he was hers alone. A wanton quiver grabbed at her gut. "Am I truly your queen, Virgil?"

"Come again?"

"During my travels, I often asked about Elusia," explained the girl. "We'd rarely stray from the zeppelin's route, but there was always the occasion to talk with the locals. Merchants, politicians, steeplejacks, slaves: I sought knowledge of the world without prejudice. They all knew of you, the tyrant of the north, patriarch of ruin. But when I inquired of your queen I was always met with confusion."

Virgil heaved a sigh, slouching forward and entangling his fingers in raven strands. "I haven't had an officially ordained queen since Ankaa."

"Then the chapel atop Galvant's Bulwark?"

"A lie."

"Oh." The homunculus crawled to his side and plopped in the lush grass. Strangely, she felt less aggrieved by the truth than expected. "The chapel was beautiful. We should return."

The sorcerer flinched at her ambition. "I'm sorry, Des. We can never return."

"Why not?" Descarta asked, oblivious to his pact. "You rule there."

"Hazael owns the blighted realm now. That was our bargain, remember? He assists me in raising Ankaa. In return, he secedes the Elusian throne. Not that I cared for the wretched place to begin with."

"Right," replied the girl, scrunching the line of black lace that spiraled her skirt. "You must have loved her deeply."

"Who knows."

"You know, Virgil."

"I know only emptiness when I think of her. The evacuated void which brings forth patriarchs of ruin."

Descarta imagined the trials he underwent for her, the unfathomable dedication hundreds of years epitomized. He fabricated a religion for Ankaa, commissioned a grand dome in her image and mercilessly plundered and killed. Even that monumental passion faded into mirthless indifference. "What of me, then? Will I too be lost to time?"

The solemn weaver lifted his gaze and delivered an empowered stare which suffered no uncertainties. "Never," he swore. "Your image might once again evade me. You might grow to hate this withered soul. The outcome will be the same. Never will I allow my bond to you to unravel."

Dimple-adorned cheeks flushed carmine. Descarta was so rapt by his cerulean concession that she hardly noticed the earth trembling beneath her. "I will do the same," she said, drawing near to him and pressing her forehead against his sleeve. The rumble returned with might a second time, setting her forward and into his lap. Her heap was a transient one, for Virgil erupted to his feet and deposited her in a bed of tickling grass. "What was that?"

"Something is wrong," arrived Virgil's somber reply. He sought the treetops and the heavens which resided there, worries made manifest by the billowing cloud of smoke thickening overhead. "Something is very wrong." Kneeling, the sorcerer caught his bewildered queen with a grim gaze. "Hide, dear. Do not emerge until I return for you."

"I would rather—"

"Please," emphasized the weaver before thieving a brief marriage of lips and dashing off into the thicket with a rare energy.

Descarta deliberated the disturbed undergrowth in his wake. Her gut was taken by uneasiness, a foreboding which told her the image of him hurrying away would be her last. How could he expect her to sit and dawdle while he addressed uncertain danger? Releasing a troubled breath, the homunculus sat up. She tried with no effect to knead the knotted stirring from her belly. "I should find cover," she whispered, casting about her surroundings for a shadowy nook to slip into. Restless orange-yellow orbs were drawn once more to his exit. She had been tutored in weaving by Virgil, in the dance of thrust and parry by Hafstagg. Virgil praised her as being precocious, able to pluck at the fabric with acumen normally reserved to decades of study. How could he expect her to idle while he faced the unknown? Resolute, the diminutive girl took to her feet and the path he'd taken. They were partners, tethered by more than an intertwined umbilical, but by fierceness of heart. Descarta vowed to never again let him face his struggles alone while she watched from without, the powerless spectator.

...

Dust swept by on angry gusts as he approached the wounded cave, its entrance cleft wide. The disfigured maw issued an apologetic groan, integrity forfeit under the shock. Debris scattered beneath his boots, remnants of the subterranean palace's violated chastity. Virgil wore a scowl as he broke the dark within. The stench of rain and lightning clung to destroyed causeways, a firm indication of weaving. This was no accident.

The raven-robed figure proceeded slowly, respectful of the dense shadows blanketing the palace. Corridors he'd traversed thousands of times had suddenly grown foreign, become a dreamscape where every alcove bared fangs. A shout pierced the tenebrous tenseness and turned corner after corner until its mellifluous pitch reached the sorcerer. The elven ring was birthed on familiar chords, a ring that had many times gifted its inharmonious hymns stitched with touching affection.

"Merill!" exclaimed the weaver, chest thudding the rapid tempo of anxiety. Caution cracked under its weight and Virgil sprang toward the source. Heavy steps carried the weaver by the eternally harsh frowns of ancient portraits, watching his progress with disdain. The row flowed beside him, haughty noblemen deriding the fallen king, and concern began its constricting crawl around his throat. Virgil knew the palace well enough to draw a map without reference. It was this knowledge that worried him. The latticework of causeways and arrises meant pinpointing the location of reverberating sound would require many a tortured squeal. Then another cry rattled his heart once more, sending him to a stumbling halt. Ankles flared their objection as he shifted direction to enter a passage he'd just passed. The second complaint was near enough for him to discern. "Away!" its shaken pitch warned the insidious snake that had slithered into his hideaway. An ajar portal radiated the restless light of flame just down the hall. It was enough indication for Virgil, who deemed the illuminated room his destination.

Breaching the entrance, his haste was snagged by a tripwire which sent him rolling into the middle of an antechamber. The spill deposited him on his back, a silver chandelier suspended overhead, casting its luminous candlelight over the room and blinding him with its sudden flash. Virgil drew to his knees, shaking away a lancing headache and disorientation. He spotted Almi and Merill immediately, the lithe sisters bound like swine for slaughter at the far end of the chamber. "Dears!" he exclaimed, concern sinking its age inducing talons into his grimace. "Have you been harmed?" They shook wheat-colored heads and thrashed in a futile struggle against their restraints. Almi whined through the rags stuffed in her mouth, widened sanguine orbs seeking Virgil, communicating the terror whose iron grip would not relent. He jolted toward his wards, a leap made crunch as he crashed into an unseen wall. The sorcerer staggered back a step, growling away the agony of his crushed, oozing nose and starting forward again.

"It's pointless, you know," rang a low, seductive voice from behind the shaken man. He spun to find Violah, adorned with the trappings of a supreme weaver and a smirk of confidence, standing tauntingly close. Fresh raven sleeves crossed over her full chest, phalanges tapping with anticipation of biting into her succulent prey. Behind her, Josiah emerged from his shroud of darkness. The rogue avoided his gaze. His guilt-sodden spheres watched the floor. From behind the columns supporting the room, a contingent of eight weavers stepped out, all following meticulous passes which perpetuated the magic imprisoning Virgil.

"How is it?" asked Violah while baring an ivory grin. "To be where I was? To know you're helpless before me?" Virgil was ignoring the supreme weaver, scanning the ground around him where a confining circle had been etched. "It's drawn perfectly," she stabbed, taking pleasure in quenching his hope. "Just as your spellbook instructed. Really, you shouldn't leave your tomes lying about. It's careless. What a mess I had to sift through."

"Violah," interrupted the scout from her side.

"Go on. They're no longer needed."

Hurrying past his subjugated ex-sovereign, Josiah held his stare ahead and followed a straight path to the bound twins. Upon his arrival, a fellow rogue emerged from the antechamber's main room, bowing deferentially and helping the bard to carry the girls through the far exit.

"Stop! Josiah! You cannot! It will break them!" boiled the weaver from his bubble. An inferno flared around him and flooded his prison with a swirling storm of flame that hissed at its shell, yearning for release. Incensed beyond reason, he scratched at his containment, nails cracking and breaking under the vehement prying. The fortress shivered around him, but the containment held, his rage doing little more than vibrating pebbles. "Return them!" he demanded as the conflagration died, palms pressed against the invisible boundary. "Return them, you wench! Sundered take you before I do! When I am free you will regret this!"

Smirking, Violah offered a mirthful clap. "Oh, what a rousing show. I did not expect you to be so passionate. Over your artificial thing, perhaps. Not those delinquent toys." A corrosive laugh shook the woman. "Josiah predicted you well. A king unfit for his throne who adores a pair of trashed slaves."

"Why are you here?" muttered Virgil in resignation as he turned to face his captor. He could not dispel his prison. Charged with an insuperable situation, he had calmed. "You wouldn't make the journey simply to kidnap my wards."

"Josiah did," the woman mused, shifting her hips. "He'll give them the attention they seek, so you needn't worry."

"And you?" inquired Virgil, volatile temper revitalized by her comment. "Why has Hazael broken our agreement and sent a conniving witch to my home?"

"To be fair, it was a poor contract. You left Elusia in a state of pure ruin. As for my presence here, well, you are a loose end, Virgil. Frayed, detestable and dangerous." She shrugged, clawed robe swaying with the movement. "Snuffing your life is a matter of security."

Dread pressed against his ribs, giving rise to pain more acute than his shattered nose or curled fingernails. If his spirit was quelled, so too would Descarta fall. "Have you forgotten?!" he thundered, rising and hammering a fist against the limit of his detaining shell. "Have you?!" he spat. "I let you live! When you, the wrecked whore, could offer nothing more than your bare chest and a willingness to be turned into a drooling concubine! I allowed you to persist!"

"You are mortal," retorted the woman, frowning at the way he besmirched her in front of her subordinates. She would have to dispose of them later. "You do not deign the worthiness of my being. Hazael does." It was the steward that pacified her after the session with Virgil, the steward who gave assurance she would not be harmed. Now, he would praise her for extirpating this decaying root of his past. "Well, then. The time for discourse is over. Permission granted to beg while I peel your flesh away." The sorceress raised an outstretched palm toward Virgil, talons hanging with menace from her robe. Excited fingertips reached toward their goal, popping sparks galvanized at their ends.

Violah let fly a high-pitched oath, snatching her hand back to clench her torso. She watched in stiff horror as her robe bounced above her bosom once, twice, thrice, four times. The supreme weaver parted her lips, a waterlogged protest escaping aside a crimson river. Her underlings looked on in disbelief when she toppled forward, leaving a scarlet smear on the magical barrier as she made her final descent. Then the fabric claimed the woman.

Behind her stood Descarta, soft frown deepened by the severity of the situation. The diminutive girl gripped the ornate, emerald-studded pommel of a sabre whose claw had gorged on stolen lifeblood. In the instant of awe-stricken quiet that followed, many thoughts bombarded Virgil: dread that she had disobeyed his wish and been dragged into danger, relief that his blooming berryflower had prevented both their demises and finally the sated blade she carried. The vorpal masterpiece had belonged to Ankaa; it hadn't been used since he discovered her cold corpse. Then the still was cleft, split by a deafening roar as his prison exploded, the vast energy requisite in detaining the weaver imbalanced by Violah's fall.

Mental backlash from their destroyed spell snapped as a whip at the surrounding mages, leaving two seizing and the rest dizzied. Virgil let his rage free, throwing his hand into an open-palmed uppercut that stretched the floor forward, skewering the nearest opponent on an earthen spike. Anger unsatisfied, he jerked his fingers apart, forming a fan out of his hand. With enthusiasm, the spike willingly spread to mimic the display, snapping brittle bone and tearing through meaty stuffing with a plopping slurp and messy spray.

Unlike her encounter with the elves, Descarta did not dawdle or freeze. Fueled by her zeal for Virgil, she followed the steps imparted by Hafstagg. She shuffled forward and spun an elegant pirouette, a feint-disguising technique whose grace shifted to brutality as she halted the spin to connect a cartilage shattering heel with brittle larynx. The blow knocked its target from his feet, leaving the subordinate rasping for breath that wouldn't come. The victim, versed as he was in weaving, was defenseless versus her sabre mastery in such tight quarters.

The adjacent weaver raised his palms, half in defense and half in attempt to conjure a nasty riposte. The noxious counter he meant to bring forth never came to fruition. A quickstep and dexterous flick of her wrist brought the thirsty sword into his chin, piercing tongue, brain and crumbling skull at its exit. Damp auburn vines settled around her face, thrown into a wild canopy by her rapid, vigorous turns.

Virgil appreciated the morbid elegance of her movements, the captivating unity of budding beauty and technique. Her glimmering chestnut locks spread about her like a flaring skirt when she threw herself into a whirl, lending to her deadly ballerina prance. He admired the contraction of her toned thighs as their strangely erotic strut glided the vivacious assoluta to a stunning close. Yanking her blade free, the spectacle risked a glance at her companion. She met his feverish gaze with confusion, then shouted and pointed the well-fed blade behind him.

Lifted from his trance, Virgil followed her warning, immediately erecting a wall of stone at his rear. There was a crash, and a frosty wave washed over him, residue from the ice that clashed with his shield.

The final of three foes that stood on her side of the earthen barrier was pulling together an assault. Descarta rushed at the weaver, desperate to interrupt what she knew would be a pernicious blast. Two strides and a keen thrust to the gut dispatched the caster, but not before his thaumaturgy manifested. A disembodied limestone gauntlet swiped awkwardly at Virgil, missing completely due to her interruption. Instead, it connected cleanly with half the pillars supporting the roof and crumbled into gravel.

The ceiling protested and unsupported stone complained in the form of harsh rumbling. Descarta was knocked from her feet,

surrounded by the deafening din of falling rock. Face pressed firmly
to the cold slate, she felt someone slip their arms around her. The
roaring torrent grew louder, insufferable. Then everything faded to
black.

...

Descarta rasped, stirring a plume of silt which sent her into a
fit of coughs and hacks. The stench of churned earth assaulted her, an
odor that always roused ambivalence in the girl. She could never
decide whether she favored freshly tilled gardens or found the
renewed dirt repulsive. Grunting, she rolled to her back, foul-shaped
debris stabbing and forcing her to sit. Quiet hung in curtains around
her, breached only by the silken moonlight that shone through
fissures in the rocky dome.

"Oh," she said, observing the curiously fractured barrier. "The
ceiling must have collapsed." She lingered for a moment, absently
toying with black frill until the numbness of shock sloughed away.
She and Virgil were fending off doom-hurling weavers when the
cavern caved in. "Virgil," mouthed the girl with less anxiety than
gnawed at her. Turning on her knees, she cast about for her amour,
finding him on his back just behind her. Descarta crawled over,
further sullying her dirty pinafore. Hovering over him, she blew a
breath of relief at the rise and fall of his chest. She smiled, a slightly
crooked rise birthed by the truest gratitude. For a third time, the
sentinel gave grand clarity to his love by playing the role of savior.
Grabbing a mud-encrusted hand, the homunculus gently stroked his
fingers, one by one. A dull glow emanated from her touch, mending
the curled fingernails before restoring his shattered nose. "How will I
ever close the defile between our deeds?"

With great care, she lifted his head to rest it in her lap, only to
have her digits tangle in the thick stickiness of blood soaked hair. A
concerned sigh caught her lips as she gingerly palmed the affected
area, weaving a stream of bluish affection to repair the trauma. "It's
not fair that you hoard the sacrifices, my Virgil. I'm left to lick your

wounds and devise ways of shoving you into peril so that I may close the gap." Finished suturing the gash, the girl admired her king. Greasy raven strands stretched across his soiled cheeks, dominating his grim visage. She calmed the mess, delicately gathering the restless talons.

"Almi! Merill!" screamed Virgil, jolting from his respite and casting about in keen mortification. Descarta gasped, jumping and toppling backward at his sudden rise. "Where are you hiding?!" he demanded from the empty darkness. His rapid breathing slowed, shoulders slumped as his consciousness was gradually pulled from the nightmare and deposited in a nightmarish reality. "Almi . . . Merill . . ." he repeated in subdued melancholy.

"Virgil," called Descarta from behind the forlorn figure. "How do you feel?" She eyed his back, finding calm in the deep swallows he inhaled. The girl waited, hands on thighs and staring inquisitively. "Virgil?" she called again, louder and with minor worry. "How—"

"They're gone, Des. Gone." Virgil willed the punctured dome to close, shuttering the twilight globe and completing the burial mound. "Because I failed as their protector." He wanted to close everything off, to return to the period when attachment eluded him. Those centuries of oblivion were nirvana when juxtaposed with the innate pain of feeling. "How do you think I feel?"

"Forgive me," whispered Descarta against his harsh tone. She fumbled her way to him until her forehead bumped his back. The homunculus swept her hand back and forth, clearing the collection of earth and pebbles and took a seat behind the weaver. "I couldn't protect them either, and now you know how unworthy I've become." Wracked by the fear of uncertainty, the dainty homunculus pulled her arms to her chest, seeking to contain the stabbing that roiled within. "I disobeyed you. Worse, you've seen . . . seen how I've changed. I'm no longer innocent, pure or anything you valued in me. I've tried to hide it, but I couldn't stand by while you perished. Quelling a life, that isn't foreign to me. I don't like it, but I'm stained. Please don't despise me. I shouldn't have deceived you."

"Dear," began Virgil, heaving a mighty sigh. "Dear, you've done no wrong."

"I am tarnished," emphasized the girl. "I succumbed to these stains and in doing so tarnished your treasure."

Another susurration escaped the sorcerer. "I am incarnadine with the blood of innocents. How could I play the condemning arbiter when hundreds of thousands have bled by my decree?"

Releasing a choked sob, Descarta leaned forward, her volume rising to a boom. Hazelnut tresses jostled about her head as it shook in fury. "Was it not grotesque?! Abhorrent?! An affront to purity?! Were you not sickened?!"

"Quiet!" demanded Virgil, the single word sealing her lips. She shivered at his tone, sinking away and into herself. Crystalline film wetted her cheeks as she took to her habitual fumbling. Hafstagg was right; he would not accept her as she was. And she could no more blame him than change her past. She began to fall deeper, to commit to the descent, when Virgil caught her. The ridges of his scorch-scarred fingers were liberating to her cheek, drying her tears and invigorating her soul. "V-Virgil?" she stammered, his touch permeating a welcome heat.

"You should not think that way," Virgil spoke as the dome of stone gradually receded. The luminous shower returned, imbuing the cerulean stare that hovered mere inches from the homunculus.

Descarta sobbed, emotions running amuck. "But—"

"No," pressed the weaver. "Through those hardships you came to accept me. If anything, I am indebted to your sacrifice." Descarta sucked in a deep breath, enamored by his stroking. She was so afraid he would discover her, and so ashamed of what she'd become. "Your dance was mesmeric, exquisite, a display of unparalleled beauty, my lovelet. I found myself awestruck."

"R-Really?" Descarta inquired, but the girl was already aflame with relief. Reduced to drowning embers, her burden flitted away on the pacifying zephyr of his assurance.

"Really," promised Virgil. "Now come, we must gather what we can and head to Vanathiel." He glanced beyond her, to the ancient blade throwing a scarlet-hewn glint in the moonlight. "Don't forget your sabre."

CHAPTER TWELVE

In Pursuit of Passerine

Descarta patted down her dress, huffing at the cloud of dust each slap chased off. He'd left with such haste she hardly had time to gather essential traveling gear, much less change into something clean. They'd marched through the dark hours, and she never thought to challenge his insistence on pressing without rest. The argument would have been fruitless, fallen on ears too transfixed to reason. How would she have convinced him to slow when his pace was set for the endangered wards? And the raven-haired sorcerer was no more approachable than a slumbering beast. He'd taken on a dour shroud since departing, eyes toward their far off destination. The companions had been moving under the star-speckled ceiling relentlessly. Beginnings of blisters were sore on her heel, a tribute to the comfort of her days settled with the weaver. The everlasting flamewheel pitched its diurnal array of violets and oranges across the grand canvas above, a celebration of the night tyrant's fall. Still, the organic spires of Vanathiel were but slivers on the chromatic horizon.

"Virgil," she started, realizing she'd been swept up by the moment and simply followed his lead. "Why are we heading to Vanathiel? Will Almi and Merill be there?"

"No, they won't."

Descarta examined the austere man. He strode with intransigent purpose, on feet surely less travelled than hers. She admired that trait. Not a childish stubbornness but a steadfast devotion to the few he cared for. The diminutive girl took comfort in knowing he would pursue her with similarly adamantine steps if she were stolen away. "Then why Vanathiel?" she inquired. "What do we need there?"

"A zeppelin," explained Virgil somberly. "Violah was in charge of Josiah, meaning he will be returning to Elusia."

"Do you think he flew back?"

Virgil nodded in affirmation. "Flights to Elusia are costly; it isn't a regular route. Even so, a long return with prisoners like Almi and Merill would be quite the trial. They are clever when it matters, and nothing pains them more than being distanced from me." The sorcerer expelled an exhausted breath. He'd thought the tumult had settled down, that tranquility was within reach. "Belligerent prisoners are dealt with by breaking them down, peeling back the layers until resistance is squashed. Josiah wouldn't use the tactic, at least not as anything but a last resort. Not with Almi."

Descarta nodded her agreement. His reasoning was sound, and knowing the maleficent despot, gleaned from experience. "So he will want them secure as soon as possible." The weaver showed no signs of replying, so she assumed her deduction was correct. "He must yearn for her," she pondered aloud.

"He does," agreed Virgil. "Josiah yearns, but not for the right reason. His chase exists purely because it is a chase, a hunt for elusive prey. When Almi denied him, he was slighted, and that has poisoned him."

"Will they be all right?" questioned the girl. She was genuinely worried for the troublesome elves. "Before the Underrise you mentioned they mutilated themselves when you sent them away."

"They will manage. For a time."

"After that?"

The sorcerer grew distant once more, traversing the realm of memories sorely unforgotten. Porcelain flesh ripped, delicate faces befouled, digits that once caressed him with utmost care crooked or severed, Almi and Merill grinned up at him toothlessly, promising they would be good girls if he gave them another chance. Explaining they'd enacted punishment for falling out of his favor. The sweet, demented fairies had done nothing wrong to begin with. "We must hurry," he said after enduring the frightful return to yore and a shudder jolting his spine.

...

Careful to avoid disturbing the snoozing maiden, Virgil eased her slender thigh from its roost across his lap. It seemed to him like her mercurial aversion to contact had been dampened considerably in the last moon. When he awoke, he had to practically pry himself from the bear trap of her arms. Virgil allowed himself an enervated smile, tempered by the dreadful turn of events. At least his shining flower had improved her condition enough to initiate prolonged closeness. While she insisted they share a bed, the girl always maintained her distance. She was fighting something, he knew, something more than his touch—for there were times when she pined for it with furious passion. Whatever her plight, he was glad she had conquered a fraction of her passenger. Virgil regarded the resting homunculus, sheets strewn about her frame in a ghostly gown. She slumbered quietly, mouth agape just enough for him to hear her rhythmic inhalations.

Much had transpired since the days of dissidence wherein she moped and snapped around the ramparts, a caged sparrow fluttering about with virulent hostility. Set against his abnormal lifespan, it should have been nothing. To him, a decade was as a week to normal humans. Yet those nine years had impacted him more profoundly than the centuries before. Gently, he lost his fingers in her hair, still damp from bathing. Virgil let their touch command him, fulfill the countless moments when he swallowed the urge to lose himself there.

Upon his wandering digits the final destination was at last realized, a peaceful garden beyond time, beyond torment. A nursery whose blossoms bore only the brightest of spores. A nursery where he could simply submit to the sublime will of her ever-soothing song. He kissed her then, gingerly conveying his thanks to the side of her head.

Berryflowers offered their aroma, as they always did when she was near. Virgil allowed himself a brief delay in her natural fragrance. He could remember the accident that had imparted her with the scent. That day, Almi and Merill capered about the homunculus containment room, tossing berryflowers in one of their more animated moods. The cavorting ended with lavender petals bobbing in select incubation tanks. Virgil walked in on Merill, standing atop Almi's shoulders in an elven totem pole, fishing contamination from the concoction of life. He scorned them then, frightened them so by his poisonous pitch and with such severe scolding that they would not risk punishment. For a tenday, the twins clung to arrises, peeked through windows or buzzed from afar, avoiding prosecution long after his ire faded. Ultimately, they made a contribution to her creation and imparted Descarta with a spice of their own.

Virgil withdrew from the mattress and her enticing fragrance, distancing himself from the beckoning call to reverie. He searched their traveling pack, sifting through sundries until he located quill, ink and scroll. The sorcerer then seated himself at a simple desk, feathered apparatus scratching meaning into blank parchment.

...

Drowsy amber eyes peered from the ghostly sheets, focused on the rapid metronome which brought words to a missive. The serene incandescence of an unhindered moon cast a bluish glow on the weaver. It was a spooky shroud, a tapestry reserved for omens and portents. "Virgil," she called from her sleepy cocoon of gossamer silk, batting weighty lids. "It's too late."

The weaver jumped at her protest, cursing an errant line across his letter. He shot his lady an apologetic smile before the ebon feather resumed its skitter across the page. "You're right, so rest."

She groaned, floundering in her wrap to sit up. The dainty floweret rubbed blurriness from her vision and huffed as she battled the tangle around her waist. "I cannot without you here. You know that."

Virgil sighed, placing a buffer of parchment atop the drying ink and folding it into thirds. "You will be fine," he assured her, rising and stowing the missive in their sack. "There is a contact I must visit before we depart in the morning. Slumber, love, and remember you are precious." They met in a brief joining and he was through the oaken portal, an elusive breeze across her lips.

Descarta swayed, exhaustion calling her to the clutch of pillows. Dearly, she wished to flop amidst a sea of fluff and dreams. But she was denied that escape as insecurity crept into her bones without her sorcerer there. Groggy, she swung willowy legs over the bed, dangling them and surveying the room. A pearlescent shimmer filtered through the sole window, casting haunting shadows across the rented room. The homunculus knew there was nothing to be afraid of. No denizens of darkness would assail her. Still, a shiver took purchase on downy shoulders, and she avoided looking anywhere threatening. So her gaze settled on their pack and the parchment jutting from its mouth. She considered the folded missive and the startled response her call invoked in the scrawling weaver. He was abnormally hasty in his rendezvous, especially so considering how he hung over her just minutes before while savoring her scent.

Leaning forward, she squinted at the letter as if it would divine the message hidden there. No such feat was forthcoming. Descarta nibbled her bottom lip, nervousness doing its utmost to ground her rear. Yet there was the worry, too, that something was amiss with the weaver. As sure as cardiac clockwork, affection prevailed.

Descarta shuffled to the sack, plucked the paper and impatiently unfolded it. As she did, the diminutive dame thanked the Maiden for the lack of a seal. Hardened wax she would have surely broken in her eagerness. Her dimples sunk plaintively as she followed the dire calligraphy.

> *Descarta,*
>
> *Forgive me, my dear, for I must finish this voyage alone. My journey is of selfishness, to rescue girls who have been less than friendly with you. To ask you to accompany me into the den of Saradin for their sake would be reckless folly. If I feel my ribbon is jeopardized, I will retreat into the fabric's prison. I cannot return from the sanctuary, but it will enable you to live on.*
>
> *Room and board are paid, so give me a week. If I do not return, assume I never will. I have also left an assortment of precious gems, better than any singular currency, and suggest you use them to purchase a place for yourself far away. You will not wither or require maintenance for at least 150 years. When the time comes, you can consult my notes. You are astute—one of your bountiful endearing traits—so I am certain you can decrypt the formulae given time.*
>
> *You are a gift, my love. A gift I have had trouble unwrapping, but one which I treasure nonetheless. Never question your capacity to overcome, for you are the incarnation of everything awe-inspiring, and of my greatest wishes.*
>
> *Yours without end,*
> *Virgil*

Just below, the phrase "Sleep, love" was scratched in an offensive runic script. The words began a crawl across the page, prompting Descarta to blink and massage the weariness from her eyes. When she opened them, the ink had just brushed her thumb.

Emitting a shriek, she tossed the missive to the floor and took a wary step back. There was a prick, a tiny needle prodding at her digit. Wincing at the sting, the girl raised her hand and squinted at it. Arcane letters stuck there, gradually fading as if sinking into her being. She wavered then, enervation overcoming her and forcing the wobbly-kneed girl to the thick maroon carpet below.

"Damn you," she cursed Virgil for his insight. It would have made less sense if he hadn't the sagacity to prepare for contingencies. Exhaustion swept over her, a pulsing spur that injected drowsiness from its magical gland. Calmness claimed her, a poisonous serenity brewed in her fantasies, of being cradled by her creator while the stare of the high sun warmed her skin.

Descarta would not be subdued without a fight. She had been instructed by the very man whose residual will sought to conquer her, after all. And it was staggering, that such an oppressive force was woven into mere scribbles. The rising spellweaver clenched her jaw, forced her lids wide and floundered about—anything to keep herself awake. An onlooker would have mistaken her for a struggling fish out of water. The gland twitched, shooting another wave of subjugation into her frame. She snarled against the cresting tsunami and forged on, shoving at the pacifying embrace with all her willpower. The stab and parry persisted for heartbeats which seemed agonizing hours until she felt a wonderful thing. The pressure to sleep faltered and retreated. It snapped at its own tail, swallowing and swallowing until it consumed itself.

The homunculus ended the confrontation facing the ceiling, chest heaving and basking in her victory. It made her feel accomplished. That she had truly progressed under Virgil's tutelage. He would not have left the trap if he thought it would fail. Grunting, she rose and heaved the loaded sack onto her back. There would be time to slake her ego later, when Virgil could praise her—after she tore into him for the insult. Feet slipped into boots and she was gone, belongings bouncing against her as she descended the spiraling stairs and verily leapt from the inn.

Tenebrous night blanketed Vanathiel's aristocratic district, made more menacing by the organic spires which rose like dark behemoths around her. Through their supreme mastery of Aether magic, the elves had crafted a capitol embodying their long-lost spiritual closeness with nature. The arboreal constructs were as hollow as the denizens of the once hallowed land, lending goliath trunks to shelter its residents. In the day, a stroll through the district would be like following a cobblestone path through an ancient forest. Under the veil of twilight, however, it was hardly compelling. Hidden stares bore from every direction, and the trees towered as many-armed golems seeking to squash intruders.

Determined strides clapped against stone-studded causeways, ferrying her under the imposing canopy and rousing the late hour. Confident in her ability to thwart any enterprising elf who thought to sweep a tantalizing morsel, Descarta pressed onward. She knew the way to the zeppelin harbor, both out of experience and because the landing tower was a beacon against the lesser districts whose lanes were paralleled by more traditional structures.

The grim watch of barky colossi retreated to her rear, and she slowed her pace to a more controlled gait. Stark against the low skyline of the trade district, she peered at the zeppelin tower as she strode. Silhouetted against the starry sky, the great inky splotch was easily discerned. Luck was with her, for only one vessel had moored until morning. She wound through the empty passages with purpose, directing herself toward the sole spire in this section of the elven metropolis. Originally, Vanathiel was no more than the area composing the aristocratic district. As foreign policy changed, additions were made for wayfarers seeking shelter or trade. This transformed the sacred city in lasting ways. The most protrusive was the mottled framework of districts, erected one by one until the city was an amalgam of design.

Emerald embellished saber flapping on her hip, none sought to accost the hurried homunculus. The girl preferred to believe it was because her affinity for the biting end of the rich pommel was unmistakable.

In little time, Descarta emerged from the mortar and limestone throughways at the base of the boarding tower. She approached the iron steps with care, flinching with each ring of boot on metal. Warehouses, shops and homes shrunk into miniature replicas below, conjuring a familiar scene. When she first made the climb, the girl was fleeing Virgil and what she then thought were the horrors he forced her into. Much had changed since that dreary day when the rise never seemed to end, the ambivalent girl glancing wistfully over her shoulder with every few steps. Now she chased the sorcerer, the ancient man who had gifted her everything and asked nothing in return. Descarta did not reject what he'd become or look the other way when confronted with his countless misdeeds.

The evils—and she could not dispute their nature—were not innate to the villainous weaver. They were woven into his soul over time, sewn thread by thread for his fallen queen. And when the time for choice arrived, Ankaa's imprisoned soul was shred to slivers for Descarta. He sacrificed centuries of labor to crystalize her dissipating spirit. Whereupon all Virgil had endured was shifted to his diminutive blossom. She refused to allow him to brook this challenge alone; even if it was for the lecherous elves who, too, commanded his heart. She and Virgil shared an essence, literally. To Descarta, it was more than an issue of death, but of a visceral need to be beside the sorcerer, to support him in her own way.

"So, what will it be?" came a familiar pitch from the platform just above. She flinched, muscles going rigid at the thought of being caught. The voice belonged to Virgil, there was no doubt. Tentatively, she crawled upward, peeking over the uppermost rung. Across the platform, cargo was heaped in preparation for loading. The crates and barrels served as a wall, allowing her to creep to just beyond where Virgil parlayed. There hadn't been a response to his question until she pressed against a gilded iron chest which reeked of rust.

"I don't have a choice here, do I?" replied the addressed party in a distinctive elven drawl.

Descarta peered around her cover, thanking the moon for throwing her shadow behind the clutter. Virgil stood a stone's throw away, talons reaching out from his robe and ravening for the gnarled corpse just beyond their grasp. Paces ahead of the weaver sat a visibly shaken elf in the rugged trappings of a hardened sailor. Like most of his kin, he was handsome in an exotic way. Albeit, that comeliness was forfeit to a jagged picket of biters and an ear lopped off at the skull. Jade orbs hovered over his fallen companion, likely concerned less for the unlucky fellow than avoiding a similar demise. The area exuded the rainy stench of thaumaturgy, a clear indication that Virgil had loosed the spell whose wake was a headless cadaver. Like the flighty wards, she had grown fond of the scent, his scent.

"You do have a choice," Virgil replied, gesturing plaintively to the mutilated captain. "I advise against it, first officer. My offer is generous, is it not?"

The elf shifted his stare to a plump pouch which sat saturated in the captain's blood. "Very," agreed the officer. "Oh, to the Sundered with it. I'm freed of one bully and taken by another. You have relieved me of a great debt and offered payment, so that places you above the bastard in my view. Though I will reiterate his concern: the lords will not be pleased with the noise at this hour."

"They have no choice. Rouse the engines. I once served on a vessel much like your own, so I will assist in preparations." He kicked the jewel bag from its scarlet puddle into a jingling roll of jangling gemstones.

The elf scooped the tumbling pouch and bounced it in his palm. "It's a deal, then. I've long wanted my own ship."

"The zeppelin belongs to me until our voyage is over," clarified Virgil, already starting up the boarding ramp. "Bring the good captain to the deck. We'll pitch him over the Ignusian stretches."

"Aye," answered the freshly pinned captain. "But the mess?" he asked, grasping a limp ankle with both hands and tugging.

"I'm in a hurry," ordered the weaver from the deck. "Leave it. You've plenty to bribe meddlesome inquisitors."

Descarta waited until the crewman disappeared onto the deck and dashed from the rusty chest. She bolted from cover to cover, taking care to favor the shadows and avoid casting her own. Then she reached her target: an oversized mooring chain, anchored taught to the platform. Ten feet separated her and the shaft where the chain disappeared into the vessel. It was there, she knew, that had to be her point of entry. As long as the pernicious fall didn't swallow her up, she would have secured her place aboard the late night zeppelin.

...

They quivered under his stare. The generously applied sedative afforded them little more. A scowl had drawn his countenance in disappointment and frustration. "Why are they here?" questioned Hazael, tone commanding the venom of his mood.

"They are my prisoners," explained Josiah, well aware of the hazardous promontory he teetered upon. "I have not treated them poorly, and I've contracted our best weavers to attend to their condition."

Hazael kneeled, lavender cloak bunching around him in a regal spume. He wore the vestments of his position well, and considered his reign as patriarch of Elusia heretofore fruitful. The realm had begun a steady recovery since he administered the poultice he and Virgil had devised to return the kingdom to prosperity. Yet this did not fit into his scheme, or Virgil's. The elves would surely suffer here, eventually perish. Moreover, he was incensed that his seneschal would go to such lengths, especially without permission. "Almi and Merill cannot be cured," retorted the sovereign while examining the twins. They seemed to be in perfect health, though he was sure that would change the second their sedative thinned. "Now answer me. And pray it is a tale both convincing and comedic. Because this scenario speaks to me, and I do not like its story. Come then, bard."

Josiah was a master of lies. To be a bard meant to sew them into reality, to embellish the truth enough to make it fantastical, to sway men. Yet the king always had a way of penetrating that façade, and the rogue knew it would be unwise to anger Hazael further. "Violah came to me," replied Josiah. "She explained she wanted to eliminate Virgil, that he was a threat to your security as our leader. I knew his location."

"So you set off without notifying me to usurp a personal pact I'd made with the man?" The sovereign shook his head. Violah tried too hard to gain his favor, something she already had. He wished she could see that, instead of pursuing increasingly outlandish attempts at pleasing him.

"She said you wouldn't have it."

"The woman was right. And you knew it." Hazael reached to pet Merill whose sanguine orbs lolled about as he stroked her hair. He didn't think himself attached to the creatures until his role as king, when he found their catlike capering a missing distraction in the humdrum monotony of the Saradin ramparts. "They were your reward, then. Where is she?"

"Plundering his manuals and artifacts, I assume. We commissioned two zeppelins. When I left, her craft was moored."

Hazael heaved a great sigh, expelling the tension that gripped his muscles. Everything about this was wrong. Virgil gave him a second chance, adopted him when he would have been an orphaned runt to an uprooted royal family. The weaver changed his destiny and offered Hazael a grab at a throne rightfully his. The imperial cast off wasn't proud of the corruption he helped to spread, but it was all for the greater good. He had stripped malign beasts from their role as malefactor kings and cleansed a kingdom befouled by its shepherds.

None of this would have been possible if Virgil hadn't plucked him from the catastrophe of his house's downfall. Even if the sorcerer was a false savior, a creature of opportunism, he still felt indebted to the ancient man. The exchange was fair: utmost desire for servitude. And Hazael was hardly treated as a slave during his centuries of tenure under Virgil. Instead, he learned to seize what he wanted and, more importantly, how to do so. Virgil was his mentor once, but now he was something far more precious, irreplaceable, an old friend.

The king rose, gathering the foamy mantle about him. His cropped platinum cut had grown into a ruler's mane that curled about his chin attractively. "You have full access to any resources necessary to heal those two. Virgil gave it an earnest attempt, but I owe it to him to try." He started toward the wrought iron slab of their cell but stopped beside Josiah. The rogue flinched, fully expecting a wealth of retribution. "You were made my steward as a trustworthy partner. I will have to rethink that."

"Your liege, I—"

"Quiet," interrupted Hazael, commanding an impervious authority. "Send Violah to my chambers when she returns. And if I find you have mistreated those two, I will have you flayed and hung." The saturnine sire left then, thick metal portal giving a shout as it slammed shut behind him. He drifted there, in the low light of the dank dungeon, and shook.

A part of him—the seneschal whose dearest cohort was an insidious tyrant—curled in on itself like an abject child hugging its knees. Hazael had hoped to restore Elusia to its prime, to a state not unlike that which Kalthused so valiantly carved. Beyond his vindication, though, he wanted Virgil to one day return to the reinvigorated realm. Now, it was impossible.

Worse, perhaps, was the hurdle he yet faced. Violah was hardheaded, unmoving in her strides to prove her worth as his mademoiselle. Her proficiency in weaving was second only to Virgil, something Hazael often pointed out to her when she arrived with her latest trophy. She made this much evident in defending Elusia during the clash five years prior. The encounter may have been planned, but her might in curbing the invaders could not have been fabricated. Truly, no resident of Elusia doubted her prowess, and they were all enamored by her. The woman had played a key role in administering the blight's antidote and easing the burden of reconstruction. Among his subjects, there was even enthusiastic talk of a sorceress queen to wed the king.

Given that, the king feared what he would think of her when she returned. Because now, he knew only scorn and betrayal.

...

Descarta likened her nervous breathing to the subtlety of a boar. Wheezing machinery clanged and complained behind her, fully drowning her heavy inhalations. The cover was apparent to the girl; yet she could scarcely remove her stomach from its mire of knots. Her vantage told the homunculus he was sleeping now, leaning against the aft of the airborne ship. Only a wooden door separated her from him, and its warped boards hardly did that. The diminutive maiden delayed there, focusing on the reliable rise and fall of a slumbering creature and the patched robe of a once venerated position. The stitching was her handiwork, while Almi and Merill had provided the constituents for dye. The result wasn't flattering—not that her captivating crow needed it. Their patchwork operation represented what they strived for, a return to glory. Like the repair, it wasn't perfect, but they had introduced stability to a man dominated by fractures.

Somewhere within the recollection, she had marshaled her courage and reached for the exit. The porcelain arm froze in its extension, white-knuckled, fingers curled anxiously into her moist palm. The sudden shift wasn't due to faltering resolve, but a looming shadow that blotted the glow of the dangling ivory satellite above. Virgil appeared like a phantom, occupying space that was, until that second, empty. "You shouldn't be here," he said, somewhere between a grating rasp and a snarl—condemning, whichever it was. "Do you wish to die?"

Descarta parted her lips to reply, to spew some vicious retort, but stopped short, snapping her mouth shut and feeling very nonplussed. The irritation that followed his timbre didn't please her. She bristled at the greeting, not an apology or a request for forgiveness. It wasn't at all what she expected, what she sought to demand.

"Very well, then," he muttered, taking a step back and targeting her with an outstretched palm.

A familiar density steeped in front of Descarta, reeking of ozone and sulfur: the precursor to weaving, when the fabric was plucked and brought to the surface. "Virgil! Don't do it! I'm sorry!" She thrust the door open and burst through, toppling the stunned weaver over. The fall ended with her atop the weaver, wispy remnants of barely contained thaumaturgy emanating from singed fingertips. "That's too harsh, Virgil," she choked, trying desperately to pacify the anguish tearing at her chest. Descarta had undermined his will, and he had intended on enacting punishment for her irreverence. But to set her aflame—it was too draconian, even for him.

"Des," spoke the supine sorcerer in a timbre far more gentle. "I thought you were a stowaway or assassin." He moved to stroke her arm, to caress her tenseness away. Instead, his charred touch burned like hot coal on her delicate flesh. She yelped a pained shriek and rolled away, ending on her knees.

Descarta clutched her smoking arm, staring at him with mortified eyes. "First you abandon me. Now this?!" she shouted. Venom started her words, a brew strengthened by the fear of abandonment, by betrayal and by rage. "How could you do this, Virgil? How? Do you think you can play the hateful demon and push me away again? Well, you can't! I know you now!" The shivering girl sobbed, auburn drapes obscuring her downcast visage as she spilled drops of torment to the deck below. "This . . . this isn't you," she sputtered between torso-wracking pouts.

Virgil crawled to her, sitting just before the girl and taking in the lamentable scene. He could be certain his dainty dear was emotionally shaken when she arrived. It was only natural, having been cast off with a mere farewell letter. That she was there at all troubled him a great deal and catalyzed manifold worries he had meant to avoid by leaving her to the relative safety of Vanathiel. More pressing was her quaking form, for he didn't value her enmity. Taking care to sheath his fire-touched fingertips, he nudged her chin with his knuckle, gingerly pulling her amber-speckled windows upward. They were brilliant gates into a roiling core, incandescent with the girl's insurmountable vigor. He offered a plaintive grin, apologetic in its lure, and spoke to her. "Forgive me, dear. Truncating the weaving at its peak, well . . ." He angled his hand to illustrate. "It wasn't intentional, I swear."

Meekly, she squinted at the display and gradually understood the situation. Then her fury resurfaced, liberated by the release of anguish. Issuing a growl, she pushed over the weaver and mounted his stomach. "How could you abandon me? Don't you love me?!" she scolded, accentuating the incisive inquiry with a strike to his sternum.

Virgil didn't attempt to deflect or block the blow. He refused to risk burning her once more. "Des," he coughed, "I did what was right for you. Only that. Which meant—"

"No!" the homunculus shouted, driving home another abusive fist. "You went too far! When you performed that vile ritual, you gave me free will! You instructed me to follow a path true to myself! And now you expect me to kneel when it matters most?! I will not! My heart is forfeit without you, so it will perish or prosper at your side! No place else!"

Frowning, the weaver regretted not taking more stringent precautions; he hadn't expected her to overcome the trap. The minor incantation should have been enough given his inherent influence over his creation. Rationality reached for him. He strummed at its rejoinders, and ultimately tossed them all. What would they mean to her, someone beset by a spirit as real and intractable as his own? Resignation overcame him, and he groaned at the throbbing which gripped his sternum and ribs. "You should be napping now. The spell should have taken you to your most favored dream." Grinning mischievously, he teased the homunculus in an attempt to deflect her turmoil. "A world dominated by lust and sweat, I imagine."

"It tried," said Descarta, dimples taking her cheeks despite herself. "I'm very stubborn." The turbulence that had taken her began to melt away under his reassuring proximity.

"And there was nothing naughty about it! It was wholesome!" she contested. Blushing, she eased her tawny tangles to his robe, a sleepless night finally catching up to her. "You're a bad man," she muttered as she pulled in a lungful of his scent. Relief captured her with its natural sedation, and weary lids began their steady descent. "But you're my bad man," she murmured from her dream borne chariot. "And you cannot leave me."

She was secure, once again moored to the spellcaster.

CHAPTER THIRTEEN

Of Elves and Appetites

The sparkling iridescence of starlight had faded. The world above was suspended in the clear and brilliant shine of early afternoon. A plateau-spotted, orange-hued domain stretched to the horizon, the zeppelin having covered ground far quicker than any landbound locomotion. Now that Ignus was below them, the flight was well underway. Virgil reflected on this, giving his weight to the aft barrier.

He'd submitted to Descarta's hidebound demand, conjured a grin that assured she would remain his side-stitched loveling. Yet he was already stirring the cauldron, brewing ways to deposit her once again in the tranquil repose of safety.

"Morning," murmured the drowsy damsel who dominated his thoughts. She approached the weaver and slipped her slender wing under his. Descarta let Virgil take the feathery weight of her chassis, emitting a contented hum against his robe.

"It's still early," said the sorcerer. "Rest a slight longer."

The tiny girl issued a moan, sweeping her head from side to side against his back. "I ache from the deck. And you aren't there to catch sleep for me."

"You chose the spot," reminded Virgil, taking care not to poison the retort by reminding her that she could be sprawled among downy pillows and tangled in a storm of silky sheets if she'd only obeyed him.

"Stop that," slurred the hardly awake homunculus. "Pillows and sheets are no good without you."

Addled, Virgil furrowed his brow and rose from his roost atop the bulwark. "I didn't mention any of that."

Descarta released a drained grunt, reverie approaching from her robed nest. "I heard it," she replied almost inaudibly. "Don't say what you don't want heard."

"What did you hear?" interrogated Virgil, turning to her and clutching her arms.

The petite spellsword whined her disapproval of being uprooted in a series of whimpers. "Downy pillows and a storm of silky sheets." A weary head-butt to the chest followed, and she verily collapsed against him. "Let me rest on you."

Willfully, Virgil eased his bushed parcel down to the rail. She wiggled into a comfortable nook, half strewn across his lap; a habit stolen from the eccentric elves.

Their peculiar dementia struck Virgil more stridently than usual. In particular, the strange way elven twins could, at times, communicate mentally due to their uncommon connection. Virgil twanged the thought, awed at the revelations its frequency imparted. It was not inconceivable she'd developed extrasensory perception under circumstances nearly identical to elven twins. They were joined just as the twins were: bound by their married ribbons.

Almi and Merill, bubbling and hopeless, surged once more to the forefront of his mind. The pool which stirred there was so wrought with unrest that he lapsed in his brooding over the wards. Every moment was one too many, an hour dawdled was an hour they could have been tortured, beaten or worse.

He'd failed the sparky sisters. He had repaid their adamant affection with oscillating attention, their fervent fascination with lonely evenings. Virgil had sent them away, sought to remove them like pests he couldn't bear to exterminate. He'd sacrificed them in favor of the maiden now occupying their beloved nook. To add acid to the wound, he'd rebuked them for toying with her mere moments before he watched powerlessly as they were stolen away. It was detestable recompense for a pair of girls who had engineered his recovery by gifting him their sweet lullaby on the nights when agony flared in his ruptured mind.

And he was certain their prime objective was to return to him, regardless the cost. The weaver made a mess of his raven hair, blowing a disgruntled sigh as he did.

"We're going to rescue them," issued Descarta from her perch, nestled within his obsidian mantle.

Virgil craned his neck to cast at her, and the golden-brown answer keenly projected her concern. The shining stare had just returned from a brief hunt for flufftail sheep, ducts sandy from chasing their dusty lope. Even if she was abnormally sensitive to his thoughts, it didn't take augmented perception to augur his discord. Still, he found "rescue" a dubious description for what he had embarked upon.

Almi and Merill suffered perpetually, ever wound within feelings of insufficiency and the looming nightmare of being cast aside. "I can never rescue them," he mused dolorously. "Only do what little I can to diminish their suffering." Virgil vented his grief in a thick outbreath. "Rescuing them would have been cutting their throats and leaving the pair in their bed of slaughterhouse entrails."

"What's that mean?" asked the homunculus, shifting uncomfortably under his censuring stare.

"You know, Des."

"But I don't," she explained, confusion drawing her drowsy countenance. "You never told me," she reminded him. "Only that they're your wards."

There was no way she'd know. He'd stripped her of the knowledge when he rendered her an artificial amnesiac.

"Sorry, dear," Virgil said as he chiseled his lips into a smile for her. She was as precious as the twins were, and granted her own special magic. He reached for the girl and hugged her to his midnight robe.

Fidgeting in his embrace, Descarta peered up at him, nap-touched gaze piercing with its invitation to a delightful future. "What's this for?"

"You're brilliant," said Virgil, kneading her back appreciatively. "An enchanting luckling, and I'd be remiss to leave you without praising the beauty I beheld."

The homunculus produced a bewildered stare, tapping her fingers accusingly on his chest. "You're doting, Virgil. What are you trying to get out of me?"

"Nothing, nothing," he honestly replied, running a relaxing circuit back and forth over her flank. "I don't want my distant demeanor to harm you."

"Oh, I'm fine," she responded, weariness escaping with a lasting yawn. Playfully, she tugged at his patchwork robe. "But just in case you had any ideas, I'll have no safety words being thrown about, you flatterer." Descarta sought his sapphire spheres, lips curled and satisfied by her teasing.

What she found there was a stirring coruscation, a boiling desire that bubbled over and threatened to swallow her up. Her obsidian repose rose and fell with the ferocious breaths of an angered beast. "V-Virgil," she protested. "I was only fooling—" Then a familiar sensation brushed her thigh at skirt's end. The black lace of her viridian pinafore retreated from his magically infused digits, a cosset that issued permeating warmth. "Virgil," came her second protest, a mirthless objection whose syllables were as crippled as her will to resist.

As the cinder-sown touch crept higher and eased its evocative claws under her dress, all resistance scattered like a fleeing flock of flutterflies. A burning conquered her frame, bored into her core, and she flushed crimson. Descarta retreated into the arousing fragrance of his robe, hiding her embarrassment while further parting budding hips in invitation.

He teased her, skirting over the highly responsive border between her thighs and where she most wanted him.

Descarta stiffened and pressed her hips forward, whimpering from her hideaway. Sleepiness had lost and lust made her its marionette, pulling at the strings that engaged a pleading grind. She yearned for the lascivious, unspeakable performance he oft enthralled her with; to once again be rendered captive to soul-wracking pleasure. She rocked more furiously then, seeking the slightest brush along her craving mound. The impassioned homunculus emerged from her nook to pout at the controlling weaver. He brimmed with hunger, a viciousness Descarta knew he was containing for the delightful moment when he would ravage her. "M-Master me," she breathed seductively, anxiousness leaking forth.

Virgil rewarded his lace-wrapped little one by slipping a finger between her honey-slickened cleft. The sorcerer danced within her, navigating charted waters like an experienced captain. She shook then, hazelnut locks jostling about as her writhing intensified. Emboldened by the unquenchable inferno in her gut, she reached to squeeze the torrid shaft beneath his robe. "I must have it," she begged between ragged breaths, the audible cry of readiness between her legs giving credence to the plea.

When he nodded his consent, she beamed with wanton appreciation and fumbled with eagerness to unbutton the barrier between her and engorged satisfaction. Lean muscles greeted her with each unclasped button, their serpentine sinews exciting the forge in her mid-section. What she unearthed there was mere embers before the inferno that seized her furnace when his fiery brand was set free.

Descarta expelled an unsteady breath, alabaster hips shaking from Virgil's constant probing. Then she leaned forward and rewarded herself with the mouth-watering rigidness she pined for. Her tongue appreciated its length, rising from the base to the tip and flicking at the delicious, salty dew that accumulated there.

The spellweaver emitted a rapt groan as his diminutive love gorged on his manhood. Descarta changed when she wished to be used—transformed into a nymph whose kiln was insatiable. And Virgil found the alteration spellbinding. The way she feverishly hummed against his rigid shaft, dancing about its length with her agile tongue. Her labored breaths were like velvet along the sensitive skin, and her molten depths called to be devoured in similar voracity.

Virgil retreated from her nectar steeped hive, eliciting a stifled protest from the girl. She paused feasting then. A gossamer thread suspended from her quivering bottom lip as she cast anxiously at the sorcerer. Her sex engine persisted, willowy limbs straightening and parting to a lusty rhythm implanted by invasive fingers. "Stand, dear," he commanded, and his magnum opus obediently put quaking legs beneath her with the reflexive immediacy of a girl trained.

She was the blossom who flourished in their efflorescent joining of egos, so Descarta made it as much a part of her as breathing or eating. Her Virgil would despoil her throughout, render the girl ravaged as kingdoms in his maleficent wake. And she would revel in her role as his willing victim.

The radiant girl edged forward, trembling elatedly. She draped a quavering thigh over Virgil's shoulder, bracing a weakened knee around the sitting man's upper back. Having presented her bare womanly center, the orange-brown panorama of Ignus confronted her prurient pose. Fleetingly, she worried some voyeuristic wayfarer enjoyed her exhibition from the terrain below. Fleeting, because articulation vanished when Virgil took ravenous purchase on her heated bottom with the controlling bite of a predator feeding. Draped over his raven-topped scalp, her lace-festooned pinafore was the hiked curtain to a performance that set its lone audience ablaze. Descarta took the fervidly working head in both hands and entangled shivering digits in his dark mane while she reeled at the frenzy betwixt her hips.

Beneath the canopy, an entrancing scent bound Virgil to her candy coating. Sucked, supped and stroked, her saccharine folds were smothered by his appetite. His mouth enveloped her savory syrup, relentlessly dining on the most ambrosial of meals. She would shudder, emit a kittenlike mew and seize up with each pass his delicious expedition took over her swollen little hill. Delightful were those moments when her rear would spasm and draw taut under his fingertips, nails nipping his scalp and seductively slung porcelain leg become rigid under his ministrations.

Administering a final kiss, the weaver tugged Descarta by the waist, maneuvering his slender sparrow to his lap, where she collapsed against him.

Descarta huffed, drawing fingertips over the scorched flesh that dominated his torso. Still ensorcelled by the sopping stimulation, she ground against him like a wind-up doll. "Virgil," she mumbled, besieged by deliriousness. "Inside me ... I ..."

Virgil infiltrated her filigree-banded skirt, trained hands travelling familiar contours as he stripped his treat of her gossamer packaging. She flushed a rosy grin and timidly covered her modest bosom, a point of insecurity for the wiry girl. Dependably, Virgil dispelled her fear by prying her arms from pink-tipped breasts and leaning forward to kiss at the downy pendants. Self-doubt dissolved, her hip-oscillations intensified, pleasuring herself on his defined washboard.

Diminutive chassis swaying, she peeled his singular garment over sinewy shoulders and pleasantly controlling arms leaving him as bare as she. Her tiny chest heaved under his suckling, attentive lips and grasping hands that dug possessively into her rear. Drunk with carnal craving, Descarta longed for him, required he fill her nethermost passion. Surrounded by the tempest of his libidinous heat, she could comprehend nothing further.

As if sensing her rising tension, Virgil's stimulating gauntlets left her swaying rump. A great pressure lanced her quivering entrance and she utterly froze. This remained the only trying step for Descarta. Her dainty physique was still growing accustomed to his throbbing girth.

"Be . . . gentle . . ." the homunculus whimpered before emitting a wounded squeal. He'd taken her by the shoulders and forced her to the base of his swollen promontory, and it to her womb. Her strained entrance flared its agonized objection, shrieked at being stretched beyond capacity—a small voice amid the overjoyed arousal that crashed into her stuffed core. If anything, the striking ache heightened her erotic hypnosis, augmented it such that her hips began a feverish foxtrot. A machine powered by unchained yearning, they jerked wildly against his pulsating shaft.

Descarta clung with zeal to her patriarch of pleasure. Pressing her bare porcelain chest against his, she caught the weaver's cerulean scrutiny, and the visceral power there corrupted her most brilliantly. Higher thought was relinquished to a muddled fog of salacious abandon, lusty grinding evolving into a piston-like frenzy. Teary eyes stared absently, her senses converging on the overwhelming churning that began in her hearth and spread like wildfire to dominate her glistening frame. His controlling claws were all over her, touching, simulating, invading every part of her at once. The enthralled nymph wound her legs sensuously around his waist, pulling him farther into her aching tunnel. Ecstatic shouts sputtered off the writhing homunculus' bliss-twisted tongue as mindless gibberish, clarion only in their raw revels.

Virgil entered her damp hazelnut tapestry where his parted maw found a blazing neck, littering the succulent flesh with hungry kisses. Her smoldering fireplace was unbearably tight, and its rocking constrictions enveloped his length with her slick elixir. The crazed delicacy wheezed husky breaths and incoherent stammering into his ear—a descent into corporeal purity that she'd learned to cherish after a year in his lap.

He could tame it no more.

A guttural growl announced Virgil's uncaged fury. Invigorated, he threw his dazed confectionery to her back. The tiny thing moaned from her trance, unremitting in her vehement gyrations, as if she'd never left his lap. She needn't worry, though, for Virgil was immediately on her, conquering his creation.

With animalistic roughness, he pinned wiry legs to her heaving chest and furiously ravaged her. The new position was deep, too deep, and she felt as though he was hammering her stomach. Screeching at his merciless bludgeoning, reality caught her and she rolled onto her shoulder to crawl away.

Snarling, Virgil snapped the lass back into place, pressing his weight into her.

"It's too—" she cried, before Virgil reentered her and conscripted all of his might into drilling the trapped girl. She didn't know whether to thrash at the keen beating she endured or swoon at the unexplainable delight it imparted. Ultimately, she did both, returning to the realm of maddening lust while squirming and howling under his especially potent blows.

Under his ministrations, heaven always found Descarta.

...

Descarta stirred within her feather-stuffed duvet, a fluffy wrapping stolen from cargo that'd never reach its destination. The girl fished for her companion and emitted a dissatisfied mumble. She was the lone occupant of the insulated repose for two. Drowned by drowsiness, she reasoned he was out entertaining his elven wards. They were reliably tenacious, coaxing him into an early stroll with each rising sun. Skipping about merrily, they would explore, gawk and shine, hands in his.

"Let them have it," she grumbled, tossing about. Descarta's schedule was idyllic: burrowing into a cozy den until Virgil bade her awake. A kiss, perfectly pressed, upon her head, and he would deliver dawn through an encircled yawn.

The atmosphere of flight found her nose then, an airy scent she recognized after years in its company. With it reality arrived: lazy days shattered by snatchers and assassins.

Casting about sleepily, she spotted the shadowy silhouette belonging to her missing sorcerer. The ascending sun set his outline with an orange glow and highlighted his dark mantle in a strange accord. To Descarta, the roles always seemed switched. In its relentless rise, the morning flare welcomed Virgil; in exchange, he warmed the creature.

She tightened the duvet around her bare frame and rose to approach his side. A residual ache throbbed in her belly, a persistent reminder of the tempestuous day before.

"You should rest, Virgil." She leaned against him, craning to peer at his sun-bathed features. Virgil kissed her head with the lips of dawn and she couldn't help but call it peculiar. He knew his kiss roused her; yet he hadn't abstained before leaving the night prior. Had he counted on her joining all along? Descarta would not pry. He would not answer. Still, she couldn't help but ponder whether he nudged her toward certain scenarios with circuitous tactics.

"I have managed on less," came his gloomy reply. "Besides," he began, before his voice failed to melancholy and his countenance grew distant.

Virgil's reticence mattered not, for his toxic lichen remained. Its caustic tail coiled around her, delivering unspoken boiling. The weaver had stirred to take Almi and Merill on their daily trot. The eccentric wards were, of course, missing. So he replaced their satin grip with the rigid bulwark, a thicket's din with an empty Ignusian sky.

"We'll rescue them," assured Descarta, giving him a nudge.

"Rescue them?" Virgil scoffed, adopting an exhausted scowl. "Where the twins are involved, there is no rescue."

Descarta frowned, absorbing his sodden aura. His murky response was baffling, a morass she did not appreciate. "Tell me," she demanded with puffed cheeks and wrinkled brow. "If we aren't rescuing them, what are we doing?"

The brooding sorcerer heaved a listless sigh. Displacing one torture with a lesser alternative was hardly rescue. What label could he issue the cause, where a dampening was all he imparted?

"Virgil?" pressed the diminutive girl from his side, knuckles prying the sleep from her lids. "Tell me."

"Don't worry yourself, dear."

The fluff-padded lass grunted, illustrating her discontent by bumping against the weaver. "You can't make these decisions alone," she scratched at his distance. "I care about them, too. Now why wouldn't we rescue Almi and Merill?"

Virgil pivoted to face her and offered a solemn half-grin. "It's good you care," he muttered. He regarded her lovingly, placing weary palms on her neck with the care one would show a priceless artifact. With that beholden touch his thumbs caressed her just below the jaw. "Almi and Merill are unique," he explained. "Wretchedly so."

Descarta wore a glum pout, witnessing his transition from saturnine to hopeless. His narrowed cerulean gaze penetrated her, locked in a contest with demons. "What is it?" she asked in a pacifying timbre, slipping a hand from the cocoon to cover his forearm.

"I cannot save them. They are eternally cursed to love no other. A beast whose heart, after hearing their bewildering confession, has always been elsewhere, unfeeling." He put forth another languid grin and let his hands fall, turning back to the vermillion panorama. "You know this much."

Infuriated, Descarta abandoned the duvet and snatched his wrist, spinning the weaver back to her firm glare. "How can you say such a thing?!" she fumed, before modesty returned with a shriek. Flushed scarlet, she scrambled to cover herself, pulling the blanket under her arms. The homunculus continued, anger tempered by embarrassment. "I-It isn't true." Clutching and fumbling at the fabric's edge, she suspended it just below her shoulders and captured his stare.

"Why are you awake, Virgil? Whose sake is it for?" Building confidence, she stepped forward, craning her neck to look up at the silent sorcerer. "Without exception, you join them every morning. You do it because you feel, do you not? Because to Almi and Merill, hopelessly attached or not, those few hours when you see only their faces are priceless."

"It isn't—"

"Listen, Virgil," she said, pressing on. "When you return, you are never downtrodden. You are refreshed, despite your complaints when they wake you. How, then, could they possibly be cursed? To delight in your company is one thing, but to know those walks benefit you . . . Virgil, that is what they've wanted, what they've found and what you falsely claim they'll never have: mutual affection."

The weaver did not contest her argument; he couldn't. Scorned as abominations by their kin, the pair exhibited an admiration for nature most elves had long forgotten in favor of city dwelling. Virgil considered it an ironic twist, a gift of purity among their fractured minds. And his hidebound homunculus was right. He favored the jaunts.

It began soon after Descarta returned, and Virgil figured ascribing the tradition to a need for attention was not incorrect. Whether by weaseling under the covers or yawning and wiggling from their nighttime nest, they never failed to rouse him. The weaver would object as they did whatever it took to drag him along. But when Almi and Merill accompanied him on springy heels he settled appreciatively into their course.

"You've always been strong willed," he mused, encircling the girl in a raven-robed hug and pressing his forehead to hers. Descarta was smooth against his arms, and he couldn't resist tracing adoring circles just below her downy dorsal. "What happened to that apprehension when we're close, dear? You aren't shivering at all."

Descarta brightened under his doting, excited not only that he didn't refute her assertion, but that he noticed the change. She wondered if her trepidation had been trivial, if he'd think her childish for imposing limitations on her own happiness. "Well, I . . ." Feeling sillier by the second, Descarta dipped her chin to hide her face. "Until you convinced me otherwise, I thought I'd deserted you. And in doing so became a person you couldn't love, one who didn't deserve you. The shaking, the uneasiness . . . it was punishment, I think."

Virgil clutched his Pygmalion project and gave her a reassuring squeeze. "You should have told me, dear. I've always held you in the highest regard. A bastion of beauty and intellect, my only lamentation was that you'd never accept me."

"You!" Descarta blushed, seeking the cover of his mottled mantle. "You can't say such things so nonchalantly!" The recluse expelled a breath of contentment then, feeling very at home within her obsidian alcove. "Thank you," she whispered against her weaver. "My greatest fear was that you wouldn't accept me."

Virgil shook his head. "I would not scorn my lovelet. Besides, I should be the one thanking you. Those years abroad have fortified your inner strength. Without that, who would I have to right me at times like these?"

"I said stop!" complained Descarta, sinking further into her hideaway. "It's terribly embarrassing."

"It is truth. I suppose I should have shown Hafstagg more gratitude for raising you where I could not."

"I'll never forget that man," said Descarta. "He was an oaf, but he protected me. He taught me how to wield a saber, how to survive. But his greatest aid was elsewhere. During the lonesome nights without you, he would visit and make me well."

It was Virgil's turn to blush, and he did—bristling in boiling rage. "What did he do to you?!"

"V-Virgil h-he," the homunculus stumbled. "I can't b-believe! Hafstagg didn't touch me! Not once!" Exasperated, she butted his chest, huffing. "On those evenings, he settled me with his chronicles of traveling as your guard." She paused, digging further, to her castle days. "I owe him much. But Virgil, without you I would not be here today. You laid the foundation for everything I am, in ways I still haven't fully appreciated. His tales helped me see as much."

His blossom's praise made Virgil proud, diminished long-seated ignominy. He'd made myriad mistakes in her treatment, and ever dreaded they would persist as irreversible blemishes of his inexperience. "You're chatty today. Did I happen to rattle something loose?" Virgil tapped at her bare back with his fingertips. "Perhaps I should administer a thorough check-up."

Descarta gasped, ducking free of her nook and scampering to her pinafore. "You're such a lewd man! I was being nice!" she whined, slipping into the emerald and black dress under veil of her duvet. "So lewd!" she shot from her tent. "A vile tease!"

Virgil grinned at the amorphous ball of cloth and flesh. They both knew she enjoyed the attention. "Are you sure I shouldn't investigate? You're so irresistibly toothsome," he joked before beginning a slow creep to the dressing lass. When he had nearly reached her, teeth deviously exposed and claws outstretched, the tempest stalled.

"Virgil," she solemnly muttered. "I'm afraid."

"Afraid? Dear, I'm only toying with you. You needn't be afraid," said Virgil, perplexed by her sudden shift. Had he went too far? No, that couldn't be; this was common between them.

"What if we're too late? They could be enduring torture while we enjoy ourselves." The girl peeked from her cover, strained countenance seeking reassurance. Virgil thought she looked smaller then, swallowed by the gloomy duvet. The same worries would have claimed him if she wasn't around to obscure the virulent doubt. But Descarta was far from inviolable herself.

"They'll manage," he said, the placating lie invoking a past better left within the rotting, pot-marked shell it inhabited. "They've been through far, far worse." A smile, broken and shallow, came forth to give substance to his promise.

Descarta peered at the weaver, piercing the farce without effort. Grief lived there, called his vacant stare and feigned sincerity home. "Far worse?" she asked.

"The past," shrugged Virgil, returning to his typical reticent disposition.

Descarta absently fumbled with the confectionary lace around her dress. "Tell me of them."

"Some things should never be revisited."

"Virgil," insisted the girl, "please. They're . . . my dearest friends, and I want to understand them." Fists clenched, she sat resolute. "Teach me of them."

The sorcerer emitted a resigned sigh. There was no point in resisting when she was like this. "Sometimes it is better to not know." With another sigh, he ventured into the dreadful archives.

...

"Your Majesty, sir, most honored," the nasal voice of a chintzy elf called from Virgil's side. "If I may have a moment of your time, sire. Evenstar."

Hazael made the subtle movement that placed his palm on the hilt of his blade while Virgil appraised the bejeweled fingers of the unctuously bowing elf. "Do I know you?" he asked.

"Oh, I would not expect you to, sire!" rattled the tawdry figure. "But I assure you, Ginyern has been at your service for years. Served you well indeed. Waiter." He punctuated the last sentence by fluttering his ringed digits.

"Served yourself, I see," scowled the king. "Tell me what you want before I show how little gratitude I have for these unnamed services."

The elf cast about nervously, darting a scrutinizing gaze at every shadow. "In the past, I've secured artifacts for your procurers. And I have something . . . perishable that may interest you. Fruit."

"There is a reason," spat Virgil, "they contact you—not me." The sorcerer hadn't missed the peculiar speech pattern employed by the elf. Someone had tinkered with this one's thoughts. Blunt objects weren't exactly surgical tools.

Ginyern nodded. "I know circumspection. I haven't fared this long by upsetting kings. Arbalest. Which is why I would not approach you if it weren't worth the risk." The elf held his hands wide, signaling his good intentions. "No daggers here, sire."

"Elsewhere, I'm sure," arrived the sovereign's rejoinder. "To the point, elf."

"A rarity, sire, I assure you. Oh, they are precious," Ginyern commented, a devious grin taking his lips. "Hoarding."

"Out with it," groaned the mage. "I have neither the time nor the patience to deal with your ... whatever it is you're doing."

"I cannot say here, sire. Lingering ears wish to hear," Ginyern explained, utilizing the alleyspeak turned elven proverb. "If you'll follow me, they're but a short distance. Boots." With that, the rogue stepped aside and executed an extravagant sweep of his studded phalanges. "The den is this way, sire," he said, indicating a seedy side street. "This way."

The expression Hazael offered made his opinion clear: he thought the king crazy to not simply ignore the hustling elf and proceed to their meeting. Virgil contested the disapproval with a look of his own, one of defiance. "You'll protect your dainty king, no? That's what grumpy stewards do."

Hazael didn't even bother arguing; he was well aware of the futility. Instead, he unsheathed his vorpal companion and equipped a most disgruntled grimace. "Let's get this over with."

To the credit of Ginyern, his warehouse was a quick stroll away and suffered no assassin infestation. Rodents and roaches, however, were bountiful. "I don't use this one often myself, so I don't keep it in order," he explained. "Should hire some urchins. Catfish." Working through a series of locks, he swung open the warehouse door to release a draft of rotten everything.

"I've followed you this far. Now tell me why you've brought me here," ordered the sovereign, peering tentatively into the dimly lit structure. "Enough fooling around."

"Twins," muttered the elf, growing very fidgety. "Elven twins. And alive. Now please, come in. Before someone overhears. Worms."

Virgil squinted in an effort to discern the seedy salesman's features under the poor light. The elf was either mortified or a practiced actor. If the dealer was telling the truth, the former was very likely. Though if he wasn't lying, that he was still alive spoke wonders for his cunning. Elves born as twins were to be executed both by Vanathiel law and religious edict. Following the dogma of elves, twins were a result of consorting with the undergods and if allowed to reach puberty, would bloom into harbingers of the end times. The true purpose behind this was that elven twins share a spirit. While they are capable of living independently, if one dies, the pair dies. This created a multitude of problems for which the elves resorted to cannily threading a solution into their prime religion. "Very well," he muttered after finally deciding to entertain the idea that the greasy thug wasn't stringing him along. The rarity of the reward would be worth the gamble.

With the sovereign's assent, Ginyern pressed forward in a hurried shuffle toward the destination. The brief course wound through a swaying forest of meat hooks which clung to the rotted remnants of past trophies. The stone was littered with detritus, chiefly decomposing entrails which could have only belonged to the deep sea fish that once lined the gutting facility turned warehouse.

"It's a temporary acquisition. Recent," explained Ginyern, discerning Virgil's distaste at being led through the muck. "No reason to clean the mess when you move as often as I do. We're here," he announced, followed by a compulsive "Snowsettle". The rogue stood before an iron-forged portal rusted with neglect. "One's feisty," the elf warned as he unbarred the entrance and swung it open. Restless rattling of chains and raspy breathing preceded the pungent attack of maggot mounds.

"Sorry," Ginyern coughed. "Before I locked them in, they collected the guts and made a swimming hole out of the mess. Restless. Please, enter," the thug grinned, nodding at the lightless hole.

"You cannot be serious," groaned Hazael. "You aren't, are you?" The steward once again sought to reason with his king. "Virgil, come now. This is nonsense. I did not think this could degrade so. We're to be played by a trickster."

"Oh, calm yourself," Virgil replied in exasperation. "He wouldn't allow the fanged beast to devour me in its lair while you nip at his neck with your blade."

An audible swallow emerged from the demented elf. "N-No beasts, sire. Twins."

The sovereign and steward exchanged a glance before Virgil stepped forward, conjuring a bobbing orb of flame and stepping through the portal. His flickering beacon cast an anxious light over the locker's innards, dancing in orangey impatience over the creatures at the far end.

An emaciated sprite battled with her chained shackles, lids clenched shut against the invasive, burning light. "Thack'ma!" the adolescent elf cursed while feebly wrestling with her restraints. "Thack'ma! Thack'ma! Thack'ma!" she croaked. When the impish girl finally adjusted to the intense light, a singular crimson sphere stabbed at the king with barbed hatred. The second of the pair remained shut, crusted and swollen a nasty purple. "Thack'ma!" the slave defiantly spat with beleaguered vocal chords, thrashing with spindly arms.

Virgil scowled, noting the dozens of bruises spotting her flesh, especially the stomach and inner thighs. The bite marks on her wrists seemed to be her own given the placement. He'd seen it many times before, children to lesser households or without a home given to slavery. The becoming ones were always introduced to the world of sexual labor. Albeit, this elf had likely seen the end of her service, injured and infirm as she was. Even the fetish-soothing allure of elven twins could only go so far. Virgil surmised her condition was the reason the swindling elf wanted to rid himself of bad stock.

The remaining twin was hardly in better condition. Shivering on her side amid a bed of entrails, the girl watched the ceiling above him eyes-half-shut. Curiously, he crooked his neck to afford him a look at the dull stone roof. Nothing out of the ordinary dangled above the sovereign. Shifting his attention back to the supine elf, he took a step closer, drawing more rattling chains and poisonous curses. The sovereign edged forward, affording the more energetic elf a wide girth as she raked from the end of her shackles.

"Etchak vlass mim," Virgil offered in her tongue, expressing his friendly intent. The rib-chested girl only fought her shackles more ferociously. He was certain the promise had been made many times before. Having arrived at her side, Virgil kneeled by the motionless twin, damning the Sundered under his breath as his floating blaze illuminated her dire condition. An infected puncture in her flank, a snapped femur and a cracked skull and jaw all did well to explain her state of quasi-consciousness. Her dirtied flesh was afire and mottled with the same signs of abuse as her sister. They were twins; this much he could confirm.

Frowning, he stood and shot a bothered scowl toward the door where the fence and steward spectated. "They are broken goods. Your poor business ethic makes me question whether you've served me at all, or whether you've picked up on my name while sniveling at the toes of your betters." The sovereign exhaled and went through the habit of running a hand through raven locks, flummoxed. "I do not know that they could even be repaired. Do you think a ruler would pay for something so thoroughly lambasted?"

Fumbling over a response to the insult, the elf ultimately remained silent, casting a nervous glance over his shoulder at the steward who waited with blade ready.

Virgil turned his attention to the less subjugated of the pair. Still snarling and pulling at her chains, she displayed impressive energy for a creature so malnourished. "Tell me, little one," he began in her language. "Would you like to come with me?"

"Thack'ma!" she slobbered once more, the elven equivalent of "fuck me". Virgil pondered the phrase. She could have been confusing it with the similar "Thack'man" for "fuck you", trying to prevent him from using her sister or the haggard girl genuinely wanted to be raped. In her state, it would not have surprised him. He'd seen many slaves shattered so exhaustively they believed they needed to be treated like property.

"Listen, you can come with me or—"

"Thack'ma! Thack'ma!" the thrall rasped as her exertions began to take effect, enervating the tiny elf and bringing her to her hands and knees where she vomited an empty stomach.

"I can see why you're eager to be rid of them," said the sorcerer, kneeling by the spasm-wracked child. He entangled his fingers in the yellow-brown mess of matted, sticky hair and wrenched his fist, pulling the girl's head with it. Tugging, he brought her to her belly while she scratched at his wrist with nail-less fingers, oblivious to the futility. "They've earned you a fortune," Virgil stated. "Yet you would risk it all to insult a king with damaged goods."

"They are rare. Gems," explained the thug. "You collect these oddities, no?" The sorcerer's quiescent disposition did not betray his anger. Thus the rogue disregarded the mention of an insult. Virgil sighed, still pinning the slave's head unceremoniously to the grime-layered stone. He didn't care that they were tortured and beaten, only that they could have been hopelessly damaged. Ginyern was correct after all. They were valuable, and their uniqueness could serve his research well if Hazael managed to stabilize the pair.

"Kill the wither-brained fool," commanded the sovereign.

Splintering vertebrae gave a cracking cry as the seneschal's pommel connected with the base of Ginyern's skull, toppling the unctuous elf.

"Done," said Hazael.

"Now then," remarked Virgil in elven tongue as he returned his attention to the elf. "What of you and your sister?"

Satisfaction lit the girl's lone crimson orb as her hindered stare sought first the sliver of tongue before the dispatched rogue's face then the fountain of red that pooled below unmoving lips. "Not yours," she stated.

"Oh, but you are," countered Virgil. "I assure you, child, your master will have no objections."

The floor-kissing elf snarled and began anew her fruitless clawing. "Thack'man," she growled.

Virgil chuckled and strengthened his firm grasp on her scalp. "Ah, you do know the proper word. Alas, the choice is an illusion. You should know by now the meaninglessness of your accord. Besides," he said as he released the captive and gave her prudent distance, "I assure you my sleeping arrangements are one hundred percent less mackerel bladder."

...

"That's horrible," Descarta somberly muttered. "They were only little things, right? How could a person hurt them so?" She was disgusted. Having learned of the innate darkness that blighted the world, she still couldn't accept that children could be subjected to such treatment.

"How? Wickedness hibernates within us all. One only requires the desire to invoke the beast," answered Virgil.

"They should be hung, dangled by their necks and strangled until their eyes pop out. Submitted to a hundred thousand unpleasant cruelties! Strip them of their skin and . . ." The diminutive girl ceased her rambling. The dourness surrounding Virgil had deepened noticeably. Descarta winced at her own harshness and shrunk away from the weaver. "I didn't, it wasn't meant for you," she clumsily spoke, twiddling with the lace of her pinafore as she did when taken by anxiety. "Forgive me?" she uttered while casting glumly at her boots.

The fallen king gloomed. Not for what she said—he'd earned every draconian punishment—but for her state. "Do not worry, dear. I have nothing if not a wealth of despicable crimes awaiting judgment."

Descarta bunched the fabric clinging to the viridian frock in her palm, admonishing herself for the haphazardly plucked curses. She had dismissed his tarnished virtues during her half-decade sojourn, pardoned them as only a throbbing heart could. The homunculus needed him to see her compassion, to know he was accepted. Beyond the cobblestone fairways of rot and blood he'd etched into nations aplenty, Virgil was a bastion of romanticism. Perhaps no one but those elves saw it, but Descarta did. And it was spellbinding enough to lift her above his faults and misdeeds.

"Virgil," insisted the girl, tugging her gleaming amber gaze upward and dimpled cheeks likewise, "you have me, and I care not how many atrocities you've committed. My passion will not relent." As she hovered there staring at the sorcerer, she understood she did not know how someone so inexplicably evil could lasso love so beautifully; only that he did.

...

"What's this?" Almi questioned, sniffing the pastry and appraising its vanilla swirls of fruit-spotted frosting. Merill likewise scrutinized her bread, timidly tapping the tip of her tongue against its glazed surface.

"What's this?" the more vocal of the twins inquired again, picking at a chunk of orange embedded in the pastry. "What is it?"

Virgil drew his lips into a slight curl; they never failed to entertain him. "Brioche," he explained while strolling through the vacant halls of his abandoned palatial laboratory. "Specially prepared bread filled with fruit and covered in frosting. You favor sweets. Quit toying with it."

"We like to toy," whispered Merill from her position at the rear of the trio.

"I'm painfully aware," sighed Virgil citing their endless mischief. "You should let Hazael be for my sake."

"Our Virgil is always busy-bee," complained Almi, taking a greedy bite of her treat and producing an agreeable grin at its deliciousness. "He should toy with us."

"Always busy-bee," chimed Merill, nibbling at the vanilla coating.

Nearly a decade and they still had trouble with the human language, Virgil considered as he strolled under the latest in a vast line of exquisitely carved arches. Their complaints were founded in his obsession, in his steadfast dedication to centuries of planning and research. His foundlings had matured into needy creatures over the last seven years, displaying an unhealthy attachment which he couldn't shake. More unsettling was the connection to the playful twins he'd unwittingly allowed himself to develop. They were a distraction—it was the sisters who'd persuaded him to cease his toiling over the cluttered atelier and join them for a break. Almi and

Merill had been given time to mend deep wounds and experience a world outside the grim dungeons they'd grown accustomed to. Not nearly enough, he knew. Virgil doubted the scars would ever disappear, and suspected the healing had nearly reached its zenith. There was little else he could do to suture the twins, so perhaps it was time to set free his foundlings.

"Dears, I've been thinking," started the weaver, meaning to bring up the idea of finding them a home before Almi perceptively curtailed the topic by snatching his arm and jerking him sideways. "What?" he asked as she chewed the remainder of her dessert.

"We like this," she stated.

The way she'd devoured her brioche while Merill relentlessly nibbled on hers illustrated that quite clearly. Virgil assumed the twins wanted the pastry introduced to their menu. "Good," he replied. "But it's not baked locally, and we need to speak about—"

"No," Almi interjected, golden curtains exaggerating the shaking of her head.

"No," emphasized Merill in a muffled mumble absorbed by her pastry.

"We like this with our Virgil," the less reticent of the sisters cooed in her honeyed timbre. "He's our Virgil, and we're his always."

An exhausted sigh escaped the sorcerer's lips. "Dears, you must listen."

"Always," drilled Almi, encircling his arm with her own and wielding a powerfully enchanting smile.

Merill joined in the display, augmenting the spell by inching forward and offering her luminous scarlet orbs. She interrupted her nipping enough to mutter, "We like this," before beginning her timid munching anew.

The weaver cast at each of the twins. They were either clairvoyant or could sense his growing distress. He had been sending them away with greater frequency as they gravitated closer and closer to him. Recently, it'd grown worse, and they'd taken on the role of sprightly satellites. "I cannot deny your allure, little ones. You are pleasant and you wield it well. More importantly, though, you are distracting. We'll find you somewhere comfortable to stay. Besides," the weaver punctuated, "you must learn to live on your own."

"No!" objected Almi in a shriek somewhere between a plea and cry. She dove against the weaver and strangled his torso with her slender arms. Even the taciturn Merill added her chassis to the embrace, brioche dangling from a worried frown. "Our Virgil is our Virgil! Only he knows us!" Almi tried to explain. "If we're sent away, you wouldn't be our Virgil!" Tense seconds of silence followed where the twins rubbed their faces in his robe before, captured by an idea, Almi shot the sorcerer a shining grin. "We'll help! We can sizzle slurpy sauce and bubble green goops! Teach us how!"

The weaver grimaced at the creature, adorably melancholy in her desperation. He could have quashed her hope by noting the temporal vacuum teaching them would create. Instead, his features softened under a defeated sigh. "You are persuasive monsters."

"We're not monsters!" whined Almi, scratching at Virgil's raven robe. Pressing her chin into his sternum, the relieved sister took on a lighter demeanor while Merill hummed contentedly against her brioche. "Virgil makes our chests tingle. We like him."

The sorcerer responded with a half-grin, showing his gratitude by patting the bantam twins' sun-crowned heads. "A bit longer, then."

...

The way he recounted his time with the elves clearly illustrated the weaver's affection-inspired turmoil. "See," said Descarta, triumphant in her tone. "You did rescue them. It might not have been your initial goal, but you healed them and gave them a home."

Virgil shook his head. "Another manner of torment. I was too aloof, blind to their kind resolve."

"Oh? Then why are they still here? How many times did you offer a disgruntled 'a bit longer', hmm?" came the diminutive girl's rejoinder. "It might not have been perfect. It didn't need to be, did it?"

Virgil sighed. Offering a morose smile, he gave her arm an appreciative pat. Time had run away from him, and in doing so he feared it had critically wounded his priorities. Fading memories of Descarta's cheerful voice escaped the sorcerer for time enough to allow the elves to introduce their own sonorous tune. Virgil grimaced, absorbing the bleak situation. He'd mistakenly relinquished the stage to his heart, and its passion had nearly destroyed him.

He wouldn't allow it to destroy her, too. The sorcerer had to regain the emotional composition that had allowed him to leave Almi and Merill in the tunnels below Galvant's Pass. Virgil brimmed with ardor for the twins. Yet reason shouted in favor of abandoning the deadly campaign to retrieve them. It was Descarta who represented centuries of discarded morality and hard work. He'd abandoned Ankaa for the special package, squandered time immeasurable to be with his creation. If he persisted in this slapdash mission, he could lose everything. Regretfully, Virgil succumbed to reason: greed would not protect Descarta. "You're right, dear. I've done enough for them. I have a responsibility to you."

"Done enough?"

Virgil sought her cheek, the long-elusive refuge fortifying his resolution with its contract of unrefined love. "This time, I'll do what's right for you, my queen." He sealed the pact by stealing her lips and impressing upon them a blazing fit of gratitude.

"Where are you going?"

"To inform the captain. We're turning back."

"What?!" exclaimed Descarta.

"We'll find a new residence and settle there. Your safety cannot be risked on Almi and Merill."

If his wistful words were tangible, the intensity would have left her flat on the deck. He planned on abandoning them for her, leaving them to the nameless punishments he'd plucked them from decades ago. "No," she muttered.

"No?" asked the weaver. "I assure you, we can find somewhere. The world is vast, as you know."

"We will not!" repeated the homunculus with growing resolve. Part of her condemned the elves for romancing Virgil—her Virgil. It quantified the twisted sisters as a threat whose elimination had gloriously arrived. Descarta would not submit to its venomous will. Damn the consequences, she would not allow another travesty in her name. It wasn't her way, and she wouldn't allow a darkened reality to control her. "We must save them," she pleaded. "You aren't the only one who will shoulder the burden of their demise!"

Virgil absorbed her words, her tiny tension-wracked frame. "They would not do the same for you."

"That's not important," she argued. She recalled her return to Virgil's palace. Before they attempted to send her to the abyss, the twins carried a look of complete defeat. As though her return spelled their demise. They were agreeable at times, even pleasant to be around. "Your elves might hate me, but they don't deserve this. They're sweet girls who just want to be with you. I cannot fault them for that." Descarta bored into her sovereign with a pleading stare of utmost determination. "I've come to terms with the thousands of candles blown out by my own existence. Don't force this one on me, Virgil. Please."

The sorcerer furrowed his brow, scrutinizing the adamant girl. He had no desire to force her closer to his ethical abjection. He had no desire to abandon two spritely blessings who had entrusted him with much more than their lives. "Do you understand what chasing them will entail? Your ribbon encircles my own, binding our essence. If I fall, you fall. The risk is doubled for us, Des."

The diminutive girl nodded, hazelnut locks bobbing with certainty. "I cannot bear to see them harmed."

Virgil thought to show her no heed. Her behest was not irrefutable, after all. When he chose to stabilize her fading essence with the souls of thousands, he gave her no choice and she despised him for it. The sparkling fairy was here now only because of that, but how far could he push her? "Very well," he sighed, though Descarta recognized a hint of relief in his grim tone.

She summoned a brilliant grin, rewarding his pliancy with a grand hug. "Thank you!" the girl crooned. She expected the weaver to simply enslave her will as he had so often in the past.

CHAPTER FOURTEEN

The Heart of Goliath

The ambassador's quarters suffocated her. Arabesque walls pressed their vengeance. The high convex ceiling sought to squash her skull. Descarta had no fond memories of the Underrise. Virgil scorned her in this very room. Almi gleefully participated in the brutal competition that could have snuffed out her life. Virgil made the ultimate sacrifice for her just beyond its hell-forged halls. There was nothing here for her, only the cresting tortures of a memory never far enough away.

"Shouldn't we be heading to Saradin?" she asked, sitting very still across from Virgil, as though the slightest movement could trigger calamity.

The weaver appraised her with a curious scrutiny. Their bond fed him then, answered his unspoken inquiry with harrowing turbulence. Virgil released a hopeless sigh when the wave passed, still gripped by its uneasy saturation. "What's upsetting you, Des?"

"I just don't like this place."

There was more to her mood, of that Virgil was certain. Their shared umbilical communicated unaltered feelings. The spellcrafter didn't force a response; if the dour girl wanted to discuss it, she knew he would listen. "We won't tarry. I only need to request Bromyr's assistance."

"Good," mumbled Descarta, peering at the threatening ceiling. "I want to leave soon."

The pair didn't speak afterward, each tending the call of introversion. From time to time, she would glance at him, curious. Mostly, Descarta deliberated the stone dome above, pondering whether her return to Saradin would produce similar results. She wasn't aware their brief stay had impacted her so, and yet it had.

"Virgil," she began, thinking her ancient lover perfectly capable of explaining the troubling unrest. She was the product of alchemy and thaumaturgy—his homunculus—so he would surely understand her every mechanism. The realization both terrified and excited the girl.

But he slumbered. The exhaustive events had finally subdued the nearly intractable weaver. Descarta admired her sovereign, for that is what the girl would ever view him as. The stark raven claws that raked at his pale chin were unkempt. The talons of his patchwork mantle, once a symbol of great power, were blunted by the same incident which left the scorched scar upon his neck. Yet he maintained the magnificent aura of a monarch, her monarch. Descarta could still envision him in his splendid lavender garb, situated beside her in the throne room. Virgil always seemed disinterested during audiences and councils. The lackadaisical king would often rely on Hazel to recount the most recent pledge or plea.

Originally, he impressed upon her a detestable irresponsibility. Descarta knew better now, had traversed the contours of his inner purpose. The clamor, the quarreling over ordinances, the disputes, even the welfare of his subjects was all peripheral, insignificant before his true goal. Though she suspected he may have also despised the residents of Elusia, those who Ankaa died for and who had all but forgotten her. The diminutive girl frowned at the snoozing man. Perhaps that was why he despised himself.

Unable to bear the dreary hush, the room's thick portal burst open in a limestone-cracking bang. A frightened oath escaped Descarta. The cry lifted Virgil from his nap and deposited him in front of his blossom, a shroud of distressed air sizzling its complaint about him.

The door moping beside him on a splintered hinge, Hafstagg towered in the damaged ingress.

"Hafstagg?" blinked Descarta. "What are you doing here?"

"Fool!" The ogre directed a shout at Virgil, bronze half-plate heaving in duress. "Have you gone mad?!"

The weaver allowed his shoulders to slouch, adopting a less tense posture. Descarta noticed no decline in the disturbed fabric that surrounded him, though. And he didn't relinquish his spot between her and the mammoth warrior.

"Des tells me I have," quipped Virgil in a pitch both complaisant and dangerous.

Hafstagg released an impatient grumble, platinum beard shaking in accord. He shot a nervous glance over the snarling demon perched atop his spaulder. "We aren't havin' time for this," warned the mercenary. "Bromyr is on his way. He's not alone, and he's not for welcoming you."

"Thack'," the warlock hissed. Hardly pleased by the possibility, he still remained rooted to the spot. Virgil would not be so easily swayed. When the hammer-hefting warrior left, it was not voluntarily. He'd admonished the weaver once too often, and the unremitting push to slough his wards sent Virgil over the edge.

Descarta didn't want to witness another confrontation between the two. "Trust him," she reasoned to the sorcerer's back. "He's only looked out for me." She reached for his closest hand, a claw contorted with harnessed energy, and took hold of it. "Trust me."

Snarling, Virgil relented. He chilled the churning flurry of cinders awaiting release and squeezed Descarta's sweaty palm. "Very well," he said. The weaver might not have liked Hafstagg, but he couldn't deny the warrior's unnecessary conviction when Descarta was involved. "We've a zeppelin moored to the Rise," explained the sorcerer as he approached the warrior-filled egress, homunculus in tow. "Get us there." A series of gravelly shouts came from behind the warrior, condemning the dawdling trio and giving substance to Hafstagg's claim.

The hulking man pivoted, giant legs flexing and propelling him into the charging crowd. Earthfolk scattered, titan and wayfarer alike knocked flat under his bowling charge. Hafstagg lifted his equally hulking bronze hammer with a menacing bellow. He forged through the group, dusty plumes and earthen cries exploding wherever his hammer connected. And it connected often.

Then his progress ceased, utterly squashed by the foray's newest participant. A boulder-sized fist crashed with the punishment of an avalanche into the warrior's breastplate, stealing his breath and sending him into a tumble that ended where he began.

"Your charge wasn't very effective," observed Virgil. He was hardly amused though, for Bromyr emerged from the silted clouds, fully taken by battle rage. When Virgil recognized the mineral-induced berserker state, he knew parlaying would be utterly ineffective.

"You cripple my Mundin! You swindle me into an impossible battle! And you dare return?!" Bromyr shook the tunnel with a grinding roar. "You will be crushed!"

"I'll help," whispered Descarta, shifting her palm to the studded pommel at her hip.

"No," said Virgil, placing his hand over hers. "Forget that. It's useless versus his armor." The weaver looked to Hafstagg. "Can you busy his underlings?"

The warrior grunted his concurrence.

"Then do so." Virgil stepped in front of the homunculus, a gesture that brought a gruesome grin to Bromyr's chiseled countenance.

"A challenge?!" The rock-king belched a mighty guffaw before stalking forward with the Underrise groaning under his incensed steps.

"Des, stay here and invoke a globe of water," instructed the sorcerer. "I will keep the brute at bay."

"What? Shouldn't I be helping?" Descarta frowned, slighted by being forced into the role of spectator. "I can fight."

Virgil would have liked to explain his stratagem. To lay its constituents in a web that praised her as integral—which she was. He wouldn't risk an outright assault. Pulling so heavily at the fabric was unpredictable in his condition, and the necessary force would likely be mutually destructive. Conjuring water was onerous here, parched as the Underrise was by a pit of roiling magma. Yet Virgil was certain Descarta, with her amplified abilities and affinity for water and wind, could glean what little moisture clung to the air.

"I'm depending on you, dear." Virgil sucked in a steadying breath and the earthfolk causeway sighed its treaty, a trembling maw awaiting his command. In darker days, he would have choked the tunnel, twisting it as an asphyxiated esophagus and crushing all within. Circumstances changed, though, and he couldn't afford to act so recklessly. Thus, Virgil stirred a second elemental will. Embers answered with an agitated sizzle, crawling over his flesh in a swarm of motes until their empowered glow nearly blotted out his flesh.

Fully prepared, the warlock left the ground in a feline pounce which hurled him toward Bromyr. He would brook the earthfolk champion no closer to his treasured lovelet.

To Descarta, her blazing weaver didn't leap. Willingly and with little effort, the earth itself set him forth, lurched to launch its master. And when, in a wreck of rocky vengeance, he collided with the stalking Impervious, she knew his chosen elements favored him. Granite gauntleted his furled knuckles. Sinuous vines of fire whistled around the weaver, a tenacious shield that, in a wondrous coalescence of hearth and stone, crystallized to spoil the obsidian titan's angry blows. Then, with a great surge, the tunnel would stretch a crag to pluck Virgil from the onslaught. For the adamantine shield was merely temporary against the untrammeled vehemence of the golden-veined earthfolk behemoth.

Like a frenzy of reverent crusaders vying for the supremacy of their warring gods, Hafstagg and a dozen of Bromyr's followers clamored around the pair. The outnumbered warrior was far from pressed, though. Virgil inadvertently severed the pack with every geyser of stone that lofted him on a slate-bound chariot. Encumbering as he was, the earthfolk would not hazard betraying their leader and his kill. So the gravel-grumbling humanoids were forced into groups and politely partitioned for disposal.

Outside the bubble of tumult, Descarta concentrated, attempting to conjure a watery sphere, and consequently understood her task. The barren atmosphere repulsed the element, turned it away with dry denial. She did not falter at its resilience; no, the difficulty imparted confidence. The neophyte weaver appreciated Virgil's trust, then—that he gave her craftsmanship with water such pedigree. To manipulate the elements required intense training, but to manifest any of the four primary planetary constituents was a feat of skill and intimacy. Shining at the subtle compliment, the diminutive girl began to cull and breed the paltry moisture surrounding her.

The five earthfolk facing Hafstagg hesitated, mortally shattered kin reduced to rubble before them.

"Fight me, fledgling pebbles!" The adrenaline flooded human took the lead, initiating a brutal rhythm with his singing hammer. The nearest titan growled its defiance, wide shoulders thrusting a tower shield at the whirling bludgeon. The aegis issued a metallic whine, and the earthfolk shieldbearer watched in disbelief as the weapon's head punctured the barrier and cracked his chest.

Hafstagg deftly pulled the hammer back, prying the mangled shield from the toppling titan. Two wayfarers approached then, titan counterparts keeping a respectful distance while their companions attempted to pry apart his stalwart defense. His new adversaries were wiry and agile, far less likely to succumb to a direct attack. So the warrior countered by lofting his bronze mallet diagonally and forcing the creatures to approach on his terms.

The wayfarers split, drawing apart to come at the mercenary from a wide angle. A pernicious bubble of still surrounded them, out of place among the din of groaning stone and clashing warlords. Then the still popped. The two bore on him with the swift stride of an elf, angling their one-handed maces like mandibles seeking to snap into the warrior and inject their virulent brew. One attacked his knee with a horizontal swipe, the other his neck, a brutal overhand.

To Hafstagg, the technique was transparent, a common feint betrayed by half-cocked appendages. At the last possible breath, they handed off stances, switching to mimic the other and coming in from opposite approaches. The silver-bearded brute expected this, and had responded accordingly, countering their progressive indirect attack with a similarly deceptive parry. When the wayfarers transitioned, the warrior sidestepped beyond the falling strike and toward the knee crushing arc to his left. A bronze sabaton connected with the assailant's willowy arm, stop kick successfully averting the incoming mace. Hafstagg's armored boot descended with a dust scattering stomp, beastly hammer spreading a similar cloud from the calcite countenance of his dispatched wayfarer. Hafstagg immediately whirled on the second of the pair who aborted its failed assault and shuffled just beyond a murderous swing.

The wayfarer and its remaining titan comrades broke toothless grins then, stalking forward with confidence. Hafstagg sensed the earthen heaving, and knew the platoon had been reunited—with him trapped between. The ogre grunted his resignation and hefted the massive mallet to his shoulder, cocked for punishment. For Descarta, the lass he learned to adore as a daughter, Hafstagg promised a grand display of dusty explosions: earthfolk fireworks.

He was airborne.

An indiscriminate limestone appendage erupted below the skirmish, setting wayfarers, titans and the displeased Hafstagg aloft. For his second of soaring, the mercenary cursed Virgil and his haphazard disregard. Then arrived the bone-splintering crack of the tunnel roof and his unceremonious clatter to the rubble strewn afterlife below.

Virgil swallowed great gulps of oxygen, the constant push and pull of his earth-given mobility enacting its toll. He'd managed a cleft in the gargantuan slab which was Bromyr's chest, supernaturally gauntleted fist proving its resilience. But the constant battering of being tossed about left him fatigued. Again he bludgeoned the rampaging Impervious, crag augmented knuckles sending a plume of jagged cracks from the original injury. With a sluggish swirl, seething fire kissed a half sphere of stone, leaving a prismatic barrier of pressurized crystal.

The many-colored shield buckled under a potent blow; its once adamantine structure had been jeopardized by weakened weaving. Before Virgil could take another earthen ride beyond his adversary's reach, Bromyr's massive fist penetrated the spray of shattered crystal. Its velocity merely blunted, the obsidian cross retained enough energy to send Virgil spinning away. Skipping to a rolling halt through jabbing rubble, the weaver emitted an agonized cough. He would have rather been hit by a stampeding mammophant.

"Careful!" Descarta issued in her youthfully buoyant pitch, concern staining the melody.

Virgil glanced first at the towering Impervious, then his homunculus. She had been fervently weaving. The gathered sweat on her brow illustrated as much. Before her hovered the sphere he requested, every bit as impressive as he would have expected. Every bit as disturbed by the exchange as its pinafore swathed conjurer, distressed ripples cast about its skin.

"I'm," a shiver seized the sorcerer, bludgeoned ribs crying out. Virgil refused defeat. Clutching his torso, he battled the discordant protest and forced himself erect. "I'll be fine," he managed, taking stinging breaths. "You've done well. Now quickly, target his fractured trunk. Send the globe at him."

Descarta nodded, at the same time worried for her injured crow and thrilled by his compliment. Through narrowed lids, she concentrated on the approaching earthfolk patriarch. As instructed, she sought the jagged crevasse Virgil had so furiously imparted.

The girl hesitated. There would be no second chances to fulfill his charge, no time for another calling. She had to succeed here as Virgil's partner, as the one he could rely on in dire circumstances, or forever fail. Descarta wished to be more than a liability, yearned to rise above the role of burdensome blossom. To become the girl he would seek for those harrowing, glorious or mundane occasions when, back-to-back, they could conquer anything together.

A rising gust answered her mental appeal, murmured its assent in ethereal notes. Magically imposed purpose replaced caprice, subjugating the urge to curl and loop around the crosshatch of intersecting catwalks. The enthralled squall rose from the rolling pit of magma, gathered its brethren and crashed into the ambassador's chambers, squeezing through the balustraded balcony in a subservient rush. The windy raiment coiled anxiously around the homunculus, swooning under her captivating call and setting russet locks and filigree-festooned frock into tantalizing undulation.

Bromyr growled an avalanche of a snarl. He was the victor, the supreme lord in this place, his molten throne. And he would brook no interference. He would pluck Virgil apart like a love-me-not flower.

A distant part of his enraged sentience told him she would inflict a far greater wound on the wretched weaver. Yes, Virgil would first watch her suffer as his precious pebble had suffered. To think Mundin still idolized the man! Thought his spoiled spellcasting admirable! Rage heightened, the titan stomped his fury and charged at the billowing girl, tunnel quaking under his massive strides.

Descarta paid him no heed, attention commanded by the cadence of meticulous weaving. She used her will as a needle, threading the contracted gale into the floating globe until it was a spinning mass of turbulent, ultramarine froth, foaming within its invisible confines.

"Des! Do it!" screamed Virgil, desperation sinking into his tone. Growling, he called once more on the elements. He'd rather risk catastrophe than witness the rampaging giant maim his blossom.

He was stopped short by a thunderous boom, an explosive power so impressive the entire Underrise moaned in complaint. Its cavernous causeways quivered, threatened to collapse out of sheer astonishment. Virgil clutched the throbbing on the sides of his head, eardrums producing a high-pitched squeal.

Downy, unfathomably downy, hands covered his, and he sought the delicate demon which occupied his hell of tolling bells. Descarta moved her luscious rouge lips, tapped her tongue to soundless words. Her hazelnut canopy was tossed about a worry-strained visage, enchanting even in its furrowed distress. An emerald strap of the offset pinafore dangled errantly from her shoulder, calling for an attentive caress to slip it back into place and, in turn, feed upon her dainty design.

Virgil blinked. She could find ways to be brilliantly ravishing in the most unpleasant of situations. He pulled his gaze from the mime in front of him and peered over her russet top to the dispatched Impervious. What he saw was nothing short of amazing. Bromyr had fallen to his knees, leaning back on goliath arms like a spiritless construct awaiting activation. Where the cracks had been, his torso was gone, simply vanished. In its place there was a gaping shaft, perfectly round and perfectly empty, extending from his chest to back. The sphere had collided with the stampeding brute and shot straight through. Descarta had, once again, strummed a spell above many master weavers—the joining of elements. It was not according to plan, but the opposition was dispatched nonetheless.

"Hey," called Descarta from below, worry-gripped timbre finally breaching the incessant ringing. "Virgil, please say something. Virgil?"

"I'm here," he answered, lowering his stare to hers.

"Oh, you had me terrified!" complained the girl. "You could have said something!"

"I couldn't hear you," rebutted Virgil as the siren faded from his head. "Your spell was deafening. Come now. Once this corpse is discovered, we'll have no chance of escape."

Descarta nodded her assent, but first scanned the demolished battlefield. "Hafstagg!" she called. "Virgil, we can't abandon Hafstagg!"

The sorcerer frowned. He knew what befell the warrior. And while it wasn't intentional, he was grateful for the inadvertent kill. "Do you see him?" asked Virgil. "I'm sorry, dear. But we'd know if the useless bastard was alive. A giant, loud-mouthed oaf such as himself is hard to miss." He instantly regretted the ill-chosen words.

The homunculus spun back to Virgil, snatching his umbral robe and staring daggers at the weaver. "Don't besmirch him like that! He protected me for you, even though it was your fault his chef died! We must search!"

Disappointment burned a tormented grimace onto the sorcerer's dirty countenance. "Fine," he spat, angry with himself for ever believing the girl could rise above his faults.

The moment a troubled scowl took his features, she regretted the poorly plucked stab. "W-Wait," Descarta begged, snatching his sleeve to stop him. When he whirled on her, the fierce tempest that churned in his leveled stare rendered her speechless. She wanted to explain, heard the pacifying apology bouncing about in her skull, but it never left her lips. His noxious glare paralyzed her.

Virgil snatched free his robe and prepared to unleash his steaming condemnation. Much like the disturbed creature before him, the weaver rescinded the complaint, snapping his jaws shut just in time to douse the unjust riposte. He wanted to lash out, to marshal a vehement verbal flaying. And he was grateful he didn't. He had coffers of boundless regret which needed no padding.

A labored sigh conquered the shrill quiescence dominating sorcerer and sorceress. Virgil counted his reserved, clement disposition as one of his greatest post-rite losses. Decades of skullduggery from the mischievous twins and he'd never neared such malign treatment. The windswept girl had pushed her limits to impress him, left herself in disarray and surely exhausted. With care, he hooked a soiled finger beneath her dress' errant support to lure it once again over her silky solstice. "We will search," the weaver submitted, wearing a plaintive grin.

Descarta craned to regard his cosseting fingers, having taken passing residence just below her neck where they wound a placating circuit. Under its influence, she relented, stepping away from stirring her saturnine cauldron.

"And Des," added Virgil, "Your display was marvelous. Again, you effortlessly impress me."

"I wasn't trying to!" puffed Descarta, executing an about face to hide her rosy cheeks. "Virgil! I've said that isn't normal! You cannot just announce it!"

The weaver allowed his morose lips to curl honestly, feeding on her brightened mood. "We're alone, dear."

"Don't mind me," coughed Hafstagg as he rose from a premature grave of dislodged rubble, effectively sundering the moment. "I'm hale. Just a knock to my head is all. Nothin' to worry about here."

"Hafstagg!" exclaimed the homunculus, bounding over to wrap his generous paunch. "I was so worried!"

"Is that what that was?" chuckled Hafstagg. "And here I was thinkin' it flirtatious chin-waggin' and touchin'."

Descarta sucked an exasperated gasp. "You two are insufferable! Insufferable! Let's just go!"

"Finally, some sense in this one," said Virgil, approaching to firmly secure her hand. "We aren't out of trouble yet. Keep that dazzling saber and masterful spellcrafting ready."

"Virgil!" objected Descarta, giving his scorch-scarred palm a squeeze. "No more! And . . . and . . ." She paused, shrinking away from Hafstagg and against her companion's raven robe. The flushed homunculus burned all over, scarlet claiming her every inch. As absurd as Descarta felt, her weaver's applause always reached deep. "And I'll give my utmost for you, Virgil," she happily whispered. "Thank you for believing in me."

The bronze-clad warrior excavated his behemoth hammer and heaved a shrugging complaint. "I haven't left," he said, smacking the clinging layer of dust from his doublet.

"Perhaps you should," offered Virgil. "The real lechery doesn't begin until we reach the zeppelin. She howls so seductively."

Descarta dug deeper into her alcove. She angled to peek at the warrior and snapped back into her retreat when she noticed his disturbed scrutiny. "He's lying!" she screamed against the suppression of her tenebrous mantle. "I've never! I'm innocent and virtuous and . . ." The truth of their frenzied flourishes drowned her denial to a mumble.

Hafstagg suffered a wobbly, stumbling course through twenty replies, all leaving his flabbergasted lips in a slobbering flurry of spit and blabber. "Ridiculous!" he finally managed, tossing his arms in defeat.

...

"The captain?" inquired Virgil from his vigilance at the zeppelin's winged aft.

"Overboard," answered Hafstagg as he returned from the task. "I'll be pilotin' from here out." He followed the weaver's dour glare, over the hastily aborted mooring cable to the furiously working earthfolk scattered about the plateau below. Siege engines were being lashed, secured, repositioned and loaded with pernicious projectiles. If even one of the missiles penetrated the blimp-suspended airship, it would spell doom for the three man crew.

"Send Des to me," instructed the weaver.

"She only just closed her eyes," contested Hafstagg. "You know she's exhausted."

Virgil gave the balustrade a white-knuckled squeeze. Briefly, he missed kingship. Missed enacting punishment for objections by servants who, apparently delirious, thought they'd foreseen something he hadn't, and that he cared to listen. The sorcerer knew Descarta needed rest just as well as Hafstagg. Was he not there to witness the girl scraping at her inner pool to invoke a feat of thaumaturgy? If the cantankerous warrior didn't fetch the girl, she'd have plenty of time for rest amid the splintered skeleton of their getaway vessel. "Send her," he repeated, austere.

"You're pushin' her—" the warrior began before Virgil shoved himself from the balcony and face to face with the towering man.

"I don't recall requesting your opinion! If it pleases you to enact revenge for my past deeds by playing the haughty father to a girl that, by my reasoning—any reasoning—is neither your offspring nor responsibility, fine! We will address that later, I assure you! Until then," Virgil tossed his arm behind him, signaling the incensed earthfolk shouts. "That is our priority!" He took in heavy, angered breaths voraciously, satisfied to have released a fraction of his building stress.

Hafstagg frowned, platinum beard sagging. He dwarfed the weaver; yet the man stood confident before him, neck craned sharply to snatch with menacing eyes. The sorcerer was correct in his pragmatism, despite his boiling. "I'll grab her," agreed the warrior, tossing in a nasty rejoinder. "And afterward I'm thinkin' you tell me of your priorities. I'm sure you've none above the lass."

Growling, Virgil grabbed the immovable brute by his half-plate contrivance. "Get her," he ordered. "And when this over, I will strangle you by your own dimwitted accusations."

"We'll see," said Hafstagg, taking a step back and walking off to wake Descarta.

Virgil let out a frustrated sigh and returned to his post, calling out to the wandering zephyrs populating the heights. He couldn't caress them with Descarta's propensity, but he would at least begin the gathering.

Moments later, Descarta emerged from the cabin, rubbing darkened candelabras and the reddened orbs within. "What is it, Virgil? I'm so very sleepy."

Hafstagg, exiting behind the slow moving homunculus, didn't miss the worry with which Virgil regarded her.

"I know, dear," he responded, partitioning a section of his mind to maintaining the lassoed wind. He retrieved her, hooking her waist and assisting the drained spellweaver up the steps to the rear of the zeppelin. "I can feel it," explained Virgil. "You need to rest, but we aren't safe yet. Once we are, I'll personally weave you to sleep." Virgil knew it'd hardly be necessary, though; she was already wavering on willowy legs. "Until then, I will support you."

Descarta nodded her compliance. She was too tired to complain. She felt as though her core had been emptied.

Virgil gave her flank a reassuring rub. He'd practically carried her aboard the vessel, but there was no other option. "Listen, love." He walked her to the railing where she could see the imminent salvo in its final preparations. "If we don't dampen their ballistae, we'll be shot down."

The homunculus nodded again, realization creeping into her groggy mire. "Instruct me, Virgil."

The sorcerer offered a smile, a solemn promise all would be well. "We're too far for a direct counter-assault. You sense it, don't you?" asked Virgil, referring to the imprisoned gusts. "I need your command of the element. I need more, a tempest at our back."

"I don't think I can," pouted Descarta, blinking at his request. "Even if I could, I feel dry inside. I'm sorry, Virgil."

The weaver shook his head. "I'll support you. Through our shared tether, I'll feed you my reserves. We'll work together."

Descarta bobbed her head lazily. She didn't think herself capable of summoning mighty storms, but she refused to deny him. The situation gave her little choice, regardless.

"It could hurt, or you could feel nothing at all," warned Virgil. "The process works like opening a valve, so it will rush into you immediately. I will only release a portion, and I will continue doing so until we've reached a secure distance. Understand?"

Another nod. This time firm, resolute. He was relying on her again, and she wouldn't let him down.

"Good. I'll begin then. And remember: let nothing through."

It happened exactly as he said it would. Raw energy unfurled within her, exploded in a deluge of puissant burning that bit at the back of her eyes and threatened to leap from her throat. Momentarily, the burning was unbearable. Then it simmered to a pleasant warmth which beamed inside of her. It reinvigorated the girl, and she whirled a pinafore flaring circle.

"Virgil! This is amazing!" Curious, she waved an outstretched hand and her favored element followed her will with no effort. "I'm not even trying! Is this how your flame answers you? Oh, I'm so light! Let's float away, Virgil!"

Virgil grinned, satisfied. He'd purposefully fed her just beyond capacity, and the surplus energy sloshed out of her shell and coated her in a temporary vim. Once extinguished, her buoyant state would follow. "We can float later, love. Stir our defense before it's too late."

Rendered incapable of a solemn reply, Descarta beamed her response. "Yes!" Jubilant, she threw willowy-soft arms wide, executing a spin on bouncing heels and reaching high. "It doesn't even object! Teach me! I bet I could fly if I wanted!"

"Please don't try." Virgil allowed himself a moment of pride. Fabricated or not, he hadn't seen her so elated since they first departed Saradin. The sorcerer watched in wondrous captivation as she followed the steps of her weaving waltz. It was superfluous; the gale would have obeyed without her display. Virgil didn't mind, for he found her playful pirouettes no less than bewitching. The maelstrom she produced was dazzling: a fury of orange-red sand kicked up from the desolate terrain and excited into a whirlwind.

"Look at it!" boasted the chipper girl, hands placed triumphantly on her hips. "No amount of arrows could ever—oh!" An enormous sharpened stake careened past her, clattering over the deck in a hazardous tumble before plummeting overboard. "That's not supposed to happen!" she exclaimed, ducking behind the balustrade.

"Feed it," instructed Virgil, once again gorging Descarta on his essence.

"I-I fwill," the sorceress slurred while rising with the footing of a drunkard. "Twake thish!" The vortex throbbed in accord, each pulsation granting greater girth. "Aaaand thish!" she bellowed, the tempest mirroring its intoxicated weaver with a thunderous groan.

Virgil tugged the swaying homunculus back down to the deck. The defense would be useless if she toppled over the aft. Her storm would have to suffice in its current delivery. She was losing mental faculties, and pushing her further could result in permanent damage—something he refused to risk.

"Hey," called Descarta from her slouched seat. "H-Hey, Vurghul."

"What is it?" Swift gusts radiated and swam over their heads, tossing her russet canopy over eyes that, to Virgil, were glistening with pearlescent seduction.

"You, you, you . . . yer shcent ish like the rain. But I shay . . ." The blabbering homunculus leaned close but never stopped, crashing unceremoniously into his lap. "I shay . . ." she slurred, rolling to stare at him from an uncomfortable repose. "I shay . . . the rain shmellsh like you!"

Wearing an amused smirk, Virgil rapped his fingertips on her inelegantly twisted back. He charged himself with archiving the moment, a rare artifact among her tangle of moods. "That's enough for now," he said.

"I am . . . a queen," she murmured, narrowing a steel glare at the sorcerer. With a grunt, she rolled onto her back, liberating her neck from its unnatural winch. "The shky queen ofh . . . ofh . . ." Descarta squinted at Virgil between heavy lids that shuttered with greater and greater frequency. "Yer right. Alwaysh right. I should shleep."

CHAPTER FIFTEEN

The Heart of a Villain

The zeppelin persisted in its course, unaccostable thanks to Descarta's momentous twister and Virgil sustaining the gusty construct until they reached the safe harbor of open skies. Behind them, the Skrillsill loped. Its whimsy-given dunes had granted passage unburdened to a vessel that, in harsher fortune, could have been assailed by worms or sandstorms.

Virgil kneaded the balustered wooden fore, scowling his distaste at Galvant's Bulwark. The monolithic fortress, a needle on the cloudy afternoon horizon, cast a menacing glower from beyond the pass which marked entry into Elusian territory. The sight aggrieved him. Its lancing pinnacle represented the beginning of a treacherous trek through a quagmire he thought he'd finally escaped.

"Why're we headin' for Elusia anyway?" asked Hafstagg from the navigation room, raising his volume over the drowning rush of mountain-swept wind. He frowned when Virgil ignored him, motionless aside from the breeze which threw his robe into tattered agitations.

"To rescue Almi and Merill," Descarta answered his question through a cavernous yawn. She plodded over, hopping atop a stool overlooking charts, parallel rules and a nautical almanac. She recognized many of the labeled territories from her travels, though much of the world was left unexplored on this particular map. There were other places, but the ship's owner likely had no use for a map outside his regular causeways.

To Hafstagg, she seemed refreshed, and that would have warmed him if she hadn't answered. "Rescue Almi and Merill?" he inquired.

"The poor creatures," she swallowed, gloomy at their mention. Descarta detailed to the warrior everything that'd happened since their capture—excluding certain lecherous encounters where she paused for a passing heat spell.

Hafstagg didn't prize them like Virgil did, or approve of their residence in a palace whose sole queen should have been Descarta. Yet he hardly wished them suffering. Almi and Merill were spritely, entertaining and, with the occasional exception, harmlessly eccentric. He granted their traumatic tale a respectful hush, appreciating the reticent sorcerer. To Virgil, the dire situation must be rending. "How is he faring?"

Descarta lifted her attention from the nautical clutter to the man in question. He'd erected a palisade of affection, a barrier wrought for her benefit. It was not inviolable, and their connection afforded her his sorrow. "Not well," she replied, frowning. The homunculus doubted he'd slept at all, while she'd wound herself in succulent slumber. "I should be with him," the sorceress declared, mostly to herself. She moved to leave, but the mercenary snagged her with another inquiry.

"And you? How have you fared?" prodded Hafstagg. "Virgil isn't seemin' to have fully recovered. Has he hurt you?"

"No!" shouted Descarta, his accusation catalyzing a drift from her glum stirring. "No," she came again less forcefully. "My Virgil is a wonderful man. Immeasurably wonderful. He's so gentle with me, and he loves me."

The warrior smirked, hanging a thumb in his paunch-wrapping doublet. "You're beginnin' to speak of him like Almi and Merill. Every man has faults—especially Virgil. Don't forget that."

Descarta looked away, wrought with disgust. "You care for me. I understand, because you're special to me, too. But . . ." Her fierce amber orbs first sought Virgil, then the grinning warrior. If he really cared, he would support her, not belittle her relationship with souring words. His superior smirk angered the girl and mismatched a rare scowl onto her kind countenance. "You will not challenge his dedication. You will not!" The livid girl clenched diminutive fists, a fuming flower before him. "Virgil accepted me when I returned! Asked nothing of me, nor has he ever! If I were out there where the twins are now, he would not abandon me! He would pursue me no matter the cost!"

"Des," sighed the warrior, grin quickly fading. He pondered whether she spoke out of obsession or experience. Virgil wasn't known for his kindness. The way he treated her was absolutely uncharacteristic of the despot. "I only want you to be careful."

Bristling, the homunculus dropped from her stool. "When I left, you looked down on me," she riposted. "Now you're the one treating him as nothing more than a villainous beast." Her blood boiled, and Descarta felt she'd explode just by sharing space with the warrior. The girl fumed a direct path to the exit, pausing before she left to get in a final word. "Never speak ill of my Virgil. I would kill for him." She sharpened her final comment with a caustic edge, warning the warrior that, if it came to it, she would side with the weaver.

The bearded man tapped his bronze sabaton, eyeing the derisive girl. She briskly sought Virgil's side, entrenching herself within his tenebrous mantle. Descarta gave her partner a nudge, reeling him from his meditations and locking an expectant gaze on the weaver. He responded by drawing her deeper into his wind-livened robe, enveloping her with the untrammeled adulation of a sovereign's highest treasure.

Hafstagg deliberated the exchange between Descarta, Virgil and himself. Their contention, her threat and the simple embrace that followed. He flashed a full-toothed grin no one else would see. Descarta had achieved her utmost yearning and found somewhere she belonged. Somewhere she could smile, be herself and be admired for doing so. An alcove all her own, whose shadowy embrace she would never give up.

The warrior nodded to himself, still grinning.

...

Suspended from the heavens, her perspective afforded Descarta a view shared only by gulls and gods. The Elusian terrain was a sprawling flatland of verdant green, clamored into liveliness by the restless summer draft. Within its mercurial murmur, the etesian wind carried an oceanic scent wed with the earthy spice of barley and wheat.

Descarta inhaled the delivery, and it returned her to the late afternoons not so long ago when she would pine to lose herself in the fields beyond captivity. She'd vaulted horizons, explored far past her incipient longing. And now she yearned to return to that place. A palatial retreat littered with dusty tomes, dilapidated furnishings and above all else, Virgil. Their demolished home was an abject remnant of the past, but it was theirs, it was comfortable and it was home. The homunculus didn't favor the uncertainty of knowing they could not return to the collapsed underground palace.

"We should prepare for docking," said Virgil from just above her as he slid digits over her flanks and around her stomach. "Are you certain you wouldn't rather turn back?"

She clad his hands in her own velutinous gauntlets, smiling at his unimpeded concern. Descarta remembered a time when she envied the twins for those events when he would, likely unintentionally, shed his mask and follow the precept of compassion. "You don't want to turn back," she answered. "Me neither. So why would we?"

The girl thought the circuitous path to Saradin curious, but she had assumed there was some tactile meaning to their meandering. "If we're to moor soon, why descend toward Dascion?" she inquired, referencing the river port just north of their supposed destination.

"Saradin isn't equipped to accommodate zeppelins," explained the weaver. He reached for her low-hanging side-ponytail, its russet fall secured by a charming green ribbon and slung over her chest. Glissading fingers worked his nervousness into the soothing cataract. "And we'll be taking a hidden route."

Descarta followed his touch from her stomach, once again cupping his anxious caress. "They'll be free soon," she assured him, seeking to quell the concern that seeped from Virgil and into her. She cast toward the postern railing at the buttresses of Saradin, then back to the water-hugging harbor of Dascion. Traversing the distance on foot would take a day or longer.

Within moments, the zeppelin quickened its decline, settling into a bobbing hover above port laborers who methodically secured its mooring ropes and prepared the boarding bridge.

Wrapped in cloaks to hide their identity, Descarta, Virgil and Hafstagg followed the ramp to confront the awaiting foreman.

"You aren't scheduled until tomorrow," he stated, scribbling the note on his log. "There's a fine for that."

"The supreme weaver isn't feeling well," Virgil said, emphasizing the venerable title. "So we returned early. I'll handle the fines after seeing her to the ramparts."

"I see," the foreman replied, glancing uneasily at Descarta. Her face was obscured by the diving sun's late afternoon shadow and an oversized hood. The man wanted her gone as soon as possible. He despised dealing with regents, their ire too easily invoked. "I won't be impeding you, then. And never mind the fines."

"You are generous," Virgil offered before leading his cohorts away from the harbor and its tense foreman. He doubted anyone would recognize him, since he spent much of his second reign barricaded in the Saradin ramparts. But he'd rather not risk an encounter. "One stop, then we set out for Saradin," he said.

...

"A bakery?" asked Descarta, confounded. She eyed the shop's swaying sign, an exquisitely carved graphic depicting a glazed loaf. The looming scent wafting from the building assaulted her with the promise of frosted treats, a familiar smell from her time in Saradin. "Why a bakery?"

Hafstagg only shrugged.

"I'm sure there's a good reason." The homunculus found the pommel of her sabre, tinkering with the largest set gem. She intentionally spaced herself from the warrior, pretending to be occupied with the waning skyline. "Hey, Hafstagg."

"Hmm?"

Descarta moved from the studded hilt to her frock, kneading the spiraling lace. "I'm sorry. I meant what I said, but I only said it out of anger. I'd do my best to avoid such a decision."

The mercenary grunted, and for a moment Descarta thought he'd take the pontificate approach once more. "You have what you were seekin', little one. I'm thinkin' I overlooked that much. Hold on to your place. Sink your nails in and never let go. And if I get in your way, well, dammit girl, cut me down."

"Finished," announced Virgil, effectively truncating the conversation. His purchase dangled at his side, a stuffed satchel still emanating steam from the kiln. "Now, we can begin our incursion."

"Why are pastries necessary?" inquired Descarta. She gave Hafstagg a smile, conveying her gratitude for his words, before shuffling to Virgil's side. "Are we going to pastry their captors to death? Are they stale?"

Virgil plucked a sugar-powdered strudel from his sack, passing it to the girl. "I just thought they'd like a treat," explained the weaver. "It's jam-filled."

She accepted the offering and took a generous taste. Her bite freed the raspberry filling which oozed toothsome tangy warmth. She issued her approval with a chipper bob of her head and delighted buzz. Licking full lips with a sanguine coated tongue, she strolled beside Virgil, with Hafstagg guarding the rear. "Delicious," she declared. "Same as the pastries I ordered in the ramparts. But should we really be bringing treats along?"

"The baker is an artisan. The artisan who prepared your sweets those years past," explained Virgil while ferrying the companions on a winding course that replaced the din of the harbor with the serene hush of residents settling in for the evening. Flagstone gave way to dirt passageways, densely situated workshops and sundry fronts to the contrast of humble homes afforded capacious lawns. The group entered the city's proximity, an area designated for the common folk when they'd finished a tiresome day of peddling wares or unloading cargo.

"Dear, even in the best accommodations, those twins are mortified. And," he said, taking a sharp turn toward an abandoned building. Its walls were dilapidated, pockmarked mortar dominated by flora. "You're right; it's a poor idea. I thought it'd cheer them up." With a frown, he discarded the pointless sack. Stepping through clinging briars and untamed overgrowth, Virgil battled his way to a sealed well. "Here."

Descarta scooped the bag and drew up beside the weaver, presenting the strudels. "Take them."

Virgil gave her an inquisitive stare, brow furrowed. "I conceded to your logic, dear. Let it be."

"Take them," she insisted, pushing the steaming treats to his chest and taking the final scrumptious chew of her share. It was unorthodox given the circumstances, but Virgil ventured beyond the call of necessity to greet his captured wards with a personal touch. Squashing the recent introduction of affection for the sake of affection in a man so often defined by melancholy would neither please her nor better him. Even awkward and inconvenient as it was. "Being there will be enough for them," chimed the homunculus. "They'll buzz and flitter about you excitedly. Proclaim how grand you are." Descarta pulled her dimples into a solemn grin, thinking of the occasions he'd put forth the seemingly insignificant extra that was, to her, inconceivably precious. "You'll be a savior. Still, this will brighten them further."

The weaver accepted the sack, uncertain what to make of a girl who, moments before, declared the treats a bad idea. "If you insist," he submitted, turning his attention to the well. A thick slab sealed the portal, secure as the day he'd melded the stone. Forged of earth imbued with his blood, it would only follow his command. And it did, issuing a chalky moan as it slid aside, revealing a shaft of impenetrable black.

Descarta peered into the abyss, the vast emptiness calling for her to dive in. It seemed to speak, to reference a revolting lexicon that urged her forward with provocative power.

"Listen," said Virgil, applying a stern pitch and firmly grabbing her by the arm. "Do not stray. Do not touch anything." The sorcerer inhaled, steeling himself for the journey. "Remember I love you, Des."

Perplexed, she cast at him, amber orbs seeking to augur the cause of his spiritually projected unease. It was peripheral, a newborn satellite that came forth and orbited the seated fear for his wards. He only stared into the umbral shaft, offering no explanation. As if conquering an unseen impasse, he tilted his head in a slight nod. "Down, then." It was hardly a warning, but it was all Descarta would receive before she was tugged to plummet into the tenebrous maw.

...

The darkness swallowed her, contained Descarta within its raven phalanges and eerie suspension. It was a lie, façade. Not an absence of light, but of everything. No sense of falling assailed her, no vertigo, only the vacant cloak of nothingness. For an unexplainable reason, for an immeasurable time, Descarta found the eldritch place alluring. She cautioned herself, but it sung to her, stroked her with persuasive harmony. And who was she to refuse its serenade? It'd be rude, unappreciative—a blighted travesty!

Something foreign encircled her waist, wound about her like a demoniac serpent stealing her special place. "No," she protested. "This is my home! Leave me be!"

The tow would not surrender its malign pull, and she found herself retreating. The dark, spellbinding stillness receded, fell and gave way to stark crimson-white undulations of the fabric. The juxtaposed reality was different here: wrongness pervaded her in a way unlike Descarta's prior visits.

"Take me back," she begged, wishing to return to the crooning nothing. "I belong there!" She slapped at the coiling snake at her waist and discovered Virgil's arm hooked there. The girl followed his sleeve, somehow astounded by its existence, to the sorcerer it belonged to. "Virgil," she gasped. "It's glorious. So serene. Come with me . . ." her voice tapered off into a longing sigh.

"You don't belong there," he replied without moving his lips. The weaver's placating pitch rebounded in her mind, transmitted directly to the homunculus. It came as a vibration that expelled her unrest. With a severed thread, it detached her from the beseeching void and returned her will.

Liberated from the song of death, she absorbed her new surroundings. Velvety fabric flowed on unseen waters, her sea-faring path an odd cleft in the material. Above and below, a strip of umber stone similar to the tunnels outside Stonenoggin extended for eternity. There was so little she knew about weaving, about the fade, about all of this.

"Consider it a magical wake, not unlike the track a worm carves in soil," Virgil answered her unspoken question with an unspoken answer. "We are not in the fabric, but its effects reach us here. Remember: do not stray."

Wordlessly, the obsidian-robed man instructed Descarta to follow. He intertwined his hand with hers, fingers criss-crossed in a web which bound them together.

The fabric ahead shivered, twanged and shifted in a disturbed chord. Virgil frowned.

Descarta sensed his sudden despair, a dropped octave that rapped at her umbilical, both shrill and worrisome. "What?" she inquired. The oddity greeted her afterward, answered in a disharmonious wail. Portions of the fabric faded and gave way to shimmering, restless shards of the physical world. Chains, taut but broken by conflicting realities, flickered between realms. Masonry appeared in rubble, floating in pieces to a three-dimensional puzzle. The apparitions contained within were the explanation for her weaver's grim shift. Ghouls, for that was the only name she had for the monstrous maidens, howled at her with abnormally stretched maws. Withered beyond the beauty they held in life, the creatures were little more than flesh draped repulsively over bone. It occurred to Descarta that the banshees weren't screaming at her, but for her. They all seemed to be suffering incredibly, and the ethereal stakes piercing wrist, elbow and stomach were at least one clear cause of that agony.

Virgil said nothing, only ushered her between the rows of clamor with a firm grasp. The homunculus caught a faint gleam above him, a swaying thread of multi-colored spidersilk catching light. It was joined by a network of similar streams, each gaining visibility as he passed the wraith it belonged to.

The weaver's fingers were oily, sweaty between her dainty digits, and he exuded trepidation. "Darling," she swallowed. "What's going on?" Descarta hoped the term of endearment would empower him, for she rarely used them.

"Do you love me?" he asked, hastening his steps through the blighted area. "Would you like to settle with me?"

"You know I want nothing more," she answered, casting about.

"Then remember I love you, as I asked. Let this simply remain a mystery." Virgil prayed she would relent, feared what would result if he detailed the arcane apparatus. Descarta rooted herself, pulling him to a halt, and the weaver knew her tenacity had taken hold. It was at times like these her treasured spark troubled him.

The sorceress looked about her, absorbing the situation. Their damned cries, their sheaves of rotted hair spread as straw over sunken skulls. "I know you've done this," she conveyed, closing to his back and placing her hand there. "The territory I've chosen has its faults. I only wish to learn of them, not judge or condemn them." When he offered no response, she gave his mantle a placating caress. Mumbling a curse, he renewed his stride, and she thought she'd been ignored. The weaver allayed her disappointment as he fled the scene.

"My heart," he started, clutching her tangled fingers fretfully. "This is my heart. It maintains me now as it has for centuries."

"Your heart?" Descarta asked, nonplussed by the analogy.

"Call it what you wish. I'm human, and it breeds life where there should be none."

"And the girls?"

Virgil sighed, growing less comfortable as the conversation progressed. "Slaves or stolen, most of them. A few trysts—naïve ones who thought it noble to give themselves to a king. Sacrificed, chained as you see them. Staked to this twisted joining of realms. One every decade to pump me with lifeblood."

"So it is by their agony that I live?" Descarta asked, making the natural connection.

"Yes."

The girl ceased her prodding there. She'd inquire further later. For now, he'd shared enough. Descarta valued his pliancy and, while less than eager, forthrightness. "Thank you," she muttered. "Eventually, I want to know everything about you, my love. No matter how dark. In return, I will not turn away." She gave the passing chambers another inspection, realizing the wailing had moved to her rear. The older cells were vacant, save for undisturbed ash and hardly enough bones to compose a corpse. "That said: I'd like to avoid causing more harm than is absolutely necessary."

The pair continued their otherworldly traipse in a few transient moments of silence. The chambers had disappeared as abruptly as they were unveiled, so Descarta occupied herself with the billowing scarlet terrain at her sides.

"They were before you," Virgil eventually spoke.

"Before me?"

"The trysts. Given our bond, unguarded thought is contagious here." The weaver gave her a smile, pulling her to his side. He'd heard her inner turmoil. "Walk at my side, dear. You belong here, not behind me." Virgil pressed on after she returned his smile. A gloomy exchange. "They thought it'd be something to prattle about, that they'd been plowed by whatever royal position I held at the time. Or they were peasants seeking a rise to nobility. I began to reject them after you arrived."

Descarta nodded, obtrusively relieved. She was grateful he felt compelled to reveal more without her prying. The girl didn't want to be a burdensome busybody. "Didn't Almi and Merill object?"

The plaintive shroud he wore saliently conveyed his regret. "I cannot count the ways I have wronged them. Taken advantage of their subservience. They would . . ." His response thinned beneath the choking oppression of remorse.

To Descarta, however, his swirling sentience unwittingly transmitted the curtailed words. They would join. He saw that it wounded them, but they would take part in the carnal thrashing simply to be with him.

His innermost troubles could not have been rendered in greater clarity then. A cavalcade thundered around her, striking from all sides with blades of serrated sorrow.

They were sweet girls, his wards. Devoted in everything.

Why could he not escape his despair? The debilitating, paralyzing, corrupting rancor which prevented all things beginning. He loved them—with a flickering heart, he loved them! If he could subdue parasitic enmity long enough to discover his blossom, why not Almi and Merill?! How he tortured, tormented, defiled and perverted their immovable ardor! He'd forever blighted himself in their captivating crimson orbs—so captivating and so cursed!

The nether-misery never breached his countenance, the calm composure of a sovereign.

Fraught by their amplified link, Descarta watched and wondered how often he endured these internal invectives. He handled this one with little outward indication. The surge of emotion was so powerful that tears he would not allow himself to shed instead blemished her cheeks. "V-Virgil," she sputtered, sobbing under the indomitable sway of his grief.

Creasing his brow, the sorcerer cast a questioning stare her way. "Dear? What's gotten into you?"

"S-Stop with those vile thoughts. You're b-better than that." Wrought by his sadness, her weeping would not yield. She took his arm and used its sleeve to wipe her face. "You needn't punish yourself," she mumbled against him. "Just learn from your mistakes and treat them properly!"

"Enough," whispered the weaver. "Enough. It is my penitence. I've attempted to make it up to them, nurtured them as they have me during the last six years. I've embraced those wonderful creatures. Well, I've tried. I'm sure it was a poor display." Virgil expelled a forlorn susurration. "But just as I would not allow myself to forget you, my dear, I cannot allow myself to forget what I've done to them. What I'm repaying them for."

"That isn't a relationship," she retorted. "It's not."

"How so?"

"I may not be as experienced as you, my Virgil, but I know a relationship is not the offspring of burden and despair. It's love; it's what you and I share. It's what you share with those elves. If you truly want to repay them, withdraw from the past. Don't forget what they've endured for you, but set it aside and put their worth first."

Virgil would not look at her. He was ashamed, mortified. Ashamed of his heretofore negligent disposition. Mortified by the possibility he'd never set things right. An exhausted susurration later, he thought of the diminutive bloom whose hand had faithfully remained in his. To the fallen sovereign, it was a keen representation of her incorruptible dedication.

"I don't have a hoard of secrets," projected Descarta. The unfiltered exchange of bare souls could be precarious, and was most certainly frightening. Still, she was grateful for the fey journey. Virgil was rarely forthcoming, so mired in his raiment of dissidence. Here, he settled. Submersed her in frozen truths he could not thaw, emotions he dared not convey. And the merging confirmed her high regard for the weaver. The homunculus wondered whether he found her depths similarly nourishing. "But I have been keeping something from you."

"It's a ravine I would never leave. Luminous throughout," Virgil assured her. To accentuate the point, he gave her feathery hand a kiss. "Now tell me, if you would."

Descarta nodded. He'd allowed her within his glacier, if reluctantly. Now it was her turn to brook his judgment, to avert her roiling gaze in shame. "When I came back to you I'd already lost my chastity. In truth, it was . . ." The girl paused, tasting descriptors for her defilement. "It was stolen."

Stolen. The anguish-saturated word gripped him and its spiny ungulae sunk deep. Upon her return, she'd assured Virgil of her fidelity. This was different, delicate, an affliction. His next footfall anchored him, and in turn, the aggrieved miss. Scarred phalanges scarfed her moist cheek and steered her tumultuous amber stare to his. "You needn't worry, dear. You've done nothing wrong, and I would not be in a position to condemn you, regardless. You are, and shall always be, unspoiled."

The diminutive spellblade slanted her head into his touch, appreciating its permeating presence. She could feel his rage, his vow to punish the fiend responsible. Yet the fiery eruption was regulated for her, contained beneath a shroud of sympathy. Virgil's vaporous control spread from his palm and permeated her. Descarta murmured content under his influence. He needed no magic to placate her. "We were north of Kaen Morr, crossing the Dhal Hinterlands when a nasty blizzard forced us to moor."

"You don't have to," Virgil interrupted. He breached her tawny velvet cascade and stroked peace into the wavy cataract.

"I want to." She closed her eyes and granted his calming caress authority. "We were lucky. A hamlet was nearby, one with hot springs. I needed to force the chill out, so I stripped and slipped in. The steam was thick. I couldn't see. And I accidentally bumped into someone." The homunculus opened her amber orbs, finding confidence in Virgil's accepting cerulean reflection. "His hand . . . ended up on my breast. I struck him, though! I struck him hard, Virgil! He berated me and left the spring, calling me a puddle-chested boar-witch." She gloomed at the worn raven talons reaching from his robe. "Am I too tainted?"

"Dear, is that all that happened?"

"I promise," she muttered. "After that, I returned to our lodging."

Virgil expelled a breath of relief. "So he unintentionally touched you, you hit him and he teased your humble chest. Des, such an exchange hardly revokes your chastity."

"Really?" replied the homunculus, still downcast and toying with an equally dark strip of lace.

"Yes, love. I thought you'd been raped. Don't frighten me like that." He stole the girl from her gloomy cauldron and once again began their otherworldly stroll. "Does it truly trouble you, dear?"

Descarta shook her head. "No longer. I thought myself corrupted. You were to be the first to touch me. You're so good to me, Virgil."

"You're pure throughout, so don't worry yourself."

"Yes, Virgil," she mumbled, feeling incredibly silly. She studied her chest, a pair of modest mounds made even less impressive by the well-endowed wards. "Am I really puddle-chested?"

Virgil answered with a frown, but inside he chuckled.

"T-This is a serious conversation! Don't laugh!"

"I'm not," replied Virgil. "I'm flabbergasted by your obsession with breasts."

"H-Hey! I heard you! You can't hide it here!" she harrumphed, clenching his hand.

Virgil caught her slight grin, a welcome crack in her insecurity. "They're lovely, dear. Sumptuous. Do I not show you?"

"You do," she responded. "But Almi and Merill . . ."

"They don't like your breasts?"

"No, Virgil! That's not it at all!" she huffed, bearing a wide smile. He had the oddest ways of brightening her mood.

"You're beautiful, Des. All of you. You're different than they are, not inferior. I might even find it more appealing." Virgil answered her grin with a libidinous flash of his own.

Her luster returned in an effervescent sheen. "Thank you for cheering me up, Virgil. I can always depend on you."

"That's right," he concurred, weaving a touch of arcane placation into her palm, drawing a delighted hum from the girl.

CHAPTER SIXTEEN

Foundlings and Fate

"We're here already?" Descarta surveyed the red and white landscape. She saw nothing that indicated they'd reached their destination. "We couldn't have traveled for more than an hour."

"The laws of our world do not prevail here, Des." He looked weary, with beads of sweat accumulating on his wrinkled brow. "We're returning to our realm. Please do not stray this time. I don't know that I can retrieve you."

Then there was emptiness again. Exultant, beseeching and controlling. This time, Descarta was prepared. She rejected it. The homunculus would not succumb when Virgil, Almi and Merill relied on her. As if outraged by her denial, the void expelled her in a disgruntled cough.

Birthed from a single point of light, Virgil's study exploded around her. Despite many days under his ever-watchful eye, it was foreign to the girl. He'd only summoned her to his reclusive nook for monthly examinations. The acidic stench of potent chemicals clung to the place and was heightened by the caustic sizzle of residual magic. Now, when she inhaled the scent, it brought to her lungs a part of their subterranean home.

Virgil had untangled their latticework of affection and approached a framed sword. It was identical to the blade strapped to Descarta's hip, a sabre of sure craftsmanship. He retrieved the artifact then turned to see Descarta, mouth agape, staring flummoxed just to his left.

"How long has that been there?" she asked.

He followed her stare to a portrait set above his desk. The painting depicted her in the ruffled saffron regalia she would wear to official affairs. "Years."

"I've never seen it," Descarta contested. "It's ridiculous. You had it hanging here and never told me?"

Virgil secured the sword to his robe, doing his best to appear nonchalant. "I'd take it down when I called for you."

"I don't know how to feel about that."

"Let's go," he said, effectively evading the topic. "We'll try the dungeon first." He breached the ironclad door enough to peer into the passage beyond, flinching at its metallic groan. When he decided the causeway was clear, Virgil motioned for Descarta to join him. With clandestine steps, they followed the hall to a spiraling stairwell floored with lavender carpet. The descent deposited them in the bottommost atrium, grand entrance to the Saradin ramparts.

The palatial spectacle was just as Descarta remembered it: a bronze-embellished image that allowed no visitor misgivings of the sovereign's might. Braziers popped low in the place of lamps, thwarting the dead velvet of night. From her vantage, she could just count the four floors opening to the atrium which provided residents an elevated view and defenders a perch to loose arrows and boiling pitch. The ironclad ring of armored sentries sounded from the higher levels, reminding her that this was not a midnight jaunt through her home, but an excursion into enemy territory. Virgil escorted her along the room's shadowy periphery. He maintained an alert eye on the lackadaisical guard stationed in a state of half-sleep by the colossal gate.

When they took the egress opposite their exit, Descarta thought they would not be accosted. Until, after several sharp turns by standard emblazoned banners, her guide issued an oath.

"S-S-S-S—" stuttered a frightened servant from just beyond Virgil. She'd been knocked to the floor, wick-burning lamp toppled to cast long, angry shades over her. "S-Sire!" she finally managed.

"Hush," Virgil ordered from atop the lass, covering her mouth. He was still, listening for any disturbance in the ramparts' natural rhythm.

Descarta recognized the servant: a woman several years past maturity who had once served her every meal. At the outset of her world-spanning journey, the lass had bid her farewell. Her freckle-cheeked comeliness persevered, a trait worthy of a mistress or noblewoman. Though she'd always been far too timid for the latter role. "Elissa," whispered the homunculus. "It's Des. We won't harm you. Just don't shout."

A petrified bob and subservient whine was enough for Virgil. "Smart girl," he muttered, slowly withdrawing his palm.

"Virgil, get off of her," murmured Descarta. The servant lay motionless beneath him, paralyzed by her predicament. Elissa wore only a thin gown of filament and fervently avoided looking at either of them. Descarta sighed. She didn't recall making eye contact even once with the woman. "She's frightened enough without the threat of you ravaging her."

"F-Forgive me, miss Des. This isn't. I would never. W-Wait. Not that I think you unattractive, sire! But only. I wouldn't," she fumbled for a deferential apology. "O-Oh, I'm so sorry."

Virgil sighed and pulled the quaking, downcast servant to her feet. "I said hush. This room, is it occupied?" he inquired, motioning toward the nearest door.

"No, sire," she replied through shivering lips. "Empty. I promise, sire."

The sorcerer escorted the trio into the room, which turned out to be vacant. Elissa stood in place with her lamp clutched close and watched her feet. Of the fort's staff, it had to be her he ran into. "How has Hazael treated you, Elissa? Were you made head of staff?"

"Y-Yes sire. B-But I never betrayed you, sire. Never. I wept for you, sire. We thought you dead."

"Good. Now tell me: where are Almi and Merill?"

"W-With you, sire?"

The weaver sighed. She didn't know, or she would have told him. "Were any extra meals prepared? Anything sent to the dungeon?"

The girl nodded, still refusing to cast anywhere but her bare feet. "Two, sire. I know not their destination, but prison guards took them. Weavers visited the dungeon this day. Is mo—" she swiftly snapped her mouth shut, biting her tongue. "Are Almi and Merill in danger, sire?"

"They'll be fine soon enough." Virgil expelled a breath, unsheathing his sabre. "I cannot risk an alarm, Elissa."

"I know, sire. I'm just relieved you're alive." She didn't lift her gaze or move to escape, only awaited her demise.

Descarta had been quiet hitherto. She wouldn't consent to cut an innocent down out of purely empirical necessity. The woman had never spoken briars to her, even went beyond her obligation to please Descarta. "Don't, Virgil," she insisted, grabbing his sword arm. "Can't you see she won't betray us?"

"We cannot risk it, dear." The weaver gently pried himself free, offering an apologetic frown. "She comprehends and does not object. If she reveals us, our survival would likely be forfeit."

"Please don't," Descarta objected.

"I will make it quick," the sorcerer responded, as if that'd slake her unrest. He clutched the servant's shoulder, angling his blade to circumvent her ribs and puncture her frantically throbbing heart.

Elissa quavered before him, rooted to her point of extirpation. The lamp rattled its protest in her trembling paws, but she did not intend to escape. "S-Sire," she sputtered. "M-May I, may I look at you?"

"Very well," agreed the weaver, allowing her that final concession.

Her inky, well-groomed forebangs lifted from their crestfallen eternity. The blood-scarlet globes that appeared bore excruciating familiarity, a saturnine glimmer too near to their origin.

Virgil thought her smile disgusting. She should abhor him, despise his every virulent element.

Descarta couldn't fathom why the woman was so utterly willing. She wasn't deliberately discarding virtue for the man, but her life. Her right to ever know happiness or a world beyond the floor she so adamantly followed. How could a blessing so precious be handled with such insignificance? Elissa was crazy, deranged—saliently unfit to make her own decisions. The sorceress started to interrupt, but Virgil was already retracting his poised blade.

"We'll bind her," he said. He couldn't smother those eyes.

The lass inhaled a gasp, alit with an exultant flicker. "S-Sire!"

Virgil gave her raven top a pat. "Quiet, girl. You're doing well here. I expect no less."

"Y-Yes, sire," she replied in an excited whispered, beaming.

It occurred to Descarta that she'd never seen them together before. Their similarity was peculiar, uncanny even. Then there was the strange way she mirrored the twins when grinning at him. And her slightly pointed ears. And the way he addressed her, as if she were more than hired labor. "Virgil," whispered Descarta. "Who is she?"

"You know her, Des. She was your personal servant," the weaver responded while pulling sheets from a guest bed. "You cannot have forgotten in the last five minutes."

"Is she your daughter?"

Virgil choked and Elissa abruptly returned to her crestfallen demeanor. The tension was dense, tangible. Virgil began to tie the sheets in intervals, crafting a makeshift rope. They'd only talked about her lineage once, and it was to clarify that she'd never speak of it again. Almi and Merill would play with her, but they scarcely had the capacity to raise her or love her. To them, parents were inconceivable creatures of which they knew nothing. Virgil had higher concerns—resurrecting Ankaa prime among them—and he was arguably less capable of fatherly duties than Merill, her mother, was of her own role. It was a miracle conception. For after decades of copulation, the twins were proven as barren as his augmentative weaving had rendered him. Thus, he'd given her a safe life: to be raised as a ward among his staff. An effortless existence, if mundane. It'd been so long since he acknowledged the girl that she stunned him. Elissa was what Merill would be if she wasn't irreversibly broken. A bashful, beautiful woman brimming with intelligence.

"I'm going to hit you, Elissa. It will be painful, but it will complete the illusion." The spellcrafter's ginger explanation lightened the truth of the act.

"Yes, sire," she said, setting her jaw.

He stood before her once more and regarded yet another dreadful lamentation. If he hadn't happened upon her, she would have forever remained a wraith dismissed. He was no longer the aloof sovereign who abandoned her. And revisiting the consequences of his disreputable past was beginning enact a vicious toll. "Does your place here satisfy you?"

Elissa tapped pensive trepidation at her clattering lantern. "I only know this life, sire. Never would I refute the wealth of your gift. It fits me, sire." The deathly hush which followed was sodden with many things, of which remorse reigned. Then, in an agonizing heave, the air evacuated her lungs. The blow to her gut was stunning, an uppercut which marshaled dizziness and white-hot searing. She swooned, begging, clawing and wheezing for the escaped oxygen. Her entrails threatened to leap from her throat, and in her daze, she cautioned them that it would not please her. If it wasn't for Virgil's steadying support, she would have toppled. From her hunched position, Elissa could only discern the tear-distorted reaches of his robe. But she knew he held her, and thought the disorienting coruscation worth a visit by his proud pinions. Briefly, regretfully, his lips met her raven crown, an unspoken apology for blunders he could never right.

The penumbral talons began their greedy creep then, eclipsing her vision and shredding awareness.

...

Once again treading the mortar morass, Descarta was finding it cumbersome to shake the odd exchange. The raven-topped, carmine-eyed girl was his offspring; that was lucid. Her mannerisms and features clearly marked Almi or Merill as the partner progenitor. Just when the sorceress thought she'd uncovered her sorcerer's secrets, another denizen was roused from dormancy. She was beginning to understand there were many more, and she'd have to bear them as they breached the depths.

She'd followed him down two more stairwells, illuminated only by the incandescent birth of lanterns spaced too far apart. Her palm hovered on his back, seeking the obsidian mantle for direction and courage.

"Virgil," she called, nearly inaudible. The scenario rapped at her with unremitting complaint. "Your daughter deserves better. She's a princess, isn't she?"

"What would you have me do?" the weaver retorted, exasperated. "I'm no more her father than you are her mother. Once, I was her king. It ends there."

Virgil was lying. Not to her, but himself. She was witness to the solemn transaction. It was not an empyrean love that drove him to spare her; for Virgil, the patriarch, had none. "The role is still there, awaiting fulfillment. Almi and Merill—"

"Merill," he hissed, "is not equipped to take care of herself. To love another. You would have me supplant the single gift I've given Elissa, a life of guaranteed ease, for what? I spared the girl because I saw her mother in her. Nothing more."

Unsettled by his hissing susurration, Descarta had to remind herself she wasn't the target of its ire. Merely a bystander waylaid by misdirected venom. She only sought to shelter him from further grievance. Why did he seek to singe himself with the irresistible destruction of sorrow? "Virgil," she started, beginning to brew a riposte keen enough to move him.

"Des, hear me," the dethroned despot muttered, and finality gripped his timbre. "We pursue Almi and Merill, not ghosts or lost causes. Perhaps afterward—" If he planned to budge, it was interrupted by the grizzly tones of ale-touched discourse just ahead.

"Those elven wenches were teases. Cavorting around with their supple bodies." Armor rattled as the turnkey grunted a harrumph. "Now we've our chance and Josiah forbids touching them."

"Wants them all for himself." Mirroring his comrade's disappointment, the other guard heaved a sigh. "Shame about the scars. I knew they weren't right."

"You'd still plow them," chuckled the first voice.

"Damn right. Bludgeon their tight snatches."

Descarta was sweating, rivulets running down her form and dampening her viridian pinafore. In a matter of seconds, the stairs had grown insufferably hot. Virgil heaved, his mantle assuming the rise and fall of an infuriated beast's mane. She moved to quiet him, to pull him deeper into the cloak of shadows. Her fingers snatched at air. She muttered an oath as he left her, growling.

There was a blast, a curse and the resounding whine of an alarm bell. Descarta turned the corner to find one guard immolated, reduced to a smoldering skeleton. Virgil was impaling the remaining jailer, repeatedly thrusting his bloodied sabre between armored plates. The man feebly fought beneath him—more of a valedictory quake than opposition—one hand jerking on the rope which spurred the whistling alarm. The homunculus expelled her frustration. Why did they even attempt to be surreptitious?

"They're mine! They're pure!" The incensed weaver shouted against the scarlet spittle that formed the knight's incoherent throes. "Untainted! I'll! I'll!" Virgil snarled as he knocked the man from his chair. The turnkey crashed with the clatter of forged metal. He twitched in a fit of spasms as Virgil, straddling his chest, plunged thumbs into his eyes.

A shiver caught her spine as Descarta watched her weaver rip the guard's sockets empty in a sloppy spray. The victim was motionless now, and she hoped he'd died before the horrid assault.

"Retrieve my songbirds," Virgil instructed her. His pitch had sloughed its maniacal inflection, but his gaze still churned. "I will crush any who impede us."

The homunculus nodded, kneeling before him to detach the mutilated man's key ring. She avoided the gory sockets and hastily plucked the jingling band free. "I'll be quick. Be safe, Virgil." Descarta kissed the weaver's blood-splattered cheek, frowning at his distant glare.

He needed rest. The mounting stress was eroding him. She hadn't seen the disparaging look in his handsome cerulean pools since the terrible winter past. With the twins' aid, she'd sealed his stubborn malady. Or so she thought. "Remember I haven't left you," she added, pressing her lips once more against his face. She gave him a worried glance before approaching the dungeon door, trying each key.

"Yes, dear," came his reply, still sitting atop the corpse. "You are here with me." It was a trained response, one she'd forced him to say again and again. Until his corrupted mind believed the truth—that she had returned, and she loved him. The lock clicked, and she cast at the weaver once more. He'd enough wherewithal to rise and remove his sabre, a propitious sign.

She smiled plaintively and trusted him to his task. The portal slammed behind her, introducing the humid, gloomy stink she'd always imagined a dungeon would exude. Only one cell was lit, so she trudged toward the restless light cast by a high-hanging lantern. When she peered inside, she emitted a startled gasp. The twins were on their sides, bound in restraining jackets. They looked at her, but their sanguine orbs hardly acknowledged Descarta beyond that. It seemed someone had at least taken care to ensure their comfort by fitting their piece of the prison with great pillows and wiping it as clean as any other room in the palace.

The homunculus almost went through the laborious task of eliminating keys before realizing the barrier was slightly ajar. She thought it odd, but shrugged, pulling the oppressive bars wide and clambering to her knees beside the twins. "Almi, Merill. I'm here to take you home," she said, smiling and only just realizing how much she'd missed the frolicsome pair. But there was no response forthcoming, only their glum stares. "Hey," she called. "Don't you hear me?"

"They won't reply," a familiar, sonorous timbre issued from outside the cell. "Sedatives. For their sake, of course."

Descarta spun and reached for her studded sabre.

"That wouldn't be wise," sighed Josiah, waving at her. He stood across the hall, leather-bound arms hanging unassumingly at his sides. "I've no reason to kill you."

"You stole them!" Descarta hissed. "Do you know the pain you've caused?!"

"Less than he has," retorted Josiah. The bard took a step forward, causing Descarta to bristle and clutch her blade's pommel. "I know of another exit. Let me take them. Virgil doesn't have to know. Why fight for them when you could have him to yourself?"

The homunculus bit her lip, censuring the passing, monstrous and downright repulsive urge to agree. The sweet sisters were more than obstacles to be cut low. "Never," she spat. "Virgil needs them, I need them and they need us."

A surge of blistering radiation blew over them, eating at the air and indicating the battle outside had begun. A portion of the sorceress' mind registered the meaning. She partitioned it, reminding herself she could not be distracted when contending with the coy bard.

"Do they?" countered Josiah. "Go on, remove their bonds."

Descarta shot him a questioning glare.

"I won't stop you."

Wary, the sorceress knelt, never showing the crafty rogue her back. For she was certain he would puncture it swiftly. Descarta first unshackled Almi then Merill, peeling the binding, oversized coats from their fragile forms. A sob escaped her throat at what she uncovered. Cuts, boils, brands and unidentifiable lesions scarred their tender olive flesh.

"Your noble king healed them, but only what someone looking from without could see. Only he saw them like this. The mutilations are as old as those elves." The rogue watched as she stroked an elven brand across Merill's waist. "That marks them as cattle, a slave."

"Why would you force this on them if you know how they've suffered?" the homunculus growled, nauseated by the extensiveness of their defacement. "They should be home, causing me mischief. Not reduced to mindless thralls."

Josiah grinned. He'd gained a small victory with their scars. He wanted to convince the homunculus to leave. Despite working with Violah, he had no desire to kill her. "Tell me, Des. If Virgil intentionally left this blight on their flesh, what did he leave beneath the surface of their tortured minds? How many perfectly mendable wounds did he ignore? How far would your immortal weaver go to make these gorgeous girls forever his?" The rogue took another confident step. Descarta did not respond this time, only caressed the repulsive elven stamp set beneath Almi's belly. "He's lived longer than the most revered of their kin," reasoned Josiah. "He knows deceit better than any of us."

Descarta rose, beholding the drooling twins with a frown. "Virgil treasures his wards more than you'll ever fathom. You have not seen his heart as I have," she declared. The diminutive girl set a resolute amber stare on the rogue. "Give them to me, or I will relieve you of them. Forcefully. I'll not fall to your cloying words, bard."

Another atmosphere-shuddering heat wave passed, followed by the screams of those caught in agonized conflagration. "He cannot last forever. Assist me and the two of you will leave unharmed. Else," Josiah drew his short sword and dirk, "you will never leave."

Descarta answered with the metallic whine of steel emptying its scabbard.

The bard's lips sagged in a dispirited grimace. "I will honestly regret snuffing such a beautiful maiden. But it seems I have no choice."

She hardly had time to deflect his incipient thrust, a flash as incisive and swift as any of Merill's fletched shafts. Descarta answered with a counter-beat, drumming thunder onto his blade, circling under and stabbing at his hardened umber leather. Josiah retracted his outstretched sword, snapping his dirk across to entrap her sabre, but she shuffled out and away, effectively breaking the tangle.

The rogue smirked, flipping his short sword into a reverse grip. "Impressive. A common fencer would have been felled by the first blow."

Descarta snarled, lace-spiraled pinafore flaring behind her as she vaulted into an expulsive ballestra. She plunged her vorpal spire at his throat, a preparatory feint that the bard nimbly and predictably circumvented by displacing her line. The diving homunculus snapped into a spin, whirling into a lithesome twist that swept her boot and blade into a back-handed blow with the blunt of her pommel. Josiah threw himself out of range, cracking his shaved head on the intractable cell wall. He growled the throb away and lunged again at Descarta who finished her deadly descent with a graceful glissade, drawing up into a neutral stance. He came in with blades poised for a low double-edged sweep at her billowing dress and alabaster thighs.

He knew it wouldn't connect, such was the articulation of a compound attack, but Josiah didn't expect her to evade his two-pronged strike by leaping between the pincers with elven dexterity. The bard just avoided her rising knee by rolling aside and into the den of pillows. Descarta rebounded off mortar and stone with elegant sureness of frame, turning about to swipe at her recovered adversary. He countered with a yielding parry, directing her sabre vertical and plucking it from her grip by use of his dirk. The disarm was a forceful tug, and her locomotion bound her to follow it into a forward stumble, rendering his brutal heel kick unavoidable as it blunted her ear.

She was sent sprawling, drowned in the stomach-turning cacophony which stabbed at her skull. Descarta emitted a half-sob, half-whimper that touched her lips with the tinny rouge film of blood and spittle.

"Sorry, Des," Josiah muttered, hardly happy with himself as he hovered over her, dirk poised to strike, "but this is the end." He jabbed the spike at her bosom. Her tear-clouded eyes afforded the diminutive girl an abstract window into her world, but it was enough to catch the finishing blow with her hand. She wailed an agonized shriek and pulled her impaled claw wide, causing the rogue to fall toward her. Josiah was utterly defenseless against her final blow. Given his proximity and descent, her palm thrust needed very little force. She'd seen Hafstagg employ it twice, and preferred to keep to less brutal methods. It was a last resort, a chilling reminder that neither life nor death were pretty affairs. She could feel his nose splinter under her upturned palm, its cartilage give way and fly as needles into his brain.

Uncontrollably sniveling, Descarta rolled the rogue off her and sat up. She rattled under her sobs, under the weight of killing Josiah, of the kick to her head and the blade ran through her hand. She regarded the latter with murky vision, stifling a bawl to tug the dirk free, only for the cry to escape anyway under the shock of her wound. The girl howled and clenched her wrist under the quavering, punctured palm as she willed the weave to suture the injury. Her head reeled, but the weave listened, mending shattered bone and ripped flesh. With a shudder, she took to her knees, wiping the rainclouds from her tumultuous amber gaze. Descarta deposited herself amid the pillows between Almi and Merill, heaving a mighty sigh. She spared energy enough to dampen the crippling pulsation that spread from her bruised ear and gripped her mind in electricity.

She blinked, staring absently at the ceiling while the pain ebbed and relented under her convincing weave. "Almi, Merill," she called. "We have no time to nap." Her quaking had been reduced to the occasional sputter. She would need to apply more intense healing later, but for now, her state would suffice. They weren't safe quite yet. Descarta situated herself between the elves, kneading firm circles on their bellies. She massaged her will in, clinging to the substance that claimed them and neutralizing the magically injected neurotoxin. When she was finished, the somber girl gave their stomachs an affectionate pat, frowning at the disfigurement.

Soft yet sordidly uneven, their bare skin revived the departed rogue's assertion that Virgil deliberately neglected their healing. It could have simply been a ploy, a snare to diminish her awareness. Still, many constituents of the weaver remained an enigma. Descarta shook her head, banishing the foul poison. "He loves me," the girl declared with confidence. "He loves them." Her dear despot guarded his past because it hurt, because he was ashamed, because he was afraid. Not because he misled her.

"D-D-D-D-D-D-D-D-Des?!" shouted Merill. The weary homunculus grinned at the elf, meaning to greet her. Yet the stare of horror the girl beheld her with admitted no such reunion.

"Dear, we're here to take you and your sister home." Descarta stroked her stomach, seeking to calm the bewildered twin, but it only drove her into a frenzied fit. A vibrating whine caught Merill's chords, seated just beyond her maw and proliferated in volume and pitch. It grew, flourished and plucked eerie disharmony from its home until it could no longer be contained. Merill set her quivering lips agape and let it boom, a wail so strident, so puissant its forlorn discord dazed Descarta. Afterward, she emerged to see Almi and Merill shivering as mortified kittens under a pile of pillows.

"She's seeing us," whimpered Merill. "She's touching us."

"They're seeing us," yowled Almi. "They're touching us."

Descarta peered at the shaking mountain of downtrodden elf and pillows, perplexed. The twins were truly aggrieved. Their sodden streams and fear-captured stares were as real as Merill's broken shriek. Yet she hadn't harmed them in any way.

"Our Virgil will never look at us again," sobbed Almi.

"Don't see us!" screamed Merill. "Only our Virgil!"

"Our Virgil will hate us," Almi lamented, hugging her sister. The woebegone elves pouted at the ancient sabre lying just beyond their mound. Each eyed its keen edge, ensnared by the scintillating gleam of the lantern above.

Merill whined and turned into her sister, rubbing grief-drenched cheeks on the girl's bare chest. "Afraid," she quietly issued from her retreat.

In response, Almi scratched placation into her whimpering twin's golden scalp. The stronger of the two still contemplated the beseeching blade with captive crimson defeat. "We must renew our vows," she spoke softly. "For our Virgil." The elf reached from the warren of pillows. Trembling but sure, her phalanges stretched for the instrument of deliverance.

"For our Virgil, everything." Almi spoke the soothing words to steady her hand as she took the pommel. She closed her eyes and envisioned him situated beside her, countenance wrought with something she could not describe beyond the way it bloomed warmth within. Merill cuddled her, flinching at every painful movement because she could not stay still under Virgil's scrutiny.

His enigmatic stare was hot. Not as the principally destructive flame he wove with equal proficiency. But as the soothing bronze of steaming apple cider that coated her furnace and afforded generous warmth. On those long departed pages when, littered with the remnants of crunchy intrusion—a toothsome sound reproduced many times to the satisfaction of cavorting twins—the powdery sheen of Evenglow would illuminate the evening sky. And the arbor all around would stretch willowy digits to make marble of the world above. It was her spellbinding playground.

She was young then, unforgivably young. Virgil would call, interrupt merriment; yet it was not unwelcome. She and her sister would sheepishly sip at the tangy apple squeeze, and it would lessen the chill to a dull ache of which only his continued attention could melt. It was on one of those days, lost within the flurry of snowy similarity, she understood he was not like the preceding shadows of captivity. She loved him.

Time had reinforced the solidarity of her love and entangled the hearts of Almi and her inseparable sister. The many-chambered conveyance of affection spoke to them, murmured with every year greater drumming for their only one. So when sent to begin a life of their own, they could only hurt. The gentle man had never caused pain before. The only pain they understood was punishment.

"Why have you done this?" their love probed. He scanned the twins' exposed bodies from head to toe. The self-inflicted wounds were a bright red latticework scattered with burns, craters and other unexplainable rips and boils. The sisters had taken every approach to vindication.

"For our Virgil," she explained. "See?" Lifting Merill's stalky arm, she pointed to a gnarly flap of flesh where a fishing lure once sagged. "We wronged our Virgil. He sent us away." She pouted, begging with carmine orbs made sanguinolent by their mutual beatings. "We punished us! Our Virgil doesn't have to shoo his girls."

"We're his girls," Merill concurred, emphasizing every plaintive word with mellifluous melancholy.

Almi basked in his sun-touched stare which had been intensified by their wretched entreaty. It bathed her in jubilance, enamored her.

The elf harnessed that empowering feeling. They could renew their chastity for Virgil. He needn't send them off again. She need only bring about the shining stare once more.

Descarta snapped her fingers around the elf's wrist. "Stop. What do you plan on doing with my sword?"

"Let go," Almi sneered. "Stop seeing us! You're like those women. Seeing and poking."

"With pokers," complained Merill from within her sister's embrace.

"You're making us unchaste," groaned Almi, tugging at the gem-embedded hilt. "Virgil didn't give permission!"

"Unchaste," echoed Merill. "Unchaste like you!"

Descarta shook her head, certain they didn't grasp the truth of the term. Their woodland romps with Virgil were hardly innocent. In seeking to eternally aggravate her, their carnal shouts somehow reached the sorceress' subterranean chambers on those mornings when salacious behest ruled them. Instead of retorting, she hardened her vice. "Don't you want to go home?"

"Only our Virgil can see us. So . . ." The hidebound elf pulled at the blade, and its promising glint accentuated her declaration. "We will be punished, and he will see us. Only our Virgil."

"That won't do." Descarta wrenched the desperate ward's wrist so that the sabre clattered free.

"You're hurting me!" protested Almi. "She's hurting me!"

"We don't have time for this," sighed the exasperated homunculus. "Your Virgil will think you ravishing creatures, will adore you unconditionally. That much is . . ." Descarta considered the multifarious blemishes upon the elf's physique. "Painfully evident."

"Don't see!" howled Almi, struggling against the wrist lock. "Virgil did not approve!"

"Listen," stroked the sorceress, attempting another approach. She had to convince them before this one intentionally broke her wrist or the spell-flinging sorcerer was spent. "I'll keep this between us. Dress yourselves," she motioned toward their folded tunics, "and Virgil won't be the wiser."

Almi narrowed scarlet slits, turning to confer with her sister. Merill only cowered, secure in her cave. The discourse was there, Descarta knew. And she assumed it was much like the bond she and Virgil shared during their extradimensional traipse. The unspoken exchange ended with Merill nodding and slinking further into her nest. "You would mislead our Virgil?"

"Only for his benefit," assured Descarta.

"Whore-radish! Slut-potato! Beany witch sprout would betray her king!" Almi renewed her struggle, yelping and growling. "Tramp-turnip infidelity!"

There was a blast so boisterous the keep yawned and shuddered. Bits of its body bounced or soared past the cell, bringing pause to the contest within. Descarta was still, suspended in worried stasis. She waited, heart pounding, for any indication her precious weaver survived. "Virgil?" she called, enervated by her own trouble stained voice. "Virgil?"

A muddy rasp responded, accompanied by the uneven shuffling of irregular footsteps.

"Virgil?"

"Des." Spoken with two slickened syllables, it incited the nominal girl's runaway heartbeat further. "Des," Virgil called again as he waded closer.

"Virgil!"

He sought the voice, a substance flickering before him as vapor through the fiery hues of some upturned world. Why was he wading through this realm of magma and heat? Everything was so numb. All he sensed was the enticing nibble of cinder on his mind, chewing at the stitches there. The feeling was nostalgic. Merill would gnaw at him like this, lightly contenting herself on his shoulder. "Almi and Merill," he called. "Have you found them?"

"They're here," Descarta answered.

Almi scampered back into hiding, coiling around her twin and pulling a pillow modestly in front of her torso. "Oh! Oh! Please forgive us, our Virgil! Don't shoo us again!"

"Don't worry, dears," the weaver consoled. "You've done nothing wrong." He staggered another step, then another. The molten pool sloshed and foamed around his boots. Yet he remained unharmed by its sizzling touch. Something important was missing. "Des, what happened? Did you create this inferno?"

She said nothing as he turned the corner. There was no pitch for the sight, no tune by which to match her horror. The cleft in his side was such that his segmented spine bared meaty ridges. He stared first at her, then the shivering pillows, eye-sockets devoured by white fire. "Oh, by the Maiden! Virgil!"

"Our Virgil!" A synchronized screech escaped the twins as they burst from the pile to clamber about him. "Des! Des! Des! Des! Des!" They buzzed around the chasm which stole fully half his flank, fretfully blinking away tears. "Des! Do something!"

"I've missed you, my little birds. You do love to flitter about." He gave them each a pat and grin in turn. "The blaze does not harm you either? You are special girls indeed, and so very beautiful."

The sisters swooned under his pat, swaying between hopping in happiness and fidgeting in despair. "Our Virgil, they were seeing us, touching us. Des, too!" Almi cried.

Merill nodded her accord.

"All is forgiven, dears." He cast at their displayed mutilation and frowned. "Did they invade you?"

"Only touched! Only saw!"

"I'm relieved, loves. You are precious creatures." He noticed the rogue's cadaver and frowned at Descarta. Her exquisite visage was bruised and swollen from chin to ear, a mottled splash of red-brown and green-purple. She did not move, only cast aghast at him with a hanging chin. "My poor blo—blo—blo—"

The nibbling mind-cinder ceased picking and bit down with jagged bayonets. Its ember muzzle severed the stitch and, subsequently, a fragment of his control. With it feeling arrived, anguish sharper than any he'd known. The sorcerer immediately fell to his knees, too drained from the mortal loss of blood to do anything but quake in its unrestrained fury. Descarta was kissing him—his soot covered face, his sweaty hair—and rigorously tossing her head from side to side.

Then he pulled a breath, shallow and more a harbinger of death than life-bringing oxygen, which wheezed out of his punctured lung. His favored element unfurled, seized the severed stitch and funneled its cauldron of molten rock, commandeering his body.

Descarta yelped and withdrew from the weaver. His touch had the intensity of coal, and the magical fire ruling his eyes now roiled with newfound vim.

Almi and Merill were on their hands and knees, petitioning Virgil, groveling and begging him to change his mind. To stay in their world. To never shoo them.

The homunculus reached toward her king. Official titles meant naught to her; she was his queen in all the worthy ways. As his chosen love, Descarta had to attempt to heal him, to somehow graft the intimidating cleft. As her fingers neared, she was interrupted by the blaze that controlled him. It began to weave Virgil anew. The girl jerked her hand back, gawking at the surreal display.

Bone cracked, began the chalky grind of mortar and pestle working in reverse to return dust to skeletal integrity. While organs stewed the wet, sloppy gush of fluid, wisps of flame operated as tiny digits to spin a cover of tissue and muscle. After returning a layer of flesh, the miraculous flame instantly died and relinquished its loom.

"Virgil?" Descarta reached out with his name. "Oh, Virgil. Don't leave me."

Merill pressed her forehead to the weaver's knee. "We'll be good girls."

"You're ever lovely girls." Virgil cradled the sides of her head and eased the elf vertical. "Ever lovely."

"Our Virgil will shoo us?" whimpered Merill from between his coddling palms.

The sorcerer shook his head. "Never again." Lightly, he engaged her lips, shedding anxiety in a relieved kiss which sanctified his pledge. Almi mewed from his lap, savoring the indirect attention. "Never," he reaffirmed, applying a cosseting trail down her neck, shoulder and shear-scarred back. Merill only stared at him. Caught beneath his touch, she was frozen. Only the darting, anxious and lovestruck, of her glistening eyes over his gave light to her tale. And he found her sanguine portrait spellbinding—a magic thaumaturgy could never reproduce. "Because I love you."

The twins both sobbed and flung themselves around him. "We love our Virgil!"

Descarta awkwardly looked away, alienated amongst the reunited trio. She was happy for them, especially Virgil. He'd committed to finding the twins tortured to death, despite his reassuring words. A pang of envy still lingered, poisoned the joy of rescuing Almi and Merill. Reasoning told her it was a silly, infantile jealousy. He'd sacrificed centuries for her and little for them.

"Dear."

Descarta looked up to see the elves slipping on crimson tunics and Virgil standing before her. Once again, his resilient robe was in tatters. "What happened back there, Virgil? I don't understand."

"I cannot explain, dear. I can hardly believe it myself," he replied. The weaver had an idea, but he was doubtful. Virgil didn't dare convey a hypothesis so harrowing without firm certainty.

"You frightened me," she murmured, slipping slender arms around him. "I thought it was over. I—"

Virgil hushed her gloom with a common pilgrimage, one that saw her mottled cheek and throbbing ear visited by his gossamer gauntlet. "We must hurry, but first." He called upon his negligible healing weave, enough to complete the restoration she'd already begun. "You fought for them, love. You could have abandoned them to Josiah."

The pacified girl smiled and sunk into his palm. It was as though tiny embers licked at her flesh, nothing like her water-inspired magic. He read her so well, and she was truly grateful. "You heard," she said.

"Only the beginning, before the cursed knights arrived." Virgil reached for her palm and brought the partially mended puncture to his mouth, weaving warmth with his lips.

The act deepened her dimple-festooned grin. His fingertips met her chin once more, and she lifted it accordingly, realizing he'd made her his marionette. Descarta didn't mind manipulation, though, not if it was Virgil pulling her strings. Whether by their connection or simple body language, he'd augured her trouble and sought to mollify it. That was enough for the homunculus.

"Have you thanked her, girls?" Virgil ordered more than asked. He still delicately balanced her chin on his fingertips while addressing the twins with his question.

"Thank you, Des!" they chimed.

Virgil again gathered the gleam of her shimmering amber pools. "I'll not forget your devotion," he stated before plucking a kiss and pulling in a delicious breath of berryflowers.

Descarta flushed rouge, but did not turn away, bound as she was by his touch.

"You are second to nothing, no one. Never feel cast aside, my dear."

Descarta nodded. The entire scenario struck her as out of place in this dungeon, with danger just beyond a collapsed passage. But she was so close to him, and he was so kind to her. She could only linger in silence and wait.

The weaver released her chin, allowing her to shyly avert her gaze. "Good. Now, there should be another exit." Virgil turned about and set to searching, with the twins skipping merrily behind. "If only I could recall the schematics," he groaned. "The other option is to blast our way free, but the odds of that succeeding without collateral damage are not favorable."

"Collateral damage!" chirped the chipper Almi as she grabbed at his raven robe. "Our Virgil is super favorable!"

"Blast it," decided Merill while hanging from his arm.

Smiling, Descarta welcomed the return of pell-mell. She started to follow, but her boot kicked Josiah's short sword. The homunculus frowned at her handiwork. She'd killed twice on this journey, and both opponents thought they were defending justice. Bromyr wanted to avenge his daughter, while Josiah pursued a goal no less personally sound. He thought Virgil an ignoble creature who would treat Almi and Merill as cattle, belongings. She murdered for her truth, and they had died for theirs. Descarta blew a sigh. She was no stranger to the grim greys that reality suffered, but she didn't have to enjoy it. The homunculus stepped over her crushed impasse, leaving the rogue to rot.

Her path lay clear. While she would avoid conflict, these needless instances of death, any who presumed to set her astray would have to be eliminated.

...

The passage was dark, damp and infested with swiving vermin: all the holdings one would hope to avoid in narrow canals. Her bared arm brushed against something slick and pestilent. She shivered in response. "Where are we?" Descarta pressed, gagging.

"Regicide is a threat to even the most righteous rulers. And Des, such leaders are rare." Virgil intensified the mote of fire bobbing above his head, granting the unsettled homunculus clearer vision. "The ramparts hold several such tunnels. Her lower passages have atrophied, gone without maintenance for decades, centuries even. The river Tethim claims this one."

"We're scared," called Almi over Descarta's shoulder, placing chilly hands on her upper back and drawing a complaint from the spellblade. "Will our Virgil hold us?"

"There's no room, Almi. I will hold you plenty when we, well." He considered their demolished den. "When we find a new home."

Descarta wondered how he could tell the twins apart merely by voice. She often labored to use the correct name when the girls were in plain sight.

"A treehouse," suggested Merill, frightfully patting her sister's tunic. "With trees. The birds sing for us."

Almi bobbed her head. "Birds like our Virgil. When he walks with us, they twip so happy! Twip, twip, twip!"

"Twip, twip!" echoed Merill. "Twip!"

The homunculus contemplated the weaver. He looked brightened by their display, even trudging through muck and mold as they were. He also looked preoccupied. "Where does this lead, Virgil?"

"I cannot be certain. We're ascending, and it's angled to the west." Virgil shook his head. "It's all very cloudy."

"Did Kalthused know these causeways well?"

The sorcerer was silent, recounting events weathered and worn until her inquiry pried them free. He stopped and steadied himself against the slimy film and deluge of uncorked memories.

"Virgil, are you hale?" Descarta asked, still troubled by his mercurial faculties. She bunched his robe against him, applying a firm grip to fortify his balance.

"I haven't seen these in so long," he explained, giving her hands an appreciative pat. "Kalthused knew these tunnels better than any." Virgil began his stride once more, observing the passing greys and greens of nature-claimed stone with interest. "He was a king worthy of admiration. Kalthused marshaled this nation to freedom from an overbearing suzerain with severe prejudice against elves."

"Wasn't Ankaa an elf? She was your queen."

Virgil recalled the woman, the quintessential elf—graceful and reverent of nature. He hadn't seen her in some time. "Yes," he replied, curiously examining her renewed image. "Ankaa was both elf and queen. She was a worthy monarch, sympathetic to her subjects' plight, tenacious and loyal to the final breath. Kalthused would often whisk her away through these tunnels so they could relax without the royal guard at their heels. She adored mixing with the townsfolk and exploring the southwestern reaches where thickets flourish."

"Do you miss her?" asked Descarta, wondering whether he was beginning to regret his decision.

Virgil strummed at his heart, seeking Ankaa there, but her melody didn't echo. "A sweet girl blooming with intellect once told me obligation was not the foundation of companionship. So no, dear. Her memories belong to Kalthused, and he passed long ago."

Descarta allowed herself a somber grin. She shouldn't have worried. "I've only met her twice," conceded the sorceress, "but she was brilliant. Ankaa must have been glorious in life."

"She would find her successor the more resplendent queen," said Virgil, following a sharp bend to the left. "And so would I."

"Virgil!" objected the homunculus, clutching her frock. "Why do you insist on teasing me?!"

Almi and Merill giggled from her rear, with the former poking at her sides. "Resplendent Des is resplendent."

"Stop that!" battled the diminutive girl as she ineffectively attempted to avoid the elf's playful tickling in close quarters. "I said—" Descarta burst into laughter, a cavalcade of giggles. "Enough!" she gasped, batting at her assailant. "It's too much!"

The weaver emitted a slight chortle, amused by the lively transaction. "The three of you feel well. That is good," he said. "But it seems we've reached the exit."

CHAPTER SEVENTEEN

Those Glistening, Maddening Rubies

"This had better not be a false alarm," groaned Hazael. "I have an early meeting with the Kaen Morr emissary. And I would rather suffer his grumpiness under full repose." He pulled his regal cloak over evening attire, swiftly pacing from the royal quarters. "Where is Josiah? He should be here, not you."

"Indisposed, sire," answered the captain of the royal guard, a fiery-haired woman who'd taken the helm when the former captain succumbed to halberd during the calamity Virgil had sown.

Hazael sighed. "You mean you cannot find him. I should have appointed you seneschal." He opened a heavy wooden egress and two plate-clad sentries came to attention as he passed. Hazael cast below the covered bridge connecting his satellite tower to the fortress' mass. The ramparts were full of boisterous troops establishing a line atop the southwestern gate. "What's the situation?"

"Unchanged, sire. The weaver remains unidentified, and he's either trapped or taken the escape route. We're removing the rubble blocking the dungeon, but that could take hours." They passed through the opposite portal, this time encountering four armored sergeants who assumed a defensive formation around the pair.

"We've archers positioned atop the bulwark in the event our trespasser knows of the exit."

"And the servant? You have not mistreated her?"

"We've followed your orders, sire. She knows something, but will not speak." The woman hesitated, a pause in her briefing. "If we could torture her, sire."

Hazael grunted, thinking of the red-eyed half-elf. As the only fragment of his predecessor's legacy, she could challenge him for the throne. Elissa was harmless, however, content in her dull position. She'd inherited a portion of her mother's regrettable malaise. "We're not barbarians. She will be given the respect she's earned through service." The entourage started down a twisting stairwell in a clamor of rattling sabatons. "I'll take the bulwark defense, then. I fear one of the fools from the Triad of Sorcery has attempted to secure our elven guests. They are an artifact of sorts. I want no arrows loosed at the girls, understood? Bows strung, though."

"Yes, sire." The captain bowed her leave and set off to issue his commands.

"Ever troublesome," sighed the sovereign, deliberating the bouncy pair. "Even with your Virgil departed."

...

The iron-forged door exploded into flight, rebounding off the adjacent ramparts and spinning to a halt across the courtyard.

"Sorry, door!" Almi bellowed from within the tunnel. "No keys!"

Virgil began to shush her, but recognized the pointlessness given the explosion he'd just employed. "We must make haste," he instructed. "There's another passage nearby."

He stalked out under the vesper cover, cohorts stepping closely behind. Virgil peered about as he prowled forward, feeling the furtive advance would be thwarted at any moment. Someone had to have known the keep enough to predict his route. As if in response, enough bows to arm a garrison were pulled taught and plucked, issuing a salvo of hissing shafts from the battlements. "To cover!" the sorcerer growled, racing toward the southwestern gate where line of sight would be obstructed. Virgil threw his arm backward, aimed high and spewed a plume of incineration. Several bowmen cried sizzling dismay, amounting to a paltry loss to the castle garrison.

Merill squealed a terrified oath, a feline wail which faltered and broke in her throat. It was a dreadful cry, one whose charnel pitch would never leave Virgil.

He cast toward the sound, and its origin arrested him with keen mortification. Almi—his sweet, bubbly Almi—had collapsed onto the cobblestone causeway. She laid face down, a hollow doll whose spiritless limbs spread awkwardly like broken pinions. The volley was auxiliary then, a threat left to a lower dimension. Flight ceased, and his toes pointed accusingly at the flowering arrow growing victoriously from her throat. Merill hovered over her twin, prodding at the shaft with tentative pats which were retracted before attempting removal.

"Almi," muttered Virgil as he approached. The name was acid on his tongue, a poisoned utterance whose once inviolate worth had already been corrupted with ruin. For each shaky step spread the sanguine spill under like-hued eyes stripped of their prized vim.

"Almi," came again the noxious word as Virgil knelt in her leaking lifeblood. With a grimace, he stroked her wheat-colored hair. There was no satisfied mew to follow, only her evacuated crimson stare.

Descarta called for him, a cry as distant as the shower of arrows pelting the stone all around. She rushed to protect the occupied weaver, and conjured a deflective barrier of wind that sent incoming arrows errant. Her attention was divided among maintaining the shield and the downed elf. She'd spotted the protruding fletching, a grievous sign that brought forth her feelings for the special sisters.

"Cease fire! Cease fire!" roared Hazael from atop the ramparts, adding poignancy to his order by slapping a bow from the nearest archer's grip. "I said cease fire!" The garrison ceased their volley, and an eerie quiet fell as Hazael and his subjects peered at the dolorous display below.

For Virgil, silence had long blanketed the tumult of escape, usurped its urgency. Attentively, he gifted Almi all the affection he'd denied her. Admissions of her worth, her ineffable worth, coiled around relentless petting. He would have remained there, stroking lamentation into her expired soul, if Merill didn't interrupt.

"Virgil, I'm sleepy," she mumbled as she draped lazily over his lap. "I don't want to nap," the timid twin sputtered, heavy eyelashes fluttering to remain open.

A choked sob shook Virgil as he administered a loving cosset to her tunic-wrapped flank. She grinned under his ministrations. It was a weary, withered thing tempered to slight dimples.

"Our Virgil always watched over us," issued the elf in a delicate murmur. "We're sorry for troubling our Virgil. We only wished—"

"Never," contested the sorcerer, squeezing her slim flank. "You were never that. My dears are precious to me." Somber dimples deepened slightly at his words, and the waning twin curled in her repose.

"We've looked only at you, only our everything," Merill whispered, rendering him captive with swiftly dimming carmine orbs. "So . . ."

All at once, those glistening rubies were brilliant, perilous, forlorn, hopeful, bewitching and heart-breaking in their emptying wane—incomparably beautiful and repugnant. "Yes, love?" choked the fallen king after a rending moment of stillness from his lap.

Merill issued an onerous breath, encircling his waist with drained arms and pressing her cheek to his stomach. "So our Virgil will make us his again?"

Virgil embraced her then, taken by an unquenchable ardor. The request made lucid her understanding of the approaching demise, and the twins' utmost wish to someday occupy the husk once reserved for Ankaa. For his wards, she was the ultimate culmination of his love, an obstacle that preceded Descarta. If Virgil were to set forth to resurrect Almi and Merill, it would appoint them his incumbent elves.

"I will," assured the sorcerer in an austere pitch. "You have earned it, my songbirds."

Merill released an elated hum and sucked in a valedictory gulp. She savored the rainy scent and, foremost, his praising promise. Had Merill the capacity, she would have beamed, wholly rapt by the final triumph. Instead, the withering floweret simply faded, content in the knowledge that, through Virgil's conviction, she would return.

"Merill," wept the weaver, smothering himself with her wheat-colored curtains. "Merill, I need you. More than you've ever needed me. I need you." The limp cadaver sagged, head lolling over his embrace, but he clenched her tight nonetheless. Remorse stole him, an acute anguish born from more than their lacerating departure. Virgil wished to rewind, to right the decades of neglect, to sow a relationship wherein he rewarded their cataract of frolicsome love in kind. "Come back to me," he pleaded, shaking the small, vacant frame. "Do as I say!"

"Virgil," said Descarta, struggling to keep her voice from breaking. "We have to go. Who knows when they'll have a change of heart?" She palmed his shoulder, giving it a supportive squeeze. Descarta yearned to mirror his display, to crawl to the twins and mourn. But she knew that would not do. No, she had to be his strength, hold herself together to prevent Virgil from crumbling. "Let's leave."

"A change of heart," repeated Virgil, traversing the time when, after resenting her captor for two years, Descarta returned him from death. With uncharacteristic roughness, Virgil snatched her wrist and tugged her atop Merill, palm pressed against the dead elf's bosom. "Bring her back!" he commanded.

"Virgil, I—"

"You revived me!" Virgil fed her, unleashed his spellpool in a wave of burning. "Do it!"

Descarta reeled at the deluge. The potency now was twentyfold what he loaned her before. A scorching hunger unlike anything she'd encountered sought to consume her, to devour her vessel like a flame-gripped moth. All of her threatened to disappear in a spray of ash. "Please," she begged, pulling at the vice around her wrist, "Please stop! You're hurting me!"

Growling, Virgil released her, tossed her arm as an apparatus no longer useful. Aghast, she immediately scampered to a distance, brow furrowed in a storm of confusion. "Virgil," she sniffled, "please understand. I don't know the spell."

The sorcerer didn't acknowledge her. He didn't acknowledge anything. The gnawing cinders returned, foregoing nibbling for ravenous bites. Tenuous sutures applied by his compassionate caretakers all popped. For a moment, ephemeral and mortifying, Virgil knew what had happened. He shot a request for forgiveness to his blossom. He meant to warn her, had followed all the proper steps to speaking.

Then rage and grief took him.

Chasms ripped through his tormented mind, conquered rationality and left only emotion. Swinging on rusted hinges, his gates roared a discordant complaint as they were flung open and the coruscation invaded.

Tears sizzled and evaporated from the weaver's cheeks. A magical orange-red glow dominated once cerulean eyes. "Almi," hissed Virgil, and a wispy stream of flame married his lips with hers. "Merill," followed a sibilant utterance, an otherworldly command that conjured a second fiery thread.

"Yes, our Virgil?" answered the elven corpses in a timbre both sonorous and sepulchral.

"Return to me, dears. Never leave."

Almi and Merill obediently crawled to him, fire-consumed orbs locking with his similarly blazing stare. "We're yours, our Virgil. Always and forever."

Descarta watched in horror as the possessed trio rose—Almi still sporting the jutting arrow. Fiery flares leapt capriciously from Virgil's body, now consumed by a scintillating shroud of fuming oranges and blues. Cinders rose around him, and the pyre grew, errant flares turning anything they touched to sand.

His marionette wards were the only exception, and they reveled under their puppeteer's will. Gleefully, the pair bobbed and spun around him. "Prance, prance, prance," they crooned in a haunting tune. "Forever prance, prance, prance!"

Virgil stood emotionless, but sobs permeated his fire. Dreadful and ghoulish sniveling which incited the undulating flames to writhe and quiver. "You would steal my sprites?! Root them before me?!"

The snarling words battered Descarta. They seeped into her spine and made clear his unchained hatred, fueled by profound sadness and manifested by fire.

Reality shuddered and howled a defiant roar before being split in twain. The space behind Virgil peeled and curled as burning parchment, an ever-expanding rupture into the fabric. The cavorting twins tightened their reanimated orbit until he brought them into his obsidian mantle. Almi and Merill craned at him expectantly, and he gifted each an inferno-glazed kiss.

"How I love you, my songbirds," he projected in the sibilance of passionate ember.

"Smite everything?" Merill suggested, rising to her toes to nuzzle his neck.

The flaming chrysanthemum shook its accord. "Everything." Virgil raised a quivering claw, phalanges contorted as his countenance—a deranged joining of agony and pleasure. He issued an arcane susurration, and the roiling wreath hushed at his command.

"Everything for you, my Merill." Concurring with his desire, the agitated inferno raged forth, taking the form of incandescent ravens. Squawking disdain, the elemental avians became a thousand splashes of lava upon the battlements, sloughing flesh and steel alike.

"Twip, twip, hurray!" Merill shouted in her haunted timbre.

"Again! More twipping!" Almi insisted, and the fiery flower bloomed further, efflorescing into another crowing quorum.

"Virgil!" implored Descarta, voice cracking as the immense heat dried her throat. "Don't give in! I'm still here!"

The call drew a raven her way, its incendiary wings folding into a dive. Descarta brought her forearm up defensively. She hardly thought it would negate the crash of lava, but she summoned a globe of water anyway. With the Tethim nearby, weaving the element came with a thought.

Plummeting death struck her sphere and shot through in a hiss of steam. The homunculus faced her end, and its otherworldly crowing promised a painful demise. She clenched her lids shut and envisioned, one last time, a quiescent night beside her one true king.

The air stirred around her, tossing hazelnut curtains free of their binding. No burning pervaded her, no meat falling from her bones. Someone sunk fingers into her arm, and she fluttered dry eyes open to see Hazael, lavender cloak billowing about him. His protective magic had saved her. The indomitable lava sent chromatic shimmers throughout the milky aegis as it swam down the sphere. The shield would not block another such attack.

"Hold on, girl." The Elusian king instructed. "The next spray will be our last."

"But Virgil," she objected.

Hazael tugged her toward him and hooked his arm around her waist. "Virgil wouldn't want you dead, especially by his hand." Without waiting for a response, the sovereign took three magically augmented bounds which deposited him and his parcel in the relative security of the inner keep.

The sorceress shook off her vertigo and scowled at Hazael. "This is your fault! You stole our elves, and now they're dead! Dead!" She sobbed, visualizing the shaft that lanced Almi's throat, and the putrid emptiness of her stolen vim. "I should kill you! They didn't need to die! They were . . ." She expelled another heart-rending sob. "You're merciless." Descarta reached for her hilt, ready to feed it once more, but Hazael interrupted with a technique too quick for her to follow.

Somehow, the tip of her own blade rest on her neck. "You will listen," the man charged, leveling his gaze on the homunculus. "If you still wish to fight me, I will return the sabre. Understand?"

Descarta nodded, not deluded to choice in her position.

"Follow me," he instructed. "Better that I explain while we walk." Hazael lowered the threatening steel from its seat. "And Des, remember the ease with which I disarmed you."

They began a course through the ramparts' innards, passing places and people all familiar to the brooding girl. "How is this helping Virgil?" she caustically demanded.

"Firstly," began Hazael, "I did not authorize the incursion which thieved your twins. I truly regret all that has transpired. Virgil maintained the pact, and so have I. Violah is pragmatic, calculative." A pensive delay staggered the explanation. "You are here, so she is dead," he surmised.

"Yes," Descarta murmured.

The king exhaled, a sodden yet brutally pithy elegy. "Was, then. She was also irrationally rapt. Unlike her, unlike your weaver, I can separate emotion from logic when necessary. It is fortunate Virgil survived. I owe my status to him." Hazael produced a mirthless chuckle. "Assuming I have a nation to rule when he's finished raging. The bastard's gotten very good at that." He glanced behind him, appraising the uncomfortable homunculus. "I'm not your enemy, girl."

"If you aren't a deceitful snake," Descarta agreed. "Yet I cannot see what this idle prattle is accomplishing." Her mind wandered to Virgil, her dear, luckless Virgil. Sentenced to ruin and conquered by grief, he needed her more now than ever.

"It accomplishes as little as a cantankerous maiden," mused Hazael. "We could canter in silence, ever-handsome king and his ever-brooding captive. Would that suit you?"

Descarta groaned, bunching lace between sullied fingers. The delightful twins were butchered by his armsmen, and he had the audacity to mock her despair. "Tell me how to fix Virgil!" she screamed, drawing glares from the nearby staff. "Take responsibility for your errors, you rotten king!"

"Watch your tone here, girl. I am king, as you say." warned Hazael, waving off an inquiring guard. "I meant no ill. The scenario is grim, so I thought to lighten the mood."

"You have failed."

Hazael sighed. She hadn't lost her venom. Given the circumstances, her antipathy was relieving.

When he set out to activate the remaining beacon, it marked the end of an arduous plot spanning centuries. Virgil discovered him those ages ago, a soiled princeling stripped of title and family. The sorcerer must have known who he was at the time, a pliable adolescent full of hatred. But his benefactor was not unfair. He was clement, a trait chiefly recognizable when his understudy would, yet again, prove his trouble with weaving. Virgil promised—delivered—a kingdom stolen, and all the training to flourish as its sovereign. In return, Hazael greased the wheels of death, acted as a stanchion for diplomatic coercion, for which Virgil had no taste. It was a macabre companionship established through tragedy. The mutual maleficence was the only meaningful connection he'd managed since the incident that set him on their dark path.

Truly, her antipathy was relieving. She'd triumphed resentment and found what his dearest friend yearned for, the love which articulated seething anxiety. Descarta feared for Virgil.

"He was right in choosing you," said Hazael. "Initially, it perplexed me, troubled me, even. You were an unknown, unpredictable constituent in our meticulous design. How he watched you, Des. With a captivated intensity I hadn't seen since he palisaded himself from his wards, and never before them."

Descarta stared at his lavender mantle, enduring the casual conversation and attempting to divine any lucid falsehoods. She had to remain vigilant, lest he pluck her strings in a way deleterious to her precious spellcaster.

"Ankaa would not have suited him. Her highness was, by his description, a woman of unassailable purity. She would have been disgusted by his uninhibited immorality. Left him, surely."

The diminutive girl frowned, pondering whether he knew she'd done exactly that: abandoned Virgil. "And me?"

"Imperfect, stained. A lost vessel who would not accept him." The sovereign ushered her into the royal quarters, where they were alone. He chortled again, still devoid of mirth. The quarters' view afforded Hazael the forward courtyard, already evacuated and rendered boiling lava. Virgil was advancing, a shambling mass of blinding fury within the stark twilight. "He'd probably committed to you at the outset. I should have recognized it back then. Accompanying you every night was not requisite for his weaving. Your happiness, comfort, training—all of it adventitious. He needed only perpetuate your health; you were a carapace, merely occupied."

Descarta stood beside him, also spectating Virgil's gradual, relentless advance. The gluttonous wreath had grown tremendously and now threatened the innermost keep, hungrily flaring at its bright-hot exterior. Saradin's garrison had relinquished attrition to the Triad of Sorcery who was faring no less inadequately. The weavers hurled bolts of lightning, summoned noxious acids and shouted empowered oaths, an enfeebled volley against the blazing ring of protection. A translucent, hive-like dome shimmered into existence overtop the intractable patriarch. As quickly as it appeared, the anti-magic field failed, raining shards of molten glass. Its conjurers followed suit, falling to conflagration. She examined the ever-growing rift in his wake, a window into the bloody hues of the fabric. "What's going on?"

"Your Virgil will smite everything. Just as his reanimated foundling instructed." The king responded, regarding the girl he once called queen. "The rift in his wake will engulf the nation, claim everything. We absolutely must seal the conduit. I need you for that."

The homunculus wore a forlorn glower, extracting his true meaning. "I'll not kill him. This nation, every nation, would fall first." Her stalwart glare told him she would not budge, even if he turned a flaming raven on her once more. And Hazael was certain he would.

"Consider this," he started, moving to tinker with the bottom of a quelled brazier. "Virgil would have murdered you back there. What happens when your heart no longer beats for him?"

"He dies," the sorceress answered.

"He dies." Hazael inclined his brow in affirmation. "I saved you both from immediate cessation." There was a distant click, a mechanical whirring and the brazier rose to display a hidden pedestal. "I could have allowed you, thus Virgil, to cease. Albeit, that would have been saving a few lives to doom everyone. Virgil has ripped the planes, and he now acts as a limiter for the fabric's expansion. As long as he is here, it must flow through him to claim this world. He now uses that dammed flood to feed feats of weaving."

The sovereign reverently removed a crystalline dagger from the dais. It awakened in his palm, heaved for breath in tenebrous pulsations. "When the real Sundered rampaged, this placed him in stasis until the weavers of the time could extract and punish him." Hazael considered her once more, a wistful creature, and then presented the blade. "He will be rendered marble, and you will persist. Virgil would want you to thrive, not fall needlessly beside him."

Descarta regarded the glowing artifact with a plaintive frown. She applied teeth to her bottom lip, stifling the implacable weeping that threatened to shake her diminutive frame. The quivering girl inspected its cruel contours, saw herself plunging the lustrous seal into his gut. "Why must I do this?" she questioned, inflection burdened with despair. "I love him, Hazael. The thought repulses me."

"Your connection with Virgil allows you access to the fabric, a feat no sorcerer of my kingdom can accomplish. The weapon cannot function in our world." He kept his reply brief, leaving Descarta to confront her dreadful mire.

Ruminating, she leveled grim amber eyes on the hungry carousal of coruscation. Her wondrous weaver was in there, suffering. Descarta struggled with her dilemma. Disdain, hope, fear then love, her chronicle under his pinions was defined by upheaval. What terrible label would she engrave upon this scenario? Regret? Sacrifice? Loss? Or would she fade alongside her darling sorcerer?

"What is required of me?" she asked, delaying the altogether lacerating quandary.

"We will first confirm that you can, in fact, enter the fabric. From there, I will escort you as close to Virgil as my admittedly insignificant power permits. Then, you will have a brief window to incapacitate him before you're no doubt incinerated." Hazael watched as she absorbed the terse instructions. The fractures in her resolve were protrusive, and he feared she would collapse under the stress at any moment. "I cannot force you to do this," he reminded her, hoping to mollify the burden.

Descarta turned inward again, seeking the rainy scent of home. She ached to be awoken by her patriarch's gossamer touch, to explore the abandoned palace at his side, marveling at his tales and imparting her own.

She'd only just begun to explore him, to nestle into his cozy cosseting and experience the most breathtaking journeys simply by catching his gaze. Decades were supposed to pass where they gravitated ever closer, until she could recite his tales as though they were her own. Until she could no longer number the times they shared a kiss wrought of unblemished passion. Until their bodies had become so intimately intertwined the slightest brush of skin set her aflame. Until they set forth, the storybook pair, on a lovers' journey to incredible new worlds.

The homunculus ached because it could no longer be. She never expected their odd relationship to go precisely as concocted by her springtime fantasies. Just a single dream would have sufficed. Things were going so well until misery intervened.

A quake seized the keep, shaking her already wobbly knees, a reminder of imminent peril. Descarta took a tentative step toward the jagged crystalline talon and inhaled sharply, rejecting tears. She would have a lifetime for mourning.

"I will do this," she woefully declared, fists clenched at her sides. "Only if you heed my conditions."

Hazael gave her an inquisitive look that signaled her to proceed.

"When we are through here, Elissa will accompany me. Of her own accord, of course. You know her, correct?"

While it was hardly an accomplishment, he probably knew her better than Virgil. She possessed many characteristics of her negligent progenitors. The most blatant would be her mother's meekness. "The seed resultant of copulation between Virgil and Merill," he replied, purposefully discarding the term "daughter".

"That is . . . a way of stating it." Descarta furrowed her brow at the peculiar wordage. "Elissa should be taught her father's merits, not subjected to the jeers his victims will unquestionably shout following this catastrophe."

"The woman was not raised as his offspring, Des. She scarcely knows him," warned Hazael.

"I'm aware," conceded the sorceress. "But she is all that remains of them. I would very much like to be her friend. Besides, we met her on the way to the dungeon. She longs to know Virgil more than you may believe."

Hazael shrugged, thinking it a poor idea. "If that is your request, I will comply."

The homunculus shook her head. "There is more. I and any who accompany me will be pardoned completely, and your coffers will fund our voyage."

"Prudent," Hazael observed. "You've imbibed some of his best traits." The king didn't mention her heart's thumping call, and how it bewitched Descarta just as blindly as her weaver's had for centuries. "You needn't fear retaliation, anyway. But you have my word. I am charged with pardoning you and your cohorts and facilitating travel. Is that all?"

Descarta wrapped trembling digits around the dagger's chilled hilt. The dormant magic incited goosebumps across her skin, a porcelain field that would never again know the pacifying warmth of her Virgil's touch.

"Take me to him."

...

A scorched gust rushed over her and stole the moisture from Descarta's cheeks. The tears gathered there, tenacious and without her accord, to renew with every momentous leap that brought her closer to the roiling inferno. Her soiled russet canopy tossed about in a tempest, and each time her kingly carrier flexed his legs for another bound, a web of hazelnut locks stole her vision. Descarta clutched the antediluvian dagger by her flank, frightfully grinding whitened knuckles about its hilt.

As she drew near, the incensed shroud reunited her with the man within. Lips drawn by a caustic scowl, cinder-drowned stare no less diabolical, her beloved sorcerer had become revenge incarnate. With a slight tilt, enough to sway the sweat down his rage-ensnared visage, he acknowledged her. His mottled robe flared menacingly, a jaw of slovenly chipped incisors awaiting the next meal. Descarta heard his weeping then. It entered her, a troubling psychosis which bore into her skull. Unhinged chuckles staggered by bottomless sobs planted his discord there. The wicked cry demonstrated just how thoroughly he had broken. Most mortifying were the wretched boils and foul, leaking lacerations claiming his exposed flesh. With fingers mangled to contortion, Virgil somehow managed to secure his sabre. She instantly knew the wounds were self-inflicted, a morbid recompense for his failure to save the wards.

Almi darted into her line of sight, revolving in a leisurely prance with no regard for the fletching still lodged in her throat. Ecstasy captured her once enchanting countenance, tarnished by her widened, fire-claimed sockets and bloody tongue that dangled, indolently and to one side, over her chin. With a fey, charnel mew she disappeared once more into the veil.

Then the living cloak lurched.

Hazael freed her, delivered the homunculus to the churning vortex on a perilous path straight to its eager craw. Hissing, the blaze spat its defense, a geyser of ravenous orange-white burning which collided with and enveloped her aegis. The scorching blast screamed irritation and hammered with unremitting vigor at the semi-lucid sphere.

An oath escaped her cracked lips. The wreath's counter-assault ruined her view. Descarta's surroundings were but scintillating hues of hatred, devouring the borrowed barrier in clouds of scattered weave.

Instinct told her to shift, so she did. The soaring sorceress had no other method of determining the distance to her target. She never expected incorporeal travel to come so naturally. Thanks to her shared umbilical, it only required a properly tuned thought. Half of Descarta was already there in Virgil. Her world gave way to the flowing crimsons and empty whites of the fabric. The popping roar of Virgil's firestorm died to tranquility.

Two footfalls: all that divided Descarta and the love of her life. Under the fabric's influence, they arrived achingly slow, and painfully clear.

The first with adamantine sureness. She would follow through, pursue her agenda even if it meant everything would succumb.

The final was stripped of determination, and she faltered. Her stride became a stumble, her stab a clumsy reach. All because of his smile. Beneath the pervasive latticework of bloodletting incisions, he welcomed her with a smile. It was neither feigned nor crazed. The simple fervor-grown grin was the same that'd graced his features when lazing at her side, stroking affection into her hair. She'd come to douse his beautiful flame, to repay his compassion with a shard to the abdomen, and he beamed at her. But no, that was not enough. For the cruel weaver, never that. He had to spread his ragged sleeves wide, an invitation to the dirge.

And it successfully struck. The dagger ran Virgil through, punched his liver and, by her weight, plunged ever deeper. Until its despicable hilt could advance no further, and seated itself against him in a bunch of patched fabric.

Dumbfounded, she regarded her quavering hands, wrapped tightly around the instrument of his end. When she agreed to the task, this was the one event she could not foresee. And no amount of divination could have readied her for the resultant sorrow. Until that excruciating moment, she expected fate would intervene and return her prized relationship. Descarta censured her ill-placed hope. Among the pantheon of heartless bastards, fate reigned unopposed.

"My blossom," choked the weaver as he hunched over her. "I'm relieved you chose to live." Openly weeping, he embraced her with untrammeled care. Descarta craned her neck to peer with boundless melancholy into his watery cerulean stare. Virgil basked in her lovely portrait, cherished the tiniest features. From her expressive dimples to her silken collar to the speckled orange-yellow enchantment of her wistful orbs—he would forget nothing. He would treasure his blossom for the whole of his sentence. The weaver reached to bless himself with a final visit to her lovely, dark-brown sheaf, but froze just as his fingers breached her hair.

"Virgil," Descarta whispered. The pommel throbbed in her grasp, spreading its debilitating magic. She cast at the artifact, at the dark tendrils originating there and creeping outward.

The diminutive girl didn't care about the world. She never meant to seal him, only release his spirit. She orchestrated this. Descarta pressed her waterlogged cheek to the weaver's petrified heart. "If I am to live, my Virgil, it will only be with you." Descarta murmured her resolution against the sweet ozone of his mantle. "And likewise, I will die only with you." If Virgil taught her anything, it was that sacrifice sanctified true love.

With a grunt, she pulled the crystalline blade free and tossed it aside.

Virgil gasped a sodden breath and collapsed. She tried to support him, but the sudden weight deposited the pair in a supine heap. "Blossom," he murmured from atop her bosom. "Why are you—" An involuntary shudder shook him. "Why?"

"Never again will you be alone," she responded. Descarta blinked. A cloud of fuzziness had begun to claim the edge of her vision. The weaver was caught by another passing quake and session of wet coughs. The hot, dampening pool leaked from his robe to stain her pinafore. She embraced her companion, extending willowy arms around his unkempt head.

"I'm sorry," Virgil lamented in an almost inaudible whisper. "I relinquished myself to despair." The waning sorcerer attempted to rise, to steal a glance at his precious queen once more. Enervated, he could only manage to drag his mutilated hand upward, affording him the opportunity to stroke her downy shoulder. "I've failed you. Return the dagger before it's too late. Live, blossom."

"You're wrong," insisted Descarta, growing light-headed. She'd closed her eyes to appreciate his ministrations. "It is because of your devotion that I would not dare carry on without you."

The only reply was his distant, labored inhalation.

She stroked the passing weaver, gently massaging her limitless love into his hair, neck and back. "You will never again be alone, my Virgil," she softly assured him. Descarta would become one with him soon. She was afraid, terrified of the swiftly approaching darkness, but she could never have thrived without him.

"You were not given permission to die," reproached Virgil.

The statement jolted her listless state and threw her into a furnace. "What, darling?" she inquired, perplexed by his virulent tone. Descarta opened her eyes to the ramparts looming overhead.

"Retreat!" shouted Hazael from nearby, drowned by immolated screams. "By the Sundered! The fires have returned! Into the keep!"

"I did not give you permission to die!" the weaver bellowed, possessed once more. "I did not!"

Then he was above her, defaced claws planted astride her head. Once again, roiling embers fleeced his gaze and flared with his screech. "You will live!"

"Virgil," she mustered, laboring to stay conscious. "I—"

"This is not permissible!" The fiery sorcerer roared.

His maw remained agape, unnaturally wide. Descarta was mystified by the liquid inferno that slinked subserviently up his arms and into the waiting cavern. The climbing veins swelled and bubbled, feeding Virgil an unbelievable amount of the fire-stuff until it tapered to tiny luminous threads along his robe. To Descarta, it resembled the forge cauldrons of the Underrise, or even the sloshing pit of magma which fueled the earthen polis. Virgil shuttered the incandescent swash and leaned to within a breath of her face.

She was too enthralled to be afraid of the smoldering his proximity brought, to refuse his mental imperative to unclench her jaws. The weaver parted his lips and set the molten tincture down her throat.

...

I never thought a kiss could so embody pure passion. He tongue-fed me the ambrosial brew, and its heat spread from my throat to my toes. Oh, the way our lips met was unforgettable. Initially, I thought he would scald my innards, but it was like swallowing sweet honey of the perfect temperature. No, I didn't even swallow. The poultice swam deep of its own locomotion, and with it came vitality. My Virgil had kissed me many times before, but this was different. It was untamed, guttural. Like it could only be unlocked by the primordial fire that ruled him.

Descarta tapped her quill. The events were only a month past, yet they seemed so far gone. The diminutive girl fought to recall the following days, but they remained lapses of tenuous sentience.

According to Hazael, I was critically sick, and recovered only after having teetered upon death multiple times. Ultimately, he kept his word. Much effort was put into medical care. There was also the ordeal of faking our deaths and ensuring our safe departure—my darling had killed many subjects and turned the outer ramparts to rubble. Though I doubt the man would have been so inclined to aid if Virgil hadn't closed the rift when feeding me life. Regardless, I think Hazael will make a true Elusian king.

"Des," Elissa feebly called from just beyond the cabin. "Sire—I mean," the downcast woman contemplated scrabbling fingers, an improvement over her feet. "I mean . . ."

Descarta glanced from her juniper writing desk, patiently awaiting the winsome half-elf. The title would come.

"F-Father won't listen," she meekly finished. "I told him it was unhealthy, just like you said." Stepping aside, the orphaned princess surrendered the ingress. "He's here," she announced.

"I'll fare. I'm not your milksop," groaned an agitated Virgil. "And I need no consent to visit my blossom. Why do you persist in treating me this way?"

Elissa flinched at his tone, but she did not yield. Weeks of tending to the man had instilled a sliver of confidence. "Your condition," she contended. "You mustn't—"

"I'll fare," said the weaver. Forcefully, he abandoned the noxious timbre and applied a pat to her inherited obsidian crown.

Descarta produced a full-toothed grin, and the elves anchored within flitted excitedly. "Our Virgil!" she blurted and hopped to her toes. Cursing, the sorceress shook her free-hanging hazelnut curtains, effectively scattering the domineering twins.

"He's here," reiterated Elissa.

"Let him be for now," replied Descarta. "I'll look after our belligerent patient."

The carmine-eyed woman risked a glance at her cohorts, quickly leaving her father and settling on the less intimidating target. "Des," she spoke, softly. "It does him no good when you, when you . . ." Elissa flushed crimson and reverted to fumbling digits. "It's very noisy."

Virgil palmed his brow, finding her comment impossibly choking. His daughter should not reference such ribald things, even if they had been boisterous.

"Sorry," offered Descarta, no less nonplussed. "I'll look after him. Nothing lascivious, I promise."

Elissa bobbed a vehement nod and hurried off, the most mortified by her awkward declaration.

The sorcerer expelled his tension in a mighty sigh. He entered the cabin and turned toward the fleeing woman, allowing the weird static his offspring had summoned to dissipate. "She is troublesome."

"You adore her," Descarta said to his back.

"That makes her no less troublesome," replied Virgil, both a concession and rejoinder. Elissa should detest him, not enter a state of panic when his injuries flare. "And I cannot look at the girl without seeing Merill there. It's rending, Des. Truly rending." Virgil expelled a wistful breath.

Something ticked within his spirit—a residual cinder that flared with each day. He dismissed it as his mind instructed, denied its existence. Then the sweet, sonorous tittering caught his ears, captivating. Almi and Merill shined excitement at him, jostled impatiently at his sides. The bantam sisters gave Virgil an expectant nudge, prodding with their chins.

"What special songbirds I have," he mused, begirding their waists with a squeeze. The sorcerer rewarded their vibrant carmine stares with a visit to sunny tops, kissing each in turn.

"We'll twip for our Virgil," said Merill, glowing.

He smiled, calling their dissonant lullaby to mind. "That would be delightful."

"Always and forever," Almi promised, scratching contentment into his raven vestments.

Descarta frowned, the silent observer, as he caressed emptiness, conversed with specters. This was his diurnal quest, an odyssey to the rejection of loss. She'd confronted him several times, and he always fervidly refuted the event ever happened. He authored these scenes to assuage sorrow, then locked them away so that every illusionary bubble remained untouched by the truth. To the man, these brief encounters were very real. Descarta pledged her utmost to fulfill her role as his affectionate stanchion. "Virgil," she called merrily.

Illusion dispersed, he turned to face his lovely confectionery. She stood in front of him, hands anxiously clasped at her waist.

Descarta curled dimple-festooned cheeks into a dulcet invitation. "I would very much like to hug my patriarch of ruin."

Virgil would not have refused her—the embellished request was purely for his benefit. So he accepted her: the dainty girl who had endured trials harrowing and deadly by no motivation but inviolable love. And that—the twisted, inexorable ardor—was by itself mesmerizing.

Gingerly, she eased herself into his intoxicating aroma, her chassis into his bandage-sheathed abdomen. Descarta mewed, content.

"You're high-fettled, blossom," he noted, likewise encircling her.

The homunculus nodded concurrence. "It's a delightful alcove. And," she peered at the discarded quill. It'd told her spellbinding tales. "I've nearly finished our chronicle. Virgil, our quest has been volatile, but you were ever vigilant—affectionate in hope and despair. I will not forget."

Virgil kissed her russet cascade. "And you, my beautifully bloomed blossom, have stirred feelings I thought forever buried." Again, he occupied her hazelnut locks, cherishing the saccharine fragrance of berryflowers. "How fares our journey?"

"Hafstagg follows the plotted course precisely," she answered, savoring the return to leisure. "Though he often questions, quibbles over your order to embark by sea."

"The brute will understand when we arrive. My only uncertainty is whether I can fulfill my vow." He pushed her to arms' length, thinking of his spritely wards, and admired the dazzling girl. "How do you feel?"

Descarta grinned, spirited by his unabashed concern. "Well enough," she said. "Almi and Merill are tenacious."

"You are acclimating well."

"Will they continue to vie for control?" Descarta asked. The deeds they compelled her to do and say were often terribly embarrassing.

Virgil gave her shoulders a reassuring squeeze. "They will, but their influence can never be manifested more than what you now encounter." He carefully unwound the viridian handkerchief she'd tied around her neck. "What of here?" he inquired while cosseting the velvety, bruise-streaked ring beneath.

"It doesn't hurt anymore," she murmured, turning away shyly while he administered the elves' most salient point of control.

"Good," he hissed, hot against her nape.

She shivered as his controlling talons seized her flanks. Her forge flared, roiled its yearning cry and she pressed provocatively into her lecherous raven.

His empress of ruin.